Regency Society

Innocence in Regency Society

DIANE GASTON

MILLS & BOON

Published in Great Britain 2014
by Mills & Boon, an imprint of Harlequin (UK) Limited,
Eton House, 18-24 Paradise Road, Richmond, Surrey, TW9 1SR

INNOCENCE IN REGENCY SOCIETY
© 2014 Harlequin Books S.A.

The Mysterious Miss M © 2004 Diane Perkins
Chivalrous Captain, Rebel Mistress © 2010 Diane Perkins

ISBN: 978-0-263-25010-7

052-0115

Harlequin (UK) policy is to use papers that are natural, renewable and recyclable products and made from wood grown in sustainable forests. The logging and manufacturing processes conform to the legal environmental regulations of the country of origin.

Printed and bound
by CPI Group (UK) Ltd, Croydon, CR0 4YY

As a psychiatric social worker, **Diane Gaston** spent years helping others create real-life happy endings. Now Diane crafts fictional ones, writing the kind of historical romance she's always loved to read. The youngest of three daughters of a US Army colonel, Diane moved frequently during her childhood, even living for a year in Japan. It continues to amaze her that her own son and daughter grew up in one house in Northern Virginia. Diane still lives in that house, with her husband and three very ordinary housecats. Visit Diane's website at http://dianegaston.com.

The Mysterious Miss M

DIANE GASTON

For Helen and Julie, who have been with me
in this writing venture from the very beginning,
and Virginia, who made our circle complete.

Chapter One

London, September 1812

Madeleine positioned herself on the couch, adjusting the fine white muslin of her gown and placing her gloved hands demurely in her lap. The light from the branch of candles, arranged to cast a soft glow upon her skin, enhanced the image she was bid to make. Her throat tightened, and her skin crawled from the last man's attentions.

This wicked life. How she detested it.

She checked the blue-feathered mask, artfully fashioned to disguise her identity without obscuring her youthful complexion or the untouched pink of her full lips. 'The Mysterious Miss M' could be any girl in the first blush of womanhood. It was Farley's contrivance that she appear so, and the men who frequented his elite London gaming hell bet deep to win the fantasy of seducing her. Escape might be out of the question, but at least the mask hid her face and her shame.

Unable to remain still, Madeleine stepped over to the bed, discreetly tucked into the corner and covered in lace-trimmed white-and-lavender linens like some virginal shrine. She perched on the edge of it and swung her legs back and forth, wondering how much time was left before the next gentleman had his turn. Not long, she surmised. She had taken more care in the necessary toilette than usual, thoroughly washing away the memory of that odious creature who had not departed too soon for her taste.

Male laughter, deep and raucous, sounded in the next room. Stupid creatures, seated around tables, as deep in their cards as in their cups, just waiting for Lord Farley to make away with their fortunes. The girls who ran the tables, tonight dressed as she was, like ingenues at Almack's, were meant to tantalise, but, for a select few, the Mysterious Miss M was the real prize.

Farley would not allow his prize to flee. She had learned that lesson swiftly enough. No matter. There was nowhere for her to go.

Voices sounded outside the room, and she blinked away the memory of how Farley had doomed her to her fate, or, more precisely, how she had doomed herself.

The next man, thankfully the last, would appear soon, and she had best be ready. She checked her hair, fingering the dark curls fashioned in the latest style to frame her face, a pale pink silk ribbon threaded through them.

Something thudded against the door. Madeleine hopped off the bed and hurried to her place on the couch. In staggered a tall figure, silhouetted against the brighter light of the gaming room. He stood a moment with his hand to his brow.

A soldier. He wore the red coat of a British uniform, festooned with blue facings and looped gold lace, unbuttoned to reveal the white linen of his shirt. If only she were a soldier. She would battle her way out of this place. She would be in the cavalry and gallop away at breakneck speed. How lovely that would be.

The soldier, who looked not more than five years older than she, swayed as he swung shut the door. Lord Farley's generous supply of brandy, no doubt.

Madeleine sighed. He might be foxed, but at least he was not fat. With any luck, his mouth would not be foul. She hated a putrid-smelling mouth. With all his lean muscle, he looked as a soldier should, strong and powerful.

'Good God!' he exclaimed, almost tripping mid-stride as he caught sight of her.

'I am afraid I am not He, my lord,' she retorted. The candles illuminated a handsome face, grinning with such good humour she could scarcely keep from grinning back.

'Yes, of course not.' His green eyes twinkled. 'And fortuitous for me that you are not, Miss…?'

'Miss M.' A charmer. She had met charmers before. The charm wore thin after they took what they wished from her.

'"The Mysterious Miss M", I recall now.' He flopped down on the couch next to her. 'I beg your forgiveness. You quite startled me. I had not expected you to actually look like a young lady.'

'I am a young lady,' she said, playing her part.

'Indeed,' he agreed, masculine approval shining in his sea-green eyes and a dimple creasing his left cheek. 'I swear you are the vision of one. England does offer the finest ladies. I find I must apologise for this humble uniform.'

He presented her with his boot-covered foot and winked at her while she tugged on it. Though properly polished, her fingers felt the leather's scratches and scrapes. From the battlefield? she wondered. When his foot finally gave up the boot, he nearly fell off the couch. She rolled her eyes.

He laughed. 'Have I impressed you with my finesse, Miss M?'

'Indeed, my lord. I cannot recall when I have been so entertained.'

He chuckled softly and swung around, bringing his face close to hers, his expression more full of mischief than lust. 'And I thought you were here to entertain me.'

She felt a smile tickling the corner of her mouth. He placed his finger on her lip and traced the edge. His eyes filled with a wistful expression that surprised her. A heat she was not quite prepared to feel made her wish to fan herself. As she wiped the disturbing touch from her mouth with her tongue, he took a swift intake of breath and gazed into her eyes so intensely that she lowered them.

He was like the fantasy she conjured up in her loneliest hours. A knight on a huge white stallion, who faced the evil lord in the joust, winning her away. Or the pirate who fought the blackguard and sailed her away in a ship with a dozen sails. He was the soldier, riding in with sabre flashing, to rid her of Farley and keep her safe forever.

Such nonsense. He was none of these, for all the splendour of his uniform, dark, curling hair and sun-darkened skin. He certainly looked the part, though, with his eyes wondrously expressive and a face lean, as if honed by battle.

Once Farley had been a fantasy, when she'd dreamed he was taking her to a marriage bed instead of the one in this room.

The soldier shrugged off his coat, and his loose linen shirt revealed a peek of black chest hair. Madeleine's eyes fixed on the wiry patch and her fingers itched to discover how it would feel.

As if it would feel any different than the other lust-filled men who forced themselves so hard against her that she pushed on their chests to give herself room for breath. She placed a hand on her breast. What fancy had captured her to give way to such thoughts?

He grinned impishly at her again, the dimple deepening in his cheek. 'You are a vision, Miss M. Like England herself, beautiful to behold. Nothing mysterious about it. In fact, I shall call you Miss England.'

'Do not be so foolish, sir. The fabric of my dress is Indian. The design is French and the style Roman. My mask is Venetian. My pearls are Oriental. I think my shoes are from Spain. There is nothing of England here.'

His finger traced the edge of the demure bodice of her dress where the fullness of her breasts was only hinted. He hooked his finger under the material and pulled it away from her skin, allowing a soft touch of what was underneath.

'I suspect,' he murmured, stroking her skin and gazing into her eyes, 'underneath you are pure England.'

'Not pure, my lord,' she whispered as his fingers did lovely things to her soft skin. 'Not pure at all.'

He slowly leaned closer so that she could feel his breath on her lips. With a gentleness she did not know existed, he placed his lips on hers and lingered there, moving so softly, she was only half-aware of him urging her mouth open and tickling the moist inside with his tongue.

She moaned and positioned herself closer to him. Her arms twined around his neck and her fingers played with the curls on his head. He tasted of brandy, but she decided she might like brandy the next time she was compelled to drink it.

He urged her down on the couch, covering his body with hers. The hard bulge of his arousal pressed against her. To her surprise, it pleased her.

Only once before had a man's arousal not filled her with revulsion. That day in the country when her father's house-guest, the Lord Farley her older sisters prosed on about, met her out riding and showed her what happens between a man and a reckless, unchaperoned fifteen-year-old girl. She had thought it a splendid joke to be the first of her sisters kissed by a man, but, all too easily, that kiss had led to delights she had not imagined.

The soldier's muscles were firm beneath his grey wool trousers. His mouth played lightly on her cheek, and Madeleine's long-suppressed desire tugged at her again. She must not allow herself the weakness. She must control her sensibilities.

His kisses trailed down the sensitive skin of her neck, and she said her rehearsed lines: 'Shall we go to the bed, my lord?'

Immediately he rose, grinning his dimpled grin. 'Whatever you command, my lady.'

He gallantly extended his hand to assist her up. His grasp

was firm and warm, even through her lavender-kid glove. As she led him to the bed, he kept hold of her hand, the gesture unexpectedly setting off a storm of yearning inside her.

Vowing to get her feelings under control, Madeleine continued her duties, turning back the covers on the bed and facing the soldier. She slowly pulled off her gloves, one finger at a time. Her fingers free, she unlaced his shirt, caressing his warm bare skin as she pushed it off his shoulders. When she unfastened his trousers, the bulge therein attested to the success of her endeavours. She tried not to watch his green eyes darken with passion.

A guttural sound emerged from his throat. Madeleine collected herself and proceeded with the task she was bid to perform. This was the moment for him to pounce on her. She must temper his lusting, so that her dress not become ripped from his impatience.

Even completely free of his clothes, he did not pounce. Instead, he simply gazed at her. All the unwanted cravings of her body rushed back as she gazed at him in return. Usually she avoided a view of the men who bared themselves before her. When Farley first seduced her, she had been too shy to look, but her gaze freely drank in this soldier's body. He was more beautiful than the drawings of Greek statues in her father's books. Her eyes widened with surprise at the pleasure of seeing him.

'Good God, Miss England,' he exclaimed. He moved toward her. With gentle hands on her shoulders, he turned her around and fumbled with the laces of her dress, his progress painfully slow.

He chuckled. 'I am woefully out of practice.'

With a resolute purse of her lips, Madeleine spun back to face him and made quick work of the laces. The dress fell to the floor. She tackled the corset next. When she let her shift drop from her body, his gaze was as rapt as hers had been, and her resolve to simply perform her task fled.

His eyes met hers. 'I feel home at last.'

He ran his hand over her breasts, his fingers barely skimming the soft flesh. Her breasts ached. How could they ache? He'd barely touched them.

'Wh—where have you been?' She would distract herself. These feelings were too disturbing. 'In the Peninsula?'

'Last at Maguilla.' His manner turned solemn and his sparkling eyes lost lustre.

Maguilla. So exotic a name, like a magic kingdom far away. But what had happened there to cause his change in mood?

Sadness lingered in his eyes, but he smiled. 'I have been too long at battle and not long enough at home to have seen what I most have missed.'

'I do not understand you, my lord.' She chewed on her lip. 'What have you most missed?'

His gaze travelled up and down the length of her. 'England,' he said in a reverent voice. 'Every hill, curve, and thicket. All lush beauty and honest comfort.'

Madeleine felt herself blush. She stilled the impulse to cover her most female parts. 'Well,' she said, 'shall we proceed, my lord?'

Quickly she climbed on the bed, her mouth set in a determined line. He followed her, more slowly than she would have guessed. That he was not so eager to slake his desire unsettled her, but not so much as her own yearning. When she climbed in the bed and positioned himself over her, she nearly burst with excitement. It felt too much like what had brought her to ruin, but she wanted this soldier. Wanted him very much.

She stiffened and panic raced through her.

He halted immediately, searching her face. 'What is wrong?'

Her heart pounded. 'Nothing. Nothing is wrong.'

He cocked his head sceptically. 'You are frightened. I do not understand. What frightened you? Did I hurt you?' He shifted to lie beside her.

She avoided the puzzled look in his eye. 'No, you did not hurt me, my lord. I am not frightened. You may proceed.'

His hand grasped her chin and brought her face closer. 'I'll not *proceed*, as you say, until you explain.'

She could not explain what she did not understand. Even when Farley had seduced her and her body responded so wantonly, she had not felt like this. So…so excited and breathless.

Was this what young women felt when they loved the man they bedded? Was this a feeling she could never have or deserve?

A tear trickled down her cheek. As it appeared from beneath her mask, he wiped it away with his finger. 'There now,' he murmured, stroking her cheek. 'No need to cry.'

'It is of no consequence,' she said, stifling a sob, furious at her tears. Farley would be even angrier, if he knew. Weeping was not in the carefully fashioned script. 'Please don't tell Lord Farley about this.'

'Now, now.' He sat up and settled her in front of him, wrapping his arms around her. 'Why would I ever do that? Come. Tell Devlin what troubles you.'

'Devlin?' His arms felt like a warm blanket around her. She wished she could remain cosseted within them and never, ever leave.

'That's my name. Lieutenant Devlin Steele of the First Royal Dragoons. Youngest brother of the very honourable Marquess of Heronvale. At your service, Miss England.' He cuddled her closer to him. 'Tell me what is wrong.'

She released a deep, shuddering breath. 'Sometimes…sometimes I wish to be what I appear, not what I am.' The tears came in earnest now, soaking the feathers of her mask.

If only she had not gone riding that fateful day. If only Farley had not seen her scandalous attire, her brother's old clothes already too small for her. If only she had known that kissing a man could lead to so much more.

She fingered the damp feathers of her mask, hoping they would dry without losing shape or she would be punished.

'Shh, now, it will be all right,' he whispered.

No, nothing would ever be all right again.

The lieutenant held her and rocked her and murmured comforting words into her ear. It was a long cry, longer than any she had allowed herself since the night she'd learned Farley had other plans for her besides marriage.

Soon enough, though, she recovered. She pulled away from him and turned so he could not see her face as she removed the mask to wipe her eyes with the linen sheet. When she turned back her mask was in place.

'Now have you finished, little watering pot?' he asked, his lovely green eyes the kindest she had ever seen.

She nodded.

'Silly goose.' He tapped her on the nose and slid off the bed to grope on the floor for his clothes. Still unsteady, he stumbled and bumped against the bedpost.

'What are you doing?' she asked.

He laughed softly. 'Getting dressed. Do not worry, miss, I will forgo your favours tonight.' He cast her a long glance, a woeful expression on his face. 'Though it may be more difficult than piquet duty in freezing rain.'

'No, you mustn't.' She pulled him back, trying to urge him back on top of her. 'It would not suit. I am expected to perform.'

'No, sweet Miss England. You have performed enough tonight.' He stood again.

Madeleine stared at him, trying not to be transfixed by the flexing of his well-defined muscles as he groped for his trousers. She could not bear it if he should leave so soon.

He turned that mischievous grin upon her, his dimple emerging. 'We must, of course, give a show for the others in the next room. Create proper noise. Make the poor buggers envious.'

She giggled.

'Not laughter. Passion. Like this.' He let out a loud moan. 'More! More! More!'

'Yes! Yes! Yes!' she returned. They both burst out laughing, holding their mouths to keep it silent.

He collapsed on the bed. 'Stop. It hurts to laugh.' He grabbed his side. 'Ow.'

She pulled his hand away. To the side of his abdomen there was a scar, jagged and still pink from recent healing.

'You were injured at...at...?' She traced the scar with her finger.

'At Maguilla? As you would say, it is of no consequence.' He smiled, but without joy. 'We chased a regiment of French cavalry until the tide was turned and their reserves chased us. I made a foolish attempt to rally the men. A Frenchman met me with a lance instead. The wound is healed now. In two days' time I return to my regiment.'

'Back to the war?'

'Of course. It is a soldier's duty.'

Two days and he would return to war. He could be injured again. He could lose his life. Never again see his precious England. And, if she knew Farley, Devlin Steele would also return to war penniless.

'Lieutenant?'

'You must call me Devlin.'

She waved her hand dismissively. 'Devlin, then. Have you won at cards tonight? I mean, in addition to winning me?'

He laughed. 'Will you be in search of my money next?'

This offended. She had principles, after all. 'I want none of your money, but you must refuse to play further. Make some excuse.'

'Whatever for?'

'The game is not honest.'

The silly men who lost fortunes to Farley while trying to win a second chance with her never comprehended. No one won her twice in a night.

'The devil,' he mumbled. 'I never thought to inquire of

Farley's reputation. I should have known better. I shall make my excuses to him. I am indebted to you. You are quite a lady.'

'Don't elevate me, sir. I am just as I seem.'

He laughed. 'You seem quite like the misses in the marriage mart. A young lady of quality.' He smiled. His eyes turned kind and his voice tender. 'Indeed, that is what you are. A young lady of quality.'

Her face grew hot with shame. 'No.'

He struggled to get into his trousers, hopping on one foot and making no progress.

She did not wish him to leave. 'Lieutenant?'

'Devlin, remember?'

'Devlin. Will England win the war?'

He momentarily ceased his struggle. 'Without a doubt. It is nearly done, I think.'

'Wellington will see to it, will he not? And you soldiers who fight the battles with him?'

'Worry not, little miss.' He ran his finger over her brow. 'England will endure.'

Madeleine reached out and placed her hand over his scar.

'Lieutenant?'

'Yes?' He had become still, too, looking directly into her eyes.

'I wish to make love to you.' She slid her fingers up his chest.

'Miss England, it is not necessary.'

She reached behind her head and untied her mask. With trembling fingers, she removed it. His eyes darkened.

She moved closer. 'I will make love to you. It will be my gift, because you must return to battle.' With one hand stroking his hair, the other moved downward. Farley had taught her where to touch to arouse. This time, with Lieutenant Devlin Steele of the First Royal Dragoons, it gave her pleasure.

He moaned, softer this time. She clasped her hand behind his head and brought him uncomplaining to her lips. Urging him atop her, she gasped as the firmness of his body bore down on her. Her heart beat faster. She would truly make love to this soldier, this kind man who had been willing to comfort her.

He eased himself inside her with exquisite gentleness, and what typically caused her to deaden all emotion gave unexpected delight. She thrilled to the feel of him filling her, revelling in each stroke, each scrape of his chest against hers, each breath on her face. The only sound she heard was the clap of their bodies coming together and their panting breath. She matched his rhythm, stroke for stroke, press for press, and the sensations he created in her became urgent, spurring her on with each thrust. His pace quickened and her need grew. She would burst with pleasure, she was sure. She would shatter into a thousand sparkling shards. She would escape herself, this life she was forced to lead, the dismal future, in this brief space of time with Lieutenant Devlin Steele.

He collapsed on top of her, his need satisfied with hers. Sliding off, he lay facing her, his eyes half-closed, his skin aglow with a sheen of sweat. Madeleine let her gaze wander languidly over his face, memorising each feature, committing each curve and line to memory. She needed to remember him. She needed to dream of her Dragoon returning victorious from the war, coming to whisk her away. She would need for him to come to her tomorrow and the next day and the next.

The fantasy would comfort, though it would never come true.

'Sweet England,' he murmured. 'Thank you.'

She kissed him again, boldly giving him her tongue, tasting him. Brandy would never again taste so vile. It would be how *he* tasted. She inhaled his masculine scent, filling her lungs and memory with it, as his seed had filled her. She entwined her legs with his. He moved away from her kiss and grinned at her as she arched her pelvis to his.

'Ah, England, you shall be most difficult to leave.' As she placed her finger in the dimple on his cheek, he pressed his fingers into the soft flesh of her buttocks. She felt his passion flare back to life and she made a primitive sound deep in her throat.

As he entered her for the second time, Madeleine whispered. 'Lieutenant Devlin Steele. I shall remember you.'

Chapter Two

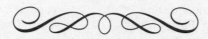

London, April 1816

Devlin Steele glanced up from the cards in his hand. The acrid smoke and dim light muted the gaudy red velvet of the gaming room. He reached for his glass and set it down again. The prodigious amount of brandy he had already consumed threatened to fog his brain.

His months back on English soil were as hazy as his present thinking. Snatches of memory. His brother, the imperious Marquess, rescuing him from the dirty makeshift hospital in Brussels. Days drifting in and out of consciousness at Heronvale, his sisters hovering around him, dispatched there to return him to health. Eventual recovery and a flight to London for a frenzy of dissipation meant to banish images of blood and horror and pain. Thus far, Devlin had managed to gamble and debauch away his quarter's entitlement. What capital he'd possessed had gone to money-lenders, but at present his pockets were flush, an unexpected surprise at Lord Farley's table.

'Your bet, Steele?' Farley's smooth voice now had an edge. His foot tapped the carpet.

Devlin stared at his cards, blinking to focus on the hearts and spades and diamonds. He had avoided Farley's gaming hell until this night, preferring an honest game, but damned if the man had not sought him out at White's. Predictable, Devlin figured, after he'd been tossing blunt all over town. Ripe for fleecing, by all accounts. A perfect pigeon for Farley.

He smiled inwardly. Farley had not yet heard the River Tick was already seeping into Devlin's boots. All the fleece had been long shorn.

'I'll pass.' Devlin barely glanced at the man seated across from him, concentrating instead on keeping his wits about him. Knowing Farley dealt a dishonest hand gave Devlin a slight advantage, if he could but hold on to it.

The cards were too good, though. Farley must be seducing him with a run of luck. He bet cautiously, against the cards, and avoided losing the successive hands. Farley's brow furrowed.

Rumour had it that Farley had lost a fortune in bad investments. Moreover, Napoleon's exile to St Helena had brought an end to the lucrative smuggling business everyone knew he ran. Farley was mortgaged to the hilt, a situation to make a man desperate—and desperate men made mistakes. War had taught Devlin that.

Farley indeed became more reckless, and Devlin stacked his chips higher.

Farley dealt the next hand, and Devlin carefully watched his expression. The man could still be considered handsome, though hard living had etched lines at the corner of his mouth and eyes. With his thin elegant nose, hair once fair, now peppered with grey, he had the look of the aristocrat he was, though his family fortunes had been squandered by an ancestry of fools. Typical of society, Lord Farley might not be a welcome suitor to the daughters of the *ton,* but, in the world of gentlemen who enjoyed his brandy, his card tables, and the young woman whose favours he doled out to the select few, Farley was top o' the trees.

Farley's fingers tapped a nervous tattoo on the table. 'Steele, I believe I could allow you some time with our Miss

M. She is delightful tonight. A Spanish maiden. Perhaps she will remind you of your service in Spain.'

Devlin peered over the fan of cards in his hand. 'I have no wish to be reminded of Spain.'

He placed his cards on the table, and Farley blanched, pushing another stack of chips to Devlin's side.

The man plastered on a smile, but a nervous twitch had commenced under his right eye. 'I think you might recollect you won a time with Miss M once before. I assure you, she remains in good figure and has added to the delights she may offer.'

Devlin remembered her. Indeed, memory of her lovely face, so pale against her dark hair, had often warmed lonely nights as the British waited for Napoleon's army to attack. Her spirit and sensibility had intrigued him more than young ladies in drawing rooms could do. Not that he had mixed in society to any great degree. Good God, he'd never even set foot in Almack's.

Devlin smiled at his host. 'I'm sure I'd be delighted to renew my acquaintance, sir. Perhaps after a hand or two.'

How long ago had he shared that memorable space of time with her? Three years and more? Just after Maguilla. What had her life been like under the thumb of this man?

Farley's brow broke out in beads of sweat. Devlin suppressed his smile. The man was in trouble. Throwing caution to the wind, Devlin made a hearty bet. The tic in Farley's eye quickened.

The cards were called, and the man on Devlin's right let out a whoop. So intent on besting Farley, Devlin had forgotten the other player. As Devlin gave up half his stack of chips, he vowed not to continue such carelessness.

'Enough for me, gentlemen. I think I shall stop before Barnes here takes my whole stack.'

Barnes bellowed with laughter. 'I'd be pleased to do that, Steele.' He gathered his winnings, leaving Farley with a scattering of chips too small to stack.

'Another time,' Devlin said, standing.

'One more hand.' Farley's voice was thick and tense. 'Don't deny me the chance to recoup, Steele. One more hand is all I ask.'

It would hardly be civil to refuse. Devlin bowed slightly and sat back down. One more hand couldn't break him, though that last loss had hurt a bit. Farley would have been wiser to quit. The man had lost all card sense. Devlin doubted he could even cheat effectively at this point. Barnes, too, was flush with his winning streak and eager to extend it.

Play was fierce. Devlin bet moderately, intent only on preserving his present winnings, but the cards came like magic. Was Farley setting him up, or had true luck shone upon him?

Caution be damned, he thought. Life's the real gamble. Devlin bet deep.

And won.

Barnes good-naturedly laughed off his losses, still ahead with his one spectacular hand. Farley slumped back in his chair, his face drained of all colour.

'You will accept my vowel, sir?' Farley's question did not demand an answer.

'But of course,' Devlin replied amiably.

As Farley wrote out his vowel, Devlin gazed around the room, into the dark recesses where Farley's girls, looking like Spanish tarts, ran the tables.

'Shall I make Miss M available to you?' Farley asked, his voice flat.

Devlin considered, sweeping his gaze over the too-opulent room. Had this place truly impressed him three years ago with its wainscoting and brocades? Now it appeared as false as glory.

Perhaps it would be preferable to seek the relative silence of the street and preserve The Mysterious Miss M as a memory.

A shout came from outside the parlour. The door opened and a burly man dragged in a girl who was beating at his chest and kicking his legs in protest. She wore a mask.

'Lord Farley,' the huge man said, 'she's brawling again.' He dropped the girl at Farley's feet. Her pale delicate fingers grabbed the edge of the table to pull herself up. She lifted her head regally and smoothed the skirt of her red silk dress. Black sensuous curls tumbled to her shoulders in a tangled mass. The lace mantilla had slipped off and hung on one of her shoulders.

'I have no patience for this,' Farley growled. 'What now?'

'She refused a patron.' The man tossed her a scathing look. 'She bit him in…a most unfortunate place.'

The girl faced Farley with her chin held high, her face half-covered by a red leather mask. 'I warned you I would do so.'

Farley shot out of his chair and with a loud clap struck his open hand against her cheek.

'The devil!' Devlin sprang from his seat to catch her before she hit the floor. Both her hands clutched her head, and Devlin supported her with an arm around her waist.

'Farley, I must protest. That was most poorly done.'

'I'll thank you to stay out of my business, Steele,' Farley snarled. 'You have no say in the matter.'

'If you strike her in front of me, I claim the right.' Devlin spoke through clenched teeth. 'You might hear her out.'

Farley rubbed his face. 'I have treated her with more consideration than she deserves, and she still defies me. I'm done with her. You found her pleasing once. Take her in lieu of my debt.'

Devlin combed her hair away from her mask with his fingers. He would leave no woman to suffer such treatment. He leaned close to her ear. 'What say you, Miss England?'

She blinked uncomprehendingly, her eyes unfocused. Suddenly her vision seemed to clear and she stared at him, the bright red imprint of Farley's hand remaining on her cheek. She smiled faintly and flung her arms around his neck.

He gazed over the top of her head to Farley. 'Your debt is settled, sir.'

A half-hour later Devlin paced the pavement in front of Farley's establishment, cursing himself. In the space of a moment, he'd tossed his winnings away and incurred further expense. All for a lightskirt with whom he'd once spent a pleasant interval. He could almost hear the Marquess ring a peal over his head. 'Brother, how many times must I caution you? Think before you act.'

Ah well, he could not very well leave his Miss England with Farley, could he? Perhaps she had some family. His winnings ought to be sufficient to send her wherever she wished to go.

At least the money bought him a little more time. Only two months left before his brother released his quarterly portion.

Two cloaked and hooded figures hurried from the alley. Devlin instinctively kept a watchful eye on them. In this neighbourhood one could easily be set upon and relieved of one's winnings. Indeed, Farley might attempt to recoup his losses. The two shadowy figures came to a stop in front of him, one carrying a large portmanteau.

'We are ready, my lord,' the other one said, breathing hard.

Devlin peered at her. In the lamplight, her face was all but obscured by the hood, and she was wrapped entirely in her cloak, clutching some bundle beneath its folds. Still, he could not mistake his Miss England.

'We?' he asked, one eyebrow arching.

'Sophie accompanies me. I will not leave her.' The resolute tilt of the young miss's head was the same defiant gesture she'd made to Farley. 'Please, we must hurry.'

'She is your maid?' Mentally, Devlin doubled the expense facing him.

'Yes, but more so she is my friend.' She glanced about nervously. 'Truly, haste is in order.'

'Haste?'

'We did not secure Lord Farley's permission for Sophie to accompany me, but I'll not leave her.'

The other woman was a wisp of a thing almost over-whelmed by the portmanteau. Devlin massaged his brow.

What the deuce. In for a penny, in for a pound. 'Very well, Miss England.' Devlin glanced around the street for a hack. 'Shall I relieve you of your bundle?'

She shrank from him. 'If you could take the portmanteau from Sophie, sir, I would be most grateful.'

'Indeed. Sophie, allow me to carry that for you.'

The maid hesitated, backing away as if it were a precious burden unsafe to hand over. He nearly had to wrestle it from her grasp. The portmanteau weighed a ton. Surprising she had strength to lift it off the ground.

'Where is your carriage, sir?' Miss England asked.

Devlin laughed. 'You mistake me for my brother, the Marquess. Perhaps we can find a hack hereabouts.'

'Please, let us remove ourselves.'

He led the way, and the women fell in step behind him, like sari-clad females of India, keeping a respectful distance.

Perhaps he should have cast his lot with the East India Company. There were fortunes to be made, to be sure, but he had no wish for foreign shores. Not after Spain and Belgium—truth was, he had no idea what to do with his life.

Devlin glanced behind him, checking on his two shadows. The memory of his Miss England's soft lips and bold tongue drifted into his mind.

A hack ambled to a stop at the end of the street, and Devlin quickened his step to arrange its hire. He assisted the women into the conveyance, and the driver stowed the portmanteau.

Devlin sat opposite his cloaked companions. 'Where shall I instruct the driver to deliver you?'

The little maid huddled against Miss England's shoulder. Miss England faced him, but he could barely make out her features. 'We have nowhere to go,' she murmured.

He rubbed his hands. 'Is there no relation who might be

persuaded to take you in?' The coil he'd gotten himself into had just developed more tangles.

'There is no one.' She turned her head, but held it erect. 'Leave us where you wish.'

Indeed, drop them into the street? They would be gobbled up in a trice. How long could he afford to put them up at some inn?

At that moment, the bundle in Miss England's arms emitted a squeak. Two small arms poked out of the wrapping and wound themselves around her neck.

'Deuce,' Devlin said.

The cloak opened to reveal an equally small head with a mop of hair as dark as her own. The child cuddled against her chest, fast asleep.

'This is my daughter, Lieutenant.' Miss England faced him again and spoke in a trembling voice, both wary and defiant. 'Linette…England.'

'Good God.'

Miss England spoke again. 'I do wish you would order the hackney somewhere away from this place. I care not where.' She grasped the child more firmly. 'Lord Farley might have a change of mind.'

Devlin instructed the driver to take them to his address. Where else could he take two women and a child when his brain was foggy with brandy and fatigue?

The passengers lapsed into silence. Miss England pointedly avoided conversation, and Devlin, angry at himself for his rash behaviour, clamped his mouth shut.

The thin light of dawn seeped through the London mist as the hack pulled up to a plain, unadorned building near St James's Street. His rooms were at the edge of the unfashionable district where the rent was cheaper. It was an area best known for housing Cyprians of the *ton* and, therefore, acceptable for a gentleman.

His entourage spilled out into the street, the little maid

grabbing the portmanteau before Devlin could reach it. He began to chuckle. To anyone passing by at this hour, the women would appear as two more fancy pieces under protection. As long as the bundle in Miss England's arms remained covered, that is.

Devlin walked to his entrance halfway round to the back.

Wait until Bart saw what he had won at cards. The sergeant's face when they came in the door would make this whole escapade worthwhile.

Devlin had once saved Bart's life on the battlefield. Ever since, the older man made it his mission to take care of him. Primary among Bart's self-imposed duties was tempering Devlin's rash, impulsive nature—a task at which he was doomed to fail.

Live for the moment. As a creed, it was as good as any.

Hmmph, more like a curse, Devlin thought. That particular creed had gotten him sent down from a school or two, but, from the time his late father had purchased his colours, it had meant survival. Now, however, it meant he had the charge of two women and a child.

He glanced over his shoulder. The women were not following. They stood on the spot where the hackney had left them, looking as lost as waifs.

Devlin cursed himself. They presumed he would abandon them. When had he ever passed by a creature in need? In his youth, one of his impulsive habits had been collecting stray animals which he'd then had to conceal from his father.

He walked back to the women. Three more strays to add to his collection.

'This way, if you please.' He wrested the portmanteau from the maid again. 'My abode is humble, to be sure, but will have to do.'

Miss England stood her ground. 'You need not trouble yourself, Lieutenant.'

'Nonsense,' he replied. 'We shall contrive something. The streets are too dangerous for you.'

With halting steps she followed him through the narrow alley. Her maid crept close behind. The sky had brightened, showing signs of becoming a magnificent day.

Devlin knocked on the door and only a moment passed before it opened. 'Good morning, Bart,' he said in a cheerful manner. 'I trust you have not been up all night waiting for me.'

'Half the night is all, then I consigned you to Jericho and took to—' Pale brown eyes in a weathered face widened.

'I've brought guests.' Devlin smiled as he dragged in the portmanteau. Bart's astonished expression was as rewarding as he could have wished. 'Not guests, really. Charges, you might say.' He stepped aside to let the women enter. 'Bart, may I present my charges.' He swept his arm in a graceful gesture. 'Miss England and Sophie.'

The little maid stepped forward cautiously and curtsied.

Devlin tossed Bart an amused glance as he shrugged off his coat. 'Where are your manners, Bart? Take the lady's cloak.'

Bart, mouth open, did as he was bid.

Devlin turned to Miss England. 'Allow me to assist you.' He stepped behind her and unclasped the fastening under her chin, removing the garment.

As the cloak fell away, the child in Miss England's arms whimpered in her sleep.

'My God,' exclaimed Bart.

Devlin laughed. 'This is Miss England's daughter...um...'

'Linette.' Miss England turned to face Devlin, and he had his first good look at her.

His memory had not failed him. Her face was almost regal in its loveliness. Her skin shone like fine porcelain, except for finger-shaped splotches of blue. Her lips were the identical colour to a rose that had grown in his mother's garden. Her lush mahogany-coloured hair cascaded down her shoulders, the perfect frame for a perfect face. She met his appreciation with a bold gaze, her intelligent blue eyes reflecting both youthful innocence and knowledge far beyond her years.

Devlin's breath left his lungs.

'I...I do not know your true name...' he managed, feeling his throat tighten at the vision of so much beauty.

She paused, her eyes searching his face. 'My name is Madeleine.' She added a faint smile. 'Madeleine England.'

He remembered the feel of her bare skin next to his, the lushness of her full breasts, and the ecstasy of her passion. His eyes swept over her as his body came alive to her again.

The child sleeping against her shoulder brought him back to his senses, a tiny girl, a miniature of the mother, very much resembling the wax dolls on his sisters' old toy shelf. The child's feathery long lashes cast shadows on the rosy cheek that lay against Madeleine's shoulder.

What the deuce was he to do with the lot of them?

Bart broke out into guffaws of laughter. 'Cast yourself into the briars again, have you, Dev?'

Madeleine lifted her chin, refusing to let it tremble in disappointment as she regarded the two men. At Farley's, her vision blurred by Farley's blow, she'd thought she dreamed Lieutenant Devlin Steele. Lord, she'd dreamed of him often enough. But when she'd blinked her eyes, it truly had been he.

She understood too well the look he'd given her a moment ago. It spoke of wanting to bed her. Foolish of her to forget this would be his motive for rescuing her. He could not be the brave and gallant dragoon of her fantasy. It had always been a silly fancy, after all, even if visions of him riding up on a tall stallion had comforted many a night.

Especially the nights Lord Farley came to share her bed.

The lieutenant ran his hand through his hair and replied to the other man's remark. 'I've not quite worked out what to do.'

She knew what he would do. He would cast them off as soon as he could. He must dislike her bringing Sophie and

Linette. Perhaps if she'd come to him alone he'd have been content to keep her.

No matter. She would go nowhere without her daughter and her friend. They depended upon her.

She avoided looking at him. 'We shall not trouble you, sir. It is light outside. I am sure we may be safely on our way.' She reached for her cloak. 'Come, Sophie.'

The slight figure was in mid-yawn, her lank yellow hair falling across her face. The other man reached out an arm for her as she staggered.

'The lass is dead on her feet,' he protested.

The lieutenant rubbed his brow, as Madeleine struggled with her cloak. The child squirmed and started to whimper. The cloak slipped to the floor. She tried to comfort Linette, swaying to and fro with her as she had done since her infancy.

'Do not be foolish, Miss England.' He picked up the cloak and tossed it out of her reach. 'You confided you have no-where to go.'

'It is none of your concern.' She attempted to pass by him to reach her cloak.

He stepped in her path and put his hand on her arm. 'You will stay here.'

She wrenched her arm away. The child started to whimper.

'You have made her cry,' Madeleine said. Much easier to be angry at him than to worry about where she would go if they did walk out the door. What would happen to Linette out there in the streets?

'I have made her cry?' His eyebrows lifted. 'Do you believe she will fare better if I allow you to leave? Do you have money enough to take care of her?'

She could not meet his eye.

He gently took her chin in his hand and made her look at him. 'You do not have money enough even for a hackney coach, do you?'

Her little girl stopped crying and stared with wide eyes at the man. 'Coach?' the child said.

Madeleine clucked at Linette, taking advantage of the opportunity to turn her back on Devlin. Inside panic reigned. Where would they go? Not back to Farley. Never back to Farley, but where? 'I do not need your concern.'

He marched around to face her again, and his voice became quieter. 'I beg to differ with you. If you will recall, it was I who intervened when Farley struck you.' He reached toward her cheek.

She shrugged him away, refusing to let him touch her. 'What does that signify? It is not the first time he has hit me.'

His hand remained poised in the air, his expression conveying acute sympathy. She should not allow herself to believe he truly cared, no matter how much the fantasy of that very thing had sustained her these few years.

The child squirmed in her arms and pulled away to grasp his fingers. The child giggled. Devlin stepped closer, and the tiny girl tugged on his neckcloth. This time when he touched Madeleine's bruised cheek, she did not draw away. Could not draw away. Speech became impossible.

'He will not hurt you again,' he murmured.

He became the hero of her daydreams again. How could she believe in him? Other young men had vowed to place her under their protection. They never returned, or, if they did return, never spoke such a promise again. Farley had seen to it. Why had Farley allowed this man to take her? Was it some sort of trick?

She glanced at her lieutenant. His eyes were warm and full of a resolve she would at least pretend was real. His face again became the one in her weary daydreams, conjured up after her toils were done and she was free to seek her bed alone. He always smiled at her in her dreams, his dimple winking at her.

Now his manly face filled her with excitement. The memory of his gentle kiss and peace-shattering lovemaking returned and agitated her. It was acceptable to dream and remember, but to let herself feel again? To hope? No, her only

hope was to contrive to support Linette and Sophie, two people she could depend upon because they needed her so.

Linette tore out the folds of Devlin's neckcloth as he leaned
down. His lips came closer. Madeleine's heart thudded against
her chest.

'I settled the lass in my cot.' The voice of Devlin's servant,
Bart, broke in, full of indignation.

Devlin smiled at the man. 'In your cot, Bart? Quick work.'

'I'll harbour no insults, if you please.' This man did not
speak as servant to master. 'If you've managed to get us any
funds, I'll see about some food. Some milk for the wee one.'

Devlin marched over to the table and emptied his pockets.
'Good news. We shall eat well.'

Bart picked up a few coins and shoved the rest back to
Devlin. 'See you try to hold on to these for a bit.' He reached
for a coat on a hook and went out the door, closing it silently.

'He is your servant?' Madeleine asked, conscious of being
alone with him once more.

As if reading her thoughts, Devlin regarded her with smouldering eyes. 'More than that, I suppose. We managed through
Spain and Belgium together.'

'Belgium,' she murmured. After news of Waterloo, for days
she had pored over the names of the dead, weeping in relief
when she finally found him listed among the wounded.

No matter. Now that his servant had absented himself, her
lieutenant would soon wish payment for her rescue.

Her heart pounded. She must not feel this excitement at
being near him. She must expect him to be as selfish and
capricious as other men. Madeleine adjusted her hold on Linette, who rubbed her eyes and flopped her head on Madeleine's shoulder again.

Devlin came near to her again. 'The child must be getting
heavy for you. Come. It is time for bed.'

Devlin led her into his bedchamber, acutely aware of blood
thundering through his veins. By God, she was more desirable
than that first, magic time with her.

As she regarded the room with dismay, he saw it through her eyes. A smallish room, furnished with a tall double chest of drawers in a style long out of fashion and a large four-poster bed with faded curtains. His old trunk was tucked in the corner, clothing spilling out.

Her gaze rested on the bed. What might it be like to share that bed with her? To tangle with her in its sheets?

This would not do. She appeared as if she would collapse at any moment. The child was no infant, nearly three years old, he'd guess. A sturdy bundle, and Madeleine had not let go of her for nearly an hour.

'Where shall Linette sleep?' she asked nervously.

'In the bed, where else?'

She straightened, her defiant chin lifting. 'My lord, I am prepared to repay you for your generosity, but I must insist on privacy for Linette. She must not be in the same room, let alone the same bed.'

He raised his eyebrows. Did she think him unmindful of the child? Did she think him so base as to take advantage of her?

'And I'm loath to leave her alone in a strange place,' she continued, her mouth set in firm determination.

He stared into her blue eyes and the breath left his lungs. He let his gaze travel down the length of her. Her red silk dress clung to her form and the weight of her daughter pulled its low neckline down lower. The attire was pure tart, but her bearing regal. The combination set his senses aflame, though he had no intention of acting upon them, ill timed as they were.

A smile not absent of regret spread across his face. 'I meant for you and the child to share the bed. Did you think I meant otherwise?'

She blushed, bringing a most innocent pink to her cheeks, her eyes downcast. 'You know very well what I thought.'

He stepped behind her and put his hands on her shoulders. The little girl's curls tickled his fingers. For a moment he let his fingers caress Madeleine's soft flesh. He held her against him, inhaling the scent of lavender in her hair. From behind her, he planted a chaste kiss on her cheek and gave her a push toward the bed.

'Sleep well, Madeleine.'

Chapter Three

The damp chill seeped through Devlin's clothing. His twisted limbs would not move. Pain had settled into a constant ache, made worse with each breath, worse still by the rancid stench of blood. Of death. Moans of the dying filled the night. The sounds grew louder and louder, until they merged into one piercing wail. An agonised sound. The sound of fear and horror and pain.

Coming from his mouth.

He woke, his heart pounding, breath panting. His vision cleared, revealing faded red-brocade curtains made moderately brighter by sunlight. What were brocade curtains doing at Waterloo?

He sat up, his mind absorbing the round mahogany table in the corner with its decanter of port, the mantel holding one chipped porcelain vase. His back ached from contorting himself on the settee. It had been the dream. He hung his head between his knees until the disturbing images receded. Had he cried out in his sleep?

The wail again sounded in his ears, coming from the bedchamber this time, not from his own soul.

He leapt from the settee and flung open the door. Madeleine paced the room, clutching her little girl. The child cried and struggled in her arms. Madeleine's red dress was creased with wrinkles. That she'd not bothered to undress before sleeping moved him to compassion. How exhausted she must have been.

The child gave a loud, anguished cry, and Madeleine quickened her pace.

'What the devil is going on?'

She spun toward him, her youthful face pinched in worry. 'She is feverish.'

'She is ill?' Devlin's head throbbed from the previous night's excess of brandy.

'Yes. She coughs, too.' Her voice caught. 'I have never seen her so ill.'

'Good God,' Devlin said. 'We must do something.'

'I don't know what to do!'

Tears glistened in her eyes. The child's wailing continued unchecked. He had not bargained for a sick child.

'Bart!' he yelled, rushing back into the parlour. 'Bart! Where are you?'

Bart emerged from his room, Madeleine's small companion like a shadow behind him. The sergeant, his craggy eyebrows knitting together, protectively held her back. The gesture irritated Devlin. Did Bart think him dangerous to young females?

'What in thunder?' A scold was written on Bart's face.

'The child is sick. We must do something.' He stood in the middle of the room, doing nothing.

'The wee one is sick?' parroted Bart, standing just as paralysed.

'Linette!' Sophie rushed past Bart and ran to Madeleine, who had followed Devlin into the room. She frantically felt the child's forehead.

'She is burning up!' she exclaimed. 'Maddy, sit down. Let's loosen her clothes. Mr Bart, if you please, some cool water and some clean rags.

'Clean rags?' Bart said, still immobile.

'Make haste!'

At Sophie's words, Bart sprang into action, drawing water from the pump and bringing it to the women, both fussing over the child. Finding clean rags was more of a challenge. He finally brought a stack of towels and bade them to cut them up, if necessary. Sophie dipped one towel in the water, wrung it out and placed it on the child's chest. Madeleine mopped the little girl's brow with another.

The child seemed to settle for a moment, but, before Devlin could relax, broke out in a spasm of coughing.

'Deuce,' said Devlin, barely audible and still rooted to the floor.

Madeleine flashed him an anxious look. 'I am attempting to quiet her, my lord.'

'I did not complain,' he protested.

Her eyes filled with tears. 'I am at a loss to do more.'

'I would be honoured to assist, if someone would instruct me.' No one heeded him.

Madeleine sniffed and patted Linette's head with the damp cloth.

Her friend regarded him with a wary expression. 'We could try to give her a drink of water.'

Before Devlin could move to the small alcove that served as the kitchen, Bart delivered Sophie a cup of water.

'Let me try to give her a sip,' Madeleine said.

Linette flailed her arms, jostling Madeleine, who spilled the water on her daughter and herself. Devlin walked to the cupboard, removed another cup, and placed in it a tiny bit of water. He handed this to Madeleine.

'Try a bit at a time,' he suggested.

She did not look up to acknowledge his act, but she was able to pour a small amount into the child's mouth. He took the empty cup and poured a bit more from the fuller one. Again the child accepted the drink.

Devlin was feeling rather proud of himself at having been so useful, when the child began another spell of coughing.

Madeleine sat the little girl on her knees and leaned her over to pat her gently on the back.

The child promptly vomited the water all over Devlin's stockinged feet.

'Damn.'

Madeleine gasped. Sophie grabbed the wet towel and wiped his feet, kneeling like a slave girl. Bart glared at him as if he were somehow solely responsible for the child's ill health.

'Enough. Enough.' He stepped away from Sophie's ministrations. She burst into tears and ran from the room.

Bart glared at him. 'Now look what you've done. You've frightened the lass.' He rushed after her.

Devlin reached for his head. Bart, he supposed, would not be inclined to brew the remedy for his excess of brandy. The child wailed again.

The sound triggered memories. Voices of dying men. His knees trembled, and he feared them buckling underneath him. The dream of Waterloo assailed his waking moments. With it came the terror that had only been too real.

Clamping down on his panic, he rushed into his bedchamber and pulled fresh stockings from the chest. He shrugged into his coat, and retrieved his boots from the parlour where he'd left them. Without a word, for he could not guarantee his words would be coherent, he rushed out of the apartment, slamming the door behind him.

Madeleine flinched at the sound and held her coughing daughter against her shoulder, still patting gently. Well, good riddance to Lieutenant Devlin Steele, she told herself, battling the disillusionment of his abandoning her at such a time.

'Was that the door?' Bart asked, coming back into the room.

'He left,' she said, shrugging her shoulders.

'Hmmph.' The man pursed his lips.

Linette settled into a fitful sleep. Though her skin burned like a furnace, Madeleine could not let go of her.

The stocky man surveyed her. Not as tall as the lieutenant and a good ten years older, he seemed solid as a rock.

His gaze softened when lighting on Linette. 'Ma'am, would you and the lass be all right if I went out for a bit? I've a mind there are some things we may be needing.'

A rock that easily rolled away. She sighed inwardly. It was foolishness to hope for assistance from any man.

But Devlin had assisted her in the most consequential way. He had rescued her from Farley, when he need not have done. He was under no obligation to assist her further, however. After Linette's distress he would surely wish them speedily gone. Madeleine's lips set together in firm resolve. He would have to put up with all of them until Linette became well.

If Linette became well.

Her throat tightened. Her child meant everything to her. She'd risked Farley's wrath to give birth to Linette and to keep her. Her daughter was the only worthwhile part of her life.

Sophie appeared at her side. 'Mr Bart went out. Do you think the master will return soon?'

'Lieutenant Steele?' Madeleine would not call him master. 'I very much doubt it. I fear Linette's illness displeases him.'

'Is Linette better? She's quiet.' Sophie leaned over and brushed the child's dark curls with her fingers.

'She sleeps fitfully and is so very hot.' She dabbed at the child's face with the cool cloth.

Sophie wandered about the room aimlessly, and Madeleine watched her, needing some distraction. The room was comfortably fitted to double as parlour and dining area, but its once-fashionable furnishings showed signs of wear. The carpet had lost its nap in places, and the cushioned seats looked faded and worn. Had not Devlin said his brother was a marquess? Perhaps the family had more title than blunt. Not that it at all signified. It was far superior to Farley's richly done-up rooms.

Unbidden thoughts of home came, mahogany tables polished to mirror finish, sofas and armchairs covered in rich velvet. No threadbare furnishings there. She could see herself bounding through the rooms, her scolding governess in hot pursuit.

Linette stirred and Madeleine's attention immediately shifted to her. It never did any good to recall those days, in any event.

'Should I unpack our clothes, do you think?' Sophie asked.

Perhaps if they appeared settled in, they might delay an eventual departure. 'That would be good. I fear I cannot help you, though.'

'Oh, Maddy, do not trouble yourself. You have your hands full.' Her waiflike friend smiled at Linette. 'You ought to lie down with the babe.'

Her arms ached from holding Linette, and she had slept only a couple of hours before the child's cries woke her. 'I suppose you are right. I will bring her into the lieutenant's bed.'

She carried Linette to the bedchamber, placed her in the centre of the bed, and climbed in next to her. The sheets and pillow held Devlin's scent as they had the night before. She had dreamed of him walking toward her to a bed like this. He would gently brush the hair from her face and lean to kiss her. She had dreamed of this Devlin many times.

It took no more than a moment to fall exhausted into sleep.

The banging of the door woke her. She immediately felt for Linette's forehead, still too hot.

'Where the devil is she? I've brought a doctor.' Devlin's voice came from the other room. 'Where's the child? Has the fever broke? Deuce, I've been to Mayfair and back. Found the doctor three houses down.'

As the door of the bedchamber opened, Madeleine had a glimpse of Sophie skittering away. Devlin charged in, a short, spry figure behind him. He had mentioned a doctor. For Linette.

The doctor wore a kindly smile in a round countenance. His coat was shabby and the leather satchel he carried was battered and worn. He came directly to Linette. 'Is this our little patient? Here, let me have a look at her.'

Madeleine rose quickly and handed Linette over to him. He sat in a wooden chair and spoke softly to the child as he peeked into her mouth and examined her all over. Madeleine watched the doctor's expression for a clue as to his thoughts. She chewed on her lip. Devlin came to her side and put his arm around her. Needing his strength, she leaned against him.

Finally the doctor handed Linette back to her. 'She has a putrid throat. Nothing to signify under ordinary circumstances, but I cannot like her fever. How long has she suffered thus?'

'This...this morning,' Madeleine stammered. Devlin squeezed her closer.

The doctor smiled, kind crinkles at the corners of his eyes. 'Well, she seems a sturdy child. A little bleeding may suffice to throw off the fever.' He rummaged in his bag.

'Bleeding?' Madeleine said warily.

'Yes, just a little. Come hold her.'

Madeleine sat on the bed and placed Linette in her lap. The doctor opened a small container and, with long pointed tweezers, removed the ringed worm.

'Hold her arm, if you please.'

Devlin stood his ground, though every impulse shouted at him to flee. He recalled the doctors placing such creatures on his arm. The memory belonged to the time of delirium and pain, when he fancied the leeches would consume him alive. Madeleine sat so composed, so resolute in assisting the doctor.

His arms prickled with the sensation now being experienced by the little girl. She was too weak to struggle, as limp as his sister's dolls when they carried them about, as he had been those months ago in Brussels.

The child will feel better after the bleeding, he reminded himself. It had been so for him.

Finally the leech fell away, satiated, and the doctor placed the creature back in its container. He packed up his bag while Madeleine tucked Linette into the bed.

The doctor took Madeleine's hand. 'You have taken good care of her thus far. Try not to lose heart. I have some powders that may assist, as well.'

Madeleine nodded, looking unconsoled. The doctor frowned worriedly at Devlin and gestured for him to follow out of the room. Devlin escorted the doctor out.

When outside, the doctor paused, glancing worriedly back into the apartment. 'The child's fever is very high. Only time will tell if she will recover.' He handed Devlin a packet of powders and gave instruction how to use them. 'I shall return tomorrow to see how she fares.' He patted Devlin's shoulder.

Devlin pushed some coins into the man's palm. The doctor placed them in his pocket, not glancing at the amount. Smiling reassuringly, he took his leave.

Devlin returned to the bedchamber. Madeleine stood beside the bed where the child slept.

'He told you it is hopeless, did he not?' she said, rubbing her arms.

Devlin attempted a smile. 'Indeed, he said no such thing. He gave me the powders and told me how to mix them. He will return tomorrow to see how she fares.'

'She will not die?' Her voice trembled.

He walked over to her and gently brushed the hair off her face. 'She will recover. You are overwrought. Come, sit. I will wager you have not eaten.' He found a chair and brought it next to the bed. 'Where did your friend and Bart go?'

'Her name is Sophie, Lieutenant.' Her voice still shook.

'And mine is Devlin.' He tapped her nose with his finger. He gazed at the little girl. 'The child will sleep, I think.'

'*Her* name is Linette.'

Devlin touched a lock of the child's hair. 'I know.'

He heard the door open and went into the other room. Bart entered, carrying pieces of wood.

'What's all this?' Devlin asked.

Bart cleared his throat. 'I took the liberty of procuring a bed for the wee one. A rocking chair, as well. The poor babe needs a place to sleep.'

Devlin smiled at him. Bart was a practical man. 'Well done, my friend.' He had not thought of such a necessity.

Madeleine stood in the doorway. 'A bed for Linette?'

'Aye, miss. And a chair to rock her in.'

The look she gave Bart was almost worshipful. Devlin's skin grew hot. By God, he was jealous. Of Bart. He wanted Madeleine's gratitude all to himself.

'Set the bed up in our room for now, Bart,' he said and received not a glance from her.

Sophie peered out from the closet where Bart slept. 'Can I help you, Maddy? What would you have me do?'

'Prepare some food for Madeleine,' Devlin said. Sophie shrank from his voice, but scurried to do what she was told.

Devlin sat Madeleine at the small table and took a seat across from her. He poured a small glass of port. 'This will fortify you a bit.'

He sat so near to her, Madeleine again became aware of the scent that had surrounded her in his bed. The lines in his face were clearly visible and told of years spent on battle-fields. Her heart gave a lurch. He was too much like her dreams.

'Drink,' he commanded, handing her the glass.

Madeleine obeyed. The sweet liquid warmed her throat, but Devlin's solicitude frightened her. The doctor must have given ominous news indeed.

He continued to speak to her in a kind voice. 'We will put the child into her bed as soon as Bart has put it together. Sophie can see to the linens. You must try to eat something, Madeleine.'

Sophie scurried from the scullery. Madeleine sipped her port, keenly aware of Devlin's eyes upon her.

Bart announced the bed to be ready, and Devlin accompanied her to the room. She placed Linette gently into the small wooden bed and carefully tucked the linens about her. The child settled, and Devlin took Madeleine's arm and urged her away.

When she returned to the table, Sophie put a plate in front of her with a fat slice of bread and cheese. Madeleine ate, because she did not know what else to do.

When darkness fell, Devlin lit the candles in the bedchamber to dispel the gloomy shadows that had crept into the room. The soft glow of the candlelight illuminated Madeleine, who looked vulnerable as she sat by Linette's bedside. She had barely moved from the little girl's side all day, though he could not fault her. Little Linette was an appealing child and it pained him to see her suffering.

Madeleine glanced at him. 'Do you go out this evening, my lord?'

He put his hands on the arms of her chair and leaned over her. 'My name is Devlin.'

'Very well. Devlin.' Her eyes drifted back to the child.

He pulled up a chair next to her. 'Now, how could I go out when our babe is ill?'

She gave him a sharp glance. 'You are not obligated to stay. I would not hold you.'

'Fustian,' he said.

She rocked gently. He wished he could convince her all would be well. He'd been trying to do so all day, but she did not believe in reassurances.

Devlin heard Bart's deep voice coming from the next room. He smiled to himself. The old sergeant was taken with that mouse of a female. It was amusing. Devlin always imagined Bart would shackle himself to some sturdy country girl to match the farm he used to dream of owning. To make a fool of himself over a wisp of a city chit amused Devlin no end.

'Devlin?' Madeleine's voice was barely more than a whisper.

'Yes?'

'I have never thanked you for...for the doctor and for... allowing us to stay.'

'Deuce, Madeleine. What do you take me for?' Tossing her out, indeed. 'Did you think I'd send you back to Farley?'

She twisted around to face him, alarm lighting her face. 'You would not!'

He stroked her cheek. 'Of course I would not.'

She turned back to Linette, but her hand went to the place he had touched. Devlin leaned back in his chair, balancing it on its back two legs. 'How the devil did you come to be at Farley's? You are too young, surely.'

She rocked at a faster pace. 'I am old enough.'

'Nonsense, you are hardly out of the classroom.'

She tossed him an insulted look. 'I am eighteen.'

'Eighteen!' he cried, unbalancing the chair and nearly pitching over. Linette stirred, whimpering.

'Shh.' Madeleine reached for the child, rubbing her back.

'Good God.' He lowered his voice. 'How old were you when you came to him?' He'd made the computation in his head, but could barely believe it. She'd been so young, and he'd made love to her. How could he have done so?

'I was fifteen.'

'Damnation!' So painfully young. He had left her there when she was younger than the silly chits making their come-out, the ones he thus far had successfully avoided. 'The man's a damned reprobate.' Devlin had bedded her, as well. What did that make him?

She gave him a sideways glance. 'You assume me the hapless victim, Devlin. Don't make me so good.'

'You did not join him willingly.' He would not believe it.

She continued her rhythmic rocking. 'Is this any of your concern, my lord?'

'Not a whit.' But that would not stop him. 'Why did you join that cheating lout, then?'

She sighed. 'This is a sordid story. Hardly of interest.'

'Of interest to me,' he persisted.

'Very well.' She paused to stroke Linette's hair. 'He seduced me. I was ruined. What else could I do?'

She made being ruined sound like getting a soiled spot on her gown. This was a rum story if ever he heard one. Farley was forty, if he was a day. Seducing a girl of her tender years—abominable. Devlin ought to have rescued her from him back then. Saved her from that abominable life.

She adjusted the blankets around the child, the candle behind her placing her profile in silhouette. His breath caught. She was a beauty. As fair as a cameo. As exotic, with her thick black curls, as a goddess from foreign shores. As skilled in the sheets as would fuel any man's dreams.

Her fingers gently touched the child's forehead. When she drew them away, they covered her face. Shame on him. Her child's life hung by a fragile thread, and he thought of bedding her.

'She will recover, Madeleine. Do not fear.'

She leaned back in the rocking chair and closed her eyes. Her silence stretched into the night, and Devlin felt guilty and useless. He watched her rock slowly back and forth in the chair. Back and forth. Back and forth.

'Devlin?' Her voice came as if from a great distance.

'Yes?'

'Do you believe God punishes sinners?'

Chapter Four

Devlin woke sharply, still sitting in the chair. The candles had burned down to stubs and the peek of dawn came through the windows. Madeleine cradled the child in her arms. The child was still.

'My God, is she…?' No, it was unthinkable.

'She's sleeping.'

Devlin's heart started beating again.

Madeleine shuddered. 'Her fever broke and she fell asleep. I thought I would lose her, Devlin. It is what I deserved.'

'Nonsense.' Weak with relief, he stretched his stiff limbs. 'She is through the illness, then?'

She nodded, her cheeks wet with tears.

While she had kept her anxious vigil, he had fallen asleep. Damned if he was not a useless sot. He stood up and, with a tentative hand, stroked the child's hair.

He kissed the mother on the forehead. 'Now you can get some sleep, as well. To bed, Madeleine, the babe can lie with us.'

He urged her up by her elbow and put an arm around her waist as he escorted her to the bed.

She looked about to protest.

He grinned. 'Now don't get in a twist. I'm too tired to

remove my clothes and so are you. We will be as proper as peas.'

She removed her slippers and laid Linette on the bed. Devlin's boots had long been tossed into a corner, as had his coat and waistcoat. He turned down the covers, and she crawled in. When he took his place next to her, he tucked her against him and promptly fell back to sleep.

When Madeleine woke, she was alone in the bed.

Linette. Where was Linette? She scrambled out of the covers and ran to the door.

Opening it, she saw Devlin seated at the table, Linette on his lap. The child giggled as she pulled on Devlin's nose. Two dark curly heads so close together.

Devlin turned his head to escape the assault on his nose. He spied Madeleine. 'Good morning, sleepyhead.'

'Deddy's nose,' cried Linette, pushing Devlin's head back with two chubby hands on his cheeks. Devlin pretended to resist.

'Would you like some nourishment, miss?' asked Bart, pulling out a chair for her.

She glimpsed Sophie perched on a stool near the kitchen alcove, looking smaller and more childlike than ever. Sophie jumped down and disappeared into the scullery.

'Our girl has made a remarkable recovery, wouldn't you say, Maddy?'

Hearing Devlin say 'our girl' gave her heart a lurch. Nor did the familiarity of him calling her Maddy escape her notice.

'She seems fit,' she agreed.

'Mama!' Linette scrambled off Devlin's lap and flung herself into Madeleine's. 'I got Deddy's nose!'

'I saw, sweetling.' She kissed the top of Linette's head and felt her forehead with her hand. It felt blessedly cool.

Bart brought a tray of tea things, followed by Sophie carrying a plate of biscuits. He set the tea service beside her and poured her a steaming cup. 'Do you want some tea, Dev?'

Devlin nodded.

Linette pointed to the biscuits, 'I want one.'

Madeleine placed a biscuit on a plate and lifted Linette on to the other chair to eat it.

'Maddy, you're a sight.' Devlin blinked at her over his cup. 'That awful dress.'

She glanced down at the crumpled red silk.

'Would you like Bart to fill you a bath? We have a tub hereabouts, don't we, Bart?'

'I believe so,' Bart responded.

Before Madeleine could think of what she wished to reply, Bart fetched the large tub, carrying it into the bedchamber while Sophie put on more water to boil. When they began to carry buckets to fill the tub, Madeleine offered to assist, but Devlin would not let her. Even Linette helped, carrying small pitchers of water, spilling more than made it into the tub. It felt all wrong to be so pampered.

When the bath was filled, Devlin brought her into the bed-chamber. Bart and Sophie took charge of Linette, but Devlin remained. Madeleine began to understand.

Devlin closed the door and leaned against it. 'Shall I play lady's maid for you?' His voice was velvet.

It was time for her to pay for his kindness. Farley had taught her how.

She cast Devlin a demure look under her lashes and strolled over to the bath. 'As you wish, sir.'

He moved closer, as smooth a motion as a stalking cat. Presenting her back to him, she lifted the long tangled curls off her shoulders. His hands slid up the length of her back. Slowly he undid her laces, his fingers light and dextrous. She remembered him fumbling with her laces all those years be-fore. Her body lapsed into a languid state. His hands slipped under her dress and ran over her skin like warm liquid.

The wrinkled red silk dress fluttered to the floor. Next came her shift. When she was fully naked, she knew he would wish to see. She turned to face him.

As she expected, his eyes feasted on her, darkening with arousal. She had learned to stand still for a man's visual pleasure.

He took time to regard her, longer than she thought she could bear. His gaze disturbed her. Not precisely as the ogling from Farley's clientele had done, but in an indefinable, unsettling way. His eyes finally reached her face.

'You are lovely.' The corner of his mouth turned up, and his dimple deepened.

The next move belonged to her. She stepped toward him and reached out her hand to caress his neck. She had not intended to kiss him, but he leaned down, and she had only to rise on tiptoe to reach his lips. He crushed her against him, standing wide-legged so she could feel his arousal pressing into her. For a moment she forgot her role and simply revelled in the strength of his muscles, the sweetness of his mouth, the feel of his hands pressing into her back, sliding down to hold her tightly against his groin. She did not realise how quickly she removed his shirt, how efficiently she freed him from his trousers, how she clung to him as he carried her to the bed.

'Madeleine.' His voice was a groan as he placed her on the bed and climbed atop her. His lips feathered her cheek and neck, soft, warm, and hungry. Her heart raced in excitement. His tongue circled the pink of her nipple, and all her senses sprang to life. She ached with wanting him.

She was spiralling out of control at the precise moment she ought to check herself. She had succumbed to the ecstasy of Devlin's lovemaking once, but that interlude belonged to daydreams. She must shield herself, protect herself from feeling, just as she'd done when required to endure the attentions of other men. The Mysterious Miss M could not be hurt, or humiliated, or betrayed, because The Mysterious Miss M felt nothing at all.

The Devlin of her daydreams was not the same Devlin whose hand now stroked the flesh of her belly, whose mouth rained kisses over her breasts. She would not be fooled, no matter what kindnesses he chose to make. Ultimately, all men served their own needs, and demanded payment for any small favour they bestowed. If they were refused, they could be very cruel.

It had been that way after the enchanted night with Devlin so many years ago. Farley had come afterwards to claim his pleasure, but Madeleine refused him. He went into a rage that left her bruised and in pain. The next day, Farley departed on one of his mysterious long trips. By the time he returned, Madeleine knew herself to be with child.

Now Devlin's hands and lips threatened to engulf her in sensation. She remained still, resolving to repay him for rescuing her, for taking in Sophie, for snatching her child from the clutches of death, but she would not allow herself to feel anything.

She pushed on his shoulders, and he lifted his head.

'Shall I pleasure you now, my lord?' She modulated her voice to a velvet smoothness, as she'd rehearsed many times.

He leaned on his elbow, his expression puzzled. 'Pleasure me?'

She deliberately slithered out from beneath him, facing him instead. She ran her finger in circles on his chest. 'I wish to please you. Tell me what I must do to pleasure you.'

He grabbed her hand and searched her face. 'What the devil...?'

She laughed, making a throaty sound Farley insisted she learn. 'Oh? Would you like me to be wicked? I can be wicked, my lord, if that is what you wish.'

He dropped her hand and sat up, rubbing his face.

She pretended to look wounded. 'What is amiss, my lord? I shall do whatever you desire.'

'Stubble it, Maddy.' He swung his legs over the side of the bed and grabbed his clothes.

'Do not be vexed.' Retaining her velvety voice, she pressed herself against his back. 'I would not wish you unhappy.'

His muscles stiffened. 'And I do not wish to play this game of yours. We are not at Lord Farley's establishment, Miss M.'

'Game?' She sat back, blinking in confusion.

He shoved his arms into the sleeves of his shirt and groped around for the rest of his clothes, donning each piece as he came to it. 'You are acting like cheap Haymarket-ware.'

She blinked at him, covering herself with the bed linens. 'I do not know what that means.'

He glared at her. 'It means lightskirt, Cyprian, dolly-mop. Shall I continue?'

Her eyebrows knitted together. 'But that is what I am.'

He grabbed at the linens covering her and yanked them away. Before Madeleine could protest, he picked her up and dumped her into the now-tepid bath water.

'How dare you!' she shouted before she remembered that men did not like it if you showed them anger.

He lunged down at her face, and she drew back, fearful of the price he'd exact from her show of temper. Only an inch lay between their lips.

His voice became disturbingly low. 'You cannot fool me, Maddy. You wanted me as much as I wanted you.' As quickly, he strode out the room, slamming the door behind him.

Dripping with water, Madeleine burst into tears, but she did not know if it was because she had angered him or because what he'd said had been only too true.

'Can you make it fit, Sophie?'

Madeleine stood in the centre of the bedchamber while her friend pulled on the strings of her dress. Though her hair, now in a braid down her back, remained damp, all other signs of the bath had been removed. Not from Madeleine's mind, however, where Devlin's angry eyes continued to haunt. She rubbed her temples.

Sophie tugged on the material of the dress. 'It is too small, Maddy, and the seams cannot be let out.'

'Oh, bother,' she mumbled.

The door slammed. Footsteps sounded in the outer room. 'Bart! Bart!'

Madeleine felt the blood drain from her face. Devlin had returned.

'Where is everybody?' He entered the bedchamber.

Sophie shrank back to a corner. Madeleine braced herself.

Surprisingly, he wore a grin on his face. He walked briskly over to her, lifted her off the ground, and swung her around. 'I have a surprise for us. Where is Bart?'

'Here I am, Dev.' Bart appeared in the doorway, holding Linette's hand. Linette had her thumb in her mouth.

Devlin released Madeleine. 'We're moving. Right now. We have to pack.'

'Did you get us tossed out of here?' Bart asked, his eyes narrowing.

Devlin clapped Bart on the shoulder, smiling broadly. 'No, I've merely secured lodging spacious enough for the lot of us.'

Madeleine's hands flew to her face. For all of them? What of sending them away?

'Explain yourself, lad.' Bart said.

'I have procured the lease to Madame LaBelmonde's apartments,' Devlin responded, grinning.

'Madame LaBelmonde?' Madeleine raised an eyebrow.

'Two bedchambers above stairs and two below. A parlour, dining room, and a proper kitchen.' He placed his hands on his hips in satisfaction. 'It should do very well.'

'A sizeable rent, I suppose?' Bart pursed his lips.

Devlin shook his head. 'Not beyond our touch, once my quarterly portion is in hand.'

Bart clucked his tongue. 'How do we pay until then?'

Devlin tossed Madeleine a broad wink before answering Bart. 'I wagered the first month's rent on a roll of the dice and won. My recent winnings should pay the second.'

'You wagered the rent?' Madeleine gasped. Visions of foolish, ruined men, their faces bleak and despairing, leaving Farley's gaming rooms flashed through her mind. She remembered the sounds of angry words, overheard years ago outside her parents' bedchambers.

'Lord Devlin is a sad gamester, ma'am,' Bart told her.

'What else was I to do with my time but play cards?' Devlin countered. 'We shall go on very well, I promise.'

Madeleine wondered about more than the rent. 'Who is Madame LaBelmonde?'

Devlin smiled at her. 'A close neighbour.'

'Close?'

'Indeed. She has found a new protector. Lord Tavenish, I believe. He purchased a town house for her. She leaves her furnishings.'

'Lord Tavenish,' Madeleine repeated. A frequent visitor at Farley's, Lord Tavenish had been well over fifty with sagging skin, and a sour smell. Would a town house be worth such a man?

Bart blew out a breath. 'Well, what is done is done.'

'Indeed.' Devlin grinned. 'We have not a moment to lose. There is a tenant interested in these rooms.'

'These rooms? Already?' Bart asked.

'The matter is completely settled. I called upon our landlord and made an arrangement with him. If we move out today, our debt to him is forgiven.'

Little Linette let go of Bart's hand and tottered over to Madeleine. 'Up, Mama.' She reached her hands up. Bart turned on his heel, muttering about setting to the task and hotheadedness. Sophie quietly crept along the wall until she, too, reached the door.

Devlin turned to Madeleine, his smile taking her breath away. She spun to face the wardrobe, gathering Devlin's clothing to pack in the trunk.

'You rented these accommodations to include us?' She could not believe it. There must be some mistake.

He put his hands on her shoulders and turned her to face

him again. 'Yes, to include you. We could not get on here, all of us, in this small space.'

She dipped her head, hiding her face from him. 'You are not obliged to house us.'

He tilted her face to him, his fingers under the soft skin of her chin. 'I am obliged.'

Not that he understood it, but Devlin felt keenly responsible for them. What would happen to them otherwise?

She shook her head.

He held her gaze. 'As you have said, you have nowhere else to go.'

She cast down her eyes.

'Madeleine, you are no prisoner here, if you wish to go.'

Her glance flew back to him. 'I do not wish to leave. You are correct. There is no place for me.' Her voice cracked.

His finger drew a line down her cheek. 'Let us not speak of this now. We have much to do.'

He watched her turn away, stooping down to hand Linette some clothing. 'Put them in the trunk, Linette.'

The laces on the back of her dress were undone. 'Let me lace you,' he said, reaching for them as she stood up again.

She twisted away from his hand. 'It is no use. The dress no longer fits.'

'Change to another then. I will leave the room if you desire privacy.'

She kept her eyes on her daughter, a doll-like miniature of herself. 'I have no other dress.'

'No other dress?'

'Well, there is the horrid red one, but Sophie washed it and it is quite wet still. I must have grown out of this one since last wearing it.'

He studied the frock, and it did indeed look unfashionably old and slightly girlish. 'A long time ago, I collect.'

'The day Farley brought me to London.'

Devlin heard the edge in her voice. How had she come to be in Farley's clutches? 'You brought only one extra dress?'

'I did not want Farley's clothes.'

Devlin raked his fingers through his hair. He had not calculated on having to purchase a wardrobe. Did the little maid and the child need to be clothed as well?

Madeleine regarded him, her eyes serious. 'Do not worry. Sophie will know how to alter it. She is clever at such things. In the meantime, if I go out, I shall wear my cloak. It covers everything.'

'We will get you clothes, Maddy.'

She lifted her eyes to him before walking over to Linette.

Later that afternoon, Madeleine held Linette's hand as she walked through their new rooms. Linette chattered, and she answered automatically, trying to stay out of the way of Devlin and Bart, busily carrying in trunks and boxes.

She had feared Madame LaBelmonde would have furnishings as gaudy and garish as in Farley's establishment, but these rooms were genteel, the golds, reds, and greens muted and beautiful. She might have chosen them herself. Would it not be lovely if this really were her house? She the mistress, and Devlin...

No, she must not pretend. But as she strolled through the rooms, she could not help herself.

She entered the parlour and ran her finger across the polished mahogany and silk upholstery. She pictured herself seated on the couch, and Devlin, on the nearby chair, reading the latest newspaper. Linette sat at her feet, playing with a doll. She ought to be doing something in this fantasy, but what? Her attempts at embroidery used to wind up in tangles, and she had never paid enough attention to sewing to know how to mend.

Sophie walked in the room in such high spirits her usually pale face was flushed with pink.

'Oh, Maddy, it is the loveliest set of rooms I have ever seen. Do you think we may really stay? Look at the furniture.

I should like to keep such nice tables polished. Do you think lemon oil or beeswax would do?'

Madeleine stared at her, not having any notion of what best polished wood, nor whether they might stay.

Sophie did not seem to notice she had not responded. 'I shall ask Mr Bart.' Sophie swept out of the room as quickly as she had come in.

'Mama, I want Mr Bart!' Linette pulled at her hand to follow Sophie.

'No, Linette. Mr Bart has much to do right now. He's moving boxes.'

'I want boxes, too.'

'Let's explore the kitchen, shall we?'

She led Linette to the kitchen where the little girl opened cabinet doors, momentarily distracted by new discoveries within. Madeleine ran her hand over the cupboard, imagining life inside this kitchen. She saw herself kneading bread, and Devlin entering, kissing her cheek, and asking for his meal.

Folly! She knew not the first thing about making bread, nor how to cook a meal.

Devlin entered the kitchen, carrying a big wooden box. 'Maddy, is the kitchen well supplied?'

She opened a cupboard. 'There are things in here. Do you suppose it is adequate?'

Devlin stood next to her and peered in the open cupboard. 'Hmm. Well, Bart will know.' He set the box down on the table and walked out.

Much later, the five of them sat around that rough wooden table, having finished a hastily prepared meal of bread from the nearby bakery and hard cheese. Devlin poured each of them another glass of wine, giving Linette, seated on his lap, a small sip from his own glass. The little girl puckered her lips at the taste, and he laughed.

Madeleine gazed at all of them. She pretended they were a

family, without a care, sharing a simple meal and pleasant conversation. The thought made her smile.

Devlin caught her eye and winked at her. 'I propose a toast.' He raised his glass.

'I want toast,' Linette said.

'To our new abode,' Devlin said.

'New 'bode,' Linette parroted.

'Hear, hear,' Bart responded.

'It is a lovely place.' Madeleine sipped her wine and swept her gaze from corner to corner.

Devlin gave her a smile. He'd had no idea that pleasing her would make him feel mellow and strangely content. He raised his glass again while Bart sliced a piece of cheese and handed it to Sophie. Little Linette banged on the table with both hands.

The mellow feeling returned. 'Tomorrow, ladies, we shall visit the mantua maker. Outfit you properly.'

Panic came over the shy Sophie's face. 'Oh, no, my lord.'

Devlin at last saw an opportunity to befriend the skittish young woman. 'Would you not like a pretty dress or two?'

Sophie shook her head and dared to glance up at him for a moment. 'No pretty dress. Nothing pretty. A bit of fabric will do, if it is not too dear. I do not presume to ask, my lord.'

'Sophie, you are part of our household. You deserve decent clothing.'

'Yes, my lord.' She slid off her stool and cleared the dishes.

Devlin rolled his eyes and caught Bart's disapproving look before the man followed Sophie out of the room.

'Do not mind her, Devlin,' Madeleine said. 'She does not want presents, I think.'

He took a gulp of his wine. Linette relaxed against his chest, still at last.

'She is afraid of you.'

He gave a dry laugh. 'Indeed.'

'It is because you are a man.'

He ran a finger through Linette's hair, brushing it off the child's forehead. 'Bart is a man, I've noticed.'

'True.' She looked quizzical.

'Well, Maddy, shall you and I visit the modiste or do you choose to be your own dressmaker, too?'

He meant to be good-tempered, but she responded with a wounded look.

'I cannot sew.'

Lord, women were difficult.

'It is of no consequence,' he said, hoping to return to her good graces. 'I'm sure we can find a skilful mantua maker. I would be pleased to see you in a pretty new dress.'

Her countenance changed, as if he had said something of great importance that had never occurred to her before. 'Of course. I understand perfectly.'

He wished he understood. Devlin poured himself more wine and drained the entire contents of his glass. It was easier to evade the musket balls of an entire French battalion than to navigate a simple conversation with a female.

'Linette is falling asleep. I need to make her ready for bed.' Madeleine rose from her chair.

'I'll carry her.' Devlin lifted Linette, and the little girl relaxed against him, a warm bundle more than comfortable against his shoulder.

He followed Madeleine into the bedchamber where they had set up Linette's bed. A connecting door joined the two upstairs bedchambers. He wanted to think of Madeleine knocking softly on that door and coming to him in the night, but, after the morning's débâcle, he was sure she would not do so.

Madeleine pulled out a tiny nightdress from the bureau. Linette's meagre supply of clothing barely filled half a drawer, and Devlin vowed to ensure the child, as well as the mother, had a pretty new wardrobe.

'Place her on the bed, please.'

He did so as gently as he could. 'Toast,' Linette murmured, opening her eyes momentarily.

Madeleine glanced at Devlin and smiled. How pleasant it felt. He had no idea domesticity could be so comfortable.

After she settled the child into bed and kissed the soft pink forehead, Devlin wrapped his arm around her and squeezed. 'She's a fine child, Maddy.'

'She is everything to me.' Her voice shook with emotion.

Madeleine leaned her head against Devlin's shoulder. His strong arm felt so comfortable, she could almost imagine he belonged to her and they were gazing upon their own—

No, she must not lapse into that particular fantasy. She must remember that Devlin wished to see her in pretty dresses, just as Farley had. She must remember that she owed him for his kindness.

'Shall I ready myself for bed as well, sir?' She modulated her voice as she had been used to doing for these last years.

He placed her away from him and looked into her face. Madeleine knew how to control her expression. She smiled, half-demurely, half-seductively. She gently caressed his neck, leaning forward so when he glanced down, a peek of the rounded shape of her breasts was clearly visible. She led him to the connecting door, pulled him into the other room, closing the door behind her.

'Shall I kiss you?' she purred, wrapping her arms around his neck. Not waiting for his answer, she stood on tiptoe and touched her lips to his.

Yes, she could do this, she thought, keeping her body in firm control. She could indeed pleasure Devlin and repay his kindness without ever pleasuring herself.

Devlin wound his arms around her and pressed her against him. Desire flared inside him, and he deepened the kiss. She reached her hands around to loosen the already loose strings of her dress. It fell to the floor, leaving only her corset and shift. He ran his hands across her bare shoulders.

So lovely. So soft. Like honey. He wanted her. Wanted to plunge into her, join himself to her and not feel so alone.

'Shall we go to the bed, my lord?'

The words echoed in his mind, from long ago.

He released her, watching as she moved toward the bed. She tossed a seductive glance over her shoulder.

She climbed onto the bed and turned to face him. 'Come, let me remove your clothing.'

He rubbed the back of his neck. And stood his ground.

'Come,' she purred, reaching her arms above her head, arching her back. 'Come, my lord.'

Devlin spoke quietly. 'You must call me Devlin. Did you forget that, Maddy?'

She rolled to her side and stared at him.

'This is not Farley's establishment.' He stared back.

She twisted the sheet in her hand.

'Go to your room, Maddy. Your daughter might need you this night.'

She sat up. 'No.'

'I do not want your favours.' Something else from her, perhaps, but not what Farley required of her.

'But you must.' A desperate look came over her.

'No.'

She scampered off the bed and gathered her dress, holding it in front of her, covering herself with it. 'Please, Devlin, you must let me make love to you. You must.' Her words came out between laboured gasps.

'No, Maddy.'

He walked to the door and opened it.

'Devlin, I am used to this. It is not difficult. I will pleasure you. It will be pleasant, I promise you.' Tears sprang to her eyes.

With every sensation in his male body, Devlin wanted to accept her offer, but he could not bear the emptiness in her seductive words. He well remembered what had passed between them that first time and this was not it.

She rubbed her eyes, now red and swollen. Her nose had turned bright pink. 'I...I wish to show you my gratitude.'

'Gratitude? Do you think I desire your lovemaking out of gratitude?'

Confusion wrinkled her brow. Devlin suspected that was not part of her practised repertoire. She clutched her dress in her hands. 'You want me, I know you do. Men like to...to... You liked it, too.'

He had indeed, but not when her eyes stared vacantly and her words were rehearsed.

'Go to bed, Maddy. Your own bed, not mine.'

She dropped her dress to the floor and wound her arms around his neck, kissing wherever her lips could reach. At least her rehearsed seduction had fled, but her desperation was no better. None the less, his body flared to life. He picked her up and she sighed in relief, nuzzling his neck. He carried her through the doorway and dropped her on to the large bed in the other room.

'No, Devlin.' She grabbed the front of his shirt, trying to pull him back. 'You do not understand. I must do this.'

He moved her hands away, trying to be gentle, but not succeeding. The demands of his body were making him harsh. 'You do not need to bed me. It is not something I demand of you.'

'But it is the only thing I can do.'

Madeleine watched him turn away from her and walk toward the door. 'You do not understand,' she whispered. 'It is the only thing I can do.'

He did not look back, but closed the door behind him, leaving her alone.

Devlin fled down the staircase and out into the damp night air. He strode through lamp-lit streets until reaching the nearest gaming house. Instead of sounding the knocker, he stood staring at the entrance. What would he find inside? Cigar smoke? Bad brandy? The luck of the draw? It was not ennui he sought to dispel this night, but the turbulence left in Madeleine's wake.

Why not accept her gratitude and bed her? He'd rescued her from Farley's, hadn't he? Taken in her child and her mouse of a maid. Provided them proper lodgings.

Devlin turned from the door of the gaming establishment and walked back to the street. When he had first met her, she had come to him, not with gratitude, but desire. Almost like loving him. He had never forgotten.

He wandered slowly through the streets, until he found himself back at the door of his expensive new rooms. The place was quiet as he entered, a single candle providing light. He glanced toward the back of the place where the two other bedchambers were located and wondered what might be occurring behind those closed doors. Was Bart holding the frail Sophie protectively, lest the 'lord' attack her in the night? Had Sophie offered her body to Bart, as well? Had he accepted?

Devlin would bet a month's blunt Bart had not made a mull of things as he had, and that, on the morrow, the little maid would gaze upon Bart's craggy features with adoration.

Devlin entered Madeleine's room quietly. The dim illumination of the street lamp shone on Linette's sleeping figure, her thumb in her mouth. Devlin smiled and gently pulled out her thumb. The little girl stirred, her long dark eyelashes fluttering. She popped the thumb back in.

Madeleine's bed was empty, and he felt a moment's anxiety, until he spied her curled up on the windowseat, sound asleep, as innocent and vulnerable as her daughter.

They were both beautiful, these charges of his, and totally dependent upon him. It frightened him, worse than leading men into battle. Soldiers knew the stakes were death, but they had the tools to fight. If he failed Madeleine and Linette, they would be at the mercy of creatures like Farley and would have no weapons with which to protect themselves.

He would not fail them, he vowed. He would see to their needs no matter what the cost.

Devlin gathered Madeleine in his arms, her weight surprisingly like a feather. He carried her to the bed.

'Only thing I can do,' she murmured, resting her head on his shoulder, much like her little girl had done earlier.

'Hush, Maddy,' he whispered. 'You'll wake Linette.'

'Linette,' she murmured. 'All I have.'

'Not any more, Miss England.' Devlin laid her carefully on the bed and tucked the covers around her. 'Now you have me, as well.'

Chapter Five

Madeleine held tightly on to Devlin's arm as they strolled the pavements of London in the bright morning sun. She pulled the hood of her cape to obscure as much of her face as possible. Still, she felt exposed.

'You will not take me to a fashionable modiste, will you, Devlin?' The thought of walking down Bond Street filled her with dread.

Devlin regarded her with an amused expression. 'No, indeed, Maddy. Would I subject you to such a terrible thing?'

That made her laugh. 'Do not tease me. It is merely that I would not want to be seen.'

'Do not worry, goose. You were always masked, were you not? No one will recognise you.' He patted her hand comfortingly.

'Of course. So silly of me.'

She took a deep breath. He did not understand. Farley's patrons did not concern her, but perhaps those she did fear encountering would not recognise her either. Surely the years had altered her?

'Where are we bound, then?' She gazed up at Devlin, so tall and handsome. His green eyes sparkled in the sunlight, like emeralds on a necklace a young man had once bestowed upon her before Farley snatched it away. If necessity bade her to walk in daylight, it pleased her to be beside him.

'Bart found a dressmaker only four streets from here,' Devlin said. 'How he should know about dressmakers foxes me.'

She laughed. 'Bart is very clever, isn't he? He and Sophie. I do believe they can do everything.'

'Unlike me, I suppose.' He smiled, but the humour did not reach his voice.

'You are the hub around which all revolves.' She spoke absently, transfixed by a coach rumbling down the street. 'Oh, look at the matched greys. How finely they step together. They are magnificent, are they not?'

'Indeed,' he answered.

She watched the coach-and-four until it drove out of sight. 'Oh, my.' She cast one last glance in the direction it had disappeared. 'What were you saying, Devlin?'

'I was remarking about how utterly useless you find me.'

She glanced at him. 'You are funning me again. What would have happened to me and Linette without you, Devlin?'

Madeleine felt her face flush. She should not have spoken so. To suggest he had any obligation to her was very bad of her. She had awoken in her own bed this morning. The only service she could render him, he'd refused.

'It is I who am useless, not you, Devlin.' She sighed. 'I am skilled at nothing...well, nothing of consequence.'

A curricle drawn by two fine roans raced by. Madeleine stopped to watch it.

'Do you like horses, Maddy?'

'What?' She glanced at him. 'Oh, horses. I used to like horses.'

'Not now?' His mouth turned up at one corner.

'I have not been on a horse since...for many years.'

'You ride, then?'

She had careened over the hills, giving her mare her head, clearing hedges, sailing over streams. Nothing unseated her. She outrode every boy in the county and most of the men.

When she could remain undiscovered, she spent whole days on horseback.

Had she not been out in the country on her mare, unchaperoned as usual, she might not have met Farley, might not have succumbed to his charm. Never riding again was fitting punishment for her fatal indiscretion.

She blinked away the regret. 'You might say I used to ride horses as well as I now ride men.'

'Maddy!' Devlin stopped in the centre of the pavement and grabbed her by the shoulders. 'Do not speak like that. I ought to throttle you.'

She tilted her chin defiantly. 'As you wish, sir.'

He let go of her and rubbed his brow. 'Deuce, you know I will not hit you, but why say such a thing?'

'Because it is true. I know what I am, Devlin. There is no use trying to make me otherwise. It is my only skill. Bart and Sophie can do all sorts of useful things. You, too. You can win at cards and go about in society. You have fought in the war. What could be more useful than that? But me, there is nothing else I know how to do.'

He extended his hand to her, wanting to crush her against him and kiss her until she took back her words. Though the kissing part might not prove the point, exactly, he admitted. He dropped his hand and, putting her arm through his, resumed walking.

After a short distance in silence, he said, 'That's what you meant last night. Saying it was the only thing you could do.'

She did not reply.

Devlin held his tongue. This was no place for such a conversation in any event. Besides, each time some handsome equipage passed by in the street, she slowed her pace a little.

He chuckled. 'Horse mad, are you?'

She pointedly turned her head away from him.

'Now do not deny it, Maddy. You are horse mad. I recognise the signs. I was myself, as a boy. Why, I liked being with the grooms better than anyone else. My brother, the heir, could not keep up with me when I rode, though he's a good ten years my senior. Nothing he could do but report to Father that I was about to break my neck.'

He threw a penny to the boy who had swept the street in front of where they crossed.

'Oh, look at all the shops!' Madeleine exclaimed. 'I had not reckoned there to be so many.'

Like a child at a fair she turned her head every which way, remarking on all the delicious smells and sights.

'You have not been to these shops?'

She laughed. 'Indeed not. I always wondered what the London shops would be like.'

'You've been in London three years and have never seen the shops?' This was not to be believed.

'Lord Farley did not take me to shops.'

This time Devlin stopped. 'Do you mean that devil did not let you out of that house?'

'Not as bad as all that, I assure you.' She patted his hand and resumed walking. 'When Linette was big enough, I was allowed to take her to the park across the street. But only in the morning, not when other people might be about. And there was a small garden in the back of the house. Sophie and I were allowed to tend it, though I mostly had the task of digging the dirt, because I did not have the least notion how to make the flowers grow. I enjoyed feeling the soil in my hands, though.'

Such a small space of geography in which to spend more than three years. 'I wish Farley to the devil.'

She gave him a look. It struck him as almost the same expression Sophie bestowed on Bart.

As they stood at the entrance to a shop with an elegant brass nameplate saying 'Madame Emeraude', Madeleine shrank back. Devlin had to practically pull her into the establishment. She held her fingers to the hood of her cloak, covering her face.

A modishly dressed woman emerged from the back. 'May I be of assistance?'

Since Madeleine had turned away, Devlin spoke. 'Good morning. Madame Emeraude, I collect?'

The woman nodded.

Devlin gestured to Madeleine. 'The young lady is in need of some new dresses.'

'Certainly, sir. Shall I show you some fashion plates, or do you have certain styles in mind?'

It irritated Devlin that the dressmaker addressed him directly instead of Madeleine, as if Madeleine were his fancy piece to dress as he wished, but, he supposed, in this neighbourhood, her clientele were almost exclusively from the demimonde.

'Shall we step into the other room?' She gestured elegantly.

He pulled Madeleine along to the private dressing room in the back. 'The young lady is in somewhat of a fix. You see, she has only the dress she wears and we were hopeful to purchase something already made up.'

Understanding lit the woman's eyes. 'Let me see her.'

Since Madeleine was acting like a stick, Devlin had no choice but to treat her that way. He turned her toward the dressmaker and removed the cloak that obscured her.

'Oh,' said the woman in surprise. 'Miss M, is it not? How delightful to see you again.'

'How do you do, ma'am,' Madeleine murmured politely, though Devlin did not miss the splotches of red on her cheeks.

'Deuce,' said Devlin.

'Why, I believe I have a dress ready for you,' said Madame Emeraude helpfully. 'Do you recall we fitted it not a fortnight ago? Wait a moment and I shall see—'

'No!' Madeleine cried.

Devlin interceded, putting his arm around Madeleine. 'We do not wish that dress.'

Madame Emeraude looked from the one of them to the other. 'I see. It is a new day, is it not? Well, I am pleased for you, miss. That other one was charming, but I shall have no business with him, I tell you, until he pays—' She caught herself. 'I beg pardon. I only meant I wish you well, Miss M.'

'Thank you,' Madeleine said, continuing to look miserable.

Madame Emeraude smiled and began to consider her, stepping around her. 'Oh, my,' she said as she saw the open laces of Madeleine's dress. 'This dress does not fit. No, no, no. This will never, never do.'

'You see our predicament.' Devlin smiled. Madeleine fixed her interest on the floor.

'Let me show you a few things I have on hand.'

Madame Emeraude signalled an assistant, who carried in one dress after another. Madeleine seemed to regard each garment with horror. They were, Devlin thought, merely dresses. A little fancy, perhaps.

As Madame conferred with her assistant, Madeleine whispered to him, 'Devlin, please do not make me wear those dresses. This one I have will do, or Sophie can make me a plain one.'

'What is wrong with them?'

'They are not…respectable.'

He regarded her, rubbing his chin. 'I see.'

When Madame Emeraude came back to them, Devlin took the woman aside and spoke to her. Madeleine watched them, the modiste nodding and looking her way. She dearly wished to leave this place where the proprietress knew her as Miss M.

Devlin came back to her. 'Madame Emeraude is ordering a hack. She has given me the direction of another dressmaker where we will go next.' He held her cloak open for her.

'I do not wish to. Let us go home, please.' This short excursion had already been mortifying.

'We will try this other place first. You need clothes, Maddy.'

In the hack she continued trying to persuade him. 'I believe

Sophie could teach me to sew, Devlin. A piece of cloth would be enough.'

He would not listen. He did not understand. Though it was exciting to be out among the carriages and shops, it was frightening, as well. She would always be face to face with what she was.

Madeleine peeked out at the passing scenery, the bustle of London with the pedestrians so intent on their destinations and the tradesmen so occupied with peddling wares. She could not hide forever. How could she rear Linette if she hid? Her daughter would have to go out into that world, too. She was determined that Linette's life be respectable, though nothing could ever change what Madeleine was inside.

If Devlin Steele was determined she should have clothes, she was determined they be respectable ones.

'Are you taking me to Bond Street?' she asked, meaning to sound merely curious, but her voice shook.

He smiled at her. 'Not to Bond Street. We are directed to a modiste who dresses the worthy daughters of our bankers and merchants.'

'Very well.' Not the fashionable part of town. No chance of encountering members of the *ton*.

They discovered a goldmine. The wealthy daughter of an East India merchant had abandoned her trousseau for one made at a fashionable address. The young woman was of Madeleine's size, and the dresses were exquisitely tasteful attempts by the modiste to expand her clientele.

Madeleine quarrelled with Devlin over the number of dresses he would purchase, wanting no more than two or three. She adamantly refused to let him include even one evening dress and would not even discuss the riding habit. His easy acquiescence in these last two matters made her momentarily suspicious, but he whisked her off to the milliner next door and a new set of arguments became necessary.

As he made arrangements for the delivery of his final purchase of several bonnets for Madeleine and one very plain one for Sophie, Madeleine gazed in the mirror.

She wore a pale lilac muslin walking dress adorned only by vertical tucks in the bodice edged by a plain purple ribbon. A blue spencer, lilac gloves, and a modest straw bonnet, simply adorned with a blue bow, completed the ensemble. She even carried a reticule.

Studying herself in the glass was like gazing into the distant past.

Devlin's image appeared behind her. 'You look very well, Maddy.'

She swallowed the surge of emotion that had risen in her throat. 'It seems like too much...'

He held up his hand. 'No more of that. We still need to stop by the shoemaker.'

She opened her mouth to protest, but as he took her hand and tucked it in his arm, he quickly added, 'Do you suppose we could convince Sophie to be measured for new shoes?'

For all his generosity to herself, his thinking of Sophie most touched her heart. She cast him a smile. 'Perhaps we should charge Bart with such a task.'

He laughed as he escorted her out the door to the street. 'Very wise idea.'

Madeleine had an illusion of being transported to the town of her childhood. The pavement was more crowded, indeed, and the shops more varied and numerous, but it was a most respectable street, and her dress indistinguishable from other young ladies shopping. Or so she thought. She still received many curious looks.

'Devlin, are you sure my appearance is acceptable?'

Devlin had noticed the admiring glances of the men and appraising looks of the women. He could not help but be proud to be Madeleine's escort. Beautiful even in her own ill-fitting frock, she quite took his breath away in her new walking dress.

'You look lovely,' he whispered back.

This news did not appear to cheer her. She furrowed her brow. Too bad some choice piece of horseflesh did not come into view to distract her.

Devlin caught sight of a shop window. 'We must go in here.' He pulled her into the shop. 'Must not forget our girl.'

They entered a toy store with shelf after shelf of dolls, toy soldiers, and miniature coaches and wagons. An exquisite wax doll with real hair as dark and curly as Linette's caught Devlin's eye. He vowed he must purchase it for Linette. Madeleine adamantly refused, saying the child was too young to care for such a treasure. He settled instead for a porcelain-faced baby doll, a ball and blocks. As he finished giving the direction for the toys to be delivered that afternoon, he spied a carved wooden horse and, thinking perhaps the little girl might be horse-mad like her mother, added it to his purchases.

Back on the street, a handsome carriage drawn by a set of matching bays approached in their direction. Devlin frowned as he spied the crest. The carriage stopped next to them. As Madeleine shrank back, Devlin stepped forward to greet its passenger.

'Devlin, it has been too long,' the fair-haired lady at the carriage window exclaimed.

'How are you, Serena?' His sister-in-law was a good creature, well intentioned, eminently correct, with classical looks and very little in common with Devlin except a connection to his brother.

'I am well, as usual,' she responded in her soft voice. 'And you, brother? We do worry when you do not call.'

'I have been shockingly remiss, but I'm fit, I assure you.'

His sister-in-law gazed curiously at Madeleine. It had never entered his mind that he'd be required to introduce Madeleine to anyone, least of all his sister-in-law, the Marchioness.

He pulled Madeleine forward, needing to exert a little physical effort to do so. 'Serena, may I present Miss England. Miss England, the Marchioness of Heronvale, my sister-in-law.'

Madeleine executed a very correct curtsy.

'Have we met before, Miss England? I do not recall.'

Madeleine, with her eyes downcast replied, 'No, madam.'

'Well, perhaps I may convey you both to your destination? I would be pleased to do so.'

Devlin suspected Serena would be very pleased for an opportunity to find out who her brother-in-law escorted unchaperoned through this shopping district. He felt Madeleine painfully squeeze his arm.

'I believe Miss England has one or two more shops to visit, but that was kind of you, Serena.'

'Are the shops worthwhile, Miss England? I confess I have never visited the ones on this street.'

'They suit me very well, madam,' responded Madeleine in a quiet voice.

'Perhaps you could recommend one to me,' the Marchioness persisted. Devlin knew her inquiry to be meant in a friendly way, but he also knew his brother's wife was nearly as fixed on him securing his future as was his brother. She wanted nothing more than to see him happily married; the Marquess wanted merely to keep his brother's fortune secure.

'I would not presume to.' Madeleine looked miserable. Only his firm hold on her arm kept her from bolting, he suspected.

A hackney coach came from behind, its driver shouting for the carriage to move on.

'Oh, dear,' said Serena. 'We had better go.'

'Indeed,' replied Devlin.

'Please call soon, Devlin. My pleasure, Miss England.' The carriage moved forward and these last words faded with distance.

'Devlin, may we please go home now?' Madeleine raised a shaking hand to her bonnet.

'No,' he said mildly, determined for her not to be made uncomfortable by her encounter with Serena. 'We need to have you measured for shoes and I must not return without cloth for Sophie.'

'Oh, yes, I quite forgot Sophie's cloth,' she murmured. A racing phaeton whizzed by. She did not even notice.

'Maddy, were you made uncomfortable by my sister-in-law?'

They walked a few steps before she answered. 'It was very improper to introduce me to her.'

'I disagree. It would have been ill-mannered not to introduce you. An insult to you.'

He glanced at her, seeing her brows knitted together and her bottom lip trembling slightly. 'A fine lady like the Marchioness should not be made to converse with one such as me.'

'Maddy, I refuse to allow you to speak so. You have studied your appearance. You could not be more presentable.' He did not yet know the story, but he would wager she'd not chosen her life with Farley. But who would choose such a life? Only a woman with no other choice.

'My appearance does not alter the fact that you should not have introduced a marchioness to…to Haymarket-ware.'

'I refuse for you to speak so,' he said.

She did not look at him. 'I will endeavour to obey you, my lord.'

He yanked open the door to the shoemaker.

After he'd ordered various pairs of shoes for her, he seemed relaxed again. By the time they'd selected several pieces of material at the cloth merchant's shop, they were back in temper with each other.

Devlin hailed a hack. As he negotiated with the driver, Madeleine noticed a gentleman across the street looking at her.

Farley.

He saw her look in his direction and tipped his hat to her. Her heart pounded wildly, and she feared she might vomit. She felt Farley's eyes on her the entire time it took for Devlin to lift her into the hack.

As they pulled away, he saluted her once more.

* * *

Lord Edwin Farley watched the hack start off down the street. He had taken to frequenting a tobacconist on this row, one of the deplorable economies he was forced to make in his constrained financial circumstances. At first he'd noticed the young lady in the lilac and blue with a connoisseur's appreciation, but when he saw it was Madeleine, he froze. All that beauty, and he'd let her fall into the hands of Devlin Steele. It irritated him beyond belief.

He'd hoped to recoup from his recent bad luck by playing until Steele owed him a bundle. The Marquess of Heronvale would have redeemed his little brother's vowels, even if the sum had been large. Everyone knew the older brother doted on the younger one. But Farley had lost instead. If that were not bad enough, he'd impulsively used Madeleine to settle his debt. Damned Steele.

The hack turned the corner and disappeared from his sight. He resumed his stroll down the pavement. Madeleine had looked quite fetching in that lavender confection. His body stirred merely thinking about her.

He'd have her back, he vowed. He'd unpeel those layers of clothing from her and bed her like she'd never been bedded before. He'd make her beg for him, make her pant with wanting him. She'd been easy to seduce as a girl. He'd only had to say a few pretty words to her, and she'd been his. He laughed, remembering how easy it had been to entice her to his room that night, her father bursting in at the perfect moment—when she'd been naked on top of him.

Yes, he'd get her back, he vowed. This time without the child she was stupid enough not to prevent. Perhaps he could make some money on the child. He knew men whose tastes went to ones as young as that. A little beauty like her mother, she would likely sell at a good price.

What revenge ought he to exact upon Steele? It would give him added pleasure to give that matter some thought.

Humming and jauntily swinging his walking stick, Farley continued on his way.

Chapter Six

The packages from their shopping expedition arrived that afternoon amid much excitement. The wide eyes of little Linette as she opened hers made all the extravagance worthwhile. Sophie, whom Devlin did not expect to break out in raptures, reverently fingered the cloth they had purchased.

'Thank you, my lord,' Sophie whispered, though she did not meet his eye while saying it.

'You did tolerably well, Dev,' Bart said, watching Sophie's every movement.

'Indeed?' He laughed. 'I am unused to such high praise from you.'

'The lass is happy. Mind you do not tease her, now.' Bart shook his finger in warning.

Devlin tried to stifle his grin. 'I shall endeavour not to.'

Madeleine was unusually quiet. She excused herself, saying she wished to unpack her dresses. Thinking of it, Devlin realised she had been just as solemn on the ride back home.

Linette held the horse up to Devlin, pulling on his trousers as she did so. 'Horse! Horse!' she said excitedly. It was inevitable. The horse captured the little girl's attention and the expensive doll was ignored. Devlin sat down on the floor.

'Shall we build a stable for your horse, Lady Lin?' He gathered the blocks together and started building.

'Wady Win,' Linette parroted.

'How much did all this cost, might I ask?' Bart's voice was deceptively casual.

'I think you had better not ask,' Devlin said ruefully. 'I thought I might pay a visit to my brother tomorrow.'

Madeleine walked back into the room. 'You will visit your brother?'

She did not need to know he intended to ask his brother for a small advance. 'I promised my sister-in-law, as you recall.'

'Oh.' She sat on the settee and watched Devlin and Linette build the promised stable with the blocks.

'Would you like me to make tea, Maddy?' Sophie asked, dropping her fabric back into its box.

Madeleine popped up. 'I will do it.'

'You, Maddy?' Sophie said. 'It is not necessary.'

'I want to. It is not so difficult, is it?'

'Neigh! Neigh!' Linette galloped her wooden horse, trying to make it jump over the blocks. The blocks tumbled.

'Now, I was building that.' Devlin ruffled the girl's hair, making her giggle. He kept an eye on the mother.

'I will do it, Maddy. Do not trouble yourself.' Sophie started for the kitchen.

Madeleine insisted. 'No, *I* will do it.'

'It is my job,' Sophie said, visibly upset.

Madeleine put her hands on her hips. 'I would like to make it. I am tired of being waited upon as if I am no use at all.'

'But, but…' Sophie burst into tears and ran out.

'That was badly done, miss.' Bart gave her a stern expression. 'The lass wishes to serve you. She credits you with sparing her much hardship.' He marched after Sophie.

Madeleine glanced at Devlin, her hand rubbing her throat. 'I did not mean to make her cry.'

Devlin understood. She wanted to feel she had some use beyond the bedchamber. He had even less to offer, except the money his brother controlled, if he could get it. If Madeleine wished to make tea, what was the harm?

He turned back to the blocks. 'Maddy, if it would not be too much trouble, would you make me some tea?'

The next morning Devlin walked up to an impressive town house on Grosvenor Square and rapped with the shiny brass knocker. The heavy door opened and a solemn-faced butler almost broke into a smile.

'Master Devlin.'

'Barclay, you never change.' Devlin did smile. 'I trust you are well?'

The man took his hat and gloves. 'Indeed, I am, Master Devlin.'

'Is my brother here?'

'He is expected directly, my lord. Shall I announce you to her ladyship?'

'If you please.'

He followed Barclay to the parlour, decorated with Serena's usual perfection, couches and chairs arranged to put visitors at ease. A moment later, the Marchioness came through the door.

'Devlin, you kept your promise. How good to see you.' She reached out her hands to him.

He clasped them warmly and kissed her cheek. 'Serena, you are in excellent looks, as usual.' His brother's wife had the cool beauty of the fine china figurines gracing the mantelpiece, disguising her warm-hearted nature. Her reserve and unceasing correctness could so easily be mistaken for coldness.

She coloured slightly. 'Do sit with me and tell me how you go on. I've already rung for tea.'

He joined her on the couch. 'I am well, Serena.'

She peered at him worriedly. 'Are you sure? You look a little pale. Do your wounds still pain you?'

He laughed. 'I am quite well. Thoroughly recovered and there is no need to fuss over me. Where is Ned?'

'Attending to some business.' Her brows knit together. 'Are you in trouble, Devlin?'

'Good God, no, Serena.' Her solicitude rivalled his brother's. 'I have something to discuss. Nothing to signify.'

The tea arrived and she poured with precision. He sipped the liquid, brewed to perfection, and thought how different this cup was from the strong, leaf-filled concoction Madeleine had made the day before.

Serena spoke. 'It was pleasant seeing you yesterday.'

'Indeed.'

'That young lady—Miss England, I believe—was lovely. Who is she, Devlin?'

He should have expected this question. He gave Serena a direct look. 'An acquaintance.'

Her eyebrows raised.

He held her gaze.

Serena glanced down demurely. 'Does she interest you?'

Did Madeleine *interest* him? Keeping her safe interested him. Making love to her interested him, but he would not explain that to Serena. At least Serena must not suspect Madeleine to be anything but a well-bred young lady, unchaperoned though she had been. She would not have mentioned Madeleine at all if she had thought her to be Haymarket-ware, as Madeleine called herself.

'She is an acquaintance, Serena,' he repeated in a mild voice.

She tilted her head sceptically, but was much too well bred to press any further.

They sat in awkward silence.

'I should tell you I have moved, Serena.'

She peered at him. 'Moved? For what reason?'

Devlin paused. 'No reason.'

'Some difficulty with the rent?'

'No.' Devlin hid his impatience with a small laugh. 'Why

do you suppose I should have difficulty with the rent? You and Ned. I cannot say who is the worse. I am not in difficulty. I am well able to take care of myself. At six and twenty I should know how to go on. I survived Napoleon's army, if you recall.'

Serena looked stricken. 'But you were so badly injured. We feared you would not live. You do not realise how close a thing it was.' She fished a lace-edged handkerchief from her sleeve and dabbed her eyes. 'And you have been gambling so. Ned was concerned because no one has seen you for days.'

'Ned can go to the dev—' This was too much. 'Good God, what does he do, scour the town for news of me?'

Serena's eyes glittered with tears. 'I believe he hears word of you at White's,' she replied in all seriousness.

Devlin burst into laughter. He sat down next to her and put his arm around her, squeezing affectionately. 'Dear sister, I beg your pardon. I do not mean to upset you. I know you and my brother mean well, but you forget I'm out of leading strings.'

She blushed and straightened her posture. 'I am sure we do not.'

'Tell me how you and Ned go on? Is my brother still managing the family affairs to perfection?'

Serena lifted her chin protectively. 'Ned has much on his shoulders.'

Devlin gave her a kind smile. 'Indeed he does. He is a man to admire, Serena. I mean that.'

'I have heard from your sisters and brother. They are excellent correspondents.'

Unlike himself who wrote little and visited less.

'Indeed? What is the family news?'

Serena, with a wistfulness in her voice, chattered on about the trifling activities of his nephews and nieces. Percy's son, Jeffrey, the eldest, at Eton. Rebecca, Helen's daughter, learning the pianoforte. All the little ones merging into a blur. He listened with as interested an expression as he could muster.

Serena doted on all the children. By far she was their favourite aunt. And he, the Waterloo Dragoon, was their hero uncle, even though he had difficulty keeping their names straight.

What a pity Serena had not had a child. Fate had no notion of fair play. She would make a perfect mother, and a loving one, as well. He suspected her disappointment in that quarter was immense.

'And you, Serena? How do you go on?'

'I am well.' A sad look came over her face.

Devlin gave her another hug. She would not wish to speak of her disappointment at not presenting the Marquess with an heir.

'Dear sister,' he murmured.

She recovered herself. 'Ned will be here directly. Will you wait for him?'

He had little choice. 'Serena,' he said, surmising a change of conversation was in order, 'do you suppose Ned would mind if I borrowed a pair of horses some morning? I've a notion to ride.'

'You will ride again?' she said brightly. He had not been on a horse since charging the French, east of the Brussels road. 'Indeed he will not mind. He will be glad of it, and I will personally ask Barclay to instruct the stable to provide any horse you wish.'

'Any two horses. I…I wish to have Bart join me.'

'Two horses it is.' She smiled.

The parlour door opened and the Marquess strode in at a quicker pace than was his custom. Devlin stood to greet him.

'Devlin, how good to see you.' Equally uncharacteristic of him, he embraced Devlin heartily.

This idol of his childhood, his oldest brother Ned, usually did not betray emotion. Ned always could be counted on to remain unflappable when his youngest brother came begging for his help out of the latest scrape. Because of those days, Devlin always felt in awe of that tall, ramrod-straight figure. He always expected to crane his neck to look at Ned. It never

failed to be a shock when he found himself half a head taller
and his brother going grey at the temples.

'What brings you to call?' Ned asked with such surprise,
it suggested he had given up altogether on a visit from Devlin.

'I wished to see you and Serena, of course, but I also have
a matter of business to discuss with you, if it is convenient.'

Ned regained that strict composure. 'Indeed. We shall go
into the library. You will excuse us, Serena?'

With a nod to his wife, he preceded Devlin out the door.
Devlin followed dutifully, feeling much like that little boy, in
a scrape once more.

Inside that book-lined room, Ned poured two glasses of
port. Devlin glanced at the shelves and had the incongruous
thought that Madeleine might enjoy a good book. Not the sort
of book to be found in this room, he supposed, but perhaps a
Miniver Press novel such as his sisters had read when they
sat by his sick bed.

Ned handed him his glass. 'What did you wish to discuss?'

Devlin sipped and paced the room, trying to figure out the
best way to present this.

'Are you in trouble?' Ned's voice was low and steady.

Devlin flashed him an irritated glance and muttered, 'You
and Serena.' Speaking more firmly, he said, 'I am not in trouble.'

His brother's face remained impassive.

Devlin took a gulp of port. 'I have moved.'

'Yes?'

'To a larger place.'

'You required a larger place?' A disapproving tone crept
into his brother's speech.

'It was too good an opportunity to pass up. On the same
street, but a much better situation.'

'And?' One of Ned's eyebrows rose.

Devlin took a deep breath. 'I am short of money as a result.
I would ask if you would advance me some additional funds
until next quarter.'

His brother did not drop his gaze, nor did his expression change, even a muscle. Devlin knew he was considering, weighing the matter silently in his head.

As a child, this silence had been a comfort. It meant Ned was reckoning a way out of his difficulties. As a man, he was less certain.

His brother stared implacably into his port. 'How wise was this move?'

'Devil it, Ned, the move is made. Whether it was wise or not is moot.'

'You engaged in this impulsively.' This was not a question but a statement of fact, a disapproved-of fact.

Devlin put his glass down on a table and faced his immovable brother. 'It is done, Ned, and I need some money to get through to next quarter. Will you give it or not?'

Ned sat in a nearby chair and casually crossed his legs. 'You have been gambling heavily, little brother.'

Devlin knew that was coming. 'As your spies have reported? I do not suppose they were present when I won back my losses?'

Ned's cronies would never have been present at such an unsavoury place as Farley's. If they had, his brother would be discussing what else Devlin won that night.

'I have heard your losses to be steep. This gambling must stop, Devlin.'

If his brother had not ordered him to stop gambling, he might have informed Ned that he'd come to the same conclusion. Now he would not give his brother that satisfaction.

'And what else might I do, Ned? What is there for me to do? The war is over, and I'm damned if I'll go anywhere else in this world to fight. India? Africa? The West Indies? I'm no longer keen on dying on foreign soil.'

Ned swirled his port and tasted the rich, imported liquid. 'It is time you took your rightful place in the family.'

'Rightful place?' Devlin prowled the room. 'What the deuce is my rightful place?'

Calmly his brother spoke, 'You need to assume the control of your estate. It should not fall to our brother Percy, who has enough of his own to oversee.'

'You know I cannot.' Devlin glared at him. 'You and my father saw to that. I cannot take control until I marry. I must subsist on what you obligingly provide me until I marry a suitable woman of whom you approve. Good God! What possessed you and my father to contrive that addle-brained plan?'

'You know why.' Ned spoke in the most reasonable voice possible. 'You lack control. You have always been devil-may-care. Father had the wisdom to know you would cease your wild ways when you had another person dependent upon you. A wife.'

'Damn it, Ned, would you have me marry merely to get my fortune? Would you have married under that fancy bit of blackmail?'

At least Devlin had the satisfaction of seeing his brother betray emotion. Ned's cheek twitched. 'Leave Serena out of this.'

Devlin felt a pang of guilt for speaking of his brother's marriage. He never knew for certain if his brother loved Serena, though he suspected she loved Ned. When he saw Ned and Serena together, there was such a reserve between them, who could tell? Had Ned married her out of duty? Pity Serena, if he had. Their father was behind the match, of course, and Ned would never have gone against their father's wishes. Two peas in a pod, his brother and father.

'I am not speaking of Serena,' he said more mildly. 'I am speaking of myself. I have no desire to marry at the moment, but I am more than ready to assume control of my property. Indeed, I long to run it. Let me take the task from Percy and work the farm. I do not give a damn if the rest of the money is under your thumb.'

It would be an ideal solution. Bart and Sophie would fit in neatly on the estate. Madeleine and Linette would be a bit more difficult to situate, but he was sure he could contrive something.

Ned regained his damned composure. 'Doing so would deprive you of an opportunity to make an advantageous match. The Season has begun and there are all manner of eligible young ladies from whom you may choose.'

Devlin clenched his fist. 'I have no desire to marry.'

Ned rose and walked to the desk by the window. He fussed with papers stacked there, glancing through them, and restacking them. Devlin would have liked to think his brother was considering his proposal, but he suspected Ned was simply showing him who was head of the family.

Ned did not look up from the papers when he spoke. 'Our father's wishes will continue to be honoured. You will receive your allotted portion on the quarter, not before. When you marry an acceptable young lady, your estate and your fortune will pass to you, and I will have no more to say of it.'

Devlin leaned down, putting both hands on the desk, forcing his brother to meet his eyes. 'Both you and Father were mistaken, Ned. You could at least let me work. As it is, you and our dear departed father have deprived me of any responsibility at all and have kept me as dependent as if I were still a schoolboy. Had I something of value to do, I might have reason to be steady. As it is, I have nothing.'

'You will have everything you desire if you marry.' Ned spoke through clenched teeth.

'But I do not wish to marry.'

The two men glared at each other.

Devlin swung away from his brother. 'You and Father never trusted me to find my own way. You knew, did you not, that he almost refused to purchase my colours?' He fingered one of the volumes on the shelf. 'I would have enlisted as a common foot soldier had he done so. Father could not force me to do anything and neither can you, Ned.'

'You are being foolish, Devlin. This is for your own good.

You have always been too wild by half and too wilful to behave with any sense.'

'You dare to say such a thing to me? Do you forget what I have been doing these past years? Do you think I have been on a lark?'

The Marquess stood. 'I know it killed our father to have you traipsing all over the continent risking your neck.'

Devlin shook with rage. 'Unfair, Ned.'

'You should have been seeing to your duty to the family.' Ned raised his voice.

'I *was* seeing to my duty to the family. How well do you think the family would have fared under Napoleon?' Devlin matched his brother's volume. 'Go to the devil, Ned.'

Ned stepped from behind the desk and faced his brother. 'Our father worried every day that you would meet your death. Not only during the war, but every day of your sad youth. You have been a rash care-for-nobody and it is past time you became a grown man.'

Devlin clenched his fists, standing nose to nose with his older brother. 'I fought for my life before I ever went to war. To be a man means more than following the dictates of a father who thought he could pull a string and have all his bidding done. When will *you* assume manhood, Ned? Have you ever had a thought of your own?'

'You are addressing the head of the family, little brother.'

'I am addressing my father. You may as well be him, Ned. You always did whatever he said. You and Percy and our sisters. You all blindly did his bidding. If he said jump, you jumped. If he said marry this young lady, you made the offer.'

'Leave Serena out of this!' Ned's eyes blazed. He shoved hard against Devlin's chest.

Devlin automatically shoved back, his soldier's reflexes operating. With his greater height, youth, and war-honed strength, he knocked his brother to the floor. 'Leave me to live my own life! I will choose when and who I marry.'

'Indeed you shall, you insufferable ingrate.' Ned picked

himself off the floor and, to Devlin's surprise, came at him with a swinging fist that connected smartly to Devlin's jaw.

'Deuce,' yelled Devlin, lunging back at him, toppling them both to the floor. They rolled, grunting and punching, knocking down a small table and sending the wine decanter crashing to the floor, red wine splashing.

'Stop this! Stop at once!' Serena cried from the doorway.

The two men paid her no heed. On their feet now, they smashed into a bookcase and books rained down from the shelves. Blood dripped from Ned's nose and Devlin's coat ripped.

'Barclay! Barclay!' Serena screamed for the butler as she ran over to her husband and brother-in-law. She pulled on Devlin's back to get him off Ned.

'Master Devlin. Master Ned.' A voice of authority seemed to boom directly from their childhood. White-haired Barclay entered the room. 'You ought to be ashamed.'

They stopped fighting at once.

Ned recovered first, dabbing his nose with the lace-edged handkerchief Serena offered him. 'Thank you, Barclay. We are quite in control again. Your help is no longer necessary.'

Devlin felt a pain in his stomach that was not the result of a punching fist. How had he wound up brawling with his older brother? He'd seen Percy and Ned in a scrap or two, always carefully kept from their father, but it was unthinkable that he should actually strike this man who'd searched all through the wounded and dying in Brussels until he found his younger brother.

'Ned, I—'

'Enough, Devlin.' The Marquess folded the handkerchief.

Serena looked as if she might swoon at any moment, filling Devlin with more guilt. Her face was pale as she righted the toppled table and tried to pick up the glass fragments. How could he have distressed her like this?

Ned straightened his clothes and brushed himself off. He glanced at his wife. 'Serena, would you leave us, please?'

'I would not wish—' she began.

'Leave us. We shall not come to further blows.' Devlin had not thought his brother could speak so softly.

With a worried look at them both, she left the room, one hand covering her mouth.

Ned composed himself and returned to his desk, showing no signs that they had been rolling on the floor moments before. 'Serena tells me you were in the company of an unchaperoned young woman.'

Devlin rolled his eyes. He might be standing before his father again. Too many times his father ignored what Devlin tried to say and went directly to whatever would hurt him most.

'Your point, Ned?'

'Did you introduce my wife to your fancy piece?'

Amazing. Ned managed to provoke his anger again. 'Ned, I assure you, I would not do anything to embarrass my sister-in-law. I have the highest respect and sympathy for her.'

'What do you mean "sympathy"?' Ned sounded ready to punch him again.

'I meant nothing.' He meant he was sorry she had not conceived a child, but this was not the time to address Ned on that subject. He had no notion how the wind blew for his brother on that score.

'Who was the woman you were with? Do you have a lightskirt who costs you?'

Good God. Did Ned wish another jab in the nob? 'She is an acquaintance who does not deserve your insults.' Devlin would say no more. He merely wished to get away from his brother. 'Ned, we have said more than is prudent. I will beg your leave.'

'Indeed? We have resolved nothing.' Ned looked like a stranger. No, he looked like their father, not at all like his adored older brother.

'It doesn't matter. I will wait for my money to come due.' He walked to the door.

Ned's mouth set into a thin, grim line. 'When your money comes due, it will be half the amount.'

'What?'

'Half the amount.' The Marquess studied his papers before glancing up at Devlin. 'You need to search for a wife. Perhaps penury will serve as an incentive.'

Devlin fought the rage that erupted inside him. How would he care for Madeleine? How would he feed little Linette? 'Damn you, Ned. You have no idea what this means.'

'Remember who is the head of the family, little brother.'

'I'll not forget.' He spoke through his teeth.

Devlin hurried out of the library and almost ran into his sister-in-law, who was walking back and forth in the hall.

'Devlin, what happened? Why were you fighting?' she whispered, her voice filled with anxiety.

He stroked her arm. 'A brothers' quarrel, nothing more. Do not worry, sister.'

She looked unconvinced. He gave her a long reassuring hug and let her weep against his shoulder a little. 'It was entirely my fault, Serena. You know how I can provoke Ned. Do not cry.'

The library door opened. An icy voice such as Devlin had never heard said, 'Unhand my wife and take your leave.'

Chapter Seven

Misery assailed Devlin as he walked through the doorway
of Ned's town house. He'd made a mess of things. What a
colossal fool, provoking his brother, though he could not precisely remember what he had said to set Ned off. They had
disagreed reasonably for a short time. How had he ended up
punching Ned in the nose, for deuce's sake?

Worse than bloodying the nose of the Marquess of Heronvale was jeopardising Madeleine's future and that of her
child. How would he care for them now?

What a damned coil. What a fool and idiot.

He set a slow pace in the direction of St James's Street.

He ought to have conserved his money, not rented the bigger apartment, not purchased as many lengths of fabric for
Sophie, as many toys for Linette. He should not have purchased an entire wardrobe for Madeleine when she argued for
only two or three dresses. Most of all, he should not have lost
his temper with his brother. He should have remained calm.
He should have rehearsed several cogent arguments why his
brother should advance him the money. Instead, he'd allowed
Ned to goad him until they came to blows.

He might laugh at rousing emotion in his brother, if only
the result had not been the halving of his funds. Ned's calm,
dispassionate control, so comforting to him as a child, irritated

him as a man. To think he used to shake with fear when Ned and Percy pummelled each other with their fists, Ned as out of control as Devlin so often was. It had been like watching the foundations at Heronvale crack and crumble.

This time it was his own would-be estate that crumbled—Edgeworth, twenty miles from Heronvale and ten from Percy's estate. His father had aimed to keep them close, tied to the land that he'd purchased from neighbours who let their property slip through their fingers.

'Land, my boy.' Devlin could hear his father's firm voice, his fist pounding the dinner table. 'If a man has land, he has a future.' His father would gesture to Devlin's plate. 'Land gives you good food and drink to fill your belly. Mind, you have never been hungry in my house.'

True, but Devlin had known hunger on the Peninsula where supplies were often low, and he had known thirst when wounded at Waterloo, waiting twelve hours in the mud to be found.

Devlin was ready for the land his father bequeathed him. Ready for work. He longed for hard physical labour. He yearned to work next to the men in the fields, as he had fought beside their brothers. Wouldn't that give Ned apoplexy!

Devlin stopped in the middle of the pavement and rubbed his brow. What good did it do to think of Edgeworth? He needed to think of Madeleine.

It would not be at all difficult to find positions for Bart and Sophie somewhere in the family. Percy, especially, had a kind heart for a person in need. Indeed, anyone would be fortunate to hire Bart. And, if he knew Bart, the man would care well for Sophie. As for himself, he could plague Ned by visiting one sister after another, never complying with the Heronvale dictates. What prime sport that would be.

But what about Madeleine and Linette? He would go to the devil and drag Ned with him before he'd allow Madeleine to return to the only profession she knew and her daughter with her. Damn, he needed money to save her from that fate. Enough money for her to live comfortably and to rear Linette.

Devlin's mind spun round and round. The only thing he knew with a certainty was that he was a damned fool and had failed the people who depended upon him.

Failed Madeleine.

Too soon he neared the lodgings. With a heavy heart, he turned the knob of the front door.

Madeleine stole a surreptitious glance at Devlin during dinner later that evening. He was unduly quiet. Something troubled him, and she did not know what. Did she even have the right to inquire?

If he were like other men, she would not care what problems he had. But he was not like other men. Would another man be so kind to her daughter? When it had been time for Linette to go to bed, it had to be Devlin to carry her up and tuck her in. For a moment she worried about leaving Linette to a man's care, but that was foolish. Devlin would not harm her.

Indeed, he should not be so kind. It made her feel she could depend on him. It was dangerous to depend upon anyone. They fooled you, then tricked you into doing what they willed.

She cast her gaze on Devlin again, and made an attempt at conversation. 'Did you have a pleasant visit with your brother?'

He glanced up and paused so long she thought he would not answer. 'I spent an agreeable interval with my sister-in-law.'

What did that mean?

'Scrapped with your brother, did you?' Bart snorted. 'That explains your black looks.'

Devlin did not banter back at Bart as was usual. Instead, he rubbed his forehead and stared down at his plate. Madeleine frowned. Bart should leave off scolding this time. Something was indeed wrong.

Sophie, her usual wary expression on her face, popped up to gather the dirty dishes. She had a cat's sense for danger.

Little had been eaten from Devlin's plate. 'Leave the dishes a bit, Sophie. I wish to speak to all of you.'

Madeleine's pulse accelerated. No good news could be forthcoming.

'Let us clear the dishes first,' Madeleine suggested. 'It will be more comfortable.' And it would delay the inevitable.

Devlin released a breath. 'Very well, remove the dishes, but return promptly, if you please.'

'I will help.' Madeleine picked up her own plate and Devlin's.

'I can do it, Maddy,' Sophie said.

'I want to help,' Madeleine countered. She was able to clear dishes, at least. No special skill needed for that. Besides, it helped quiet her nerves to be busy.

Madeleine returned to her seat next to Devlin. He had poured small glasses of port for all of them and his eyes held such a pained expression, the fear rose in her once more.

What other kind of bad news could there be, except she, Linette and Sophie would have to leave? She clenched her hands together in her lap.

Devlin toyed with his glass of port. He cleared his throat. 'I visited my brother to request an advance of the money due me in two months' time. We have wound up a little short—'

'Because of my dresses.' Madeleine moaned, misery and guilt swirling inside her.

He held the glass still. 'Not only your dresses, Maddy. My mismanagement is primarily the blame.'

'Now, lad…' Bart began, an uncharacteristic soothing tone in his voice.

Devlin cleared his throat. 'You see, I had decided the way out of our difficulties was to make the request of my brother. Unfortunately, I had not counted on the Marquess refusing.'

'The man refused?' Bart's thick eyebrows shot up.

'I fear so.'

'No worry, Dev. We shall manage.' Bart nodded his head as if convincing himself as well as the others. 'We can practise some economy. We shall do nicely.'

Devlin gave a dry laugh. 'You have not yet heard the worst of it, my friend. Not only did my brother refuse an advance, he cut my allowance in half. I do not see how we can go on at all.'

Bart's mouth opened. 'Half?'

'What does it mean, Maddy?' Sophie leaned over the table to whisper to her.

'It means you and Linette and I must leave.' Madeleine's hand went to her throat. She thought her words would strangle there.

'No,' Devlin protested. 'It does not mean that.'

'Oh, perhaps not today,' she went on. 'We should have a little time to make other arrangements. Nothing hard-hearted about it.' Her voice trembled now.

'Maddy.' Devlin grabbed her hand. 'It does not mean you must leave.'

She met his gaze. Along with pain, she saw a tenderness that took her breath away.

'I do not know how, Maddy, but I will take care of you.'

She blinked.

He turned back to Bart and Sophie. 'I think I should be able to find you both positions with some member of my family.'

'I will not leave Maddy,' Sophie cried.

'And I will stay with you, lad. We have endured worse than this.' Bart lifted his glass in a salute.

Devlin looked from one to another. 'We did not have women and a child to care for in those days.'

'We will take care of ourselves.' Madeleine lifted her chin in a show of bravado she could not feel.

'How, Maddy?' Devlin said. 'You have no means of income.'

Bart stood and held his glass high. 'We are in this together, do we agree? We solve it together.' He stared at them until they all lifted their glasses in return.

'I could take in laundry,' Sophie said in a quiet voice.

Devlin laughed. 'I hope it does not come to that, little one. I thought I might speak to some people I know tomorrow. Perhaps someone can find a use for me.'

'If there's labour to be done I can do it,' Bart said.

Madeleine toyed with her glass. 'There are three or four men who would pay much for time with me.'

They all stared at her.

'It should not be difficult, I think. I can give you the names and you can find out how to communicate with them.'

'Good God, Maddy.' Devlin's face drained of colour.

Madeleine gave him a surprised look. 'It would pay handsomely, I am sure.'

He spoke through clenched teeth. 'I do not give a deuce how well it would pay, you will not bed other men on my behalf.'

'Not on your behalf, but for us all.' He could not prevent her from doing her part, not when she was the cause of the problem.

He slapped his hand on the table. 'I will hear no more of this.'

Sophie's eyes grew wider. With a nervous glance, she slipped off the chair and skittered into the kitchen. His arms crossed against his chest, Bart regarded Madeleine and Devlin with a disapproving expression.

Madeleine continued. 'I believe it would bring in a good sum of money.'

He stood up and leaned over her. 'No.' He strode out of the room.

She followed him. 'Why not?'

He wheeled around to face her. 'You have to ask?'

'Devlin, it would not be difficult for me to do this. It is not as if I have not done it before.'

His eyes flashed.

'What objection can you have? It is the perfect solution.'

'You will allow me to solve our problems, Maddy. You will not do it by lying on your back.'

He did not need to speak to her in such a crude manner. 'It is what I do best, if you recall.'

'Deuce,' he said. 'And where shall you perform this lucrative act? In this house? With Linette in the room?'

'Of course not!' How dare he suggest such a thing. 'I have always kept Linette out of the way. Sophie would take her.'

'Much more proper,' he said, the corner of his mouth turning down in contempt.

'I have told you, I am not proper.'

'And where would Bart and I be? Collecting the money at the door?'

'Do not be absurd. I cannot talk to you. You do not see reason.' She stalked off.

How could he not see she must resolve the difficulties she had placed him in? She owed him that much. It was not that she wished to bed anyone, except...except... No, he must recognise how much she was indebted to him. He had rescued her from Farley. For that she would do anything for him. Anything.

She ran up the stairs, but he came right behind. At the top of the stairs, he caught her by the shoulders and spun her around.

'We will finish this, Madeleine. We will not solve our financial woes in this way, do you hear? You will not speak of this again.' He dug his fingers into her shoulders.

'How is it that you could object, Devlin? You know what I am.' She lowered her voice.

He made a strangled sound. 'Do you think I wish to think of another man's hands all over you?'

She stared at him. The hands of many men had touched her.

His fingers slid down her arms. 'Do you think I could accept money for another man to bed you?'

She swallowed. 'Farley did.'

'I am not Farley, Madeleine. I thought you understood that.'

He stood so close, all she needed was to stand on tiptoe and touch her lips to his. She could smell the port on his breath and the taste of it resonated in her mouth. The wish to taste it on him was almost too difficult to bear. He made no move to close the gap between them. It was clearly her choice.

His hands rested gently on her arms. Those hands had once caressed her bare skin. She craved the joy and terror of his body joined to hers. Her feet arched and raised her higher. He uttered a guttural sound and closed the gap between them, his mouth plundering as if he were a man starved. Her own hunger surged as she pressed herself against him and wound her arms around his neck. His lips travelled to her neck, sending sensations straight to her soul.

She wanted him again with all the wantonness of her wretched body. The body that had betrayed her and led to her deserved ruin. She had learned to erase all thought and all feeling in order to play the role Farley bid her play, but Devlin made her tremble with longing. He tore away the safety of her detachment.

She struggled to speak. 'Do you want me, Devlin?' Her voice sounded more controlled than she felt. 'Do you wish to bed me?'

He stilled. Straightening, his eyes narrowed. Her knees began to shake as his silence grew longer.

Finally, he spoke, his tone cold. 'Am I able to afford you, Miss M?'

He turned and hurried down the stairs and out the front door.

* * *

At the town house in Grosvenor Square, the Marquess of Heronvale pushed food around his plate. The cavernous dining room echoed with the clink of his silver fork against the china.

He glanced at his wife. She looked absorbed in her own thoughts, the corners of her eyes pinched with unhappiness. A ball of misery sat in his stomach where food should have been.

He had disappointed her once again, more inventively this time. Indeed, rolling on the floor, trading punches with his youngest brother could hardly have lowered him further in her estimation. Especially since he had lost the fight.

Humiliating.

She had probably championed Devlin, in any event. He could not blame her. She was at ease with his brother in a way she was not with him. There was so little emotion between Serena and himself he would have been surprised if she had taken his side. Serena undoubtedly would think him too severe with Devlin, that a marquess should wield his power with more compassion.

But Devlin had infuriated him with those comments about his wife. Success with women came as easy to Devlin as riding, shooting, gaming. His youngest brother did everything without effort, as well as without thought, while he, the bearer of the title, had laboured for every accomplishment.

How well he remembered Devlin's birth. He had been home on school holiday, old enough at ten years to take charge of Percy, Helen, Julia, and Lavinia during his mother's confinement. He smiled inwardly at his less-than-learned explanation to his sisters and brother of exactly what would transpire during the birth. From the moment he'd held the newborn baby in his arms, Ned had been full of pride in this littlest brother. He made a solemn oath, that day, to always protect and defend him.

Devlin had made keeping that vow a challenge. A more reckless individual had never been born. It had been no surprise to Ned that Devlin joined the cavalry. Had Ned not been heir, he might have served his country as well, fighting at his brother's side, but all he could do was bring a near-dying Devlin back home.

'Ned? Is something troubling you?' Serena's sweet voice broke through his reverie.

'What?'

'I thought you might be troubled.' She averted her eyes.

'No, I am not.' She would think him weak, for certain, if she knew his thoughts.

'I beg your pardon,' she murmured.

He wished more to beg pardon of her, for his abominable behaviour, but did not know quite how. It seemed to him the silence between them was a condemnation.

'You disapprove of my dealings with my brother,' he blurted out.

Her eyebrows flew up in surprise. 'I would not question your judgement.'

'You think me too harsh.'

'I would not presume…'

He dismissed her words with a shake of his head. With trembling fingers, she picked daintily at her food.

After eight years of marriage, his wife remained a stunningly beautiful woman, her restraint the epitome of what became a lady. He could not complain. She was biddable, even when he pressed his carnal urges upon her, something he did as rarely as he could tolerate. The marital act was too painful for her sensibilities, but she craved children and he wished to give them to her.

Another failure on his part.

Ned drained the wine from his glass for the third time. 'Do you go out tonight, Serena?'

She jumped at the sound of his voice and barely glanced at him. 'No.'

It was his turn to be surprised. She had lately developed the habit of accompanying friends to the evening entertainments, the ones from which he begged off with increasing frequency.

She pressed her fingertips against her temple. 'I shall retire early. I...I have the headache.'

He had made her ill. He poured another glass of wine, wanting to express his concern, to offer to get her headache powders, to escort her up to her room and help her into bed.

He did none of those things.

'If you will excuse me...' She rose and, without waiting for a reply and probably not expecting one, left him alone in the room.

A footman entered and moved quickly to clear the table. Ned gestured for him to take away the plate from which he had barely eaten. When the man set the brandy in front of him, Ned began to see how much of that bottle he could finish.

Chapter Eight

Devlin picked a secluded chair at White's far from the bow window. He intended to sip his brandy in peace, away from the curious passers-by in the street. He wished to steel himself before circulating among the gentlemen of the *ton* in another attempt to procure employment. But what reason was there to expect this afternoon to differ from the last two weeks? He had made inquiries with the few of his senior officers still alive and exploited every imaginable family connection.

He might as well have bivouacked in a field. In fact, he would have preferred it, sharing cold, damp nights and bawdy soldier's tales with men who knew life could end with a musket ball the next day.

'May I join you?'

Devlin glanced up. The elegant figure of the Marquess stood before him. He shrugged his assent.

His brother signalled for a drink and settled in the comfortable chair across from him. 'How do you go on, Devlin?'

How did Ned think he went on? He and Bart had counted every coin that morning. They had a few days' escape from the River Tick, no more.

'Tolerably well,' he said.

Ned regarded him with a bland expression. What lay beyond that inscrutable countenance was a mystery. Devlin could wait out the silence, even if his brother never spoke.

Ned did not betray a thought, let alone a feeling. 'I understand you have inquired about employment around town.'

Devlin cocked his head, ever so slightly.

The waiter placed a glass before Ned. 'Without success, I recollect.'

Devlin favoured him with an ironic grin. 'I am pleased you are so well informed. Unfortunately, there seems to be a surplus of men such as myself. Soldiers needing work.'

'A pity.' Ned raised his glass to his lips.

'It does not help that the men from whom I seek employment instead contrive to introduce me to their daughters.'

'Indeed?'

Damn his brother's implacability. 'It was not you who spread the tale of our father's peculiar arrangement for me?'

Ned's eyes flickered with surprise, not guilt.

Devlin laughed. 'Not you, I collect. A sister, perhaps?'

Ned's control returned. 'Helen is a likely suspect.'

'Likely,' Devlin agreed. 'She has a crony in town, I believe.'

'And meddling proclivities.'

For a moment the ease between them returned and Devlin could almost forget that his revered brother had unwittingly placed a young woman and her innocent daughter in jeopardy. Ned would disapprove if he knew of Madeleine, but would he be less tight-fisted? Pride prevented Devlin from revisiting his monetary request on his brother. He was less sure why he did not confide about Madeleine.

'How is Serena?' he asked instead, seeking neutral ground.

The Marquess's eyes narrowed. 'Well.'

Serena was not neutral ground, then. Had Ned's anger something to do with Serena? Devlin studied him. The Marquess's bland expression had a hard edge.

'Good God, Ned. Is there some trouble between you and Serena?' The sudden thought burst into words.

Ned's face turned to chiselled granite. 'Mind your loose tongue. Your voice will carry.'

'I am sorry,' Devlin mumbled. Deuce, he had managed to blunder into more disfavour. If others had heard his ill-conceived words, the rumour-mill would carry the tale throughout the *ton*. He glanced around the room, but no one seemed to have given them the least heed. He hoped.

Ned had not looked around, but maintained his damnable composure. What a soldier he would have made, thought Devlin. He would bet Ned could face down a battalion single-handed without flinching. But would he be able to muster enough emotion to strike? A soldier eventually had to tap into rage. Until their fisticuffs of a fortnight ago, Devlin would not have believed Ned capable of rage.

Devlin felt light-headed. He ought not to have imagined battle. Images, sounds, and smells enveloped him. The thud of horses' hooves, the cry of battle, the smoke and smell of musket fire. Men screamed. Horses squealed. Metal clanged against metal before thrusting into flesh. Blood sprayed and the stench of death grew stronger.

Devlin pressed his fingers to his temple.

'Are you unwell?' Ned's voice held genuine concern.

Beads of perspiration dampened his forehead, as if the day had not been cool. The incessant thunder of French cannon echoed through his brain and his vision blurred into smoke-filled chaos. He could see the men, the shapes of their noses, the yellowed colour of their teeth, the stunned expressions as his own sabre sliced their throats.

'Dev, you are white as death. Let me summon a doctor.'

At his brother's voice, the images dissolved as suddenly as they had come, leaving his emotions in tattered pieces. Devlin suppressed an urge to laugh. As in childhood, his brother had rescued him, this time from his own personal demons.

'No doctor.' Devlin's voice was not quite steady. 'I was woolgathering for a moment.' He stood. All notions of grovelling for employment fled. 'Would you excuse me, Ned? I must leave.'

The brow of the Marquess wrinkled slightly. 'Are you sure you are not ill?'

Devlin's mouth lifted at the corner. 'Poor, perhaps, but not ill. You needn't worry.'

'I have my barouche. I will take you home.'

'Not necessary, brother. The walk will do me good.' His heart still pounded and his hands trembled. All Devlin wished to do was flee. He touched Ned on the shoulder and hurried away.

A light rainfall greeted him on the street and he closed his eyes for a moment, savouring the cool droplets pattering on his upturned face.

'Good day, Steele. Been at White's, I see.'

Devlin opened his eyes and met the affable grin of Lord Farley. He merely nodded and made to continue on his way.

Farley put a hand on his arm. 'Pray, what is your hurry? Come with me to my establishment. I shall buy you a drink.'

'I think not.' Again Devlin tried to leave.

'Come. You may give me news of Madeleine,' he persisted.

Devlin shrugged off the man's hand. 'I think not.'

Anger flashed through Farley's eyes for a moment before the amiable expression reappeared. 'How does she go on? I hope she still pleases you, but perhaps you have tired of her.'

Devlin's emotions were ragged enough to plant his fist squarely in the centre of Farley's face. He pushed past.

The man fell in step with him. 'I say, Steele, I hear you are seeking employment. Consider working for me. I could use a skilled gamester, and, I promise you, I would compensate you generously. I am again flush in the pockets, you see.'

Devlin stopped, his fingers still curled into fists. He'd heard the tale of Farley's change in fortune. 'Tell me, would my employment include fleecing green boys—like young Boscomb? He put a pistol to his head after a visit to your tables, did he not?'

Farley's eyes narrowed but his grin remained. 'An unfortunate incident.'

Devlin attempted to walk on, but Farley kept pace. 'Perhaps, if you are in need of funds, you would return Madeleine to me. In return for the money you won from me, of course.'

Devlin's fists tightened. If he'd had his sword in his hand, he would relish the sound of its steel plunging into Farley's gut. Devlin gritted his teeth. 'Do not speak of her.'

'Oh?' Farley remarked casually. 'She has become troublesome to you, perhaps? She has a habit of doing so. I assure you, I know precisely how to deal with her.'

Devlin spun toward Farley and, with the strength of both arms, shoved him away. Better that than attacking and killing him. Farley fell, splashing into a puddle on the pavement.

Farley struggled to rise. 'You have ruined my coat.'

Devlin leaned over him. 'I'll ruin more than your coat if you dare speak to me again, Farley.'

He turned his back and crossed the street, not heeding the stares of others walking by.

Madeleine stood in the hall, pushing the broom here and there, wondering how one contrived to get all the dust into one spot so that one could use the dustpan. She decided to experiment on a little pile of dust, but couldn't work out how to hold the broom and the dustpan at the same time. Linette sat in the corner galloping her wooden horse back and forth, while her doll sat abandoned on a parlour chair.

Bart had accompanied Sophie to the dress shop. How could any of them have guessed that little Sophie would be the only one to find paying work? Bart searched each day for labour, coming home talking of scores of veterans like himself lining up for one job. And Devlin. More lines of worry etched his face each day.

When Madeleine and Sophie took some of her new dresses to the dressmaker in the hope that they might return them,

Sophie came home with a large package of piecework, Madeleine with the dresses she had sought to sell.

She struggled with the sweeping. She was determined to do her part. While Sophie sewed and Bart and Devlin searched for work, she would care for the house.

Madeleine tried a different way to hold the broom, sticking it under her arm and levering it against her hip. She pretended to be a simple country housewife. She cleaned the house and tended the child while her husband—Devlin, of course—tilled the earth. Their lives were a quiet routine of hard work, peaceful evenings in front of the fireplace, and nights filled with loving. Madeleine leaned on the broom and sighed. How wonderful it would be.

She should not waste time in fancy. This silly habit of hers did not do her credit. She needed to solve her problems such as they really were. She needed work. Employment as a housemaid would not be the means, she supposed, although housework had never seemed difficult for the housemaids she once knew. They sped through chores with no apparent effort.

She jabbed at her pitiful pile of dust with the broom, scattering it everywhere except into the dustpan. 'Deuce.'

As she uttered this unladylike but Devlin-like epithet, the door opened and Devlin walked in, his head bent and his shoulders stooped. When he saw her, he smiled, but his eyes remained sad. 'What the devil are you doing?'

'Sweeping.' She looked down at the floor. 'Or trying to do so.'

'Deddy!' Linette popped up from her corner and propelled herself into Devlin's arms.

'How's my little lady?'

Linette wrapped her little arms around Devlin's neck. 'Deddy play?' She batted long lashes and smiled sweetly.

'Not now, Lady Lin.' He put Linette down and the child ran back to her toy horse. Devlin rubbed his forehead. He turned toward Madeleine and again smiled.

She stepped over to him to take his hat. 'You are wet.'

'It is nothing. A little rain.'

'Let me help you remove your coat.' She reached for the lapels. He held her arms and stared at her a moment before clutching her to him.

She could hardly breathe, he held her so tight.

'Do not worry so, Devlin. We shall come about.' She wound her own arms around his neck.

Linette ran to them, arms raised. 'Me! Me!'

Devlin scooped her up and enveloped them both in a hug, the kind of coming-home greeting she had imagined a moment ago, but infused with pain instead of pleasure.

'Come into the kitchen, Devlin. I'll make you a cup of tea.' She liked the sound of that, the housewife giving comfort to the labourer.

'I want biskis!' Linette cried.

Devlin, holding them both more loosely now, gave her a perplexed look. 'Biskis?'

'She means biscuit. I believe we still have a good number that Sophie made.'

He smiled. 'Tea and biskis it is, then.' Still carrying Linette, he followed her into the kitchen.

Bart and Sophie entered from the rear door as Madeleine poured Devlin's tea. Devlin merely raised his eyebrows to Bart, who shook his head.

'These are hard times.' The sergeant frowned.

Madeleine bade Bart and Sophie sit for tea and 'biskis', and, amid Sophie's protests, she served them all. Linette had climbed upon Devlin's lap. While the others traded news of their efforts of the day, she surveyed the scene. Their situation was dire, but the moment filled her with peace.

Her family, she thought. She put a hand to her brow. She must not think of family.

'Perhaps I have something of value to sell,' Devlin mused. 'I must have a stick pin or something with a jewel in it. Or perhaps my sword would fetch a good price.'

'You must keep the sword.' Bart nodded his head firmly. 'To honour the others.'

'You are right.' Devlin's voice was barely audible.

'I could try another shop to sell the dresses,' Madeleine offered.

He winced. 'Yes, you could.'

Sophie rose and dropped a few coins into Devlin's hands. 'My earnings, sir.'

Madeleine watched the look of pain flash over his face, replaced by a gentle smile for Sophie.

'Thank you, indeed, little one. This is a welcome contribution.'

Sophie flushed with pride.

He stood, having drained the contents of his cup and set Linette upon a chair. 'If you all will pardon me.'

Madeleine watched him walk out of the room, his tall figure ramrod straight. A moment later the front door closed.

Later that evening when she was putting Linette to bed, she heard Devlin's footsteps on the stairs. He entered his bedchamber. Half-listening for sounds from his room, she sang softly to her sleepy daughter. Within a few minutes, the child's eyelids fluttered closed. She kissed Linette's soft, pink brow, tucked the covers around her, and tiptoed over to the chest. Quietly opening the top drawer, she removed a small package wrapped in cloth.

Madeleine tapped lightly at the connecting door between her room and Devlin's. Without waiting for an answer, she entered.

He sat on the edge of his bed, bare-chested, his elbows resting on his knees, his hands clasped together. He glanced up.

'May I speak with you, Devlin?'

He nodded.

She walked over to the bed, handed him her parcel.

'What is this?' He took it in his hand.

'Something for you to sell.'

He unwrapped the cloth and lifted a delicate gold chain with a teardrop pearl. In the cloth were matching pearl earrings.

'These are lovely. Where did you get them? From Farley?'

'No,' she said, indignant that he should think so. 'They were mine before I met Farley. You may sell them.'

He stared at the jewellery and at her. 'Not quite yet, Maddy. Keep them for now.'

She carefully rewrapped the package.

'I have been thinking.' He rubbed his hands together. 'I have depended upon all of you too long. Poor Sophie, her fingers sore from sewing. You, ready to sell your treasures. Bart, searching for labour I'd not ask an enemy to perform.'

She stroked his cheek. 'I have caused you this trouble.'

He clasped her hand and held it.

Suddenly shy under his gaze, she glanced down. Her eyes rested on his chest and widened. 'Devlin, you have scars.'

His torso was riddled with them. Now, thinking about it, she realised she'd felt rough areas on his chest, that day she had touched him and almost made love with him. She had not looked, however. Now, so close to him in the candlelight, she recognised the long scar from the injury in Spain, but there were so many others, short and jagged.

'It is repulsing, is it not?' he said.

She touched one of the scars with her finger. 'Oh, Devlin, how could you think such a thing?' With gentleness, she traced it, still pink from healing. 'What happened to you? How did it come about that you have so many?'

'Waterloo.'

She placed her palm against his firm chest. 'I know it was at Waterloo. I should like to hear what happened to you.'

He rose, walking over to his window. 'The tale is not fit for fair ears.'

'Fustian. Nothing about me is fair.' She followed him. Standing behind him, she marked the scars on his back with her fingers. 'You had to endure this. It cannot be worse for me to hear of it.'

He turned to face her. She placed her hands on his shoulders as he gazed at her. The green of his eyes turned soft as moss. 'I have a proposition for you, Miss England.'

She stiffened, pulled away, but he held her firm.

'Not that kind of proposition.' He took her chin between his thumb and fingers. His expression turned serious again. 'I will tell you about Waterloo on one condition.'

'What condition?' She could imagine no other condition but bedding him. He meant a proposition, after all, no matter how he coloured it. When he touched her like this, she dared hope for it.

He gave her a light kiss on the lips, which merely gave her an urge to kiss him harder in return. 'I will tell you about Waterloo, if you tell me about how you came to be with Farley.'

She pulled away and rubbed her arms. 'Nonsense. I told you already that he seduced me. What else is there to tell?'

He crossed the room and picked up the cloth wrapping her necklace and earrings. 'I want to know how a girl who owned these came to be in Farley's gaming hell.'

She turned away. She had never spoken of her past to anyone, not even Sophie. In fact, she chastised herself if even a thought of the past invaded her mind.

She faced him. 'Very well, I will tell you, but not this night. I do not wish to speak of it this night.'

'You have a bargain, Maddy.' He returned to her, kissing her on the cheek. 'I do not wish to speak of any of it tonight.'

The chaste kiss disappointed her. She wished something else from him. She wished to pretend she was the farmer's housewife readying for bed with her husband. There was no Farley, no Waterloo, no shortage of money. Just days full of useful toil and nights filled with love.

He walked back to the window and stared out at the street for countless minutes. She knew not whether to stay or leave, but she did not want to leave him, especially with the weight of all their problems on his shoulders.

'Sophie is teaching me to sew.' Her voice sounded foolish in the face of his troubled silence.

But he turned to regard her with a kind look in his eye. 'That is very well. Had you not learned before?'

'Oh, I was taught, but I did not heed the lessons.'

He chuckled. 'Your head too full of horses?'

She smiled. 'Sadly, you are right. I never could keep my mind on much else.'

He sat on the window seat, his long legs stretched out before him. 'I know precisely what you mean.'

She sat next to him, tucking her legs beneath her and leaning against him. His arm circled around her shoulders. 'It is a pity that I could not procure employment in a stable. I could do all manner of things there.' She sighed.

He became silent again, and she struggled to think of some other topic to converse upon. She rested her hand on his knee and in a moment, he covered it with his own warm, strong hand.

'No, I shall find the way,' he murmured.

She snuggled against him, the moment acutely precious.

Devlin lifted his hand to her hair, stroking gently. Her locks felt like spun silk beneath his fingers. He inhaled the faint scent of lavender in her hair, and recalled that fragrance from his first meeting of her. After Waterloo, when fever made him delirious and his sisters bathed his forehead with lavender water, his Miss England swam through his dreams.

He had never expected to see her again, and here she was, more wonderful than he could have believed.

He snuggled her closer. She tilted her face to him, the pupils of her eyes wide, her pink lips moist and irresistible.

He kissed her, tasting the sweetness of her, wanting to remove every pain and care from her life and resolving once again to do so. No matter what he must bear.

As his lips gently rested against hers, she whispered, 'Devlin, I…'

He moved to the tender skin beneath her ear.

'I will make love to you, Devlin.'

He stopped and searched her face. 'Only if you truly wish it.'

She cast her gaze down. 'I do wish it. I know it is wicked of me.'

Lifting her chin with his finger, he forced her to meet his eye. 'It is not wicked.'

'But it is,' she insisted. 'I know it is.'

'Well, then, I must be damned indeed.' He ran his lips over her brow. 'I wish that much to make love with you.'

Her face flushed pink. 'It is different for a man.'

'And how is it different, sweet goose?' He pulled the pins from her hair, freeing it to tumble over her shoulders.

'It is no shame for a man to take his pleasure.' Her countenance was solemn. 'Men even boast of it.'

The truth of her words shamed him.

He drew his fingers through her hair. 'Women are made to feel the pleasure, too, Maddy. They are merely expected not to speak of it.'

'Do you truly believe so?' Her wide eyes made her appear as innocent as a young virgin. As she must have been, before Farley.

He smiled. 'I do indeed.'

She gazed at him, a dreamy look on her face.

'Come.' He led her to the bed.

She followed almost shyly, like a bride on her first night. He was determined that she should feel every pleasure he could provide for her. He wanted to show her that lovemaking could be beautiful. Enlightening. Forgiving.

He undid the laces of her dress and gently peeled the cloth from her skin. She released a long breath. Next came her corset. As he pulled her shift over her head, she raised her arms, bringing them down again around his neck. Clinging tightly to him, she kissed him.

Though he throbbed to mate with her that instant, he kept his kiss light. He sensed she also could succumb to the passion of the moment, but he held her back. All she'd known was frenzied, impersonal coupling. He wished to show her more. He wished to show her love.

And he wished to savour each moment of it.

She unfastened his trousers and slid her hands under the cloth until she'd pushed them down to his ankles. As she stood again, she slid her hands up his legs, torso, and shoulders, nearly causing him to abandon his resolve to proceed slowly. He captured her hands in his own and tasted her lips at leisure.

Lifting her on to the bed, he settled beside her, letting his eyes drift down the naked length of her.

Miss England, he had called her that first time, half in jest. She was still so very much like the homeland he loved. Peaceful and pleasing. Exciting and teasing.

He slid his tongue down her neck and covered the rose of her nipple with his mouth. She moaned and arched toward him.

Not yet, Miss England, he thought. This must be a journey with so languid a pace every part would be savoured and committed to memory.

As dawn tried to poke its fingers through the thick morning mist, Devlin sat in shirt and trousers, staring out the window. Madeleine rolled over in the bed, making endearingly incoherent sounds as she did so. His attention shifted to her.

Her beauty took his breath away, as it had that first moment he'd seen her in Farley's gaming hell. Her dark hair such a contrast to her fair skin; her long eyelashes, so like Linette's, full against the pink of her cheeks. He memorised her image, just as he had done before returning to Spain.

The eyelashes fluttered and she opened her eyes. The smile she gave him, so peaceful and satisfied, tugged at his heart.

He would see that peace stay with her forever, no matter what the cost to him.

'Good morning,' she said, sleep making her voice raspy.

'Did you sleep well?' He already knew her reply. While he had hardly captured two winks all night long, she had slept as sound as a kitten.

'Indeed.' She stretched, arching her back and extending her arms above her head. 'And I have the feeling that this will be a lucky day. Today you will find the solution to our problems.'

'I have done so already.'

She brightened, sitting up straight. 'You thought of it in your sleep?'

Sleep, indeed. 'I thought of it last night, but I only decided this morning.'

She sprang from the bed and rushed over to climb into his lap. With her arms around him, she rested her head against his chest. 'What is the solution, Devlin?'

He closed his eyes. As if lances were piercing his skin again, he steeled himself against the pain.

'I must marry.'

Chapter Nine

Madeleine's heart pounded. Marriage had figured too prominently in her fantasies of late.

'It was my father's plan.' Devlin's voice vibrated through her body, but it did not soothe. 'And it is the only means I have of solving our problems.'

He held her more tightly. 'You see, Maddy, I am a wealthy man. My father bequeathed me a fortune, as he did my sisters and second brother. Ned, of course, has the title and all the entailed property and is as rich as Croesus, but my father saw that each of us would prosper.'

'I do not understand. You are wealthy, but your brother refuses you money?' He made no sense.

He laughed drily. 'There is the rub. My father thought me unfit for my property and wealth. Ned controls the lot until I marry a lady of whom he approves.'

She buried her face into his chest so he would not see. Her fantasies had indeed been foolish. He must marry someone of whom his brother approved. A lady such as the beautiful Marchioness. Not one who came as the prize in a game of cards.

She took a deep breath. 'So you must marry.'

'Marriage shall steady me...or so Father believed. I have resisted, Maddy. It seems an abominable reason to marry.' He squeezed her, his strength conveying his frustration. 'It is too

soon for me, in any event. I have just done being a soldier. I
do not wish—' He broke off.

Madeleine pulled away and retrieved her clothes from the
floor. Suddenly conscious of her nakedness and ashamed of
even more that that, she donned her shift, aware of his eyes
upon her. She glanced at him and he averted his gaze. Tossing
her hair over one shoulder, she slipped into her dress and
fumbled with the laces. Devlin came and tied them for her,
the light touch of his fingers sending shimmers of pleasure
down her back.

'It is because of me...' She felt sick inside, unsure if it was
because Devlin would once again pay the price for her freedom, or because he might think of bedding her, but never,
never would he think of marrying her. 'I will not allow it.'

'You have no choice.' His voice was bleak.

'I could leave here.' She set her chin firmly. 'You would
not need to marry, then.'

He turned her around and held her arms firmly, forcing her
to look at him. 'You would be driven back to Farley. Or
worse. Believe it, there can be worse.'

'I will never go back to him.' She shuddered at the thought.
'I will find employment. I am already learning to sew.'

He regarded her with tenderness. 'Yes. I am proud of your
efforts, but, even if you attain Sophie's skill, it is but a pit-
tance to earn. I counted her money, you recall.'

'I will contrive something.'

'No, you will not. I have been around this in my mind in
all manner of ways.' He released a ragged breath. 'I must
marry.'

Someone else. Some other woman. A lady.

'You are not responsible for me,' she continued, struggling
to keep the misery at bay.

He brushed a lock of hair off her forehead. 'But I am,
Maddy. I am responsible for the lot of you.'

'I could walk out. You could not stop me.' She glared.

He shook his head. 'Do not be foolish. You must think of Linette.'

She closed her eyes. He was correct. She would sell her soul to spare Linette a future like hers.

Pulling away, she went to Devlin's bed and smoothed the covers they had disordered, trying not to recall the wanton pleasure of loving him. Her carnal pleasure had come at great cost.

He spoke from behind her. 'I will see to both of you, Maddy. A snug little house for you. Whatever you want. School for Linette. I will make her future secure, and you will not want for anything.' He turned her around to face him. 'It is the only way. I will not permit you and Linette to suffer.'

His countenance, so sincere, with a look so loving, caused tears to prick her eyelids. 'I cannot like being a burden to you,' she said lamely.

He gathered her in his arms, holding her tightly against his chest. 'You will never be a burden. My wealth is such that I may easily afford to provide you and Linette a life of ease.' He took a deep breath and his chest rose tighter against her. 'But I must have a wife to do so.'

He would be that rich? But he had been satisfied to count pennies and seek common employment. Why had he done so?

Her mind seized on an anxious thought. 'Is there a woman for whom you have already spoken?'

He petted her hair. 'No, my sweet, there is no one else.'

She glanced up at him. His green eyes were soft, though tiny lines of worry etched their corners. She lifted her fingers to feel the rough stubble of his beard. Her childish fantasy of a pirate whisking her away flashed through her mind. Would that it could be true, that this unshaven, half-dressed, hot-blooded man would whisk her away. Not send her away, as fate decreed.

His eyes darkened with passion. Adjusting his hold on her, he captured her lips. The kiss, rough and as yearning as her heart, sent fire through her. She uttered a deep, needful sound and grasped at his shirt, wanting to tear it away from where her hands longed to touch.

His hands untied the laces of her dress as he backed the two of them against the bed. She let her dress slip to the floor, not caring if she stepped on it. He lifted her on to the bed and moved back to rid himself of the shirt and unfasten his trousers. She lifted her shift. He climbed atop her and she relished the weight and nearness of him. His male scent filled her nostrils along with the more primitive smell of desire.

He kissed her again and she arched to him, wanting to join with him, the need more urgent now that she knew this golden time with him would end. She whispered for him to proceed with haste, and he made ready to comply.

'Mama!' Linette's plaintive cry sounded through the door.

'Deuce,' Devlin muttered.

'I have to see to her.' Madeleine said, fighting her body's craving to do otherwise.

'I know.' Devlin sighed and moved off her, grabbing her dress, which she hurriedly donned. He worked the laces as she headed for the door.

He stopped her at the door with a quick, regretful kiss. 'See to the child. I'll come below stairs soon.'

With one glance back, Madeleine opened the door to her room and headed for the outstretched chubby arms of her daughter.

Devlin dragged his hand through his hair and stared at mother and child, desire still churning through him. He closed his eyes and took deep breaths. Arousal faded little, but calm did not return.

He watched Madeleine tend to her child with confidence, efficiency, and calm good humour. How could she manage that when his body still throbbed with wanting her?

Lord, he did not want to leave her when their passion flamed like this. Marrying would not have to cause this to end, would it? He could continue to visit her, still warm her bed.

He quietly shut the door.

No, he would not see her again after the damned marriage. It would be too cruel to this hapless future wife for their marriage to include a mistress.

The wretched course he had decided upon was the correct one. The only one. But it sickened him all the same. To damn another lady to a future without love merely to secure his fortune was detestable, but not to do so meant damning Madeleine and her child to a living hell.

He prowled the room, unable to quiet the storm of emotion inside. He must give up Madeleine. It was the only way to ensure her a good life. Marriage was his only choice.

The walls of the room closed in on him, and his breathing quickened. He shut his eyes and yearned for escape, for freedom.

Until Waterloo, soldiering had been his freedom. Living by his own wits with men who understood what was essential in life. Making the most of each day. Grateful for food, shelter, the occasional warmth of a willing woman. Laughing and drinking and sleeping under the stars. Surging with excitement, raging against the enemy. Testing skill, courage and luck. He would trade everything to go back to those days in Spain.

What blithering nonsense. Those days had vanished with Waterloo.

A heavy fatigue overtook him, but he proceeded to shave and dress. He would put the best face he could on this day, for Madeleine's sake.

Below stairs, he walked past the dining room and smiled. Their little household rarely supped at the table there, except for the last meal of the day. He liked the informality of the kitchen where they gathered as equals in this venture to survive.

That would vanish, too, with his decision. When his money flowed again, he would be master.

As he neared the kitchen door he heard Madeleine's voice.

'Sit, Sophie. Please do. I will tend to the meal.'

Sophie's inevitable protest dissolved into a fit of coughing.

Madeleine looked up as he entered. Linette clambered over the chairs to get to him.

'Deddy!' The little girl jumped into Devlin's arms.

'Devlin,' Madeleine said, 'please tell Sophie to sit and allow me to do the work. She is ill.'

'I am not ill.' The little maid, sallow-faced with dark circles under her eyes, choked on her words and turned her head to cough some more.

Devlin opened his mouth, but had no chance to speak.

'I cannot see how she fooled Bart. He never would have gone out had he known.' Madeleine fussed at putting bowls on the table.

'Deddy play?' Linette batted her long lashes at Devlin.

Madeleine whirled to the child. 'No, Linette, sit here and eat.' She swept over and took the child from Devlin's arms.

She put Linette back in her chair, raised high by a wooden box upon which Linette now stood, not sat. Madeleine continued, 'Dev, please do something. Sophie will not listen to me.'

As if to prove Madeleine's words, Sophie pushed her hands on the table to raise herself. Devlin pressed his fingers to his brow.

'All of you, sit!' he commanded.

The three sat, like obedient soldiers.

He glared from one to the other. 'Linette, do as your mother says. Eat. Maddy, stop fussing. If you wish to ready the meal then bloody do it.' He softened his voice for Sophie. 'Little one, do not exert yourself. It is foolishness when Maddy is capable of a simple breakfast.'

Sophie did as she was told, coughing softly, eyes downcast.

Madeleine rose to pour a cup of tea for Sophie and Devlin. 'You need not have snapped at me.'

He glanced at her, regretting his burst of temper, but her

eyes held the hint of a smile and a softer expression that spoke of what had passed between them the previous night.

'I apologise.' His eyes held hers for that moment. He hoped she knew he was sorry for more than a fit of temper.

Between coughs, Sophie said, 'I need to tend to my sewing.'

Madeleine started to protest, but Devlin shot her a glance to keep quiet. She spooned him a bowl of porridge.

'You need sew no longer, little one. We have had a change in fortune. In fact, I intend to return your earnings to you.'

Sophie's eyes grew wide. 'We have money?'

'We will by this afternoon, I expect. I will call on my brother again. He will give me the money this time.' He cautiously took a spoonful of the lumpy porridge. Perhaps by the morrow they would be feasting on boiled eggs and ham.

'You see, I will do as my brother wishes and he will advance me the money.' Devlin would leave further explanation of their change in fortune to Madeleine, not knowing how to tell Sophie about his need to marry.

'May…may I continue with the sewing?' Sophie asked, her eyes darting warily.

He leaned to her and placed his hand on her arm. 'You may do whatever you wish. I do shout and bluster, but you are a free woman, Sophie. Not mine to command.'

Madeleine stood behind him with the pot of tea. She brushed against him as she poured.

'Where the devil is Bart?'

'Gone to find work,' Madeleine said.

'Deuce, you did not stop him?'

'He left before I came down.'

Bart would be out searching for some sort of back-breaking labour, or something so dangerous, only a few of the out-of-work war veterans would compete for the job.

'He went to a lead factory in Islington,' Sophie said, before a cough stopped her.

'When?'

She held her throat, as if that would hold back another coughing spell. 'An hour or more, I think.'

He could hire a hack and catch up to him. Devlin took a quick sip of his tea and rushed off to warn his sergeant not to risk his neck another time for Devlin's sake.

He found Bart at the factory door where he and others hung about, hoping to be chosen for a job. The factory billowed black smoke and flecks of black ash covered the pavement and buildings. How could anyone abide such dismal surroundings?

'Come on, Bart. Let us get you out of this damned place.' He gestured his friend over to the hack.

Bart did not leave his place in the ragged line that had formed. 'It is honest work, Dev, and pays well.'

'You no longer need to break your back. Our fortunes have changed.'

Bart stared at him, hands on his waist. After a moment he abandoned the line and walked over to the hack.

Devlin explained the whole business as they rode back. Bart responded with a grim expression. 'It is right enough, Dev, but I do not like it all the same.' He shot Devlin a suspicious glance. 'Are you certain you have thought this through?'

Devlin nodded, frowning. 'This is not one of my impulsive acts. I have sat up half the night figuring this. We are mere days from having no blunt at all. What else can we do?'

The two men stared at the buildings passing by, the only sounds the horses' hooves on the cobblestones and the shouts of vendors selling their wares.

'When the time comes,' Devlin said at last, 'I want you to stay with Madeleine.' He did not have to explain what he meant.

'We have not been apart since Spain. I'll not desert you now.' Bart's thick brows knitted together in one straight line.

Devlin regarded his friend with a wan smile. 'Sophie will

not wish to leave Madeleine, I expect, and I doubt you will wish to leave Sophie. Am I correct?'

Bart did not answer, but neither did his craggy brows move from their stern expression.

'I can only do this if I know they remain safe.' Devlin's voice became low and insistent. 'I must depend on you to look out for them. I will not be able to see to it myself.'

Bart stared at him as the hack neared St James's Street. 'I will do as you say.'

That afternoon, Madeleine was alone in the house. Linette napped. Sophie, who had insisted herself fully recovered, went to return her sewing to Madame Emeraude and get another batch. Bart accompanied her, so she need not carry the basket.

Devlin left to see the Marquess, to announce his decision to seek a wife so as to release his allowance.

Madeleine hated this solitude. Busy all morning, she had given herself no time to think of Devlin searching for a wife. And leaving her.

Now there were no distractions.

The only fantasy she could muster was of Devlin in a church with a beautiful lady like the Marchioness at his side, saying his vows. If she shook off that unwanted reverie, she saw him facing the same lady in his bed.

She grabbed her sewing and settled herself in the parlour's window seat. The day was clear, the kind of day she once might have spent on horseback, galloping over the hills near her home. Those days felt as unreal to her as her fantasies about Devlin. She frowned over her stitches. Sophie had helped her design an apron to protect her dresses during the day. They had found an old bedsheet to make it with. Stitching was laborious, but she was determined to finish the garment when she was not needed helping Sophie with the dresses.

Sewing simply did not occupy enough of her mind, and

this morning of all mornings she did not wish to think. Devlin would marry and she would be sent away.

She supposed she should be grateful that he intended to take care of her and Linette. It was a good fortune, a perfect solution to all their problems. Perhaps Devlin would visit after he wed. Lots of men kept mistresses, she knew. Several had offered her a *carte blanche*, but Farley inevitably found out and they never offered again.

She refused to rank Devlin the same as those odious creatures who used to drool over her. He was not like them. Being with him was so different than being with other men. So wonderful. Devlin was a man like no other.

She turned back to her stitches. Perhaps if she became truly skilled at sewing, she and Sophie could earn enough for a little place to stay, enough to feed and clothe themselves and Linette.

Devlin would be free.

Madeleine concentrated on speeding up her sewing, necessary for a seamstress. She tried very hard to keep the stitches the same size and close together. Sometimes she would forget to use the thimble and push on the needle with her bare finger. More often, she poked herself with the needle's point instead of moving her fingers away.

For a few moments, the effort consumed her mind, but a noise in the street distracted her. A shiny barouche with a splendid pair of matched bays pulled up in front of the house. The horses were as fine as any she had ever seen. What stable had bred them? she wondered. They were identical in size, their markings so similar one would suppose they had been twins. She wished she had seen them in motion.

The knocker of the door sounded, and she jumped. She peeked out the glass to see who knocked. An unknown man stood there. The driver of the elegant equipage?

She opened the door.

The man who stood before her was more refined than any she had ever seen. His buckskins and driving coat were so finely tailored they looked moulded to his well-formed frame. His eyes, regarding her with a startled expression, seemed familiar, as did the set of his chin.

'I was given this as Lord Devlin Steele's direction.' He eyed her as men usually did, but without the typical prurient gleam.

'Lord Devlin is not presently at home,' she said.

He stepped past her, across the threshold, though she had not given him leave to do so. Her heart beat in alarm and she was acutely aware of being alone in the house.

She straightened her posture. 'Perhaps you would wish to leave your card.'

He removed his hat. 'I wish to wait.'

She bit her lip. She dare not betray being alone. His eyes still carefully assessed her.

'Who are you?' His question was more like a command.

She bristled. Smiling with bravado through her nervousness, she said, 'Forgive me for not introducing myself. I had thought it proper for visitors to announce themselves first.'

His eyes flashed at her insolence. She supposed he was not one accustomed to having his behaviour questioned. She smiled again and cocked her head as if waiting.

'The Marquess of Heronvale,' he said impatiently.

Her smile vanished. Devlin's brother.

'You are?' he commanded again.

She waved her hand as if his question was foolish, but curtsied politely. 'Miss England at your service, my lord. I am the...the housekeeper.'

'Indeed?' His eyebrows lifted in a top-lofty expression and his eyes flicked up and down her person once more.

She took a breath. 'Lord Devlin intended to visit you this afternoon, my lord. Perhaps you might find him at your residence.'

He made no move to leave. 'I will wait for him.'

She took his hat and showed him into the parlour, where he stood continuing to watch her. She scooped up her sewing from the window seat and twisted the material in her hand, wishing she had finished the garment so it could cover her pale yellow muslin dress.

'I shall bring tea.' It sounded like what a housekeeper might do. He still stood, watching her.

As she moved to leave, his voice stopped her, sounding less imperious. 'Tell me, Miss England. My brother...is he well?'

An odd question. 'Yes, he is. Very well, my lord.' She curtsied again and hurried out the door.

The Marquess watched the retreating figure, wondering what to make of this surprise in his brother's household. Housekeeper, indeed. The young woman—lord, she looked more like a girl—was a breathtaking beauty with startlingly blue eyes and dark unruly hair. Where had Devlin found her? He had heard no rumours of his brother forming a liaison.

He strolled around the room, intrigued, as well, with the genteel furnishings. The place must have commanded a respectable rent. With this 'housekeeper', it was easy to see why Devlin wished to move. And he could see why his little brother had overspent his due. A woman of Miss England's face and figure would not come cheap, as her tasteful new attire could attest.

He'd not reckoned on his brother living with a mistress, had not conceived the notion even when Serena reported seeing Devlin with a woman. Devlin had introduced Serena to her as if she were respectable. Devlin should have told him about her.

He should not be surprised Devlin had not. Ned wandered over to the window. He would have disapproved. He would have given Devlin a list of cogent reasons why keeping a mistress was irresponsible and he would have reminded Devlin of his duty.

Ned had often thought about keeping a mistress himself. There were times when his masculine urges raged in a manner he could not inflict upon his delicate wife, and a willing woman would have easily slaked his desires.

But he had not.

In any event, Devlin had no business keeping a woman. He had no fortune of his own to command. Ned stood again and peered out the window. He had planned merely to assure himself Devlin was not ill and be on his way. He pulled on the bell cord.

Miss England appeared at the door. 'Yes, my lord?'

At least she played her role of housekeeper well. Puzzling, she spoke like an educated miss. Still, her youth did not make sense. She could be no more than nineteen.

'Please have someone instruct my tiger to walk the horses.'

'Yes, my lord,' she replied.

He watched from the window to see it done and was surprised when Miss England went from the house to speak to his tiger.

A few minutes later, she entered with a tea tray. She poured the tea prettily and offered some lemon cakes, as well. He noticed tea leaves swimming in his cup.

He could not resist baiting her. 'Tell me, Miss England, how long have you been in my brother's…employ?'

'Not long, sir,' she replied, an edge to her voice.

'He had not spoken to me of having a housekeeper.'

She did not lower her gaze at this question. She smiled instead. 'Indeed? Do gentlemen discuss such matters?'

He narrowed his eyes, 'Was it you whom my wife met with Devlin—Lord Devlin?'

Her cheeks flushed. 'Yes, my lord. She kindly spoke to me.'

He ought to wring Devlin's bloody neck. How dare he put Serena in such a position, to speak to one such as this Miss England? He glared at her.

But at the moment she looked more like a timid young girl, nervous and uncertain. It was difficult to maintain his anger.

'May I be excused, my lord?' Her cheekiness had fled, at

least. He wished to ask more questions, but could think of none.

'Deddy?' A small voice sounded from the doorway, and Miss England turned pale.

Ned turned to come face to face with a tiny child, no more than a baby, rubbing her eyes and yawning.

The very image of his brother.

Chapter Ten

Ned stared at the child, a doll-like little girl who clutched a wooden horse in her hand. Even the toy was like one Devlin had carried with him at that age. She had blue eyes instead of green. Even so, this little girl was a female version of Devlin twenty-five years ago. The child stole a wary glance at him and ran to Miss England, who scooped her up in her arms.

'I want Deddy,' the child said.

Miss England flushed.

'Daddy?' Ned asked, raising an eyebrow.

The young woman blinked rapidly.

'The child's word for papa?' Perhaps the child had picked up the Scottish term from the faithful Bart.

Her eyes darted. 'No, indeed, for a…a…toy.' She looked at the girl. 'Go above stairs now, sweetling. Mama will be up directly.'

The child flung her little arms around Miss England's neck. 'No!'

Ned remembered that feeling. Chubby arms clasping his neck, the awesome knowledge that such devotion could be directed at him. His littlest brother, following him everywhere when he was home on school holiday. Worshipping him. Needing him.

'She is Devlin's child.' He did not ask.

A panicked look flashed across Miss England's face. She recovered quickly, meeting his eye. 'She is *my* child.'

Her child? She looked barely old enough.

The little girl studied him with wide lash-fringed eyes. 'Who zat, Mama?'

'He is the Marquess,' she responded.

His title would mean nothing to the child. But it would warm his heart if he again heard a childish voice call him Ned.

The little girl squirmed and her mother set her down.

Ned squatted to the child. 'And what is your name?'

'Winette,' the shy little voice said, a thumb popping into her mouth.

'Winette?' He looked to Miss England.

'Linette,' she said.

Ned smiled at the child. 'That is a splendid horse you have, Linette. May I see it?'

Linette thrust the hand holding the horse in Ned's face.

'A splendid horse, indeed. Does your horse have a name?'

She released her thumb. 'Deddy's horse.'

Ned glanced at Miss England. Her hand had flown to her mouth. With a halting gesture, he touched Linette's dark curly hair. His brother used to run to him for comfort, he recalled. Ned would mop up his tears and stroke his hair just like this.

'Markiss play?' the little girl asked, cocking her head and batting her eyelashes.

Ned laughed and ruffled the child's hair, a smile lingering on his lips. Yes, he would like to play again, to sit on the floor and gallop a wooden horse.

He stood instead. 'I shall take my leave, *Miss* England. Please tell my brother he shall hear from me.'

'Yes, my lord.' She hurried to fetch his hat and gloves and to open the door for him. The child hovered behind her, and he gave the little girl a final smile as he walked out of the door, his barouche pulling up in front of the house.

Linette ran out the door, pointing. 'Horse! Horse, Mama!'

Miss England rushed out to grab her. Ned caught the child first and held her until Miss England took her hand. Regretting he had to leave the child, Ned continued towards the barouche. He stopped, a thought interrupting the plan half-formed in his head.

He turned back. 'Miss England?'

She hesitated. 'Yes, my lord?'

'Are you married to my brother?'

Surprise flashed across her face and she blushed deep red. 'No, my lord.'

He continued on his way, climbing onto the barouche and snapping at the rungs while his tiger leapt on to the back.

From an alleyway across the street, black eyes watched the retreating vehicle and glanced back at the mother and child re-entering the house.

What was meant by that tender scene? Lord Farley wondered. The Marquess of Heronvale going all mawkish over Madeleine's child? Perhaps the man's fancy ran toward young ones. Rumour said he had no fancy for his ice-maiden wife.

Farley tried to calculate what small fortune a marquess might spend for the rare chance to dally with such a child. He rubbed his hands at the thought.

Perhaps he should have sold the child to settle his debts instead of giving up Madeleine. Madeleine had become so much more difficult since the child was born. He should have got rid of it straight away.

Cursed chit—Madeleine had vowed to slit her own throat if he so much as touched the child, and he'd decided to keep her happy. He'd counted upon her being grateful enough to come willingly to him, like the first time when she'd been flushed with delight. That was what he desired again.

Farley leaned against the lamppost. He removed a pinch of snuff from its box and inhaled it. After a spasm of sneezing, he glanced back at the door she'd walked through, recalling the sway of her hips. She was made for seduction. If ever there was a woman created for passion, it was Madeleine.

So why did she withhold that passion from him? It enraged him. He thought he'd taught her a lesson when he forced her to become the bribe in his crooked games. He'd intended to offer her only a few times, but she'd made him a tidy profit. Men would come to his establishment every night, hoping to win time with her, especially if he offered her only every now and then. Then they returned often, losing more blunt each time.

While she was fat with child she'd earned him nothing. If he'd been in London he'd have dealt with her before it had grown too big to get rid of, but one did not refuse an emperor's summons or, to be more accurate, one from an emperor's emissary. Not when the emperor paid well for information gleaned from brandy-loosened tongues and gentlemen desperate to settle gambling debts.

He should have taken her to France with him, but that night before he left she'd angered him, and it had suited him well enough not to set eyes on her for a while. Besides, she'd become something of a patriot. More than once he discovered her poring over newspapers filled with stories about the war. If she had discovered his business dealings with Napoleon, she might have been stupid enough to pass the word to some fool willing to put country above fortune.

Stepping out of the alley onto the pavement, Farley gazed once more at the apartments where Madeleine lived with Devlin Steele. He thought of her naked beneath Steele, and his own loins ached.

He'd have her again, even if he had to kill to get her.

Madeleine paced the floor, wishing Devlin would hurry home and dreading when he would.

What could be worse for Devlin than the Marquess of Heronvale learning of her existence and that of her child? She knew what could be worse—his suspecting the child to be Devlin's.

Oh, she should never have opened the door. He would have gone away none the wiser had she not.

Linette walked up to her. 'Mama? Where's Markiss's horse?'

'Gone, Linette,' she said for what seemed like the hundredth time. Linette had not stopped speaking of those cursed horses. They were beautiful animals, she had to admit.

After what seemed like hours but could barely have been more than one, Devlin walked in. Linette reached him first and was lifted into his arms.

'Markiss's horse! Markiss's horse!' Linette chattered.

Madeleine tapped her foot in impatience.

Devlin frowned at her. 'My brother was not at home, so we remain penniless.'

'He was here.'

Her words were drowned out. Linette grabbed Devlin's cheeks and yelled, 'Markiss's horse!' as if getting louder would help.

'What the deuce is she talking about?' Devlin asked.

'I told you. Your brother was here. He came here, Devlin. He saw Linette. Markiss. It is her way of saying the Marquess.'

'Good God,' Devlin said. 'What did he want?'

'To see you.'

'For what purpose?'

She lifted her arms in frustration. 'I do not know. He did not confide in me.'

'Good God. He met you?'

'Of course he met me.' Her voice went up an octave. 'I have told you.'

She knew it was a terrible thing for Devlin's brother to learn of her existence. Still, it stung to realise Devlin thought so, as well.

Devlin set Linette down, putting his hand to his brow.

'You need not worry.' She lifted her chin. 'I told him I was the housekeeper.'

He threw his head back and laughed, the sound bouncing off the walls of the hallway.

Madeleine glared at him. 'It is not a jest, Devlin.'

Grinning, he drew her into his arms, even though she tried to pull away. 'You are nothing like a housekeeper.'

She pushed at his chest. 'Be serious. What are we to do?'

Linette ran up with her toy horse. 'Deddy play!'

'Not now, Lady Lin.' Devlin continued to hold Madeleine. Linette pulled at his trousers.

'We do nothing, Maddy,' he said. 'Ned would know of us sooner or later. My brother always discovers my secrets.'

Madeleine settled against him. As long as her presence remained a secret, she had an easier time pretending. In the full light of day, however, her existence was a shameful one.

Madeleine rested her head against the comforting beat of Devlin's heart.

'Are Sophie and Bart here?' His deep voice resonated in his chest. It was like feeling the sound, as well as hearing it.

Madeleine did not move from his warm, strong arms. 'They went to Madame Emeraude's, but that was a while ago. I believe they may be dallying.'

He chuckled, producing more interesting vibrations. 'They are the unlikeliest pair.'

No, she thought. *We* are. A man of Bart's class may marry a girl, no matter what her reputation. A lord may not.

The next morning Devlin woke, tangled in Madeleine's embrace. He stared at her face, inches from his and, in sleep, looking innocent as a lamb, so very young and vulnerable. His heart ached with tenderness for her.

She had not come to him in the night. He'd been restless and eager, desire heating his loins until he could wait no longer. He crossed the room, opened the door, and lifted her into his arms. She'd not protested when he carried her to his bed.

He intended to make love to her this morning. More than once, if the child slept long enough. Knowing he must give her up made him hungry for her, as if he needed to get his fill of her while he could. Enough to sustain him for the rest of his life.

Her eyes fluttered open, immediately filling with tenderness. A heartbeat later those eyes registered alarm and then, slowly, carefully, turned blank.

'Shall I make love to you, Devlin?' She spoke in that sweet voice that sounded as if it came from someone else. Her hand slid across his scarred chest and descended, nearing to where he was already hard for her.

He caught her wrist. 'Do not trouble yourself, Miss M.'

He had not expected to see this side of Madeleine again. He'd resigned himself to a limited time with her, but he expected her passion. Had not that much passed between them?

It angered him, made him want to teach her a lesson. He could show her how a man takes what he wants. He could climb atop her and force her to love him, before their time ran out.

Devlin sat up and ran a hand raggedly through his hair. His heart pounded and his throat tightened so that he could not take a breath. The walls of the room closed in on him and he heard the beat of the French drums, the pounding of horses' hooves charging. Retreat! he thought. Run. Ride. Gallop until your lungs feel like bursting and you are safe behind the line.

He swung his legs over the side of the bed and searched for his clothes.

'What are you doing?' Madeleine's modulated voice trembled a bit.

He could show her his anger, but he would be damned if he would let her see this panic that so frequently beset him.

'I am going out.' He left the room, still buttoning his trousers.

Madeleine, her breath coming rapidly, waited a few moments before donning her nightdress.

The previous night had been more than her daydreams could have imagined. He created sensations in her that she'd not known possible. Her body had responded to him, and she had performed all the tricks she had been taught to perform. But this time she had *meant* them. She had wanted to share her pleasure with him, wanted to feel him under her hand and her lips, wanted to bind him to her forever.

She must not allow herself to love him. She must give up foolish dreaming and prepare for leaving him. She must hope that the lady he wed would be worthy of him, and that he would eventually fall in love with her and be happy.

Such a thought was too miserable by half.

Madeleine opened the door connecting her room and Devlin's. Linette still slept, but in a short space of time the sun would send its fingers through the window to poke her awake. Madeleine hurried to dress herself and to drag a comb through her unruly curls. In the scratched mirror, her lips looked swollen from Devlin's kisses. She lightly touched her breast, remembering how his hand had felt there the night before, remembering the ferocity of their lovemaking.

Her body sprang to life. The light from the rising sun increased its brilliance. The sounds of Linette's breathing grew louder. From the open window, she could smell dampness in the cool morning air. She could not afford to feel so alive again. She vowed to tame the desire he aroused in her and to become dead again. As she had been at Farley's.

After all, leaving Devlin would be a little like dying.

Devlin strode through the streets with only one thought in his mind. To run. To ride. To be on horseback again with the sensation that nothing could catch him. No man, no musket ball, no blue eyes that stared blankly through him.

He quickened his pace as he neared his brother's stable. Entering, he called a 'halloo' and walked past the gleaming berlin carriage, a well-sprung curricle, and what appeared to be a brand new barouche. The smell of hay, so long missed, came back to comfort him.

A squat, wiry figure emerged from the most distant stall, wiping his hands on a rag. 'Yes, sir. What is it, sir?'

Devlin peered at him as he walked closer. The man was about his age and familiar. 'Jem, is that you?'

The man broke into a wide smile. 'Lord Devlin, well I'll be. Good to see you again, sir.'

They had grown up together at Heronvale, separated by their stations in life. Jem had been born to the stable, while Devlin belonged in the great house with its portrait hall of ancestors, its armour and family silver. When he and Jem met in the horses' stalls, however, they were of one mind. Horses. They could spend hours talking of horseflesh. On horseback, they rode for miles.

Devlin reached out his hand, which Jem accepted with hesitation. 'What are you doing here, Jem? By God, I have not seen you in years.'

'Yes, sir, since you went off to fight the Frogs.' Jem glanced around proudly. 'His lordship gave me the running of the stable here.'

'Indeed?' Devlin surveyed his surroundings again. 'Well done, Jem. He could not have chosen a better man. How goes it with you? You are well, it seems. What of your mother?'

'Passed away two years ago, I'm sad to say.' Jem's mother had worked in Heronvale's kitchens. She had been a jolly, generous soul.

'I am sorry. I had not heard.' Devlin felt guilty for not having known, not having even thought of her in that many years.

'I'm married now, sir,' Jem said, a proud expression on his face. 'I have a son and another babe on the way.'

'That is excellent news.' It was on the tip of Devlin's tongue to tell all about Madeleine, Linette, Bart and Sophie, but it could not be right to do so. Jem had a real family. His was not.

They stood awkwardly for a moment before Jem asked, 'And how can I be serving you today?'

Devlin had almost forgotten his purpose, though it now seemed less necessary to thunder away on horseback at breakneck speed. 'I had a fancy to ride this morning. Did the Marchioness send word of me using the stable?'

'She did, m'lord.'

Devlin clapped the man on the back. 'Show me your animals, Jem, and help me select the best bit of blood.'

As they toured the stable, Devlin selected Ned's black gelding, the only horse to truly tempt him. He spied another spirited animal, a mare.

'Jem, I have another request…'

From the kitchen where she washed the morning dishes, Madeleine heard the front door open. Devlin's voice roared, 'Bart!'

She ignored it and returned to her chores. Sophie had become more accustomed to Madeleine's insistence on helping with the work. The little maid's success as a seamstress helped her relinquish her hold on every menial task that needed to be done. That and the fact that her cough had become no better.

Linette came barrelling into the kitchen.

'Mama! Mama! Horses. *Horses.*' The little girl pulled her by the hand and there was no refusing. Madeleine followed, though she preferred to avoid Devlin.

Linette led her out the front door to where Bart was holding the reins of two of the most beautiful horses she had ever seen. The gelding was so black the sun on its coat reflected blue. The mare was a rich chestnut. The steeds' eyes shone with intelligence and good breeding. Their superior long legs impatiently pounded the cobblestones of the street.

She noticed the mare was saddled for a lady to ride.

Linette squealed something incoherent, and it was all Madeleine could do to keep hold of the child's hand.

'What are you about, Bart?' she asked.

'Dev asked me to hold them.' Bart scooped Linette up in his free arm, cooing to the child, 'Now, lass, pet the nose gently.'

Linette was in raptures, hardly able to be contained in Bart's arm.

Madeleine smiled at her daughter's enthusiasm. 'What is this?'

Devlin appeared at her side, responding to her question in a low voice. 'Have you forgotten what riding horses look like, Maddy?' He reached for Linette.

He was dressed in riding gear: buckskins clinging to his muscular thighs, top boots gleaming with polish, a riding coat of deepest blue. Her heart caught in her throat and she turned away from him.

'Horses, Deddy!' the child cried.

'Indeed, Lady Lin.' He grinned at Linette and placed her on the back of the black horse, holding on to her as he did.

Linette looked tiny atop the huge steed. 'Devlin, please take her off. She is too little—'

He spoke stiffly. 'I'll not let any harm come to her.' Without turning toward her, he continued, 'Madeleine, you will accompany me for this morning ride?'

The lady's horse was for her? A thrill rushed through her, replaced by trepidation. She should not spend time with him.

'I have no clothes.'

'Yes, you do. On your bed is the riding dress.'

She had refused the riding dress at the modiste. He had ignored her. 'I told you I'd have no need of riding clothes.'

'You were wrong. You need them now.'

More useless money spent on her. Perhaps if he had simply given her the money he spent on clothes, she could have found her own place to live and he would be free not to marry for her.

She crossed her arms in front of her chest. 'What else did you buy that I asked you not to?'

'The evening dress.'

'The evening dress!' Her voice became shrill.

'And shoes to match.'

She gritted her teeth. 'Useless waste of money.'

Devlin spoke firmly. 'Madeleine, change into the riding dress and return here forthwith. We will ride.' It was a command straight from a battlefield.

'Yes, my lord.' She turned and made sure she did not rush up the steps and into the house.

Once out of his sight, her anger blazed. She stomped into her room, and saw the riding dress laid out on her bed. It was an elegant outfit, a deep crimson, the colour rich and luxurious. She fingered the fine weave of the cloth and could not help but admire the garment's excellent cut.

She picked up the matching hat. A single feather adorned it, curled into a crescent to accent her chin. The hat had netting she could pull down over her face.

She had never expected to ride again. Indeed, she had settled in her mind that giving up horses was fitting punishment for fate to bestow upon her. When Lord Farley had first seen her on horseback, she had worn her brother's outgrown breeches and shirt instead of a proper riding dress. His old clothing was tight on her newly emerging curves. Now she knew how such garments must have inflamed Farley's senses, and she'd had no sense to restrain herself.

Yes, it was a fitting punishment to never ride again.

She walked over to the window and peered out. Devlin was now astride the black horse with Linette seated in front of him. He urged the horse into a sedate walk and she could hear through the closed window Linette's squeals of delight.

Devlin looked as if he were born to the saddle, and, as he held Linette protectively in his arm, Madeleine felt her heart yearn for him.

No. She must refrain from such feelings. She would ride,

as he commanded her to do, but she would not allow herself to feel a thing. Not for him. Not for anything, except her daughter. She would not allow herself to care about how the horse felt beneath her, how the hooves pounded in her ears, how the wind beat against her face.

She turned back to the bed and began undressing.

A quarter-hour later, she allowed Bart to toss her into the saddle. She remained silent while Devlin handed Linette down to Bart and they cantered through the London streets.

They made a solemn pair as they rode next to each other through neatly kept streets, still quiet at this early hour. The shops made way for rows of houses, each larger and more elegant as they progressed. She did not ask where they were headed.

Devlin finally spoke, though more to himself than to her. 'I have not been on horseback since...since Belgium.' His voice was flat, expressionless.

Her mouth dropped open in surprise. She must have tugged on the reins because the horse broke its gait. She hurriedly righted it again, but remembered the battle's evidence on his chest and back. In spite of her resolve to be angry with him, her throat tightened with emotion.

'We are here,' he said. They had stopped in front of a large stone gate.

Hyde Park.

Beyond the gate was a landscape of green, a fantasy of countryside in the midst of a city. 'Oh, my,' she gasped.

'It is early. No one will heed us at this unfashionable hour.' His horse led the way.

So many years ago, it had been her girlish wish to gallop down Rotten Row in Hyde Park, while her sisters had merely aspired to sedate afternoon drives.

As she and Devlin rode, Madeleine tried to imagine row after row of fashionable equipages with beautiful ladies and finely dressed gentlemen perched on the seats. The less prosperous would stroll along the pavement. She admitted to curiosity about such a sight, even though she had disdained the role of passenger. In those innocent days, however, she had never expected to feel like a trespasser in a world to which she no longer belonged.

Devlin led her to a dirt path where it was clear they could let the horses have their heads. Rotten Row. There were a few other riders, and Devlin ignored them. Madeleine pulled the netting of her hat over her face.

'We will race.'

He was back to giving commands, was he? Well, she would do as he commanded. She would race.

She did not wait for his command to begin. She pressed her knee into the horse's side. The mare leaped into motion. Madeleine leaned forward almost flat against the horse's neck. She inhaled the mare's scent, heard the panting of the mare's breath and the pounding of her hooves. Madeleine's heart ignored her bidding to play dead and leapt with delight. For the first time in years, she felt exhilaratingly free.

Other hooves sounded and Devlin's horse, neck pumping, pulled alongside. She glanced at him. His beaver hat was gone, and his hair blew wildly around his head. His eyes, too, blazed with excitement.

She urged her horse faster. Joy overwhelmed her and she laughed out loud. She glanced at Devlin, his horse neck to neck with hers. He grinned. They ended the course together.

They slowed their horses to a walk. Devlin, breathing as hard as his horse, circled around Madeleine. He gazed at her. To Madeleine, the green of the park faded and was replaced by the green of his eyes. She held his gaze, memorising it. No matter what her resolve, she vowed to remember the passion she saw in his eyes, the passion that mirrored her own.

A slow grin came over his face. 'Shall we do it again?'

Before she could figure out what the *it* could be that they would do again, he launched into a gallop. She recovered quickly and urged her horse on his heels. He smiled proudly at her when she caught up. Again they finished the course together.

'I won,' he said, a smug look on his face.

'You did not,' she countered. 'I would have been a length ahead if not for this infernal saddle.'

His brow wrinkled. 'Is something amiss with the saddle?'

She felt herself redden. 'No, I…I am accustomed to riding astride. Or I used to be.'

His expression turned solemn and she suspected he could imagine the scandalous picture she made in those days.

A bird fluttered noisily out of a nearby bush, startling Devlin's horse. He quieted the animal and glanced at Madeleine. Her face was flushed and her blue eyes sparkled. No matter what happened to him from this day forward, he would never regret this moment with her. Nor would he forget.

They remained that way, staring into each other's eyes, their mounts restless underneath them. Neither looked away.

More riders arrived in the park. Some greeted Devlin and tossed curious glances toward Madeleine. She held her head down.

'Perhaps we had best head home,' he said.

'Perhaps.'

He rode to retrieve his hat and led them to the gate. She followed closely.

They returned through the most fashionable streets, to streets full of shops, to their own nearly respectable address.

Madeleine spoke, 'Why did you hire horses today?'

He glanced at her. 'They belong to my brother.'

'The Marquess?' Her voice was anxious.

'Yes, but do not worry, Maddy. I have my brother's permission.' It was not entirely accurate, but he had Serena's permission, and Ned would never counter her wishes.

They lapsed back into silence.

Soon they neared their street. Madeleine asked, 'Why did you do this?'

'Fetch the horses?'

'Make me ride with you.'

He frowned. How could he explain what he did not truly understand? He had not meant to invite her. At first he had meant to escape her. 'I did not wish to ride alone.'

'You could have taken Bart with you.'

To Bart horses were like tools, a means to get a job done. His wish to ride was more ephemeral. A last chance for freedom? Bart would never have understood.

He had not even thought of Bart, though. He had wanted Madeleine. Who else would understand the need? The pleasure?

'I wished it to be you.' His voice had turned low and he was not sure if she heard him.

As they rode up to their apartments, Linette's face disappeared from the window. A moment later she was out the door, tugging away from Bart's firm grip.

'Horse! Horse! Mama. Deddy.'

'Hello, my darling,' Madeleine called to her.

'Me, too, Mama. Me, too.' Linette cried, squirming to get free. Even a strong man like Bart could barely hold her.

'Bring her here, Bart.' Devlin reached down and scooped the child into his arms, holding her securely in front of him. 'Maddy, come with us.'

Devlin, Madeleine, and Linette rode sedately to the end of the block, quiet at this hour, and back again. The little girl's delighted laughter filled the street.

'More. More.' Linette shouted.

'Enough for today, Lady Lin.'

Bart reached for the child. Devlin slid easily off the horse and turned for Madeleine, holding her firmly by the waist to assist her to dismount.

She looked him directly in his eyes and whispered, 'Thank you, Devlin.'

He held her there, suspending the moment.

When he finally slid her down his body to touch the pavement, Madeleine blinked, turned and took Linette from Bart.

She allowed Linette to pat the horses and say goodbye to them.

'Would you return the horses, Bart?' Devlin asked.

Bart nodded, taking hold of the reins. 'Dev, a note was delivered for you. It is on the table inside the door.'

Devlin, his emotions in a tangle, ran up the steps and into the house. He had not wanted that time with Madeleine to end. He removed his coat, gloves and hat, and picked up the envelope.

Madeleine and Linette came inside, and Linette ran to the window for her last glimpse of the horses. 'Bye bye, horses!'

'What is the note?' Madeleine asked as she pulled off her hat. Her hair tumbled down to her shoulders.

He handed her a piece of paper.

Her eyes grew wide. 'It is a voucher for Almack's!'

'Serena certainly lost no time procuring it for me.' He wrinkled his brow. 'The other paper is an invitation,' he said, though she was paying little attention. 'No, a command, really.'

'A command?' She gingerly fingered the voucher.

'We are commanded to dine with my brother and his wife this evening, at their town house.' He tapped the card against his palm.

'You are?' She said absently.

'*We* are,' he corrected. 'You and I.'

Her face turned pale. 'No.'

Chapter Eleven

'Oh, yes,' Devlin said. 'The invitation is very specific. It is for us both.'

'I will not attend.' Her voice sounded as if she were being strangled. 'I will not expose myself to...to a society dinner where I do not belong.'

Devlin saw the rising panic in her eyes. 'It is a private dinner. You and I are to dine with Ned and Serena, *en famille*.'

'No.'

Devlin rubbed his brow. What the deuce could Ned be thinking of? It was not like his brother to play games. Impossible to believe he would invite Madeleine to his home to dine with his wife. Ned might not love Serena, but he certainly would never deliberately cause her any discomfort. And, then, there was the matter of the voucher to Almack's. An invitation to bring his mistress to dine, and a blatant entry into the marriage mart in the same package. It made no sense.

Madeleine stared at him, her chin now tilted in defiance, anxiety lingering in her eyes. He looked back at the card, not so much to read it again as to collect his thoughts.

He wrinkled his brow. 'I think the voucher must mean Ned intends to give me the money, but...' he glanced up at her '...I cannot understand why he wishes us to dine.'

'I will not go.'

'I do not think there would be any harm in it.'

She crossed her arms over her chest. 'I will not go.'

Devlin attempted a cajoling smile. 'You would find use for the evening dress.'

She threw the voucher at him and fled up the stairs.

As he bent to retrieve it, Linette toddled in from the parlour where she had been on sentry duty at the window. She pulled on Devlin's sleeve, her little mouth turned down and her big blue eyes mournful. 'Horses gone.'

Devlin almost smiled, even amidst his confused thoughts. He picked her up. 'That's right, Lady Lin. Horses gone.'

Linette flung her chubby arms around Devlin's neck. He clung tightly to Linette. The freedom and joy of the ride with Madeleine receded. Walls blocked his escape and the air seemed in short supply.

Run, he heard himself shout. *Run*. He was on horseback again, this time screaming for his cavalry to withdraw. They had gone too far, drunk with the carnage they'd wrought on the French, still swinging their sabres into retreating backs, until the pounding of fresh French cavalry sounded in his ears.

He opened his eyes and caught a glimpse of himself in the hallway mirror, Linette's curly dark head leaning trustingly on his shoulder.

He took a deep breath. 'Come on, Lady Lin. Let us see if Sophie left us some lemon cakes in the kitchen.'

Madeleine flung herself dramatically on the bed. As a child, she might have indulged in a fit of angry tears, but now she knew tears achieved nothing.

She rose and unbuttoned the riding dress, choosing her yellow muslin to wear. After fastening the laces, she picked up the riding dress again and held it to her nose. It smelled of horse. She closed her eyes. The ride had been glorious. The exhilaration, the freedom of speed, Devlin, hatless and grinning beside her.

Another memory to store. She pored over every detail, fixing each in her mind. With another whiff of the lingering scent, she laid the garment carefully on top of the trunk at the foot of her bed. Later she would brush it off as she had seen Sophie do, and she would hang it up to air out.

The door opened. 'May I come in?'

She stiffened at his voice. 'You might have knocked first.'

Devlin closed the door and leaned against it, his legs crossed at the ankles. 'You might have refused me entry.'

She picked up the riding dress and brushed it off with her hand. It was something to do, to look busy.

'May we talk, Maddy?'

He looked appealingly long limbed, taut with strength, but infused with gentleness. She did not wish to see him thus. She closed her eyes, but that only brought the memory of him wild-eyed on a galloping horse. She shrugged.

'First, let me assure you that the decision is yours. I will not mention this matter again, do you understand?'

She nodded, but did not look at him.

'I do not know why my brother made this invitation, but I cannot believe he would mean any harm. He is a good man.'

'I am not so certain of that.' The Marquess represented danger to her, even though he had been gentle with Linette.

Devlin continued, choosing not to argue the point, 'The invitation must have something to do with Ned advancing my money, or else why would he include the voucher? I think that in order to get the money, we must do as he says.'

She stiffened. 'I do not have to do as he says.'

He softened. 'Of course you do not. But I wish that you would. Nothing is more important to me than securing your future. And Linette's and Sophie's and Bart's.'

'Why?'

He looked surprised.

Her vision blurred with useless tears. 'Do you wish to go to Almack's and search for a wife?'

She watched one of his hands clench into a fist, then relax again. 'I do not *wish* to do so, but I must.'

'I cannot like it,' she said lamely.

One corner of his mouth turned up in an ironic smile. 'I cannot like it either, but we must do it for Linette's future.'

Did he mean this, or was he saying it because he knew she would do anything for Linette's sake? Her child was more important than all the rest of it. Even more important than Devlin's happiness, though it killed her to have to make that choice. She truly wanted to believe that Devlin cared so much for Linette, but men had said many things to her over the past years and she'd learned not to believe any of it.

'Linette is my concern, not yours.' She strode to the window and looked out.

He came behind her and put his hands on her shoulders. 'I have told you before. You all are my responsibility. You. Linette. Sophie. Even Bart. What kind of man would I be if I did not see to your well-being? But I need the means to do so.' He gently rubbed the tender skin of her neck with his thumbs. 'My brother controls the money, so I must do as he says for the time being. It is the price of my independence and your survival.'

'He is making you marry and you do not want to do so!' she blurted out. 'And the fault is all mine.'

He put his fingers to her lips to silence her. 'I choose to do this. Ned does not make me. Just as I will not make you go to this dinner, though I want you to do so.'

With all her heart, she did not want to go. She did not belong in polite society, and she did not trust the top-lofty Marquess, even if he did show a soft spot for her daughter.

It was unfair of Devlin to ask her to do such an unsuitable thing. How would she endure it? Madeleine pursed her lips. She had managed more unendurable things. She could manage this.

'Very well, I will attend your brother's dinner. For Linette's sake.'

'That is also why I attend,' he murmured, gazing into her eyes with a softened expression. 'Madeleine,' he whispered, his lips inches from hers. His fingers gently stroked her cheek.

The passion flared inside her, making her ache for him here in the middle of the day with the whole household up and busy. She had lost all claim to respectability with her wantonness. Worse, she had tied herself to him with her body.

He leaned closer. She felt his breath on her own mouth. She wanted him again, felt urgent for his kiss. She considered how to loosen his buckskin breeches.

Small steps pounded on the stairs. 'Mama, Mama!'

Devlin took a step back, a rueful smile on his lips. 'In here, Lady Lin.'

The Marchioness of Heronvale felt uncommonly nervous as she waited with her husband for the arrival of their dinner guests. She was anxious that her new guest approve of her, a silly worry. Since when did one concern oneself with the approval of a...such a woman?

Her husband's plan filled her with excitement, but she was afraid to even think of that, so huge were the hopes that could be dashed. So she thought instead about how scandalous it was to invite to their respectable home a woman whose attachment to a man involved carnal matters. Serena put her fingers to her cheeks to conceal her blush. What would Devlin's woman be like? What would be different about this woman that she could hold a man by bedding him? Serena felt almost unbearably wicked for pondering such things. What would Ned think of her if he knew?

Rarely did Ned require her to face the carnality of the marriage bed. When he did, all she managed to feel was anxiety that she would displease him. Displease him she always did, though he was too much of a gentleman to tell her so.

She wondered if Ned would look upon this mistress of Devlin's in that sensual way she had often glimpsed at the opera, where young dandies eyed gaudily dressed women in the pits.

It frightened her unbearably that Ned might do so, just as it frightened her to think he might have a mistress of his own. He gave her no signs of doing so, but how would she know?

As usual when she let herself dwell on such matters, she felt her eyes sting and her throat tighten. Ned would not approve if she looked as if she might cry. She steeled herself to assume a placid expression.

'My brother is late.' Ned stood at the mantel where the clock had chimed the half-hour.

Ned was always prompt, sometimes embarrassing Serena when they arrived first at a social gathering. She could never convince her husband that the time on the invitation was not the time one was expected to arrive.

She opened her mouth to make an excuse for Devlin, but shut it again. For some unknown reason, Ned lately became angry whenever Serena spoke on Devlin's behalf.

She was glad, though, that Ned had decided to advance Devlin his allowance, but it puzzled her why Devlin had now decided to pursue a wife when he was obviously involved with this mysterious woman, Miss England. It was hard to reconcile the idea that the pretty girl she'd met with Devlin was a wanton demimonde sharing his bed.

Barclay appeared at the door. 'Lord Devlin and Miss England,' he announced.

Serena rose, her heart pounding with excitement.

Devlin entered, looking handsome in his evening attire. It had been a long time since she'd seen him dressed so. His plain coat of black superfine complemented his dark hair and superbly fit his soldier's broad shoulders. Still, he managed to wear the formal clothes in that careless manner so typical of him. Serena fixed her gaze upon the young woman who stood a step behind him.

She was dazzling. Her hair, as dark as Devlin's, was piled high on her head. Natural curls framed her face and caressed the nape of her neck. She wore a delicate pearl necklace and matching teardrop pearl earrings. Not at all the jewellery one would expect of a mistress, more like a set Serena had received on her twelfth birthday.

The gold silk evening dress Miss England wore was cut in classical lines and free of adornment except for matching gold beading around the neckline and hem. Serena had seen more revealing necklines on the *ingénues* at Almack's, but this young woman's figure was such that a man's eye would certainly be drawn to that part of her. Serena glanced hurriedly at Ned, to see his reaction. He merely lifted an eyebrow.

'Ned. Serena. How good to see you!' Devlin spoke with cheerfulness. 'Let me formally present to you Miss Madeleine England. Miss England, the Marquess and Marchioness of Heronvale.'

The young woman curtsied perfectly to each of them and then stood regally, directly meeting their gazes. 'I am pleased to renew your acquaintance.' Her voice was cultured and correct, indistinguishable from one who'd had a respectable upbringing.

'Good of you to come,' Ned said stiffly. He turned to Devlin, just of hint of worry in his eyes. 'Are you well, brother?'

Devlin rolled his eyes. 'Good God, Ned, I am no longer at death's door, you know.'

Serena watched Miss England glance in surprise at Devlin's comment, concern flashing across her face. Devlin caught the look and disarmed it with the hint of a smile.

Serena was fascinated.

Barclay entered with a tray of aperitifs. They were still standing. Serena was embarrassed at her lapse of manners.

'Barclay, Miss England and I will sit on the sofa. Come, Miss England, let us sit and become better acquainted.' Serena led her guest to the sofa. The two women sat and accepted the small crystal glasses from the butler.

Serena had no idea how to converse with this beautiful young woman. 'I hope our coach brought you here satisfactorily.'

Miss England smiled cordially. 'It was kind of you to send it.'

'Well, we could not have you walk, and Devlin could not hire—' Serena stopped. It was poor manners to refer to Devlin's lack of finances, especially since Ned was the cause.

Miss England seemed to ignore her embarrassment. 'Indeed. It was most generous.'

Serena listened carefully to the expression in Miss England's voice. She was not sure what she expected—for the girl to be nervous? She did not seem so. For her to be insolent and mocking? There was none of that. Miss England seemed perfectly composed.

'I must also compliment you on your appearance,' Serena said, searching for conversation. 'Your dress is lovely.'

Miss England blushed at this and seemed for the first time to look ill at ease. What woman was not pleased with a compliment to her clothes?

'Thank you,' the girl murmured.

Serena's distress increased. She was not handling this well at all. She glanced to see if Ned noticed, but he was deep in conversation with Devlin. It pleased her to see the two brothers not slamming fists into each other. Ned loved Devlin more than he did anyone else in the world, Serena knew.

'They had a disagreement, I believe,' Miss England said, turning her head toward the two men.

The directness of this statement surprised Serena. She would never have mentioned the topic to anyone. 'Yes, they did.'

Miss England gave a faint smile. 'Perhaps Lord Devlin lost his temper with his brother.'

'I believe my husband provoked the trouble,' Serena said. 'It seems forgotten now.'

Barclay announced dinner.

'I will escort Miss England,' Ned said, bowing to her and holding out his arm. Serena felt a pang of jealousy. The young woman took the offered arm and waited until Serena, escorted by Devlin, walked ahead of her.

Devlin gave Serena a brotherly squeeze. 'Tell me, Serena, what is this about?'

She blinked. 'What is what about?'

He frowned at her. 'You know very well. This invitation.'

She bit her lip. 'We...that is, Ned... We wished to see you.'

He tossed her a sceptical glance. 'Fustian,' he whispered. 'Why did you invite Maddy?'

'So you would come?' Her answer came out like a question.

They entered the formal dining room with its crystal chandelier glittering from the candle flames. Serena wished they had set up a small table in one of the more cosy parlours, but Ned had wanted Miss England to see the opulence of the house. It was odd, though, that the young woman seemed to accept the frescoed ceiling, long mahogany table, and multi-piece silver service as a matter of course. Serena had instructed the servants to set the table so that they sat at one end. Ned at the head, of course, and she to his right. To his left sat Devlin and Miss England.

Serena watched the young woman throughout dinner. Miss England never hesitated over her choice of cutlery, and she seemed completely at ease with having servants present the food. The conversation was confined to topics of general interest, upon which Miss England conversed easily, but Serena noticed that she never spoke unless she was addressed first.

Serena also watched Devlin. He checked Miss England often, concern or pride alternating in his face. She looked at Ned, whose expression never changed. Serena was struck with a pang of envy so strong she feared she might burst into tears right over the chocolate truffle.

When the port appeared, Serena was relieved to leave the dining room to the men and return to the parlour with Miss England.

Miss England selected a single chair, waiting politely for Serena to sit first. A small fire had been lit in the fireplace to ward off the chill of the damp spring night, its hiss and sputter loud in the silence between the two women.

'Would you like tea?' Serena asked finally.

'No, thank you, ma'am.' The young woman remained composed, her hands folded in her lap.

'I do wish you would call me Serena.'

Miss England glanced at her in surprise. 'I would not presume.'

'But you are Devlin's friend, and he is so dear to us.' Serena fingered the lace trim on her dress.

Madeleine's nerves were beginning to fray. She had managed the role of guest long enough. 'I am not Devlin's friend.'

This pretence seemed even more dishonest than those she was forced to enact for Farley. It was shameful for her to even set foot in this house, more flush with money than Farley could have wrested out of her in one hundred years. She wished she could excuse herself and run.

Instead she regarded the Marchioness. What could have induced this high-born, titled lady to entertain her? To ask for the intimacy of first names? There was no sense in it.

The beautiful blonde woman in her pale blue dress edged in delicate lace looked even more uncomfortable than Madeleine. Madeleine suspected the Marquess was behind this visit, and his wife compelled to go along. But why?

It certainly did not help matters that the Marchioness looked as if she might cry at any moment. 'I apologise, ma'am. I did not mean for my words to distress you.'

The Marchioness smiled faintly, blinking. 'Do not concern yourself about me. I fear I am proving a poor hostess.'

Madeleine blinked in surprise. 'Why should you be a good hostess? You ought not be compelled to entertain me at all.'

Her hostess looked up. 'Compelled? I assure you I was not compelled. It was my idea to invite you to dinner.'

'Why?' It was presumptuous of her to ask, but the word simply burst out of her.

Distress again pinched her ladyship's brow, and she gave Madeleine a pleading look. Madeleine felt a different kind of shame for distressing such a lady. Lady Heronvale had truly laboured to be kind. There had not been a moment when she had shown even a hint of the disapproval Madeleine deserved.

Madeleine glanced around the room, her eyes lighting on the figurines on the mantelpiece. 'They are Meissen, are they not?' she said, trying to find something comfortable to talk about.

'What?' The Marchioness still looked distressed.

'The figures on the mantel. They are Meissen.'

'Why, yes they, are.' Her ladyship's eyes widened with surprise.

Madeleine smiled. 'They are lovely.'

After nearly half an hour of more awkward conversation, Ned and Devlin entered the parlour. The brothers looked congenial. Madeleine did not know if this boded good or ill. In any event, what more pain could the Marquess inflict than making Devlin leave her? Devlin would leave her no matter what. The Marquess could not, after all, know her identity.

Ned surveyed the parlour and elected to stand near the mantel, upon which he leaned casually. The leg nearest the fire felt too much heat, but he ignored the discomfort. He had a good view, a position of power.

He had been pleased to be able to converse with his brother in an amicable way, though he sensed Devlin's wariness. He glanced at his wife and perceived her discomfort, as well. Miss England was more of a puzzle. She seemed serene, poised, untouched by the tensions crackling throughout the room.

Ned rubbed the elegant carving of the mantel with his thumb. The time had come. He met his wife's eye. She inhaled sharply. He would bring Serena her heart's desire.

He looked down on the young woman who should never have been invited to his wife's home. 'Miss England,' he began in a mild voice, hoping it sounded friendly.

She lifted her gaze to him, the impassive expression still in her eyes.

'What think you of our house here in town?'

A flicker of surprise showed in her face, but she quickly changed her expression to one he could not read. Mocking? Melancholic? 'It is a magnificent home, my lord. Very fine.'

He smiled. 'I am pleased that you think so.'

She returned his smile. 'I did not realise you sought my good opinion.'

That statement must be sarcasm, but he could not tell for certain. He ignored it, clearing his throat. 'This house pales in comparison to Heronvale. Heronvale is a piece of heaven.' Ned glanced at Devlin. 'It was a marvellous place to be reared, was it not, Devlin?'

Devlin's eyes narrowed suspiciously. He lounged in a chair, but one leg crossed over the other swung with nervous energy. 'It had fine stables.'

Ned laughed, hoping to dispel his brother's tension. 'My brother saw little of Heronvale except on the back of a horse. Did you know that, Miss England?'

The smile was fixed on her face. 'Indeed.'

This woman gave up little of her feelings, Ned thought.

'Miss England is an accomplished horsewoman,' Devlin said.

'Is that so?' Ned remembered the child's excitement seeing the horses of his curricle. He had assumed her passion for horses had come from her father. 'You and my brother have that in common, then.'

Miss England shrugged her reply.

This was like fencing with an opponent reluctant to reveal his skill. Perhaps he should begin the attack.

He strolled over to a decanter of claret, lifting it to offer its contents to the others. Devlin shook his head and Serena mumbled 'No, thank you.'

'I should like some,' Miss England said, and Ned had the foolish impression that they had each chosen their weapons. He handed her a glass and poured one for himself. He took a sip.

First lunge. 'Did you know my brother is a wealthy man, Miss England?'

Her glass pressed against her lips and her taste of the wine was long and delicate. 'Is one wealthy who has no money to spend?' Parry.

Riposte. 'You know, then, that Devlin must marry?'

Her brows lifted. 'For his wealth, he must marry, unless you declare otherwise.' Well parried. Too well parried.

'He must marry. His heritage demands it. Do you under-stand?'

She stared at him, bringing her glass to her lips again.

Ned abandoned the fencing and indulged in a rare display of anger. 'His behaviour with you has been irresponsible. Un-becoming in a gentleman—'

Devlin rose from his chair. 'Enough, Ned. These are words to be spoken to me in private. I will not have you do so in front of Madeleine.'

Ned took a step toward his brother. 'You took a mistress when you knew full well you could not keep her in clothes or jewels—'

'She does not want—'

Ned closed the distance on his brother. 'You involved a child, Devlin. A child. How irresponsible is that?'

Serena gasped.

'You know nothing of this matter, Ned. I have said I will find a wife, what more do you want? I'll accept my bloody heritage and be damned, but you owe Madeleine an apology.' Devlin's eyes blazed with anger. 'She has done nothing to deserve these words of yours.'

'She has borne a child, has she not?' Ned paced back to

the mantel. Devlin stood his ground. Turning to face them again, Ned saw the alarm in Serena's face. Miss England looked on, alert.

'The home you have contrived is no place for a child,' he said. 'The little girl needs comfort and education and a solid moral foundation. You cannot give that to her, Devlin.'

'I can and will take care of the child. Why do you think I agreed to marry? You've left me no other way to take care of them, have you? Well, brother, you may bet on it that Madeleine and Linette will be well cared for.' Devlin's fists were clenched and his body poised for a fight. 'By me.'

Ned paced the floor. 'You cannot provide her a good home. What will the child learn of life in a household like that, with you arriving at odd hours to warm her mother's bed?'

'Damn you, Ned. You have stepped too far over the line.' Devlin's face became a rigid, angry mask. Ned thought this might be how he appeared galloping toward a company of bayonet-wielding Frenchmen.

'Ned?' Serena's fingers crushed the fabric of her dress.

He glanced from Serena to Miss England, her hands folded demurely and her gazed fixed on them. Damn his brother for compromising that young woman.

And damn himself for being glad of it.

He would not back away now, not when he had come so far. He slowed his breaths and moderated his voice. 'I do apologise. I did not intend to ring a peal over your head.'

Devlin's hands curved into fists.

'Serena and I wish to help. It is why we invited you here.' Miss England raised her head.

'We believe it would be advantageous to everyone, if you agree with our proposition.'

Devlin still glowered, but showed a hint of curiosity, as well.

Ned went on. 'We wish to adopt the child and raise her as our own...'

Chapter Twelve

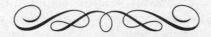

'Good God, Ned.' Devlin turned away from his brother and drew a tense hand through his hair. Ned wanted the child? 'What right have you to propose such a thing?'

He heard the Marquess take a deep breath. 'I am head of the family, you might recall.'

'What the deuce has that to do with it?' Devlin swung back to him.

Ned made no effort to respond, simply staring back.

Devlin's mind reeled with his brother's words. Ned thought he had seduced Madeleine. Thought she pined for dresses and jewels. Thought he could take Linette from her.

'Serena and I realise—' Ned's voice was steady and reasonable '—that there may be talk about our raising your child, but we are prepared—'

'*My* child?'

'Linette.' Ned went on. 'Such talk would disappear as soon as something more interesting came along. So I would not—'

'My child?' Devlin repeated, raising his voice.

'Of course,' Ned glanced at him and continued talking. 'It would be no time…'

Devlin stared at his brother, impeccably dressed in white breeches and superbly cut black coat. His hair, flecked with grey, remained neat and orderly. Did his ever-perfect brother think he'd seduced Madeleine, got her with child, then abandoned her to go off to war? Only a cad would do such a thing.

Devlin longed to explain to Ned he was not that sort of man. Explain that Madeleine had been Farley's prize. That the child might be anybody's. Serena might blush, but how scandalised could she be? An occasional tumble with such a woman was expected of young men. His brother might lift a disapproving eyebrow, but he could not damn Devlin's character. Yes, all that was needed to clear his name was to expose Madeleine's life under Farley and shame her in front of Ned and Serena.

Devlin tried to keep his voice steady. 'What causes you to think the child mine?'

Ned gave him a look of exasperation. 'She looks like you.'

'She looks like Maddy.' A vision of Linette flashed through Devlin's mind. Her curly dark hair always falling from its ribbon. The clear blue innocence of her eyes. The pouty mouth when she did not get her way. So much like Madeleine. From his first glimpse of the child, his heart had reached out to the little girl. She was Madeleine as a child.

'She is the image of you at that age,' Ned countered. 'If you do not believe me, come to Heronvale and check the family portrait in the music room. She is even named for you. She was obviously conceived during your leave from Spain. The timing is correct. How you supported them in your absence is a mystery, but there is no mystery about the fact that she is your child.'

'My child.' Stunned, Devlin made his own calculation. His one brief encounter with Madaleine. The child's age. He'd never considered.

Madeleine stared down at her lap, her knuckles turning white as she gripped her hands. The Marquess's words echoed as if emerging from a distant cave. Saying he wanted to take Linette. Saying Linette was Devlin's child.

She stood and spoke with cold rage. '*My* child.'

These men were no different than Farley and the ones he had sent to her bed. They all wielded power over her. The power to control her life, to violate her body...and to steal from her all that was dear. This rich Marquess controlled with his title and money. What chance had she against such weapons? Even Devlin, for all his pretty words, held her life and her daughter's in his hands. He could crush them both in an eye blink. He could cast them into the street. Abandon them to his brother.

Send them back to Farley.

Madeleine's body trembled. Panic mixed with rage. Three sets of eyes stared at her. The Marquess's with a look of impatience. His wife's with tears rolling down her cheeks. And Devlin's with confusion and surprise.

Madeleine held herself erect, lifting her chin high. These people would not see she feared their power. Indeed, she would not fear it. She would defy it. No one would take Linette from her. No one.

She let a faint smile cross her face and spoke again, her voice mild. 'Linette is my child.'

And, as they stood poised to hear more, she bolted. She ran out the mahogany parlour door, down the white marble stairs and through the hall, glittering with gilt. She heard Devlin shout her name. Heard the Marchioness wail, and the Marquess call for someone to stop her.

No one did. She flung open the front door and ran out into the street. She cared not that she held her skirts high away from her ankles, nor that the silk slippers scuffed roughly against the pavement. She would get to Linette first. She would grab Linette and Sophie and run.

She had only a vague notion of which direction to take, but trusted that her need to protect Linette would lead her home. Shouts sounded from behind her. She dared not look back. She'd always been fleet-footed. None of the lads she'd grown up around could best her in a race and no one would best her now.

'Maddy!' It was Devlin's voice.

She ran faster, past the elegant houses and neatly swept streets, ghostly in the lamplight. Ahead was a jumble of carriages, polished and shining, clogging the street. Elegantly liveried footmen milled about. Candlelight blazed from a house and, as she neared it, Madeleine heard sounds of music and revelry coming from the windows. She also heard Devlin's shoes pounding behind her. Coachmen and postilions glanced curiously in her direction. There was nothing to do but head straight for them. She plunged into the crowd.

Devlin's lungs strained and his legs ached as he pushed himself into greater speed. His months of recovery had robbed him of more strength than he had known. Madeleine was in sight. He gained on her slightly when she disappeared into the throng of vehicles and men lounging in front of the elegant town house. A satisfactory crush by the looks of it, but he had been out of society so long he could not even remember whose house it was. He only knew Madeleine would draw attention to herself in her flight. He must catch her before danger befell her. What could she be thinking of running into the night alone and unprotected?

He slowed, trying to get a glimpse of her in the confusion.

'Lord Devlin?' A man panted as he came up behind him.

Devlin greeted him with relief. 'Jem. Help me find her.'

Bless Jem. He asked no questions, but immediately ran to search from the edge of the line of carriages. Devlin headed through the jam where he'd seen Madeleine disappear. The commotion ahead of him told him he was close.

'Hey, missy, what is your hurry?' Men's voices laughed. 'Stop now, missy.'

Would she appear to be a lady to them? The coachmen and postilions would be whiling away the hours of waiting with a bit of drink. Boredom and drink were dangerous companions. He glimpsed her, seeing only a bit of her gold silk before men closed behind her, calling after her. Were they grabbing at her? Please no. They would not molest her here in Mayfair. St James's Street was the danger. Not Mayfair.

She turned, giving Devlin an anguished look. Jem had circled behind her. He caught her in flight.

'It's all right, Maddy. Jem is a friend,' Devlin said to her, as she struggled to get free. 'You are safe with us.'

'Let me go,' she cried. 'Let me go.'

Jem did let her go, but not until Devlin had her firmly in hand, one arm encircling her waist.

Devlin saw one of the footmen look curiously in their direction. He thought it prudent to avoid further trouble. 'Come, let us get away.'

Jem led them to the entrance of an alleyway. Madeleine thrashed and kicked as Devlin half-dragged her into the alley. 'I want to go.'

Devlin kept his arm tight around her waist. 'Jem, can you send the carriage? I assume you made it ready for us.'

'Yes, sir.' He ran off.

Madeleine squirmed and struggled in Devlin's arms. 'Let me go,' she cried feebly. 'Let me go.'

He leaned her against the cold stone wall and secured her with his body, his arms embracing her. Her struggles quieted, but she trembled against him, her breath ragged.

'You are safe now, Maddy,' he whispered in her ear. 'I will not hurt you.'

'You will let him take Linette,' she cried.

'No, I will not,' he spoke soothingly in her ear.

'He will make you do it,' she insisted. 'Just as he makes you get married.'

The truth in that statement stung. Ned held the power over his fortune, and he needed that fortune to safeguard Madeleine and Linette. Devlin had no means to combat him.

A few weeks ago Devlin would have bet his entire fortune that his brother would never to do anything so dastardly. Now Ned was like a stranger, capable of anything.

Trying to sound confident, he assured her, 'Ned will not take Linette from you, I promise.'

'I am sick to death of gentlemen's promises.' She spat out the words. 'Promises mean nothing.'

'Mine do,' Devlin insisted, offended and hurt that she would think him like other men, after all they had been through.

She met his eyes, her own a challenge. 'Do they?'

What was the use? She would not believe him. He cursed Farley and every man who had failed her. He cursed himself. It had not occurred to him to take her away from that life when he first met her. Had he done so, she'd have been spared years of suffering, of rearing her child in such a scandalous place.

Her child. His child, perhaps? Had he left his own flesh and blood to Farley's evil whims? Perhaps Ned's ill opinion of him was well deserved.

Her struggles ceased, but though his body was pressed against hers, he felt her distance.

The carriage pulled up with Jem on the box beside the driver. Devlin walked her to it.

She looked up. 'I will not ride in *his* carriage.'

'Do not be foolish, Maddy. Let us get out of here.' Curious bystanders started to gather, doubtless trying to see the crest on the side of the vehicle.

'No.' She tried to pull away.

'Enough of this,' Devlin said, more to himself than to Madeleine. He picked her up and tossed her into the carriage, jumping in behind. 'Go!' he shouted to Jem.

The carriage lurched, and Devlin fell against her. She pushed him away. Crossing her arms over her chest, she huddled against the side of the carriage, as far away from him as possible. A tear trickled down her cheek.

Feeling miserable, Devlin rubbed the back of his neck. Her dress was wrinkled and dirty, her shoes near tatters, her hair half-tumbled from its pins.

She glanced at him briefly before turning back to the curtain.

'Maddy?'

She did not respond.

Devlin took a breath. 'Linette…is she…is she my child?'

Madeleine shut her eyes and focused on the rhythmic sounds of the horses' hooves against the cobbles. She had intended for this moment never to come.

She turned to him. 'I do not know.'

There was little light in the carriage, and she could only dimly see his face. She could not read his expression.

She continued, 'She could be your child.'

He made a sound, an aching one. 'How? From that first night, I suppose, but how could you know?'

He meant how could a woman who had been with countless men say that one of them fathered a child? She winced.

'I do not pretend to know.' She had promised herself never to believe Devlin fathered her child. She'd always told herself naming her Linette was in memory of a man who had been kind to her, nothing more. But sometimes, when she gazed upon her daughter, she believed otherwise.

'It is possible, nothing more.' She felt her throat tighten. The memory of that night, both with him and afterward, was etched in her mind.

'I was a foolish girl. You undoubtedly will think me so.' She attempted a light tone to her voice. 'When you left that night, I did not do as I was supposed to do. I did not wash myself. I fancied it would keep you with me a little longer.'

She heard his breath quicken.

'And when Farley came to me, I refused him.' She winced at this part. 'I had never refused him before, and he beat me soundly, but he did not bed me. The next day, he left. He was gone a long time, more than a month.'

Those rare times when Farley left had been the best her life had to offer in those days. She was guarded against running away, but none of his lackeys dared touch her and the gaming hell ran without her as the prize.

'Maddy.'

He reached for her, but she twisted away. 'By the time Farley returned, I knew I was with child. I hid the fact from him as long as possible. He wanted to get rid of the baby, but I threatened to kill myself if he did.'

'Maddy, I'm sorry.' Devlin reached out to her, but she pushed his hand away.

'Linette has been reward enough. I ask for nothing more.'

'I should have been there to help you.' He sounded anguished.

How like a man to be sorry for what he had not done, though he probably gave not a thought to it until this moment. Did Devlin think his regret made any difference to her? He had not believed Linette to be his child and looked for excuses not to believe so now. His words were empty.

'I will not let the Marquess take Linette,' she said. 'Sophie and I will take her away this night. You need not trouble yourself further with us.'

'You will not leave, do you understand?' He spoke sharply. 'It is not safe for you.'

'You cannot make me stay.' She twisted toward him. 'Unless you plan to hold me prisoner like Farley did. Under guard every moment.'

'He kept you under guard?'

'At first. After Linette was born, he guarded her.'

'Damn.' The word barely reached her ears.

They rode in silence, the creaks of the carriage and the sounds of the horses' hooves filling their ears until the carriage came to a stop. Jem hopped down from the box and opened the carriage door. Devlin lifted Madeleine out.

'Wait for me, Jem,' Devlin said.

'You are going back?' Madeleine said, fear creeping back.

'I need to speak to my brother.'

They would plot the stealing of her child. Devlin would

give Linette to the high-minded Marquess and flawless Marchioness.

'Do you keep me here? Do you alert Bart to guard the door?'

He attempted to take her by the elbow, but she pushed him away and ran hurriedly to the door. He caught up with her there, pulling the key from his pocket. He gripped her arm with his other hand as they entered the house. The hallway was lit with two candles, the rest of the house, quiet.

Devlin took her by the shoulders and forced her to look at him. 'Nothing is changed, Maddy. I promised you that I would take care of you and Linette, and I will fulfil that promise. I will not take Linette from you, nor let my brother do so. I promise you on my honour.'

She glared at him and tried to back out of his grasp. 'More talk of promises.'

He kept his grip on her shoulders and kept in step with her. 'You must stay here, Maddy.'

'You do not command me, my lord.' She backed into the wall.

He moved towards her still. 'I must command you in this. There are dangers out there for you and Sophie and Linette. Men like Farley and far worse. You would not be safe if you left, and I would not be able to protect you.'

'I am not safe here.' He was too close now, his hands on the wall and his legs spread apart like a cage entrapping her. 'You would give my child away.'

He gave an exasperated bark. 'Damn it, Maddy. I will not.'

She stared at him as he loomed over her. His features blurred in the dim light. More vivid was the scent of him, the warmth of him.

He rubbed his cheek, rough with stubble, against hers and brought his lips near her ear. 'You may not believe my promises, but I will believe yours. Promise me you will not run away. You will stay here until I have the means to set you up in your own house, wherever you wish.'

Her breath quickened, swelling her chest so that it touched his with each breath. She wanted to believe him. Wanted to believe he was the soldier returned from the war to rescue her, to whisk her and her daughter to a pretty little cottage where they would live happily forever.

His lips touched the sensitive skin of her ear. 'Promise.'

She squirmed under the sensations his lips created, making her press against his pelvis. She forced herself to place her back flat against the wall.

She also forced herself to think realistically. It was more likely he would barter her child to his brother. Linette would be wrenched from her arms and sent to live in the Marquess's house, and Devlin would be free to pursue whatever pleasure he wished. Linette would have sugared treats and pretty clothes and a pony of her own. There would always be a fire warming her room and food filling her belly. She would learn to call the kind-hearted Marchioness 'Mama' and the Marquess, who had looked upon her with such tenderness, 'Papa'.

A sob escaped her lips. Devlin gathered her into his arms and she soaked his jacket with her tears.

'Promise you will not run away,' he murmured. 'Let me keep you safe.' He lifted her chin and placed his lips on hers.

For a moment she melted into him and allowed him to pet her and taste the tender interior of her mouth. For a moment she believed him. Catching herself, she struggled in his arms, wrenching her face away from him. He released her, pain written on his face.

She ran up the stairs without a backward glance.

Devlin returned more than two hours later. The candles in the hallway were burned to nubs. He pinched them out before ascending the stairs. His heart pounded in his chest.

Had she stayed?

When he had arrived back in Grosvenor Square, his brother and Serena still sat in the parlour. Serena's eyes were red with crying. She twisted a damp handkerchief with her fingers. His brother poured from an almost-empty decanter of brandy.

Serena had gasped when he reappeared.

'She is safe at home,' he announced.

He then endured his brother's lecture, watching the clock on the mantel pass midnight, wondering all the while if Madeleine waited for him, or if she had run. He declared to Ned that he, not the Marquess, would care for Madeleine and the child, had explained that their care was his whole motivation for marrying. He accepted Serena's shocked protests regarding such a marriage plan and allowed his brother to exact from him a promise to disengage from Madeleine and her child after his marriage. Ned rang another peal over his head about the destructiveness of debauchery and the necessity of relieving Madeleine of the disreputable status of mistress. Devlin had resisted the temptation to tell Ned the promise was unnecessary. Ned renewed his offer to adopt the child. Serena even proposed the unlikely option for Madeleine to become the governess.

Before Devlin bid Ned and Serena goodnight, Ned had discussed with him the financial obligations of engaging in courtship. They had come to agreeable terms.

Now, as Devlin mounted the stairs to where his two charges should be sleeping, his pockets were weighted with gold coin and a promise had been extracted from him to accompany Serena to Almack's the coming evening. All of which seemed of no consequence at all.

Devlin paused upon the top step, trying to sense if he would find Linette's little bed unoccupied, drawers void of contents, trunks bare.

Madeleine gone.

He knocked gently on Madeleine's door and opened it. The lamplight from the street provided dim illumination to the room. The light rested on Linette's bed.

The little girl slept peacefully. Her long lashes brushed the tops of her chubby cheeks and her little pink lips moved around the thumb tucked securely in her mouth.

He leaned over to watch her. My child? he asked himself.

He still could not see it. The little girl looked like a tiny, innocent Madeleine, before she'd encountered life's ugliness. Devlin reached out his hand and brushed his fingers through the child's dark curls.

Did it matter to him if she were his child or not? Would he feel the same ache in his heart at the prospect of losing her if he knew her to be from the seed of some other man?

He would never know.

Devlin glanced toward the larger bed, expecting to see Madeleine looking similarly peaceful in sleep, but the bed was empty. His heart accelerated and panic rushed back. Had she gone? He pressed his fingers against his temple.

And felt the point of a sword sharp in the small of his back.

Chapter Thirteen

'You will not take my child, Devlin.'

Madeleine pressed the point of the sabre into Devlin's back.

She had waited in the shadows of the room for over an hour. Each moment he had been away convinced her he was plotting with his brother to take Linette. She was furious with herself for being too cowardly to grab her child, wake Sophie, and flee.

She had finally decided that if Devlin returned home and went directly to his room, he was worthy of her trust. But if he entered her room, thinking her asleep, it would be to take her daughter. And she would be ready for him.

She had taken the sword from where it rested against the wall in his room, unsheathed its curved blade, and waited in the darkness. When he entered, she moved like a cat, silent and predatory, until the sword's point rested against his back.

'Maddy.' He started to turn.

'No!' She pushed on the sword. Its sharp point pierced the cloth.

He became still. 'I was not attempting to take her.'

'I do not believe you.' She kept pressure on the sword.

'I kept my word to you. Remove the sword.'

Her hand trembled. His coat ripped.

'You are piercing my skin, Maddy.' His voice was mild. Deceptively so, she thought.

'Why did you come in this room, if not to take her?' Madeleine's voice quavered. She had not truly intended to draw his blood.

He did not answer. He remained very still for what seemed to be an eternity. 'I merely wished to look at her.'

Something wistful sounded in his voice, and Madeleine faltered. Perhaps it mattered a trifle to him that Linette might be his child. Her grasp on the sabre relaxed slightly.

Devlin whirled around, his movement so swift she was not sure how he achieved it. He grabbed her wrist and wrenched the sabre from her grasp, catching the hilt of the falling sword in his other hand.

She cried out.

He whipped the sword to point at her. Madeleine shrank back. His face held no expression at all.

'If you must use the sabre, Maddy,' he said in a rumbling tone, 'it is not for stabbing, but for cutting and slicing.'

The sword whirred as he cut and sliced the air, fluttering the lace of her nightdress. He pointed the sword inches from her nose. Her heart hammered painfully against her chest.

Ever so slowly, his eyes not leaving hers, he lowered his arm so that the blade pointed to the floor.

'Now, heed me, Maddy.' His eyes narrowed. 'I offer you my protection. That includes Linette and Sophie, as well. You may accept or leave. You know the world you face if you spurn my offer, but perhaps you would prefer the dangers of the street...' he paused and blinked '...to me.'

Madeleine's heart slowed and she allowed herself to breathe, her thoughts a hopeless muddle.

She dreaded the idea of leaving him. Dreaded the thought that he would marry. She had persuaded herself he would steal Linette from her. How could she have thought that? He had rescued her. He planned to marry to support her and Linette. But how could he not have accepted the offer his brother had made? Linette would receive everything as the child of the Marquess.

'What is your wish?' he snapped.

Her wish? What she could not have. Her throat constricted, with frustration and despair. 'I will stay with you.'

He whipped the sword blade up into a salute, then turned and left the room.

Madeleine collapsed on to her bed and squeezed her eyes tight. She had cut him and made him bleed. She had torn his clothes.

She heard him slamming and banging things in his room, as well as the muffled sounds of swearing. She lay in the darkness and listened. What would happen in the morning? The one time she had totally defied Farley he had beaten her senseless. She had done so much more to Devlin. His forgiveness was impossible.

The cuirassier rode his midnight-black steed over a mass of writhing blue-coated bodies. Sunlight glinted off his metal breastplate and the sharply honed blade of his sword. The wind whipped the horsehair plume on his helmet while his black moustache quivered. The Frenchman laughed, and the sound echoed, merging with the moans of the wounded. The stench of war's carnage filled Devlin's nostrils, and he struggled to run, to retreat, but bloody hands clasped his ankles, holding him fast. Escape was impossible.

The huge Frenchman, a grin showing his yellow teeth, slowly raised the sword over his head and brought it down, closer and closer—

'No!' Devlin cried.

Hands grabbed him and shook him.

'Devlin, wake up! You are dreaming. Wake up!'

He fought, bucking and rearing and pushing the hands away. The voice became more urgent. 'Wake up!'

He opened his eyes, expecting to see each face of each man he had ever killed.

He saw Madeleine. She was straddling him, her nightdress hiked above her knees. Her hands were clasped around his wrists and he pushed against them, trying to free himself.

'It was only a dream, Devlin,' she said, her tone soothing.

He stared at her. *Madeleine*. Was she real? Perhaps she was the dream and if he closed his eyes again, the faces of the dead would return. He widened his gaze. His sheets were damp with sweat and his heart pounded like the drums of the French.

'There is no danger now.'

Madeleine. He ought to be furious at her, he dimly recalled, but he was so damned glad she was here. He relaxed his arms and, by so doing, caused her body to lie flush against his nakedness. As the last wisps of the nightmare evaporated, he turned his face from her, ashamed of his terror.

Madeleine stroked his hair. 'There, there.' She spoke as to a child awoken by dreams of goblins. 'It is all gone now. Nothing to signify.' Her lips touched the sensitive skin of his neck. Her body was warm, like a blanket.

'It will never go away,' he mumbled.

The first light of dawn shone through the window and the clatter of workmen's wagons testified that ordinary life proceeded, in spite of his private horror. His eyes moistened. Madeleine took his chin in her hand, turning his head to face her and kissing each eyelid.

Relief and gratitude washed through him, leaving him drained. He lifted his head to kiss her and tasted the salt of his tears on her lips. If only his world could consist solely of this. Why could life not be as simple as a man and woman making love?

She moaned softly and opened her mouth, giving, yet demanding more. Devlin pulled her nightdress over her head, his hands sliding against her smooth skin and full breasts. He was hard and urgent beneath her and desperate to feel the comfort she offered. He lifted her slightly and, as if she anticipated his desire, she gave him access.

Devlin's world became simple. Madeleine was here and his body pulsed with the sensation of her. Her hair tumbled forward, her curls tickling his face. Her pink lips parted with passion and her eyes half closed. She felt warm and smooth beneath his hands, her breasts soft on his chest. He grasped at her, feeling greedy and fearing she, like all that was beautiful, would disappear and he would fall into the cauldron of destruction and death from which he would never escape.

'Madeleine,' he growled, his need for her primal.

She gasped, and he felt her convulse around him. He exploded inside her, pleasure and peace filling him.

She relaxed, lying next to him and gazing at him. Devlin wanted nothing to break this moment.

Her blue eyes searched his, concern filling them.

He attempted a smile. 'I am quite all right now.'

Her concern did not disappear. 'I have heard you restless in your sleep before this.'

The nightmare came often enough. 'And you did not offer this comfort?' he joked.

The familiar masked look came over her and her body tensed. 'You had only to ask, my lord.'

'Shh, Maddy,' he whispered. 'I meant only a poor jest. Do not spoil this moment.'

She slipped away and reached for her nightdress. The moment had been spoiled. 'Your dream,' she said, thrusting her arms through her sleeves. 'Was it of Waterloo?' Her tone was almost conversational, but she had brought back the horror with the word.

Waterloo.

'I do not wish to say.' He spoke through clenched teeth.

'You promised you would tell me of Waterloo,' she reminded him. It sounded a scold.

'You promised me you would tell me of Farley,' he countered, mimicking her tone.

'I will,' she said. 'But first you must tell me of Waterloo.'

He turned his back on her. He felt her move toward him on the bed. Her fingers touched the sabre cut she had inflicted.

He wished to run from the memories, as he tried to run from the visions that plagued him at odd moments during the day and the dreams that tortured him at night, the ones drinking and debauchery had never quite erased.

'And if I do not, do you impale me with my sword again?'

She inhaled sharply, then kissed the wound she had made. 'I am sorry, Devlin.'

His words made him feel small.

'You carried the sabre that day, did you not?'

Damn her. She would not leave it alone. Well, she would hear it, then. All the horror. She would see what kind of man had lain with her.

'It is not a story for delicate ears.' Let it not be said he did not warn her.

'My ears have heard much that is not delicate.'

He had forgotten for a moment that her world had contained its own version of hell.

He took a deep breath. 'First there were the guns…'

French cannon had thundered and pounded destruction through the allied ranks before the relentless rhythm of the drums signalled the first French infantry assault. Devlin again heard the screams, and saw bodies being torn apart.

Wellington's motley mix of untried Allied troops was far outnumbered by the thousands and thousands of French, resplendent in new glittering uniforms, eager to bring glory to the emperor who had miraculously returned to them.

By the time the order came for the cavalry to charge, Devlin and his men lusted for French blood. They became drunk with vengeance, wreaking destruction on French infantry who broke and ran. He remembered the exhilaration of slashing his sword at men who were merely trying to run to safety. The air reeked of blood and sweat, gunpowder and grass. He told Madeleine how he rode over bodies and their severed parts, over men still moving and men who would move no more.

She listened. He sat facing her, his legs crossed in front of him on the bed. She kept her eyes on his, but he saw nothing but the memories.

'The killing did not last,' he said.

She reached over to him, placing her hand on his arm.

'The cuirassiers came.' He closed his eyes, again seeing them, hundreds of them mounted on fresh horses, shiny in their gold-tasselled uniforms. 'They rode slowly at first, then picked up the pace, like rocks tumbling from a cliff, faster and faster, until, raining down so fiercely, they bury you. I called out for the men to retreat, but they did not hear me.'

She squeezed his arm.

He met her gaze. 'Our horses were blown. We were no match for them. The cuirassiers had their revenge. My men screamed and died as the French infantry had done at our hands.'

'You watched this?' she asked, her voice hushed.

If he shut his eyes again, he would see it still. 'I was alone for the moment, the dead on the ground around me. Only for a moment…'

'Oh, Devlin.' Her hand stroked his arm, sending shivers.

'I was not alone for long. A French officer mounted on a huge black horse headed toward me. There was no escaping him. I was hampered by the dead and dying, you see. My horse could not manoeuvre.'

Devlin could still recall the man's chipped and yellowing teeth, each pockmark on his face, the glee of victory in his near-black eyes.

'Did he attack you?'

Devlin gave a dry laugh. 'He attacked my horse.'

Poor Courage. Courage had been a clod-footed, stout-hearted animal with an instinct for battle. The horse had saved his life more than once.

'That is the best means of crippling cavalry.' He gave a half-smile. 'We are nothing without our horses.'

Madeleine did not smile back.

He rubbed his hands. 'The Frenchman slashed at my horse with his sword. Skilful job, it was. Threw me off. Almost lost my sword. I managed to recover it, but he'd already had a go at me.' He fingered one of his scars. 'I cannot fathom why he did not finish me off. He jabbed at me. I rolled in the mud to escape him, while my horse screamed and stumbled nearby. Not exactly a heroic end.'

'But it was not the end,' she said.

'He meant it to be. I can still hear him laugh at my feeble attempts to fend him off. I kept rolling, until I rolled into an irrigation ditch. He slipped at the edge and tumbled down on top of me, impaling himself on my sword.'

She gasped.

'I heard the Frenchman draw his last breath, and my horse fell dead across the ditch, entombing me with my dead enemy.'

'Oh, my.' Her hand went to her mouth.

Devlin, suddenly chilled, wrapped the bed's blanket around him. Again he felt the cold mud seep into his back and the still-warm blood of the Frenchman soak his chest.

A tear trickled down Madeleine's cheek. Devlin was surprised at the tear's effect on him. Something near pain, near pleasure.

He would spare her the real horror. The sounds of the battle raging above him. The cries of the dying and wounded. The cold bleakness of the endless night, looters rustling above him. The stark terror that he would be discovered and killed for his silver buttons and leather boots.

'Bart found me the next day.'

'How did he find you among so many?' she asked, her voice raspy.

He gave her an ironic smile. 'I was quite hidden from view. He found my horse.'

'Your horse?' Her eyes widened again, this time with surprise.

'I had remained in the ditch, under the horse, under the Frenchman.'

'Devlin...' she whispered, reaching to stroke his cheek.

He moved away, not from her sympathy but from the memory that provoked it. 'I do not remember much of the rest. Bart carried me to Brussels. Then Ned came. Days had passed, I've been told. Ned brought me home on the yacht, to die at Heronvale.'

'But you did not die,' she said, as if that had been of some significance.

'That is it,' he whispered. 'Why did I not? Why great numbers of other men and not me? I killed many. Why did that damned Frenchman not kill me?'

Madeleine watched his face break. He squeezed his eyes shut and grimaced. She wrapped her arms around him and pressed his head against her breast. Sobs racked his body and his breath came in heaves.

'So you could save me,' she told him. 'That is why the Frenchman did not kill you. So you could save *me*.'

He drew away from her and stared, stunned.

Madeleine looked upon him and filled with tenderness. She memorised each line on his face. She repeated his words in her head so she would never forget what he had endured. The incident at his brother's faded. She pushed it from her mind. There was no stabbing him with his sword, no conspiring to steal her child. There was only the need to ease his suffering, his pain and guilt. And to think of how close she had come to losing him.

He leaned back against the bedboard and took a deep breath.

'Do you feel better?' she asked.

He nodded.

'Nothing helps more than a good cry.' She smiled. A good

cry had never helped her, but it seemed the proper thing to say.

He smiled back, this time wide enough for the dimple to crease his cheek. His eyes were still red and puffy, and his nose bright pink. She thought, perhaps, he had never looked so appealing. She smoothed his hair, her heart tender for him.

There was a jiggle at the connecting door and it opened. 'Mama?'

Linette stood in the doorway rubbing her eyes. Devlin hurriedly wrapped the blanket around him. 'Mama?' she said again, finally finding Madeleine.

She trotted to the bed and climbed atop it. Madeleine gathered her in her arms. 'Good morning, my darling.'

'I heard you and Deddy.' The little girl peered at Devlin who clutched the blanket around him. Linette touched his damp cheek and looked puzzled. 'Deddy cry?'

'A little,' explained Madeleine. 'He had a bad dream.'

Linette scrambled out of her mother's arms and into Devlin's, giving him a big hug. 'There, there,' she said, patting his back. 'All gone now.'

Devlin's gaze caught Madeleine's, his eyes moist again.

'Thank you, Lady Lin,' he said. 'I think I am better now.'

Linette grinned in triumph. Devlin fingered the dimple in her cheek.

'Young lady, shall we get dressed for breakfast?' Madeleine asked, her throat tight with emotion. 'Bart and Sophie will be expecting us.'

The child jumped off the bed. 'Deddy come, too,' she said imperiously as Madeleine took her hand.

'I'll be down directly.'

Madeleine glanced over her shoulder before walking back to her room. He remained on the bed, staring back at them.

A half-hour later, Devlin entered the kitchen. He overheard Bart asking, 'Did his brother advance him the money?'

He sat at the table. 'Indeed he did, my friend.'

Madeleine spooned some porridge into a bowl and poured him some tea.

Devlin glanced at the bowl with dismay. 'Today you must replenish our larder, Bart. Bacon and boiled eggs for breakfast tomorrow.'

'Bacon, bacon, bacon...' sang Linette, a white moustache of milk on her lip.

'And wages for you both,' Devlin continued.

Sophie, whose eyes had remained downcast when he entered the room, looked up with awe.

Bart turned red. 'Now, I was not asking about my wages, but there is a matter I wish to discuss.'

'What is it?'

Sophie slipped out of her chair and retreated to a stool in the corner.

Bart fidgeted with his spoon and for once avoided glancing toward Sophie. 'I...er...um...'

'Out with it, man,' Devlin insisted.

'I wish to arrange for the banns to be read.' He gripped the spoon. 'For Miss Sophie and myself.'

Except for Linette's incessant song about bacon, the room went quiet as the significance of the words penetrated.

Devlin glanced at Madeleine, who had frozen, looking pale.

'Well,' gulped Devlin. 'I see.'

Poor Bart and Sophie stared at them warily and Sophie looked about to cry.

'Why, it's wonderful news!' Madeleine jumped out of her seat and rushed over to hug Sophie. 'We were taken by surprise by it, were we not, Devlin?'

'Yes, surprised,' he agreed. He followed Madeleine's example, clapping Bart on the back. 'God help our Sophie, marrying this crusty fellow.' They all laughed except Sophie, who rarely expressed that much emotion. She did manage to smile.

Devlin reached into his pocket and pulled out a pouch of coins. He counted out a generous amount. 'Here you are, with extra for a betrothal gift.'

'No, it must be three times what you owe,' Bart protested, pushing the stack of coins away. 'You must save the money, Dev. We mustn't go short again.'

'Nonsense.' Devlin pushed the stack of coins back and sat in his chair. 'Now that I intend to assiduously follow my brother's wishes, he will continue to fund me.'

Linette, attracted by the coins, climbed on Devlin's lap, now singing nonsense words. She peeked inside the pouch. Devlin let her pour the coins on the table.

'See? We are flush in the pockets again.' Devlin gestured to the pile of coins.

'Fush,' Linette said, intently concentrating on stacking the coins as Devlin had done.

Madeleine watched Devlin finger Linette's soft curls, the expression on his face soft and tender. She stared as he gingerly kissed Linette on the top of her head.

'If it is agreeable to you, we should be about the business.' Bart had spoken. Perhaps he had spoken before, but she had not heard and, apparently, neither had Devlin.

'By all means,' said Devlin. He pushed a few more coins to Bart. 'Here. This will pay to fill our cupboards and settle our accounts. Will you see to it?'

Bart laughed and, as tenderly as Devlin behaved with Linette, reached out his hand to Sophie and assisted her from the stool.

'I want to go, too!' Linette cried when she saw Bart and Sophie leaving.

'No, Lady Lin,' Devlin crooned to her, holding her on his lap as she tried to propel herself out of it. 'Stay with me a bit. Would you like a walk in the park while your mother cleans up?'

'I want to ride your horse.' Linette turned to face him, and she played with his neckcloth and gave him her most appealing expression.

'The horses cannot come today,' he said. 'But we might see some in the park.'

Madeleine felt a chill run down her back. She did not wish to believe he might be conspiring with his brother, but the park would be an excellent place to hand over Linette.

She took a deep breath, deciding to trust him. 'You will have a lovely time, Linette.'

Chapter Fourteen

Devlin stood at the entrance of Almack's with Serena on his arm. He had never attended the assembly room, too occupied with Spanish battlefields or, when in town, with pursuits of a baser nature. The room itself was unexpectedly plain, but the pale-coloured dresses of the *ingénues* gave it the appearance of a formal flower garden in full bloom. In his youth he might have relished the prospect of gathering a bouquet, but, on this night, one suitable flower would be sufficient.

Dozens of female eyes fixed upon him, the older ones coldly calculating, probably tallying what they'd heard his fortune to be. Younger eyes might be assessing other attributes as well, but would likewise not be insensible of his monetary worth.

Devlin thought he heard the pounding of cavalry hooves, but his mind played tricks on him. The sound was merely the buzz of so many voices over the music. Perhaps the analogy to an impending battle was more apt than a flower garden. He certainly felt like the target of a frontal assault.

Truth was, he entered this room with as much intent as the flowers before him. He only hoped it was possible to find a biddable female who would welcome marriage to a man whose heart was engaged elsewhere.

Madeleine.

She had offered to play valet for him, but he had undressed her as quickly as she tried to dress him. He could still feel the heat of her body next to his, still feel the raw rush of pleasure as he entered her—

'Devlin?' Serena shook his arm.

Serena had been speaking. He forced himself to attend to her.

'We must greet the Patronesses first of all.' Serena led him into the room, seeming to know in just what direction to go. Had Serena met Ned in these rooms? Perhaps Ned had scanned the flowers with as much detachment as Devlin, since his blossom had been previously selected for him.

Serena led him to where the Patronesses held court. Three in attendance this evening, all looking more ordinary than he had expected. He would not have picked them from the crowd, except perhaps for their vigilant eyes.

'Dear Serena,' one said as they approached. The woman extended her hands to Serena and seemed genuinely glad to see her.

'Maria, how glad I am you are here,' Serena responded in kind. She nodded to the two other ladies who were busy scrutinising Devlin.

He hoped his neckcloth had remained in place and that they would not notice the mended place on his long-tailed coat. He had insisted Madeleine repair the damage she had done, although she begged to have Sophie do it. Devlin wanted to assure Madeleine that her sewing was equal to the task. She had laboured hard to learn the stitches, after all.

Serena urged him a step forward. 'Lady Sefton, Lady Cowper, Mrs Drummond-Burrell, allow me to present to you Lord Devlin Steele, who is Heronvale's youngest brother.'

Devlin bowed to the ladies and managed to push a little charm into his smile. 'It is an honour, ladies.'

'We have not seen you here before, Lord Devlin,' Mrs Drummond-Burrell said, her eyebrow raised suspiciously.

'I have not previously had the pleasure.' Devlin met her gaze and tried to sound sincere.

Serena spoke quickly. 'Devlin—Lord Devlin—was with Wellington. He is recently recovered enough to come to town.'

Serena had drilled him in the proper topics of conversation, which were pitifully few. He hoped oblique references to war wounds were included as acceptable. Not that he wished to speak with these ladies of such matters.

'Indeed. I believe I recall the story,' Lady Cowper said. 'Heronvale fetched you from Brussels. Is that correct?'

'Yes, ma'am, I am indebted to my brother.' Talk of the battle was thus avoided by mention of the rescue.

Lady Sefton took his arm. 'I am certain Lord Devlin did not come here to discuss such unpleasantness. He came to meet our young ladies, is that not so, sir?'

'I am found out.' He smiled.

Mrs Drummond-Burrell tilted her chin in the direction of an exquisite blonde creature surrounded by a group of fawning gentlemen. 'Amanda Reynolds is the current Diamond, I believe. She is not within your touch, however.' The Patroness sniffed. 'Your brother might have tempted her, but not an untitled younger son.'

'You spare me from wasting my time. I am grateful to you.' He bowed.

The Diamond would not have tempted him in any event. The fire within such a lady was as much an illusion as the sparkle of a gem. Devlin preferred the burning passion of a dark-haired woman with fine blue eyes.

But he must not think of Madeleine while here. If he did, he would never find a woman needing marriage and not much else.

'How about Lady Allenton's daughter?' Lady Cowper suggested, glancing pointedly at a plump, rather frightened-looking girl.

'Hmmph!' snorted Mrs Drummond-Burrell. 'She lacks wit,

sense and beauty. Her fortune is impressive, but that is the
end of it, and Lord Devlin has no need of her funds.'

'Come, my lord.' Lady Sefton, still holding his arm, pulled
him away. 'We shall introduce you to many young ladies
before the night is over. I suspect they will be eager to add
you to their tally of partners.'

So Devlin met many agreeable young ladies, danced many
pleasant dances, and gradually felt more and more depressed.
Some of the *ingénues*, particularly the youngest ones, were
insecure and full of anxieties, others blatantly forward, as if
already composing an engagement announcement. None were
Madeleine, however, and all suffered in the comparison. He
longed to be at Madeleine's side, even if merely seated in the
parlour watching her struggle with her sewing. He longed to
bounce Linette on his lap and hear her delighted squeals.

That morning he'd held Linette up next him at the mirror,
their heads together. He saw identical shapes of the brow,
identical dimples. For his child and her mother he would perform his duty.

He begged leave of the forgettable creature who had partnered him in the last country dance and joined Serena, seated
with Lady Sefton among the matrons.

Serena regarded him worriedly.

Lady Sefton smiled. 'You are doing very well, Lord Devlin.
I believe you have made an impression on our young ladies.'

'They are quite lovely.'

She laughed. 'Charming, sir! You shall have your pick, I
am sure.'

He frowned. 'This is my first evening among society,
ma'am. I mean only to enjoy myself.'

Serena avoided his eyes. He supposed she knew he was
lying. Or perhaps she continued to disapprove of his decision
to marry.

'Would you ladies like some refreshment?' He may as well
be useful.

'An excellent idea.' Lady Sefton nodded.

Devlin walked to the room where the refreshments were served. The ladies had requested lemonade.

'Steele! Upon my word, it is you.'

Devlin turned to see who spoke to him. A slim man in an impossibly high collar and tiers of intricate neckcloth grinned at him.

'Duprey.'

The young man smirked. 'Steele, I have not seen you since you were sent down from Oxford, I declare. Been up to no good, I expect.'

Robert Duprey had been a particular stickler at school, always eager to turn in a pupil who deviated from the rules.

'I've been in the army, Duprey.'

'Indeed? Well, I suppose that makes sense. Keeps you out of trouble, eh?' He laughed the same squeaky laugh he'd had in school.

'You have the right of it.' Devlin picked up the two glasses of lemonade.

'I say, have you tried the orgeat? Dreadful stuff.' Duprey took a sip.

'I beg your pardon,' Devlin said, stepping around him.

Duprey followed him into the ballroom. 'I say, who is that creature seated with Lady Sefton? She is perfection.'

'My brother's wife.' Devlin strode away. He served the ladies their lemonade and idly surveyed the room.

Duprey sauntered over to converse with a young lady dressed in a pale yellow gown. Devlin watched her as she spoke to his old schoolmate. She seemed familiar to him, the way she moved, the expression on her face. She had brown hair, facial features of no distinction, a passable figure. There was no reason he should recall an acquaintance with her.

Devlin walked back to Duprey and stood at his side.

'I did not mean to leave you so abruptly, Duprey,' he lied. 'I thought you meant to follow.'

Duprey gave a snorting laugh. 'I say, I would have appreciated a presentation to that exquisite angel; that is, before I knew who she was.'

The young lady attended this conversation composedly, pale blue eyes resting on each speaker.

Devlin favoured her with a smile, and received one in return. 'Perhaps you would present me…?'

Duprey clapped the heel of his hand on his forehead. 'Oh, indeed.' The man waved toward the young lady. 'My sister, Miss Emily Duprey. Or I should say, Miss Duprey. Our other sister finally legshackled some viscount a year or so ago. Piles of blunt. Emily, Lord Devlin Steele.'

'Miss Duprey.' He bowed to her.

'Lord Devlin,' she murmured through downcast lashes.

Miss Duprey was at least in her twentieth year, Devlin guessed. Perhaps if she had seen one or two unsuccessful Seasons, she might welcome an offer such as his with pragmatism.

'Do you enjoy yourself this evening, Miss Duprey?' he asked.

'Oh, yes, indeed,' she replied. 'Almack's is always agreeable, don't you think?'

'I have not had the pleasure of attending before this night.' He smiled at her, sure now he'd not met her before.

Her brother piped up, 'Steele was at Oxford with me, Em. That is, until he was sent down and joined the army.'

Leave it to Duprey to place him in a negative light. The lady's countenance remained complacent, however, so hopefully his less-than-pristine past would not disfavour him in her eyes. Devlin secured the next waltz with Miss Duprey and took his leave of her.

When he presented himself to Miss Duprey for the dance, her mother took far more interest in him than the daughter had, but the dance was pleasant enough. They made predictable conversation. Devlin knew Duprey stood to inherit a barony, not a lofty title. He knew little else about the family. If they had married one daughter well enough, there might not be a need to seek a title for the other.

The rest of the night dragged on. Devlin was surprised to see the Diamond, Miss Reynolds, eyeing him curiously. Perhaps she had not yet heard he was a younger son. Everyone else seemed to know his situation and fortune, accurate to within a pound. Devlin ran into a couple of acquaintances, including one fellow officer he had known slightly when in Spain. He supposed the few officers left alive would be, like he, searching for a wife. There was little else for a former soldier to do.

When Serena had finally indicated that they might leave without disgrace, Devlin was grateful. As they waited for their carriage, Devlin found himself standing next to the Diamond. Serena, acquainted with the aunt who chaperoned Miss Reynolds, made the introductions.

'You did not seek a dance with me, Lord Devlin,' the Diamond said, while her aunt and Serena chatted together.

'I am afraid I was warned that the competition would be too stiff,' he replied.

She laughed and grinned conspiratorially. 'A dance with any gentleman serves to cause worry to those truly in the running.'

Her carriage arrived and he bid her goodnight.

When he and Serena finally were seated in her carriage, Devlin breathed a sigh of relief.

Serena glanced at him warily. She hesitated before speaking. 'I hope the evening was to your liking.'

He gave a sardonic smile. 'It was up to my expectations.'

'You did well,' she faltered. 'You danced many dances.'

'I did indeed.' He crossed his arms over his chest and retreated into his own thoughts of the evening, thoughts he would not dare speak aloud to Serena. How boring the evening had been. And how he hated himself for performing his expected role, when he would have rather been with Madeleine.

Serena glanced at Devlin, sitting silent and sullen next to her in the carriage. She had detested this evening, having agreed to accompany her husband's brother only because her husband wished it. She could not help but think of the beautiful young woman Devlin had brought to their house and how Devlin had gazed at that beauty throughout the evening. Miss England seemed perfectly suitable to Serena. She was polite and well mannered and obviously educated. Surely those things would make her suitable? What did it matter if she had come from trade or something equally as shameful?

Serena wished she could discuss the matter with her husband, but she dared not. He had been in such a temper about his brother, she might aggravate the situation if she interfered. Besides, she never interfered with her husband's affairs. She never even knew what they were.

Ned would not understand if she talked with him of her conviction that Devlin loved this mere girl whom he had kept secret for so long. Ned should make Devlin marry the girl. Surely it would not be too scandalous for the family for a younger son to marry a mistress who had already borne him a child? Why did Ned not consider it Devlin's duty to marry Miss England?

She feared she knew the answer to that question. Ned still wished to adopt the child. Of course that was the reason. He still hoped to convince Miss England to give him her little daughter, because his wife could not bear a child of his own.

Tears welled up in Serena's eyes. Sniffing the tears away, she fussed in her reticule to find her handkerchief.

Devlin turned, looking concerned. 'What is wrong, sister?'

'Nothing,' she mumbled.

'Fustian,' he said. 'Tell me what is upsetting you.'

He put his arm around her and leaned her against his shoulder. The comfort almost opened the floodgates, but Serena refused to give in to the impulse to weep.

'I…' She searched for something to say, something other than the real reason for her tears. 'I…I cannot like this search of yours for a wife. Your heart is engaged elsewhere, I am convinced. It…it seems dishonourable.'

He stiffened. 'I have no other choice. I need to support her and the child. How else may I do that? Your husband controls my money, so I must do as he bids.'

'I still cannot like it,' she murmured.

'I cannot like it either.' He gave her arm a fond squeeze. 'I promise you I will be honourable to whomever I marry, Serena.'

'Oh, Devlin!' she sighed.

The carriage pulled up to the Marquess's town house. Devlin hopped out and turned to assist Serena.

He walked her to her door. 'Thank you, sister, for accompanying me. I could not have endured this evening without you.'

Serena did not know what to say in return. She knew she would attend another such evening if Ned required her to do so, but she felt sick at being a part of something that boded so ill for everyone.

Devlin stepped into the hall with her and gave her a quick peck on the cheek before leaving. As Serena turned to the stairs, she saw Ned staring down at her. Her heart quickened. He had waited for her! She hurried up the stairs, his eyes watching her every step. As she neared the top, he turned and walked into his bedchamber, shutting the door loudly behind him.

When Devlin returned to his apartments, Madeleine was sitting on the stairs, hugging her knees.

'I waited for you,' she said.

He gathered her into his arms with the overwhelming feeling that he had arrived home where he belonged.

She drew him into his room. 'Tell me of Almack's.'

He kicked off his shoes and unbuttoned his coat. She helped him remove it.

'I shall play valet again,' she said. 'But, please, tell me of Almack's. Was it beautiful? Tell me of its decorations.'

He tried to remember enough to answer her questions. 'It was plain. Indeed, I cannot recall that there were any decorations to speak of.'

Madeleine gave him a sceptical look as she untied his neckcloth. He must be joking with her. She recalled her sisters rhapsodising about the day they would attend Almack's. At the time, she thought it silly, but she'd always taken for granted that her future would include visits to 'the seventh heaven'.

'Do be serious, Devlin. I truly wish to know of it.'

He exercised his neck, free of its confining collar. 'I speak the truth. The assembly rooms were plain, nothing to signify. Seating around the edge. Plenty of space for dancing.'

She sighed, exasperated. 'Very well. Tell me of the dresses. What did the ladies wear? Were the dresses beautiful?'

He sat on the edge of his bed and removed his stockings. 'The dresses were of light colours, mostly. Lots of white.'

'Well, of course.'

She thought about the young ladies in dresses of white or pale pinks, yellows, and blues. Privileged, protected, caring only for the clothes they wore, the parties they were to attend, the prospective husbands they were to meet. Had he met a young lady there this night? Had he been attracted by her beauty and poise? Her unblemished reputation? It did not bear thinking of.

She hung his coat and picked up the scattering of clothes he had left on the floor. As she turned back to him, he was pulling his white linen shirt over his head, leaving his chest bare. She must become accustomed to the thrill of seeing him so, his muscles defined, the hair of his chest an inviting shadow.

She must also become accustomed to the idea that another

woman would claim the privilege of running her hands up that expanse of male beauty. She brushed his jacket. 'Tell me of the music, then. Was it wonderful?'

He stood, barefoot, bare-chested, clad only in his knee breeches. 'The music? The orchestra played dance music. You know, country dances, waltzes and such.' He walked to her, placing his hand on her shoulder.

'Waltzes?' The scandalous dance in which ladies and gentlemen touched each other. Had he touched one of Almack's elegant ladies in a waltz? She began to regret her curiosity of this night. 'I suppose you danced the waltz?'

'Indeed,' he murmured, turning her around. She refused to look at him. 'It is now accepted at Almack's. Have you not had the pleasure of dancing the waltz?'

'My duties at Lord Farley's did not include waltzing.'

He lifted her chin so that she was forced to see his eyes in the candlelight. He placed her hand on his shoulder and took her other hand in his. 'I shall show you the steps.'

He counted out the steps. Back step, side step, together. Forward, side, together. His hand at her back guided her as he performed the steps slowly, gradually increasing the pace. Back, side, together. Forward, side, together.

Soon they were swirling around the room, and Madeleine was swept up in the dance and the pleasure of being in his arms. He hummed the music. Bump, bump, bump. Da, da, da. She laughed at how silly he sounded, and he continued louder, smiling at her.

As they twirled to the music he made, he drew her flush against his chest. With only her thin nightdress between them, she felt as well as heard his resonant voice. Her hand moved to his neck, her fingers into his hair. The music stopped when his mouth found hers and a new tune commenced, a new rhythm that carried them into his bed and relieved them of the remainder of their clothing.

This was a dance she still feared a little, but so much more did she crave it. His hands on her flesh. His tongue dancing with hers. The excitation when he entered her. The transport when her pleasure exploded.

The climax of the dance left her panting.

'That is not precisely as the waltz is done at Almack's,' he said.

She smiled. For the moment, she would pretend she was his exclusive partner in this waltz, and would content herself with that fact. 'It is a lovely dance,' she said.

Chapter Fifteen

As time progressed, Madeleine's days were spent in glorious domesticity. She could almost pretend she, Devlin and Linette were a family. She and Devlin shopped together, purchasing various sundries they'd previously done without, finding treats to bring home to Linette. They took Linette to the park. They sat in quietly in the parlour, Devlin playing with Linette and her wooden horse, Madeleine stitching laboriously. Soon, however, it became necessary for Devlin to make afternoon calls, shortening the illusion. Every evening was taken up with some splendid event. This night it was the Elbingtons' Ball, purported to be the event of the Season. Invitations were highly prized.

Madeleine helped Devlin dress as she'd done each night he left her in search of a woman to marry.

As he tried tying his neckcloth for the third time, he said, 'Maddy, we must talk of the future.'

She could not think of the future. Her mind was too filled with the present, with the idea that another woman would be in his arms tonight, dancing the waltz, perhaps planning a different future with him.

He went on, 'I think the country, don't you? A place for you to have a horse, and Linette a pony…'

'Whatever you decide, Devlin.'

What did it matter, after all, when another woman would spend both days and nights with him?

Madeleine smoothed the lapels of his coat and stood back to survey her handiwork. He looked dazzlingly handsome in his black coat, snowy white breeches and linens. How could any woman resist him? She kissed him goodbye and sent him off, pretending good humour, and returned to sew by candle-light, feeling empty inside.

When Devlin entered Lady Elbington's ball, the noise and crush was as unwelcome as the memories of battle. Indeed, settings like this one, with its noise, bustle, and discreet forms of indiscretion, were now the only places unwanted memories of battle threatened to intrude. Madeleine had chased them away from other parts of his life.

Hearing the faint echo of French cannonade in the rumbling of the voices, Devlin scanned the room. Miss Reynolds gave him a meaningful look from the far corner. He made his way to her side, where two gentlemen half in their cups paid court to her, undoubtedly drawn by her fair hair and skin, and the décolletage of her gauzy lime gown.

Amanda Reynolds and Devlin had developed an under-standing of a peculiar sort. Neither had any particular interest in the other, but each found the other to be of use. Miss Reynolds used Devlin when she needed to rid herself of the unwanted attentions of other men, or to make her chosen suitor jealous. Devlin used Miss Reynolds as protection from young ladies who might pin hopes on him. As long at his attention seemed at least partially engaged by the current Dia-mond, no matchmaking mama fancied her daughter his fa-vourite.

Devlin bowed to her. 'Is this my dance, Miss Reynolds?'

'I do believe so, sir,' she replied. Some poor hapless soul had lost his moment with her. He suspected it was the young buck approaching whose eyes bulged with anger.

As they began the set, she thanked him. 'I do not know when I was in such need of rescue.'

Miss Reynolds delighted in the dance as she appeared to delight in every activity associated with courtship. When the set ended, Devlin caught the eye of the Earl of Greythorne, the gentleman Miss Reynolds hoped to bring up to scratch. Greythorne looked daggers at him.

'My rival has arrived,' he said.

Miss Reynolds grinned. 'Looking deliciously jealous. My thanks to you again.'

Devlin delivered Miss Reynolds to a group of her friends and made his way to Miss Duprey, feeling faintly guilty at the pleased expression on Miss Duprey's face as he approached. It would not be a disservice to her to engage her in a loveless marriage, would it?

He bowed to her. 'Good evening, Miss Duprey.'

She smiled shyly. 'Lord Devlin.'

He chatted with her in the inconsequential ways expected— of her health, her family's health, the weather. He engaged her for the supper dance, which happened to be a waltz. When her next partner came, he withdrew.

Devlin went in search of Serena, who he knew would be seated among the dowagers. Ned had taken to accompanying Serena and Devlin to the various entertainments. Very unusual of him, Devlin gathered from Serena. Ned spent little time in the card room, instead staying within sight of his wife, though dancing rarely with her. Devlin presumed the main purpose of Ned's presence was to keep watch over his younger brother, but it was not well done of Ned to so ignore his wife.

Devlin found Serena and sat beside her.

She cast him a look that barely disguised her concern. 'You dance often with Miss Reynolds.'

'We have become friends of a strange sort,' he replied. 'She relishes all this nonsense and I—' He was about to say that he detested it, but caught himself in time. 'Worry not, sister, there is nothing in it.'

While he tried to decide which of the young ladies present would be safe to dance with, Serena's gaze never left the couples performing the set. A wistful expression came across her face. Curse his brother for neglecting her.

'Are you engaged for the next dance, Serena? I would be honoured, if you are not.' The music had stopped. He stood and extended his hand to her.

'Devlin, you need not waste your time dancing with me,' Serena said.

'Indeed,' came a cold voice behind him, 'you ought to look to the unmarried ladies, not the married ones.' Ned moved beside Serena. The look he gave Devlin was stony at best. 'I will dance with my wife.'

'Ned.' Devlin forced a cheerful tone to his voice. 'What a surprise to see you on this side of the room. I all but forgot you were here.'

His brother glared.

'Serena, I leave you to your husband.' Devlin bowed and walked away.

The Marquess had lately become damnably ill-humoured. Steady Ned had become a man of erratic moods. No telling when he might erupt. Those days when Devlin could pour all his troubles into his brother's willing ear had vanished. Devlin could not even bear to ride to these evening events in Ned's carriage. Accompanying the silent Marquess and Marchioness was too unpleasant by half. What had so changed this brother he idolised, Devlin could not understand.

He collected Miss Duprey for the supper dance. She kept her eyes demurely downcast except when he spoke to her. Her blue eyes were her best feature, Devlin thought. If he were hard pressed to describe her, he could say only that the rest of her was unremarkable. Conversation with her was easy enough, though no different than with the other young ladies he partnered. He listened with half an ear.

'Do you go to Vauxhall Gardens this Wednesday, Lord

Devlin? My mother says we do not, but others have talked of it.'

Vauxhall. Good God, why had he not thought of it before? He could never take Madeleine to Covent Garden or to Almack's, but he could take her to Vauxhall! With the black cloth masks so common at Vauxhall Gardens, they could dance under the lights and watch the illuminations. They could stroll along the hedged paths or seek shelter in one of the grottoes. He quickened his step with happy anticipation.

'Do you go to Vauxhall, then?' she asked again.

He had almost forgotten her presence, even though he held her in the dance. 'I had not planned to go,' he said. But he began planning an excursion now.

He escorted Miss Duprey into the supper room and seated her at a table with some friends of her acquaintance. He offered to fill her plate, to which she pleasantly agreed.

Making his way through the crush around the sideboard, he heard a voice hail him.

'Steele?'

Devlin turned and saw a ghost, a most welcome ghost. He'd last seen Christian Ramsford struck down on the battlefield and had mourned his loss, but this was truly Ramsford, walking toward him.

'Ram,' he rasped, at first grasping the man's hand in greeting, then ignoring all propriety and embracing him in a hearty hug. 'Ram, I thought you dead.'

Ramsford gave an ironic smile, but his eyes glistened as Devlin supposed his own did. 'I thought you were long since put to bed with a shovel, as well. So, I suppose all those bottles of brandy consumed in your memory were for naught.'

'Damn, brandy's never a waste.' Devlin took a good look at his friend, outfitted in a superbly fitting coat of black superfine. Though the penniless son of a country vicar, Ramsford's size and presence always had commanded attention.

'What the devil are you doing here?' Devlin asked. A London ball was the last place he expected to find Christian Ramsford.

'Both my uncle and my cousin had the misfortune to drop dead.' Ramsford's voice was almost mournful. 'My father inherited.'

'Good God, Ram. You are heir to an earldom.' Devlin grinned at him.

His friend shrugged. 'I am escorting one of my sisters, and am also directed to consider the succession in my family line.'

'Come, I must select some food.' Devlin grabbed Ramsford's arm and pulled him into the throng around the food. Ram took a glass of champagne off a tray, downed it, and took another.

'You will sit at my table. I insist.'

Ramsford shrugged again, but followed him to the table where Miss Duprey sat. Devlin introduced him to the young people who had joined her, noticing the curious glances from the ladies present. Devlin was suddenly impatient to be rid of all of them for the sole company of his old friend.

Finally he was able to deliver Miss Duprey back to the ballroom. He drew Ramsford aside again. They stood near the open windows where the night breeze cooled the room and spoke of the war.

Amanda Reynolds, temporarily detached from Greythorne's grasp, boldly approached. She entwined her arm in Devlin's. 'You have all but deserted me this evening, sir.'

Devlin knew he was being used again. Miss Reynolds's true concern was the presence of a new gentleman, whose admiration she had not yet procured.

'Doing it up too brown, my lady,' Devlin said.

He introduced Amanda to Ram and realised the once-penniless vicar's son had the greater chance with her. He left them conversing in a strained manner until a red-faced Greythorne came to collect her. Before she was too many steps away, she turned, giving Ramsford a backward glance.

Devlin collected Miss Duprey for his second dance. Knowing that two dances was the limit propriety would allow, he then felt free to make his escape. After saying his goodbyes to the hostess and Serena, and ignoring his brother, he left the ball with Ramsford.

The two men found a comfortable tavern near St James's and spent several hours there toasting comrades they would never see again. The tavern, smelling of hops, gin and male sweat, was nothing like ones he and Ram frequented in Spain, but the camaraderie was identical. Devlin had missed it acutely.

When the night was well advanced, they finally emerged into the chill night. Devlin embraced his friend. The drink had turned him maudlin, but he was too foxed to feel embarrassed. He stumbled his way home, his baritone voice singing one of the raucous ditties still echoing from the tavern.

Near his residence, a man stepped in front of him. 'Good evening, Steele. I see you've had an entertaining evening.'

Devlin squinted, bringing the figure into focus under the lamplight. Farley.

'Bugger off.' Devlin shoved him aside, almost losing his balance. He was directly across the street from his apartments. It penetrated Devlin's foggy mind that Farley must know where he lived, that he was lurking in this neighbourhood for that very reason.

'Bugger off,' he said again, staggering as he started off across the street.

A whim had sent Lord Farley to spy on Steele this cool, mist-covered night, a whim and the frustration of an empty bed. The gaming hell's full coffers were not satisfaction enough.

Farley had known for weeks where Steele had taken Madeleine to live, had made it his business to know. Indeed, he knew all about Steele, his falling-out with his brother, his need for money, his search for a wife. The time was ripe to get Madeleine back.

Lord Farley gave one final glance toward the retreating figure of Devlin Steele and disappeared in the growing mist.

Chapter Sixteen

Madeleine was startled awake by a slamming door and pounding feet on the stairs. She'd dozed off while wrapped in a blanket on the windowseat of Devlin's room, where she worriedly waited for him. He'd never been so late before. He burst in the room, swaying as he swung around, looking for her.

She shot up in alarm, dropping the blanket. 'What is it, Devlin? What has happened?'

He clutched at her, pushing her nightdress half off her shoulder. His breath smelled foul with drink.

'Maddy.' His voice rose in urgency, but his words slurred. 'Promise me never to go outside unaccompanied.'

'I do not, unless for a little walk with Linette.' She pulled away from him. She had never seen him this way.

'No more. Promise me!' He shook her by the shoulders.

Why treat her in this manner? He was like a stranger. 'What has happened?'

He let go of her and rubbed his forehead. 'Nothing has happened. Nothing at all. But you will obey me in this. You will do as I say.'

Madeleine folded her arms across her chest, massaging sore shoulders. 'You are foxed.'

He glared at her. 'I am not foxed.' He took a step toward her, touching the wall for balance. 'Merely a bit disguised.'

She edged away from him. 'I have no wish to engage in a conversation with you when you are foxed.'

'Oh, stubble it, Maddy, and get into bed.'

She straightened. 'I will not.'

He held his hand against the wall and looked as if he would slip to the floor at any moment. 'I said get into bed. I cannot stand up much longer.'

Having enough of his behaviour, she marched past him, avoiding his attempt to grab at her. 'I will sleep in my own bed this night.' Reminding herself in time that slamming the door might wake Linette, she closed it quietly behind her.

Once in her own room, she leaned against the post of her bed, squeezing her eyes shut. She must remind herself that men disappoint. It had been foolish to believe Devlin an exception. She crawled into her lonely bed, its linens cool against her skin. His body would not warm her this night.

Devlin woke in his clothes, half sprawled across the bed, a whole arsenal of French cannon pounding in his head. Rain darkened the sky and he had no idea of the time of day. He sat up, and the room started to spin. As he waited for it to come to a stop, he tried to stop his thoughts from spinning, as well. What the devil had happened last night?

He remembered Ram. He remembered the two of them drinking toast after toast to dead comrades. He remembered shouting at Madeleine, God help him. He could not remember how he got home.

Devlin gingerly put his feet on the floor and took careful steps over to the wash basin. He splashed water on his face and rinsed out the foul taste in his mouth. He poured the pitcher of water over his pounding head. Still dripping, he glanced about the room.

He could not recall telling Madeleine about meeting Ram. He'd shouted at her, though. Why?

Devlin fumbled through his trunk for a worn pair of trousers and an old shirt. He flopped into a chair and tried to pull on his clothing. His head spun around like a child's toy top.

He sat bolt upright. Good God! He had got drunk and shouted at Madeleine. What else had he done?

As he took careful steps into the kitchen, he resolved to set about correcting his wrongs. Still struggling to recall what wrongs he needed to correct, he warmed himself in front of the fire. The kettle was hot and he brewed himself some tea, wondering where the others were.

Where Madeleine was.

Bart entered the room and shot Devlin a disapproving look.

Devlin waved his hand. 'I know. I know. I've been a wastrel. A miscreant. A scapegrace.'

Bart pursed his lips. 'Well, you've upset the lass.'

Devlin gaped at Bart. 'I did something to upset Sophie?'

'Not Sophie,' Bart huffed. 'Miss Madeleine.'

Devlin groaned. 'You do not know what I did to upset her, do you? I confess I remember little of it.'

Bart cut a piece of bread and handed it to Devlin, who accepted it warily, taking a cautious nibble. 'The lass did not tell me the whole, but I collect you were drunk as an emperor.'

Devlin chewed a piece of crust. 'Indeed.'

Bart opened his mouth. Devlin stopped him. 'Before you jump down my throat, I was with Ram.'

'Captain Ramsford?' Bart's expression changed to surprise. 'He is alive?'

'Alive and very well. I thought him dead, too. I saw him fall…that day.' He lifted his mug of tea and his hand shook.

'I'll be damned.'

'We left the ball together and found a friendly tavern.' He paused, taking a sip of tea, and closing his eyes. 'There were many toasts to be made.'

'By God, I'll drink to the fellow myself.' Bart opened a

cabinet and removed a bottle. He poured a generous supply in a glass for himself and a dollop in Devlin's cup.

'To Captain Ramsford.' Bart raised his glass.

Devlin clinked his cup against Bart's glass.

Right at that moment, Madeleine walked into the room. She stared directly at the bottle on the table and then to the two men. Bart quickly drained the contents of his glass and hastily exited. Silently, Madeleine walked over to the kettle.

'There is tea brewed in the pot,' Devlin told her.

Without a word, Madeleine put a half-teaspoon of sugar and a mere drop of cream into her cup and poured the tea.

As she turned to leave, Devlin put a hand on her arm. 'Stay a moment, Maddy.'

She sat, her face expressionless, her posture rigid.

Devlin's stomach roiled and he took a bite of the bread, hoping to quiet it. He gave up the idea of telling her about Ram. It would sound like excuse-making. He needed some explanation, however, but what to say when the events were obscure to him? Worse, he had this awful feeling of foreboding.

'I remember little of last night, except that I behaved badly toward you.' He lifted her chin with his finger.

She swatted it away.

'I apologise, Maddy. I am sorry.'

Madeleine tried to avoid his intent expression. It conveyed a sincerity she could not quite believe. 'Apology comes easy when you do not know what it is for.'

He took her hand and stroked it, holding it in his grip when she would have pulled it away. 'I apologise for being drunk and for shouting at you. That much I do remember.'

She wished he would not touch her. His green eyes reflected the fire in the stove, his hair was tousled, and he had not yet donned his waistcoat and coat.

'Maddy,' he murmured, his voice low. His arm drew around her, pulling her close. 'Maddy.' The cotton of his shirt was cool against her skin, but a furnace seemed to burn inside her. His lips hovered over her ear, his warm breath tickling. 'What injuries did I inflict on you, my love? I wish to make amends.'

How was she supposed to tell him of his ridiculous dictate to be chaperoned, or his abominable order to get in bed, when his lips sent shivers directly to...to that part of her body that craved him? A true lady would not run her hands under his shirt. A true lady would not kiss him back. A true lady would not position herself upon his lap, straddling him, wanting him.

'Deddy!' Linette burst into the room.

Madeleine pushed away, but Devlin would not let her escape. Linette flung herself at Devlin and scrambled into what scant space was left on his lap.

'Deddy!' she shouted directly in his ear.

He let go of Madeleine and grabbed his head.

Madeleine chuckled. 'Linette, do not scream so. Deddy has the headache.'

'Poor Deddy,' Linette crooned, only a fraction lower. 'I will kiss it and make it aaallll better.'

Linette pulled down Devlin's head, squeezed it between her chubby little hands, and gave him a big smack of a kiss right on his crown.

'Dam— Dash it all.'

As he lifted his head and Linette beamed at her apothecary skills, Madeleine laughed.

He managed a wan smile. 'I think I shall be right and tight now, if I may only finish my tea.'

Linette stood on his lap to reach the mug. Madeleine tried not to laugh at his pained expression. Linette handed Devlin the mug. 'You slept all day,' she scolded, settling in his lap.

'I have no idea of the time.' He glanced at Madeleine.

'Near three o'clock,' she said.

'Da— Dash it. I have an engagement.'

Madeleine's smile faded. A peculiar feeling settled in her stomach. 'Do you need any assistance dressing?' Her words sounded stiff, even to her.

He gave her a pained expression. 'I can manage, I think.'

'I...I don't mind helping.'

'I want to help!' Linette jumped up and down in his lap.

'Linette!' He grabbed the child. 'Stop it!'

She stopped. Fat tears gathered in her wide blue eyes. Her lower lip trembled. Devlin, his head still pounding like a hammer to an anvil, felt like a cad.

He wiped a trickle of a tear from her cheek. 'Don't cry, Lady Lin. Jumping on me hurt me a little, you see.'

She sniffled.

He shot a look of appeal to Madeleine, who simply stared at him.

'No more crying now,' he said to Linette in a soft voice. He brushed the little girl's hair with his fingers.

Madeleine spun around and ran out of the room.

A few minutes later, Devlin hurried out of the house, barely pausing to close the door behind him. Soon after, Bart and Sophie took Linette to purchase beefsteak pies and sweetbreads for supper. Madeleine was left with nothing but her thoughts.

She went to the kitchen and filled a bucket from the pump. On her knees she attacked the floor, rubbing the hard bar of lye soap on the brush and scrubbing the wood, rinsing it with wet rags. She'd watched Bart do this job and it seemed not too difficult, but the lye soap stung and reddened her hands. She dipped them in the cool water. She considered what delicate white hands the lady Devlin called upon would have, and scrubbed harder.

She could barely help thinking about Devlin's afternoon calls. What clothes did the ladies wear? Were they all as elegant as the Marchioness? Did they smile prettily at him?

Had Devlin selected a lady to marry? He had not said so, but she sensed it was true. He had become quieter, no longer describing the entertainments he attended or the people he encountered.

What did *she* look like, this woman he must have selected? Was she beautiful? Intelligent? Accomplished?

Madeleine pressed the scrub brush down more firmly, the scraping sound drowning out her thoughts. Unbearable thoughts. She attacked the floor as if scrubbing dirt that had accumulated over eons. The apron covering her dress became damp from where she knelt, but at least she was being of some use. The pungent odour of the soap, the smell of the wet wood, the rhythm of scrubbing back and forth, even the sting of the harsh soap, distracted and somehow soothed.

Perhaps this was how people endured lives of drudgery. In any event, she vastly preferred numbing herself with hard labour than willing herself numb from the labour she had once been compelled to endure. Until Devlin rescued her and showed her joy.

Madeleine threw the scrub brush in the pail, splashing water on the floor. She would not think of Devlin. She would think of nothing at all.

A knock sounded at the door, firm and officious. Callers were rare at the house. In fact, the Marquess had been the only one. Madeleine hastily wiped her hands on her apron and rose. Cautiously, she peered from the parlour window and saw familiar matched bays harnessed to the elegant carriage bearing the Heronvale crest. He had come for Linette, after all.

Madeleine quickly stepped back from the window, her hand flying to her mouth and her heart pounding. Perhaps if she stood very still, he would think no one at home and would leave.

The knocker pounded again. She heard a voice. 'There seems to be no one at home, my lady.'

Through the slit in the curtains, Madeleine saw the Marchioness lean out of the carriage.

'I am sure someone is at home, Simms. I saw movement at the window. I shall knock myself.'

The footman descended the steps from the house and assisted the Marchioness out of the carriage. Beautifully dressed in a deep green walking dress, spencer and plumed hat, she seemed to float up to the door.

More knocking. 'Miss England, are you there? Please open the door.'

The Marchioness's behaviour was most improper. Ladies of rank did not knock on doors, nor did they visit this part of town. Only extreme foolishness or some urgent situation would explain it.

Blood drained from Madeleine's face. Devlin!

She ran to the door and flung it open, throat tight with anxiety. The Marchioness's hand was poised to knock again and the delicate blonde gasped with surprise. Madeleine could not speak.

'May…may I come in?' The lady's trembling smile did nothing to allay Madeleine's fears.

She stepped aside for the lady to enter. The Marchioness turned to the footman. 'Thank you, Simms. You may wait with the carriage.'

The footman bowed and, with one eyebrow arched, gave Madeleine an appraising look before retreating.

Madeleine closed the door and faced her visitor. 'Please tell me…has something happened? Is Devlin…?' She could not make herself coherent.

The Marchioness blinked her eyes in confusion. 'Devlin? I have not seen him.'

Madeleine's muscles, all taut for disastrous news, relaxed measurably. 'You have not come to tell me Devlin is hurt?'

The Marchioness blushed. 'No. Indeed not.' She cast down her eyes. 'The matter I have come upon is personal.'

Madeleine nearly laughed in relief. Devlin was not dead, or hurt, or married. She pressed her fingers to her temples, only then realising her hair hung in damp clumps around her face. She tried to smooth the tangled mess.

The Marchioness cleared her throat. 'May I speak to you for a moment?' She glanced toward the parlour.

Madeleine peered at her. 'I will not give up Linette. Devlin promised to make that clear to you.'

The lady blushed again. 'This is not about...I am so sorry... My husband meant no harm to you, I assure you.'

Madeleine regarded her with scepticism. 'He wished to take my child.'

The Marchioness's eyes pleaded. 'He did not realise. I do pray you will forgive him.'

'Forgive him?' Madeleine said, her voice rising. 'I doubt my forgiveness would be worth a farthing to him.'

The lady straightened and gave Madeleine a direct gaze. 'You sorely misjudge my husband, Miss England. He is the best of men. His interest in your child, misguided as it was, was motivated solely by a desire to please me.' Her voice changed to one of conviction and authority. 'May we retire to the parlour, please?'

Madeleine nodded coolly, though somewhat abashed at her lapse in manners. She led the Marchioness into the small parlour, shabby looking compared to the one in Grosvenor Square.

'Some tea, my lady?' she asked with inbred hospitality.

'That is kind of you,' the Marchioness replied, a slight tremble to her words.

As Madeleine rushed to the kitchen, she glanced at herself in the hallway mirror. She was a fright, her apron wet and dirty where she had knelt. Her hair had escaped from its braid and was a tangle of wayward dark curls.

She set the kettle on the fire in the kitchen and pulled off her apron. The blue cotton day dress she wore would have been presentable had it not been soaked with water. Madeleine measured out the tea and poured the water into the pot. She attempted to rebraid her hair, wishing she had pins to bind it into some sort of submission. She found a few lemon biscuits to add to the fare and hurriedly assembled the tray.

She entered the parlour and placed the tray on the table next to the Marchioness. As Madeleine poured the tea, she noticed the lady twisting her fine lime kid gloves in her smooth, delicate, ivory hands. Madeleine handed her the cup and hid her own beet-red hands in the folds of her skirt.

'How may I be of service to you, ma'am?' Madeleine asked, determined to display good breeding, though not feeling gracious inside. Indeed, this interview was too puzzling by half.

The Marchioness's teacup rattled in its saucer. 'I do wish you would call me Serena.'

'I would not presume, madam.'

The Marchioness looked so disappointed, Madeleine thought the lady might cry. She felt a sudden sympathy.

'Perhaps you ought to tell why you have come,' she said in a soft, inviting tone.

The Marchioness burst into tears. 'I have nowhere else to turn. I do not know what to do.' She rummaged in her reticule and pulled out a white linen handkerchief, edged in elegant lace. She turned away and dabbed at her face.

Madeleine wrinkled her forehead in concern. 'Are you in trouble of some kind?'

The Marchioness shook her head, fair tendrils shaking.

'Is it your husband? Has he hurt you in some way?' Madeleine would not put it past that man to be cold and cruel to his wife, not after his treatment of Devlin and, above all, his eagerness to steal a child.

The Marchioness's head shot up. 'My husband is the best of men. There is no more honourable a man on this earth. He is nothing but good to me, always.' Her face crumbled again. 'It is I who am at fault. I am a poor wife. I cannot please him in the most basic of ways.' She dissolved into tears again.

Madeleine went to her and, crouching next to her chair, took her hand. 'Now, you mustn't cry. Whatever it is, I am sure Devlin can help put it to rights. He will be home shortly.'

The lady's eyes flashed pain. 'No, not Devlin. You.'

'I?'

'There is no one else I can ask. You are the only one I know who can help me.'

Madeleine stared at her in confusion. 'It is not my position to help a lady. I am the lowest of creatures, I assure you. What could I possibly do to help you?'

The Marchioness looked directly into Madeleine's eyes. 'You must teach me how to seduce my husband.'

Chapter Seventeen

Madeleine gaped in disbelief.

The Marchioness twisted her handkerchief. Her words came out in a rush. 'You see, I have been such a failure as a wife. I…I do not know how to give a man pleasure *that way* and my husband…he is very dear to me, you see. He is patient and makes no demands at all, but he cannot bear to bed me.'

Madeleine returned to her chair, collapsing into its cushion.

Tears poured down the Marchioness's cheeks. 'He knows I pine for children, and that is why he sought to adopt your daughter. For me! To make me happy. A wretch such as myself who cannot please him!'

Madeleine took a fortifying sip of tea.

The Marchioness sniffled, even that managing to sound ladylike. 'I thought perhaps if I had lessons in lovemaking, I could learn how to please him. I would be a willing pupil. So, you see, I thought of you.'

Madeleine's breath quickened. The Marchioness knew of her past? Perhaps the Marquess had discovered her identity. Had Devlin told him? Her cheeks burned in mortification. Surely neither of them would have spoken of it to this lady.

'Me? I know naught of love between a man and his wife.' Madeleine's voice was tight.

The Marchioness twisted her hands nervously. 'Not *marital* love, exactly. The other kind.'

Madeleine pretended calm as she took another sip of tea.

The lady continued. 'You see, it is clear Devlin is besotted with you. It fairly took my breath away, the manner in which he looked upon you that awful night. You are not married, so the attachment must be of another kind.' Her voice turned low and tentative. 'At least that is what I thought.'

Devlin besotted with her?

The Marchioness continued, 'Please help me, Miss England...Madeleine. Where else might I turn? I have not been exposed... That is, I have led so sheltered a life. I am not acquainted with anyone else who might...'

Madeleine understood. Only an improper female could speak of such matters. Ladies of the *ton* would not sip tea while chatting about the most effective way to arouse a man. Madeleine's stomach clenched with the memory of how she had learned such lessons. Farley had taken her step by step through what she must do to bring a man to pleasure. Over and over. Again and again. She had learned where to touch, what to say. Such lessons should never soil the ears of so delicate a lady.

She glanced at the Marchioness, who regarded her with a hopeful, pleading expression. Madeleine was unconvinced that the fault of the lovemaking rested upon this creature's shoulders. The Marquess showed no warmth.

She bit her lip. The Marquess had been kind and gentle to Linette, she remembered. Perhaps there was a bit of his brother in him.

She sighed. 'Very well, my lady. I shall try to help you.'

The lady's smile was beatific. 'Please call me Serena.'

Madeleine laughed in defeat. 'Serena, then.' If she were about to provide sexual lessons to a Marchioness, she might as well be thoroughly improper and use the lady's given name. 'Shall we go above stairs? I do not think I can discuss such matters in the parlour.'

Serena sprang to her feet.

Madeleine brought her into the bedroom she shared with Linette. Serena glanced around the room, her eyes resting on the child's bed. 'Is this where you and Devlin...?'

'My goodness, no!' Madeleine replied. 'This is the room I share with Linette...sometimes.' She added, 'Do you wish to see Devlin's room?'

'Yes.' Serena nodded firmly.

Madeleine groaned inwardly. How much more improper could they be? She opened the connecting door and they walked through.

Devlin's room looked as if a whirlwind had been trapped inside its walls. Madeleine had forgotten she had not set foot in his room since stalking out the previous night. She had not straightened the linens, nor picked up his clothes.

Serena's eyes grew wide with wonder. Her gaze fixated on the tangle of sheets and blankets on the bed.

'Let us return to the other room,' Madeleine said firmly, ushering her back through the door.

Serena spoke excitedly. 'When I was young, my bosom bows and I would sit upon my bed for a comfortable coze. Shall we do the same?' The fine lady planted herself cross-legged upon the bed. She pulled off her hat and spencer, placing them on the side table. Madeleine had no choice but to join her.

Madeleine faced Serena's bright, eager countenance. Serena looked as youthful as she must have been with those bosom bows.

Where to begin?

'Have you and the Marquess ever had...um...have you bedded?'

Serena leaned forward with enthusiasm. 'Oh, yes, indeed, but I fear I did something wrong, because it was so very *painful* the first time, and somewhat so every other time. My husband obliged by being very quick about it, so as to not distress me overmuch.'

So the Marchioness had not experienced the pleasure of lovemaking. Madeleine felt sorry for her. But was a lady supposed to experience the kind of frank pleasure she knew with Devlin?

Serena stammered. 'I...I am not sure I can explain all that happened. I was so nervous, you see.'

'That is of no consequence,' Madeleine said hurriedly. She had no desire to hear the details of the Marquess and Marchioness in bed. 'I must think a moment where to begin.'

She glanced at Serena, feeling the wiser, though the lady was at least ten years older. Madeleine had vastly more experience, but what did she truly know of love between a husband and wife? Farley had not taught her about that kind of love.

She closed her eyes and thought of Devlin. He had shown her all she would ever know of love. She set her chin firmly and began. 'I think you will find that lovemaking is very easy. Composed of easy parts.'

After all, it took a mere glance from Devlin to set Madeleine's senses aflame.

'First,' she said, 'you must look at your husband. Make sure he knows you are doing so. No glancing away, until you are certain he has felt your eyes upon him.'

'I shall look at my husband,' Serena repeated.

What else made the blood thunder through Madeleine's veins? When Devlin touched her.

'Next, you must find reasons to touch him,' she said in an authoritative tone. 'Take imaginary fluff off his clothing. Brush his hand with yours. Arrange his hair with your fingers. Just touch him in ordinary ways.'

Serena's eyes glittered excitedly. 'What does that do?'

What it did for Madeleine. 'His body will come alive to you.'

Serena nodded. 'What else?'

'Well, you must contrive to get in bed with him.' Perhaps that was too obvious.

Serena's expression turned bleak. 'How can I do that?'

Goodness, Madeleine had forgotten that Devlin had resisted her initial attempts at seduction. Her cheeks grew hot as she recalled how she'd thrown herself at him. What had finally induced him to accept her?

His nightmare of Waterloo. 'You might pretend to have a bad dream. Would he come to you if you called out?'

Serena frowned. 'I doubt he would hear me.'

'Then you must go to his room and wake him. Seek his comfort. He would wish to comfort you, would he not?'

'Perhaps.' She sounded uncertain.

'Of course he would!' At least Madeleine hoped so. She had not been able resist Devlin's need for comfort. 'You must insist on not being alone. You must contrive to stay in his bed.'

Her pupil nodded resolutely. 'Then what?'

Then let nature dictate the next course, unless the Marquess and Marchioness had somehow thwarted nature. This was becoming absurd. 'You must cling to him.'

Tears formed in Serena's eyes. 'Will he allow me to?'

Madeleine took a deep breath. The Marchioness was truly an innocent. What man would refuse such a creature? Had any man ever refused to touch The Mysterious Miss M? Serena was so much more beautiful. 'You must ask him to hold you, then. He will not refuse, believe me.'

'What then?'

What happens after should need no lesson, if they both allowed what comes naturally to man and woman.

Madeleine's pupil needed very explicit instructions. 'If you feel the time is right, you remove your clothes, remove his clothes, and make love to him.'

'How?' She gave an anguished cry.

There was a limit to how much she would discuss. 'Serena, merely touch him all over. Anywhere. Kiss him. It will suffice, believe me.'

'What if it does not?' Serena's lip trembled.

'Then, what have you lost? You will have tried, after all. Would you wish to go on with the rest of your life, thinking you might have had happiness if you had only seized the chance?'

Unlike Madeleine, Serena had every reason to expect happiness, but Madeleine pushed that thought away.

Serena set her jaw firmly and sat up ramrod straight. The lady had made her decision. Madeleine smiled inwardly. Finally she felt useful.

Devlin had endured his promised calls to Miss Duprey and Miss Reynolds, mainly because he had hit upon the idea of bringing Ram with him. He still felt like weeping with gratitude to have found his friend left alive.

Ram's presence this day prevented Devlin from feeling too much obligation toward Miss Duprey, and, since Ram and Amanda Reynolds had taken such a dislike to each other, the sparks flying between the two of them diverted Devlin from his sour stomach and still-aching head.

He begged off Ram's invitation to pass more time in the tavern and made for home. As he neared his apartments, he tried to recall what had disturbed him so the previous night. Some ominous presence he could not grab hold of. He glanced toward his building. His brother's carriage was pulled up to the front.

Devlin broke into a run. What was Ned doing here? Why would his brother visit? To take Linette?

'What goes on here?' he snarled to the coachman.

The man looked puzzled. 'I've walked the horses, m'lord.'

Devlin jumped on to the side of the carriage and peered inside, ready to confront his brother.

The carriage was empty. 'Where are they?' he demanded.

The footman pointed to the house.

Devlin bounded into the house and found the parlour empty. The kitchen floor was dotted with puddles, a bucket and scrub brush lying in the middle of the room. Voices sounded above him.

Giggles?

He tore up the stairs. 'Ned! Ned! Where are you? By God, if I find you...'

He flung open the door to Linette's room.

Two female heads popped up in surprise.

'What the devil...?'

Madeleine and Serena sat on the bed, looking like two little girls caught in mischief.

'Hello, Devlin,' said Serena, who broke into giggles.

He scowled. 'Where the devil is Ned?'

'Ned?' Serena gave him a puzzled look. 'At White's, I should think.'

'Then where the devil is Linette?' Women. They made no sense.

'Linette went with Bart and Sophie to purchase some meat pies for supper. I suspect they may have also made a stop at the confectioners,' Madeleine said, barely concealing mirth.

Devlin put his hand up for her to stop talking. He rubbed his brow. 'Then Ned did not take Linette?'

'No, indeed!' a shocked Serena said. 'How absurd.'

'How could you think such a thing?' Madeleine scolded.

Serena bussed Madeleine's cheek. 'I think perhaps I should take my leave.'

Madeleine looked regretful. She reached for Serena's hat and helped Serena place it becomingly on her head. Then she assisted her into her spencer. The two smiled at each other.

'Would you mind telling me what the devil is going on?' Devlin said.

'Oh, Serena is leaving.' Madeleine smiled.

'I surmised that.' He touched his forehead. 'Why the devil is she here?'

Madeleine gave him an impatient glance. 'Devlin, I do wish you would not swear.'

'Damnation, tell me why my sister-in-law is visiting my… is visiting here.'

Serena swept over to him and gave his arm an affectionate squeeze. 'A mere afternoon call.'

He gave her a sceptical look. The two women walked down the stairs, arm in arm, chatting companionably. Madeleine rushed ahead to the parlour to gather Serena's gloves and reticule. Serena gave her a big hug, and Devlin thought he heard Madeleine whisper, 'Good luck.'

Why the devil was Maddy wishing Serena good luck?

Madeleine stood at the open door as the footman assisted Serena into the carriage. Serena waved out the window. Madeleine watched for several minutes after Serena had gone out of sight.

'She's left, Maddy.'

'I know,' Madeleine said in a dreamy tone. 'I was placing her in memory.'

The Marquess sipped his sherry and gazed absently out the window as he waited for his wife to appear for dinner. His heart was sick with grief, but he promised he would reveal nothing. He had seen a glimpse of the Heronvale carriage on St James's Street, near Devlin's residence. He had casually checked with Jem to see if Devlin had the use of it, but, as he feared, it had been Serena.

He gulped the remainder of his sherry. His wife having an affair with his brother? How much more painful could it be? Damn Devlin! Pretending to court one young lady while setting up housekeeping with another while dallying with his brother's wife. Ned squeezed the crystal wineglass, shattering it in his hand as Serena entered the room.

'Oh, my! What happened?' She ran over to him, behaving as if she cared that he bled.

'It is a trifle,' he said, wrapping his finger with his handkerchief. He twisted away, refusing to be duped by her solicitude.

She pulled the bell, and Barclay appeared. 'Some bandages, Barclay, if you please. And I'm afraid there is broken glass.'

'Immediately, my lady.'

Barclay returned almost at once with a basin of clean water and the bandages.

'Sit down, Ned,' Serena commanded, 'so I may tend to you.'

He opened his mouth to protest, but she took his arm and pushed him gently into a chair and knelt in front of him. Perhaps if he endured her ministrations he could dispense with them as soon as possible.

She held his hand over the basin and carefully removed his handkerchief. 'You have a piece of glass piercing your finger.' She placed her delicate finger and thumb around the piece of glass and pulled it out, dipping his finger into the soothing warm water. Patting his finger dry, she unrolled the bandage and wrapped it around the wound.

Ned could not bear another moment of this. In a voice tight with restrained emotion, he asked, 'Where were you before this?'

She glanced at him anxiously, biting her lip. He steeled himself for her lie.

'Ned, please do not be angry. I called upon Miss England.'

'What?'

'I know you will think it dreadfully improper, but I have worried about the girl since that night she ran out.' Though she was finished wrapping his finger, she held on to his hand, stroking it with torturous gentleness.

He pulled his hand away. 'Was my brother also there?'

'He arrived as I was leaving.' She stood up, but, before she moved away from him, did an unexpected thing. She stroked his cheek.

'Shall we go in to dinner so that the glass may be cleaned up?' She extended her hand to him, so he had to grasp it as he rose out of the chair. Then she took his arm and leaned against him as they walked to the dining room.

Dinner was an excruciatingly confusing affair. He halfway believed her story about visiting Devlin's mistress. It was the sort of kindness Serena might undertake, but he sensed she was not telling all. Throughout dinner, he felt her gaze upon him. Whenever he looked up, she gave him a smile, not at all like an unfaithful wife—or at least how he imagined an unfaithful wife would act. In addition, she looked extraordinarily beautiful. She wore a silk dress of the palest pink. A matching ribbon threaded through the loose curls of her shining hair. There was high colour in her cheeks and sparkle in her blue eyes.

'Where do you go this evening, Serena?'

She sighed. 'I have decided to stay home. I am sick to death of society.'

He raised a sceptical eyebrow. 'What of Devlin?'

She gave him a puzzled look. 'Devlin? Oh, can he not manage on his own now? He seems to get about well.'

Ned fixed his attention on his buttered lobster. When she spoke like this, he could almost believe her. After all, Devlin had his young lightskirt…and that beautiful child. He had no need for Serena.

What gnawed at Ned the most was that Serena ought to prefer his younger brother, with his easy, ne'er-do-well ways. Devlin could charm with a mere smile. Ned had always marvelled at that ability because he so thoroughly lacked it. What did he know of charm? Serena had married him because it was what her father wished. It had been a splendid match on both sides, true, but Ned had loved everything about her from first sight. It mattered not that his father had dictated the marriage.

He glanced up. Serena sat with her fork poised in her delicate hand, her eyes on him. After a long moment, she cast them down with a flutter of her long lashes. Ned grew warm.

'Do you retire early, then?' Ned asked, though it did not help his sudden flare of heat to remind himself of how Serena looked amidst white sheets.

Angelic.

'I am not tired,' she replied. 'Merely tired of the noise and crowds and gossip. Do you go out tonight, Ned?' She looked at him again, her gaze hopeful.

But for what? Did she hope for him to be gone? Or to stay? By damn, he'd not give her the satisfaction of wishing him away.

'I prefer a quiet evening. You know that, Serena.'

She tilted her head, pursing her perfect rosebud of a mouth. 'You have put yourself out in society very much, these past weeks.'

And how could he not? To avoid the parties and balls meant leaving Serena to Devlin.

Ned's jaw muscles clenched. 'To keep an eye on my brother.'

He took a long sip of wine. Her brow creased, looking disappointed.

She excused herself shortly thereafter, to leave him to his port. As she walked by him, her hand slid across the back of his chair, her fingertips lightly touching his back. The sensation remained long after she departed.

He went straight to his room after that, carrying a brandy decanter with him and freeing himself from his neckcloth as soon as he crossed the threshold. His valet appeared to assist him out of his coat and waistcoat. After his man hung up the clothing, Ned dismissed him.

He kicked off his shoes and sat in the worn leather chair that had been in this room for as long as he could remember. Stretching his legs, he poured himself a generous supply of brandy, but his hand hurt like the devil when he picked up the glass. No comfort in brandy if it brought pain. After draining the contents, he set down the glass and replaced the decanter's glass stopper. He hoped the brandy would help him sleep.

The drink fulfilled its promise, and dreams drifted though

his slumber, disturbing dreams of Serena and Devlin and losing them both.

A soft voice called his name. 'Ned? Ned?'

He opened one eye and shot out of the chair. Serena stood in front of him, her pale hair and thin white nightdress glowing in the faint light from a branch of candles behind her.

'What has happened?' he cried, sure that only something dire would bring her into his room of her own accord.

Her hand swept through her long silken tresses. 'It was awful, Ned.'

'What?' He could not help it. He reached for her.

She seemed to crumble in his arms. 'The dream.' She shuddered. 'I could not find you anywhere. You were gone.'

Returning to the chair, he settled her on his lap. She cried softly against his shoulder.

'Shh, my love,' he murmured. 'I am here now.' He stroked her hair, inhaling the rose scent that always lingered there. She felt soft and warm, and his loins ached with a need he could scarce bear not filling. She'd best leave soon or he could not vouch for his control.

Her breathing finally relaxed. Not knowing if he wished her to stay or to go, Ned asked, 'Are you ready to go back to bed now, love?'

She grasped his shirt tightly. 'No, please. May I sleep with you? I cannot bear to be alone.'

When he placed her in his bed and stripped out of his clothes, he could have sworn that she smiled.

Chapter Eighteen

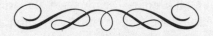

'Dearly beloved, we are gathered here...'

The sonorous voice of the rector echoed through the small church. Tears streamed down Madeleine's cheeks.

Sophie looked beautiful as she never had appeared to Madeleine before. She supposed beauty had led to Farley's interest in Sophie, but by the time Madeleine got to know her, fear had obscured the girl's looks. This day, standing next to her stalwart protector, Sophie looked radiant.

The dress Sophie had fashioned for herself was a vision of pale pink that swirled like a cloud whenever she moved. The colour put a bloom in her pale cheeks. Madeleine had woven a crown of tiny pink roses, the same colour as the dress, for Sophie to wear in her shining gold hair. Sophie gazed upon her loving groom with all the wonder and innocence of a virgin.

The clergyman droned, '...signifying unto us the mystical union that is betwixt Christ and his church...'

Madeleine was grateful beyond all measure that her friend had found the love of the good, solid Bart. She also envied Sophie painfully.

The humble furnishings of the church suited the parishioners—shopkeepers, merchants and other working people, useful people. It was not dissimilar to the church in her home parish where she used to receive angry glares from her governess for her fidgeting. As a child, she'd never been able to sit still for Sunday services. Now, what she would give for the peace of that country church. Perhaps if she had attended to her vicar's sermons, she might have avoided her sinful life.

Sophie coughed, bringing such a look of loving concern to Bart's face that Madeleine nearly started weeping again.

'Wilt thou have this woman to thy wedded wife, to live together after God's ordinance in the holy estate of matrimony? Wilt thou love her, comfort her, honour and keep her…'

Madeleine glanced at Devlin. Linette's tiny hand nestled in Devlin's strong one as they stood in front of the altar. He had never looked so handsome. He wore a simple morning coat of tobacco brown. Except for the superior cut, his clothes could not be distinguished from the style worn by Bart and other men walking about their business in this neighbourhood. He'd chosen attire that did not outshine the bride and groom.

Madeleine sighed. Truth was, Devlin looked exactly as she'd so often fantasised him, an ordinary man with whom she might share a cottage and a simple life. She shook her head. It was nonsense to hope. Soon she would never see him again.

Linette pulled away from Devlin's grasp and lifted both hands in the air. Automatically, Devlin reached down and picked her up. She leaned her head against his shoulder.

Madeleine's throat tightened. How would losing Devlin affect Linette? He had become so much a part of her world.

'…keep thee only to her, so long as you both shall live?'

Bart responded in a strong, firm voice. 'I will.'

Madeleine imagined Devlin standing before an altar making these same vows. It would be a grander church, of course, St George's, perhaps. Would his bride, like Sophie, radiate innocence and suppressed passion? Would Devlin look upon her with the same astonished joy as that written all over Bart's face?

It did not bear thinking of.

Devlin turned toward Madeleine. His eyes, which he quickly averted, were filled with pain.

'I now pronounce you man and wife,' the rector concluded, raising his voice as if there were a church full of people to hear. 'You may kiss the bride.'

Sophie blinked rapidly and Bart's face turned beet red. He bent toward the tiny woman, his movement tentative, but he raised Sophie's chin with a gentle finger and placed his lips lightly on hers. They held the kiss for a long time until Madeleine thought she might break down in sobs from the pure beauty of the moment.

Bart and Sophie put their marks in the register, and the small party left the church to walk to a nearby inn. Devlin had arranged a private parlour for a proper wedding breakfast for the five of them. The room was comfortable, a place where Sophie and Bart could relax. Breakfast consisted of all manner of fare: chocolate, sliced ham, boiled eggs, pastries, sweetmeats and dishes of berries and cream. Devlin proved an excellent host, keeping up cheerful banter, so that Madeleine was able to laugh when she otherwise might have dissolved into tears. Even Sophie smiled, though Devlin's gentle teasing made her blush.

Devlin had secured a room for the night for the couple, stocked with wine and other delicacies. He had offered them a wedding trip, but Bart refused. Neither had family to visit, Bart explained, and unfamiliar places would only unsettle Sophie.

Madeleine hugged her little friend tightly when they said their goodbyes. Though it was for a mere night, the marriage meant that she and Sophie would never have quite the same relationship as before. Sophie clung to her for a moment, whispering in Madeleine's ear, 'Oh, thank you, Maddy. I am so very happy.'

Evening shadows darkened the bedroom while Devlin sat with Linette, trying to encourage her to sleep. Her eyes were red and puffy with fatigue from the excitement of the day, but stubbornly she refused to keep them shut.

After leaving Bart and Sophie to their wedded bliss, Devlin had been loath to return home. He had insisted upon taking Madeleine and Linette to the nearby shops where he showered trinkets on a reluctant Madeleine and an eager Linette.

Linette's bed was now littered with a family of handsome horseflesh. A mare, stallion and filly, finely painted with acute accuracy and beauty, were nestled next to the child, but were not helping sleep. Linette checked and rechecked to see if they were tucked in properly. Devlin made up stories about them, setting their antics in the rolling acres of Heronvale, where they galloped and frolicked and got into mischief.

Linette's eyes widened and twinkled, but did not close.

'I believe you need nice, dull nursery stories.'

Devlin glanced over to see Madeleine in the doorway. His heart leapt into his throat. No more than a silhouette in the dim light, the curved lines of her body made his pulse quicken.

'I can remember none of them. We need to purchase a book, I suppose,' he said, trying to ignore the alluring scent of lavender that always surrounded her.

'Perhaps if you sang to her.'

He gave her a soft laugh. 'If I sang to her, she might never sleep again.'

'Fustian. You have a fine voice.'

He reached out his hand. 'Come. You sing to her.'

Madeleine walked over to the bed, and he nestled her in front of him, wrapping his arms around her and resting his chin on her shoulder.

'My sweetling,' she said, fussing with Linette's blanket, 'you must try to sleep now. It is very late.'

Linette gave her a mutinous look.

'What if we sing to you together?' Devlin asked.

Linette nodded, eyes stubbornly open.

In a quiet baritone, he began, 'Hush a bye. Don't you cry. Daddy's gone for a soldier...' Madeleine joined in with her sweet clear voice, 'When you wake, you shall see all the pretty little horses...'

Neither of them could remember more of the song, so they repeated the lines over and over until Linette's eyes finally grew heavy. Devlin admired her will. The child clung to her happy day.

It had been a happy day indeed for Bart and Sophie, but for Devlin, one of excruciating agony. At the church, the vow Bart spoke to Sophie was the same one he would soon speak to a woman he did not love. He would never feel the unrestrained joy that shone on Bart and Sophie's faces when they were pronounced man and wife. By that time he would have packed Madeleine and Linette off to some comfortable cottage, never to see them again.

'...Daddy has gone for a soldier...' Madeleine sang. As Devlin accompanied her, the words echoed in his mind, *Daddy has gone...has gone...has gone.*

Linette's eyes remained closed, surrendering to the inevitable, as he would ultimately do.

Madeleine rose from the bed, a finger to her lips. He followed her silently out the door, which she closed soundlessly.

'Finally.' She sighed. 'I thought she would never sleep.'

Devlin could not speak, his emotions too raw. The faint pounding of French drums touched his ears.

Madeleine smiled at him. How did she remain so calm when life was a shambles? 'You must be late dressing for the evening. Shall I assist you?'

He stared blankly. 'I am not going out.'

Her shoulders relaxed slightly. Perhaps she was not so calm after all.

'I would not leave you alone, Maddy.'

As soon as he'd said it, the irony of those words struck him like the Frenchman's lance.

He stroked her hair away from her face and leaned down

to touch his lips to hers. Her arms wound around his neck and he lifted her, kissing her as if she were the air he breathed.

How could he ever let her go?

In the days ahead, he vowed, he would savour each moment with her. He would provide her with as many pleasures as he could contrive. Dancing at Vauxhall. Riding in Hyde Park. Searching nearby shops for whatever she fancied.

This night he would love her with every muscle in his body, every sinew, every nerve. He would give all of himself, and glory in her response. He would show her that, although they must part, his love would endure throughout eternity.

Devlin swung Madeleine into his arms and, like a groom might carry his bride over the threshold, he carried her into his bedchamber.

The next evening, the air was chilly as the boatman's oars splashed rhythmically into the Thames. With shaking fingers, Madeleine adjusted the black mask covering her face. Wearing a mask again reminded her of her nights with Farley, although this soft cloth rested almost like a caress against her skin. With a shiver, she wrapped her paisley shawl more tightly around her shoulders. When they reached the dock and Devlin assisted her out of the boat, the night air felt warmer.

She took Devlin's arm as they walked to the arched entrance of Vauxhall Gardens. He grinned at her, his matching mask making him resemble a devilish bandit. In his trousers and coat, he might have been any young man about town. He'd promised her anonymity, more important to her than a night of music and dancing, or a chance to again wear the golden evening dress he had purchased for her.

People from all walks of life crowded the entrance, many masked like she. Shop girls, she imagined, and clerks, maids and footmen, all mingling freely in their finery, differences of class obscured by the darkness. Was it the chance to pretend or the chance to hide that led others to conceal their identities? For Madeleine, the need to hide provided the chance to pretend. She vowed to pretend that life existed only within these intriguing walls, at least for the space of this one night.

Devlin paid the six-shilling fee, and they stepped through the entrance.

Madeleine gasped. She had stepped into the heavens. Glittering lights shone everywhere like stars come to dwell on earth. Not stars, really, but Chinese lanterns hung everywhere in the elm trees flanking the Grand Walk. The faint sound of music grew louder with each step they took.

'What shall we do first, my love?' asked Devlin, holding her tightly against his side. 'There is much to see.'

'I hardly know.' She glanced around her as they came to the Grand Cross Walk.

'Let us walk the paths, then, 'til you fancy to stop.'

Devlin took her for a stroll down the South Walk with its arches and painted ruins. He kept a wary eye on the young bloods waiting to pull an unsuspecting female into the darker byways. Plenty of men ogled her, and he was glad the glittering surroundings caused her not to notice.

The music was near as they wandered through the Grove, strains of Haydn contributing to the magic that was Vauxhall. As they walked past the supper boxes, Devlin noticed several familiar faces. This had been deemed the fashionable night for the *ton*, he supposed, but who decided one night over another was a mystery to him. Emily Duprey had told him she would not be in attendance. He was pleased. He wished to forget her existence for this one night and pretend there was no one but Madeleine.

Wearing the mask gave him a freedom he would not otherwise have enjoyed. With the mask, he could stroll through Vauxhall, brushing elbows with earls and dukes, Madeleine proudly on his arm, not hidden in the apartments near St James's. He was merely a man escorting his woman, not a gentleman with his mistress. In anonymity, he and Madeleine were like all the other strolling couples.

He smiled at Madeleine's delight, as they passed each new

sight on the South Walk. She swore the painted ruins looked so real, she could walk into them. He wished they could walk into them and never return.

But the South Walk ended, returning them to the Grove. 'Time for us to dance, my love.'

He led her toward musicians playing in a balcony near the supper boxes. The conductor started a waltz just as they arrived, as if he were signalling their appearance. Devlin took Madeleine in his arms and, smiling down at her joyous countenance, whirled her to the strains of the music.

A short distance away in a supper box nearest the dancing, the Marchioness of Heronvale tugged at her Marquess's arm.

'Ned, did you see? I believe that is Devlin and Madeleine.'

He circled his arm around her waist. 'Madeleine, is it? Informal, are you not?' He nuzzled her neck, more interested in the scent of her hair and the softness of her skin than in two people dancing.

'Do behave, Ned,' she scolded, making no effort to move away. 'Look over there. It is Devlin, I am sure.'

He glanced where she had indicated. 'Wife, they are masked.'

'I am sure it is they.' She pulled him out of the box. 'Come, dance with me. We will get closer to them, and you will see. She wears the same dress as she wore to dinner.'

He needed no coaxing to hold her in his arms. These past nights together had been filled with a passion he had not dreamed existed for him. He knew not what had caused the transformation, nor did he care. Happiness was too tame a word for what he felt.

In his gratitude, he would do anything for her. Anything. Even dutifully dancing her near the couple who gazed at no one but each other.

Serena stood on tiptoe and whispered in his ear, 'See, it is they.'

Ned took the opportunity to hold her closer. He agreed it could be Devlin and his Miss England. He recognised the look in the man's eyes. It reflected what sang in his own heart. A pinprick of guilt pierced his happiness, for if that were his youngest brother, Ned's dictates forced the loss of that love. Now Ned understood how that would feel.

'Forget them, Serena,' He murmured gruffly. He clasped her against him in a manner that would get them banned from Almack's forever and would help him not think about the decisions he had forced on his brother.

Serena laughed, a sound more beautiful than the music. With a wicked gleam in her eye, she rubbed her hips against a part of him that now ravenously craved her.

Ned forgot about his brother and turned his thoughts to private recesses of the Gardens where two lovers might retreat. He swept Serena to the edge of the dancing area and led her by the hand to the narrow pathway of the Dark Walk.

Devlin barely heard when the music ended, barely registered the other dancers moving off the floor. Dancing with Madeleine had been magical. Stopping had been like coming out of a spell. She shook her head, as if sharing the same feeling.

He glanced around him. He was not two paces from Amanda Reynolds. Momentarily fearing she would recognise him, Devlin shifted away from her sight. He quickly realised it did not matter. Miss Reynolds would not trouble to notice someone dressed as gentry.

Madeleine uttered a weak cry and pulled at Devlin's arm, as if ready to bolt. She was also looking at Miss Reynolds and he had a moment's anxiety that Madeleine knew her, as well.

'What is it, Maddy?' he asked as she pulled at him.

'Oh, please, let us leave,' she cried, fear etched on her face. 'It is Greythorne.'

Devlin put his arm around her protectively and rushed her away from the dancing area. Finding a quiet spot near a fountain, he sat her on a bench. She trembled under his arm.

'What is it, Maddy? What frightened you.'

She gulped in air. 'Greythorne. I saw Greythorne.'

'You know him?'

She nodded, rocking back and forth.

A sick feeling came over him. 'From Farley's?'

She nodded again. 'Farley banned him from me.'

A man as depraved as Farley banned another from bedding her? 'Why?'

She shook her head, moving away from him.

He drew her closer, blood draining from his face. 'Tell me, Maddy.'

'No. I cannot.'

Devlin thought about Amanda. 'I need to know, Maddy. You must tell me.'

She looked at him worriedly. 'You will not confront him?'

His worry increased. 'Is it so bad?'

She nodded.

'Good God.' He rubbed his forehead. 'Very well, you have my word I will not confront him.'

She twisted her hands in her lap. 'I cannot speak this out loud.'

She knelt on the bench and whispered into his ear, in painful detail, the violence Greythorne had inflicted upon her to fulfil his perverted desires. He had read of such practices, having perused forbidden copies of de Sade's *Justine*. He had witnessed such cruelty during the war, but to have it inflicted upon Madeleine? Rage coursed through him. He clenched his fists, regretting giving his word. Greythorne would not live otherwise.

As if reading his mind, she warned, 'You promised, Devlin.'

He relaxed his hands and caressed her cheek with his finger. Folding her against his chest, he rocked her to and fro as he might have done to soothe Linette.

'Greythorne will never hurt you again,' he murmured. And the man would not hurt Amanda either. Devlin resolved to warn her before tomorrow's end.

'I know.' She cuddled against him. 'It was merely remembering.'

Well he knew about that. 'Let us not let this spoil our evening. Come. We will avoid Greythorne and get refreshments. Our enjoyment need not end.'

He rose from the bench and tugged her to her feet. She came into his arms and he kissed her tenderly. She clung to him for a moment before taking his arm and strolling back to the revelry.

'I want to dance with you again,' Madeleine said, pulling him back to the place from where she had so recently fled.

They danced each waltz and strolled along the paths, enjoying each sight. They sat at one of the Garden's restaurants and ate paper-thin slices of ham, and the tiniest chickens Madeleine had ever seen, washing them down with arrack. When the bells rang, they watched Madame Saqui walk the tightrope.

When it was time for the fireworks, Madeleine hurried Devlin to the best vantage point and fairly jumped up and down. The display began, exceeding all her expectations. Rockets exploded in the air. Sparkles rained down as if all the stars in the sky suddenly fell. Catherine wheels hissed, shedding shards of lights as they spun. Words appeared as still more star showers brightened the sky. The air smelled of sulphur, and the acrid smoke blurred the scene, but still the fireworks boomed and burst in the air.

Devlin's hand dropped from Madeleine's arm. She turned to look at him, to share the excitement. His hands covered his ears. His eyes were clamped shut, a look of anguish on his face.

'Devlin, what is wrong?' She grabbed him as he started to sink to the ground.

He regained his footing with effort, but his whole body trembled. 'Have…to…leave.' The words barely escaped his lips.

She pulled him through the crowd, hurrying toward the

gate. He allowed her to guide him, barely looking up, lost in a nightmare world she could only imagine.

'We are through the gate, Devlin,' she said as if speaking to a blind man. 'Let us go to the boats.'

When they were safely on the water and the sounds muffled by the cool air and the lapping of the oars, he relaxed a fraction. They pulled off their masks and he finally looked at her as if really seeing her.

'Devlin, please tell me. Are you ill?' She still held his arm tightly.

He gave her a wan smile. 'I am afraid the war came back to me.'

She stroked his cheek.

'The sound of the fireworks. It was like the cannon. And the smell...I...I thought I was there again.'

She hugged him fiercely. 'I am so sorry. I did not think. We stayed too long.'

He put his arm around her and she rested her head on his shoulder. 'You could not have known what I did not know myself, but it is all right now, my love.'

He held her close against the chill of the river air. 'I am sorry to have ruined our evening.'

She took his hand in hers. 'It shall always be a magic memory for me.'

As they neared the shore, Madeleine felt a shiver that had nothing to do with the night air. It was a premonition.

Her time with him was nearing its end.

Chapter Nineteen

The next day Devlin called upon Miss Amanda Reynolds as early as propriety would allow. He had borrowed Ned's curricle and meant to induce her to ride with him, the only way he could think to speak with her alone.

'A delicious idea,' she exclaimed. 'Greythorne usually appears at this time and he shall be told I am gadding about with you.' She clapped her hands merrily. 'Give me a moment to don suitable clothing.'

She left the parlour in a rush, obviously not noticing the serious look on his face.

Hyde Park was nearly empty this early hour. Amanda prattled on about Greythorne, the poor refreshments at Vauxhall, and the ball being held that evening. She enquired politely after his friend Ramsford, but in a way that quickly went to a change of subject.

Devlin scarcely heard her.

He drew the horses to a halt. 'Let us walk a little.' Handing the ribbons to Ned's groom, he lifted Amanda from the vehicle.

He seated her on a bench set a little away from the path.

'I must talk with you, Amanda.' They had become friends enough for given names, at least in private.

'So serious, Devlin,' she said with mock solemnity. 'Not some contretemps with the our dull little Miss Duprey, I trust?'

'No.' He took her hand. 'I am afraid it is a topic that is quite improper, but I must pursue it with you.'

An anxious twitch appeared at the corner of her mouth, but she continued to smile. 'Improper? La, you intrigue me, sir.'

Devlin took a deep breath and dove into the tale of Greythorne's predilections.

Her smile quickly fled. She blushed and turned pale by turns. She stared at him with wide eyes or glanced away in embarrassment. His own words sickened him and he could not still images of Greythorne inflicting these debaucheries on Madeleine.

Amanda Reynolds, cosseted darling of the *ton*, could not have imagined half of what he told her. He regretted having to impart these sordid vagaries of intimacy to her and tried to describe the whole to her without graphic explicitness. At the same time, the matter needed to be understood. Amanda must realise the kind of man she intended to marry.

When he finished, she shook her head. 'Such things are not possible! Why would you tell me this?'

He took her hand. 'Believe me, I did not wish to relate these matters to you, but when the knowledge of this came my way, I had to warn you.'

'How did you hear of this?' she stammered.

Devlin rubbed his brow. 'I cannot tell you. Suffice to say that I know of it from one who was his victim.'

She raised her brows.

'I will not say who it might be, so do not ask.'

She rose to her feet. 'I want to go home.'

'Of course.' He offered her his arm. She shrank from it.

They walked silently back to the curricle. He lifted her into the seat and climbed in himself, taking the ribbons while the groom hopped up on back.

When he pulled up to her town house, he said, 'I am truly sorry, Amanda. I had no wish to hurt you.'

She tried to smile at him, but her eyes were pinched with anxiety. 'I suppose I should thank you.'

He lifted her down to the pavement. 'You do believe my tale, don't you?'

'Oh, yes, I believe you.' She sighed. 'Why should you risk your reputation otherwise? I could ruin you for talking of such things to me.'

Devlin shrugged. 'I confess, I did not consider that.'

She did smile, then.

Devlin regarded her anxiously. 'Has he offered for you?'

She shook her head. 'Not yet.'

'Refuse him.' It was simply said.

Her smile fled. 'I will.'

Devlin watched her enter the town house. A horseman rode up beside him.

'Rather early for the Hyde Park set.'

It was Ram. Devlin still felt his heart swell at the sight of the friend he'd thought he lost.

He ignored Ram's comment. 'Good to see you, Ram. Calling upon the Diamond?'

Ramsford gave a snort. 'Don't be absurd. She would hardly find my presence creditable.'

Devlin tossed him a sceptical look. 'If you are not engaged, follow me to my brother's stable so I can rid myself of the curricle.' He had promised to call on Miss Duprey and would value Ram's company.

'I am not engaged. This gentleman's life is totally devoid of purposeful activity.'

They proceeded at a comfortable pace, Devlin feeling the company of his friend an effective antidote to dashing the dreams of the season's Diamond.

The visit with Miss Duprey was pleasant, but without a moment of interest. There was not one thing about her to dislike. Nothing to anger or irritate. Nothing to arouse any form of passion. For that he was grateful. He wanted passion from no woman except Madeleine.

Drums rumbled in his ears as he thought of giving up nights of loving her, days spent in her company. He almost felt as if the darkness would descend upon him, as it had at Waterloo, and he would again be alone with his pain with no one to see his suffering. No one would notice his life ebbing into oblivion.

He glanced at Ram seated across the room, conversing with a young lady also calling upon Miss Duprey. Perhaps some day he would tell his friend about Madeleine and Linette. Then at least one person would know that a piece of Devlin Steele lived and flourished somewhere in England.

'You are quiet today, my lord.' Miss Duprey's voice broke through the drum rolls. 'Are you unwell?'

Her discernment of his mood and her concern were to her credit. She might be bland, but at least she was not insensible.

'I apologise, Miss Duprey. I was merely woolgathering.'

She poured a cup of tea and handed it to him. 'If you are in need of a friendly ear, I am available.'

He gave her a wan smile. 'It is nothing, I assure you.' The drums grew louder. All the thoughts that swam through his head were none he could confide to her.

She cocked her head, a gesture that inexplicably appealed to him. It puzzled him how he'd singled her out for his damnable plan, but then a gesture, such as this, a fleeting look, a trill of her laughter, caught his notice and surprised him each time.

A quarter of an hour later, he and Ramsford departed the lady's parlour and walked to his brother's stable where Ram had left his mount.

'I should call upon the Marchioness, Ram. Are you game to keep me company?'

'It cannot be more of a deadly bore than the last place,' Ramsford said in a dry voice.

When they followed Barclay to the front parlour, the sounds of male and female laughter met their ears. Serena had other callers, no doubt. Perhaps she had given up on his brother and accepted the attentions of one of the many men who sought her.

As they stepped through the doorway, however, the only people present were the Marquess and Marchioness, standing quite close to each other, faces flushed.

Ned strode up, hand extended. 'Dev, good to see you.'

Devlin took his brother's hand, as surprised by the warm handshake as the friendly greeting. He introduced Ram, and presented him to Serena.

'I have seen our new Lord Ramsford many times. How lovely to meet you. You are most welcome as a friend of Devlin's.'

Ned sent Barclay to arrange refreshment and begged leave to speak to Devlin alone.

They entered the library, and Devlin could not help but remember the heat of temper that flared when he last set foot in the room.

'Forgive me for leaving your friend, but I wished to speak with you. Serena and I leave tomorrow for Heronvale. I...I have some business there and she accompanies me.' Ned's face flushed red.

Why should his brother bother to explain this? And why show embarrassment?

Ned gestured to one of the leather chairs in the room and Devlin sat. He poured them each a small glass of sherry.

'There is nothing amiss, I hope?' Devlin took the glass.

'No...no, nothing amiss. All is well.' Ned looked away, but Devlin thought he saw a grin on his brother's face.

'I doubt we will return before the end of the Season,' Ned continued, seating himself in the chair adjacent to Devlin's. 'I thought I should check your...your progress, so to speak.'

Ned's tone and demeanour might be convivial, but he remained thoroughly in control of Devlin's future.

'I have made no commitments as yet.' Devlin tried to sound matter-of-fact.

'The Season will be over in a matter of weeks.' Ned's voice turned tense.

Devlin released a fatalistic breath. 'I have made a selection.'

'And who is the lady?'

'Miss Emily Duprey.' It was as though a cage door closed upon him. Speaking of this out loud to his brother made it all too real. Too final.

'Indeed?' Ned sounded surprised. 'I had thought your interest lay with Miss Reynolds.'

Devlin met his brother's eye. 'My *interest* lies elsewhere.'

Ned had the grace to look faintly ashamed.

Devlin took another sip of the sherry. 'Miss Reynolds and I have an odd friendship. We harbour no other form of attachment.'

Ned fiddled with the stem of his glass. 'I know little of the Dupreys. Malvern, is that the property? A barony?'

'Yes.' Perfectly acceptable, thought Devlin. His brother ought to approve.

'Well...' Ned paused. A softness came into his voice. 'Have you settled Miss England and the child?'

Push the sword in deeper, brother, thought Devlin. 'Not as yet.'

Ned rose and walked to his desk and busied himself writing. He came back to Devlin and handed him a paper.

'This will allow you to draw money in my absence. You will need extra funds to procure a proper place for your...your charges. She must be well situated. Perhaps in Chelsea.'

Devlin accepted the draft and responded in a cool voice, 'I thought the country to be a better choice.'

Ned sat again and spoke as if they were settling some piece of property. 'Much better for them to be among an assortment of the middle classes. You do not wish for there to be questions about them. A ''widow'' and child will not draw attention in Chelsea.'

'No attention at all,' said Devlin mechanically, wishing to blurt out that Madeleine needed the countryside so she could ride. More so, he wished to tell his brother that sending away Madeleine and Linette was tantamount to destroying his own soul.

Devlin glanced at the bank draft. His eyes widened. Ned had written an uncommonly generous amount.

'We do not wish them to suffer,' Ned said softly.

Devlin eschewed a hack and slowly walked home. A persistent drizzle fell, turning the day uncommonly cold. The weather suited his mood.

When he opened the door to his apartments, Linette squealed, 'Deddy!' and bounded into his arms. His eyes moistened as he hugged her to him.

Madeleine appeared from the kitchen, wiping her hands on that abominable apron she wore.

'She has been asking for you all this day. I am nearly mad with it.' She smiled in amusement.

He drew her into the hug. Clasping them both to him, he thought he would be the one to go mad without them. When he loosened his grasp, Madeleine stared into his eyes. With a gentle finger, she wiped moisture from the corner of his eye.

'Come, let me take your hat and coat,' she said. 'You are damp and chilled.'

He put Linette down, but she continued to cling to his legs. 'Play horses with me.' She tugged at his trousers.

He patted the child's shiny curls. 'In a moment, Lady Lin.' Madeleine helped him out of his coat. 'Maddy, I would like to speak with you. Not this moment. When you are able.'

She smiled at him, but the emotion in her eyes was solemn. 'I am in the midst of learning how to cook dinner. Sophie and Bart are teaching me to make boiled beef and oat pudding. Does that not sound delicious?'

'Indeed,' he said, kissing her lightly on the cheek and allowing Linette to pull him into the parlour where her toy horses awaited.

There was not time enough to speak alone to Madeleine until well into the evening after Linette finally lapsed into slumber. Madeleine came into his bedchamber to set out his clothing.

'She is becoming more difficult to get to sleep.' Madeleine raised his evening coat, examining it carefully.

'We need to purchase a book of fairy stories,' he said.

'Indeed,' she agreed. 'Why, I can hardly remember when I last read a book. There is much I ought to read for myself. My mind is in sad need of improving.'

His spirits rose, but only a bit. It was something he could do for her. 'We must go to a bookshop. You may select whatever you wish for yourself and Linette.'

She blushed. 'Please do not countenance my hasty words. I do not expect you to—'

He raised a hand to silence her. 'We will go there tomorrow. I think if we go early you should feel comfortable.'

She was always more concerned about being seen with him than he was with her. For his sake, he supposed, although no one would look upon him with disfavour for being in the company of a beautiful unescorted female. They would merely assume he had an arrangement with her.

'I have brushed your evening clothes,' Madeleine said.

He was expected at the Catsworths' ball this evening, as were Miss Duprey, her brother and her ever-present mother. Amanda, Greythorne, and, thankfully, Ram also planned to attend. Devlin was especially concerned about Amanda Reynolds having to encounter Greythorne.

Devlin stripped down to his small clothes. 'Thank you, Maddy.' He fingered the cloth of his jacket. 'Well done.'

It was painfully ironic that Madeleine acted as his valet when he dressed for these evening entertainments.

She turned to get his clean shirt and he grabbed her arm. 'Sit with me a minute.'

Her eyes lingered on his bare chest, but she dutifully sat next to him on the bed. He should have planned for a neutral setting. The bed brought too many ideas to his head.

He leaned against the pillows and settled her in front of him, his arms around her, her soft hair tickling his chest.

'We must talk of where you will live,' he said.

She stiffened.

'There is little time left,' he continued.

'I told you that it is of no consequence to me where you place us.' Her voice seemed determinedly devoid of emotion.

It was detestable that she must be sent away where he would never be able to check on her, to make sure she was safe. He would never know how she fared. How his daughter fared.

He buried his face in her hair. 'Forgive me, Madeleine.' His body shook. 'I have made a mull of all of it and I cannot make repairs. Forgive me. I never meant to hurt you, to bring you to this end...'

She turned around, coming on to her knees in front of him. She took his face in both her hands. 'Oh, no, you mustn't say so!' She pressed his cheeks firmly. 'You saved us, Devlin. *Saved* us. What would my life be like—Linette's life—if you had not rescued us? Even Sophie. Would she have had any chance for the happiness she now possesses? You did this for us.'

She brushed his hair with her fingers and gazed tenderly at him. 'I shall be grateful to you my whole life. I shall never forget you. Never stop loving you.' Her hands flew to her mouth at these last words.

'Maddy,' Devlin managed, his arms going around her. To hear her say she loved him was unbearable, yet at the same time his heart soared with happiness. Madeleine loved him. She was not merely repaying him with her body. She loved him and, by God, he loved her in return. 'Maddy.'

He could not help himself, needing to show her his love. He rained her with kisses, freed her from her clothes and what few were left of his own. He poured himself into her, desperate to make the moment last, knowing it would be fleeting.

By the time he walked into the Catsworths' ball, almost too late to be fashionable, he moved in a haze of sexual satiation. His soul remained with Madeleine, but his body walked dreamlike through its paces. She loved him, and nothing else seemed the least important.

'Stee-eellle,' slurred a nasally voice. A tottering Robert Duprey grabbed his arm. 'M'sister's awaiting you. Bad form to neglect the chit. Ought to declare y'rself. Common knowledge, y'know.'

Devlin shrugged him off. 'You are presuming, sir. And you are drunk.'

Devlin might next have sought out Miss Duprey, but her brother's insinuations, correct as they might be, angered him. He went in search of Amanda instead. It was never difficult to find her, since she shone more brightly than the other marriage-mart hopefuls. He spied her across the room. Greythorne was speaking animatedly to her, looking very cross. Devlin took a step toward her, but Ram appeared at her side. Ram clamped his fingers into Greythorne's arm and, a moment later, led Amanda into a waltz.

Devlin's throat tightened. He was turning maudlin at seeing his friend assume the role of protector over the fair Miss Reynolds. He glanced around the room and spied Miss Duprey and her mother. She did not see him.

Stepping back, Devlin turned on his heel and fled the ballroom, seeking the chill air of the evening...and home.

Farley hid in the shadows outside the Catsworth town house. Steele would be there. It was *the* event of the evening, after all. The ball would last into the wee hours, but he could stand the wait. He had decided to shadow Steele this night. If the opportunity presented itself, he'd plunge a knife in

Steele's back. With Steele out of the way, Madeleine would have no choice but to return to him.

Carriages continued to arrive and a bustling of people crowded the pavement and the entrance. Farley hardly noticed the man walking in the other direction. It was not until the man disappeared around the corner that he realised the figure had resembled Steele.

Impossible. The ball had hardly started.

Farley would wait. Steele was bound to leave at his usual time and Farley then would be ready.

Chapter Twenty

'Oh, my!' Madeleine cried as she entered Lackington's bookshop on Finsbury Square. She had not imagined so many books to exist in the world.

'Devlin, this is impossible. I will not know how to look.'

He patted the hand holding his arm. 'We shall ask for assistance.'

They walked up to a large circular desk with four clerks behind. Two were idle at this early hour.

'May we assist, sir?' one asked.

Devlin asked the grey-coated clerk to escort them to books suitable for young children. They made a few selections, Aesop's Fables, one book both could recall from childhood, among them. Devlin then requested they be shown the equestrian section. He had in mind that what Linette would enjoy most of all would be a book with engravings of horses.

Unfortunately, such books also captivated Madeleine, and he, of course, could never be uninterested in such a subject. They pored over volumes containing a wealth of information on breeding, riding, equestrian care. They examined fine engravings of handsome horseflesh, arguing energetically over which volume would be most pleasing to Linette.

* * *

When their selections were made and they readied for their departure, Devlin glanced at the large store clock. It read half past one.

'We have been here almost three hours,' he told Madeleine as they stepped out the door.

She grabbed his arm and squeezed it in pleasure. 'I was not aware. Time passed so swiftly.'

The streets were bustling and Devlin looked about, realising the fashionable shoppers were out in abundant numbers, people he'd hoped to avoid, but only because they would distress Madeleine.

Her hand trembled as it clutched his arm. They stepped onto the pavement. Two ladies, one young, one middle-aged, approached.

Emily Duprey and her mother, Lady Duprey.

It was impossible to avoid them. Damn his carelessness. The most efficacious solution would be to pretend he did not see them. They, in turn, would ignore the beautiful creature on his arm, relegating her to a part of a gentleman's life that bore no speaking of.

Miss Duprey glanced up, a shocked look on her face. Devlin felt Madeleine hesitate.

Deuce. He had hoped to spare Madeleine this moment. Walking by would convey that Madeleine was his mistress. Miss Duprey was no naïve miss. At her age she was bound to be realistic about the dealings of men. She could weather the sight of him with a prime article on his arm, as could her mother. But could he bear Madeleine's humiliation?

He could not.

When they were abreast of the two women, he smiled and gave them a small bow. 'Lady Duprey, Miss Duprey, good afternoon.'

The two ladies gaped. Lady Duprey appeared as if she would pop a blood vessel.

Devlin remained undaunted. 'May I make known to you Miss Madeleine England? She has accompanied me to this excellent bookshop.' He stepped aside to present Madeleine, who grasped his arm so tightly it hurt. 'Miss England, Lady Duprey and her daughter, Miss Duprey.'

Madeleine gave a stiff curtsy. 'How do you do,' she said, her voice barely audible.

Lady Duprey hissed, muttering under her breath, 'This is the outside of enough.' She pulled at her daughter.

Miss Duprey paused and gave a shaky nod of her head. As her mother hurried her off, she turned and took one last brief glance at Madeleine, the shock still plain on her face.

After they disappeared through the doorway of the bookshop, Madeleine went limp beside him. He dropped the wrapped package of books as he caught her, easing her to sit on some nearby steps.

'Maddy,' he exclaimed, alarmed. Retrieving the books, he sat next to her. 'I am so sorry. Shall I get a hack?'

'Give me a moment, if you please.' She hugged her knees and rocked, hiding her face from him.

Passers-by began to take notice.

'I shall secure a hack.' Devlin hurried to the street and waved a hand to an approaching hackney coach. He almost carried Madeleine to the vehicle and bundled her inside.

'I am recovered now,' she said in a weak voice, her hand covering her eyes.

'Damn.' He rubbed her arms bracingly. 'There was no call for them to look at you such. They could not know…'

'It is of no consequence.' She continued to shield her eyes, and he feared she was crying.

'I am sorry for that, Maddy. You have probably deduced who they are.' He expelled a tense breath. 'Believe me, I would not for the world wished you to encounter the lady I…I mean, the one I…'

'Oh, no.' Madeleine felt her moan emerge from the depths of her heart. It was worse than she imagined. Much, much worse.

Devlin continued, 'Damn them. Their treatment was rag-mannered in the extreme. You appear perfectly respectable.

You could have been my cousin or Ram's sister, for God's sake. They had no right to treat you so.'

She lowered her hand and gazed out the window of the hack. 'They had every right, Devlin.' She took a breath and faced him, looking directly into his eyes. 'They are my mother and sister. They thought themselves rid of me after I shamed them so.'

He stared at her, speechless.

The calm of fatalism descended upon her. 'Let us not go home just yet. Ask the driver to drop us in the park. I once promised to tell the whole of my story. You shall hear it now.'

He rapped for the coachman to stop.

They found a bench in the park. Devlin protested that she would be chilled, but Madeleine assured him the brisk air served her well. They sat in silence.

'It is unusually chilly for June.' He drummed his fingers on his knee.

She smiled at him, capturing his hand and squeezing it. Nearby, a bird flapped its wings, aiming for the sky. She fully expected any regard he had for her to also take flight.

'I grew up in Wiltshire,' she began, 'though I suppose your acquaintance with Emily has told you that. I was the youngest. There was my brother, my oldest sister Jessame, Emily, and me. I believe my mother was tired of children by the time of my birth. She bothered little with me. Our father had no interest in any of us, I do not think. In any event, I was a difficult child. Wilful. I never heeded governesses, or tutors or anyone. I was sent down from the few schools I attended. All I ever wished to do was ride my horse.'

He placed his hand over hers. 'You could be speaking of my childhood, you know. Except my father took an intense interest in every niggling aspect of my life.'

'But your life has been worthwhile. Mine has...' She cleared her throat, and took a deep breath. 'I was fifteen when Farley came to visit. He had some business with my father, I know not what, but my older sisters were allowed to take meals with him, while I was confined to the nursery. I cared not for stuffy dinners, but my sisters teased me about it ceaselessly. When Lord Farley saw me out riding one morning, I was ripe to have some revenge upon them.' She glanced at him, blinking rapidly. 'But I have told you this part.'

His gaze searched her face. She'd once spoken lightly of Farley's seduction. 'I suspect there was more to it than the trifling occurrence you made it out to be.'

'I suppose.' She crossed her arms over her chest. 'It was a fine jest on my sisters, you know. The man they spoke of incessantly was paying me attention. Imagine. *Me*. He spoke pretty words to me.' She hugged herself tightly. 'I had no idea the impression I made in my brother's old clothes. The shirt had become tight around my chest, and I could barely lace up the pants. I thought nothing of it. I simply loved to ride like a boy. In those days I'd wished I was a boy, for boys could do all sorts of exciting things, like race and be soldiers and such. I hated to sit still for sewing or pianoforte or French lessons.'

He regarded her, tenderness filling him. He wished he might have ridden over the countryside with that young girl.

She continued. 'Lord Farley told me later that my clothes would have aroused any man. I should have known that, but I never paid attention when the governess talked of such things.' She bit her lip. 'When Lord Farley kissed me, my only thought was that I had achieved something my sisters endlessly dreamed about. I could not wait to tell them.'

She stood up and paced. 'Lord Farley suggested we retire to the hunting box nearby. His kisses were not unpleasant, and I was eager to try anything, so I did.' She stared at him. 'He showed me more than kisses. I do not know how it progressed as it did, but I made no effort to stop him. My body responded to him, Devlin.' She stopped to see how her words affected him.

She sunk back next to him on the bench. 'I vowed never again to allow myself such feelings.' She stared straight ahead of her, as if the bushes and trees held her fascination. 'And I never did, until that night with you.'

He put his arm around her, laying her head on his shoulder.

It took several seconds for her to continue. 'He told me to come to his room that night. I did, of course. It was so exciting, you see. At the worst possible time...my father opened the door.'

Madeleine pulled away from him and buried her face in her hands. 'I knew I was doing wrong. I knew it was sinful. I deserved for my parents to send me away. It was only fitting.'

'The deuce it was,' he muttered. 'At your age, they ought to have had Farley drawn and quartered.'

'Oh, no. I enticed him, you see. Both he and my father said so. It was not his fault. A man cannot be expected to control those...those urges.' The expression on her face was resolute. She believed this nonsense.

Devlin grabbed her shoulders and made her look at him. Though his grip was firm, his voice was soft. 'Maddy, a gentleman must control such urges. Did I not do so when you first came to stay? It was not easy, believe me.'

She blinked and knit her brows together. 'But I seduced you, too. When...when I wanted to make love to you, you could not resist.'

He could not help but smile. 'Goose, you did not seduce me. There was no need to resist when we both were willing.'

She shook her head. 'You do not understand.'

'I understand Farley took advantage of an innocent girl.'

She shrugged. 'I suppose it makes no difference. When the deed was done, my fate was ordained.'

He stood and extended his hand to her. 'Come, let us walk.'

She rose and took his arm.

He kept her close beside him. After a while he said, 'I still cannot believe your parents allowed you to be carried off by Farley. Surely they must have known who he was.'

'Indeed, they did. My mother told me she always knew I

was a shameful girl. She said I deserved to be with such a man. I was so foolish, I thought he would take me to Gretna Green. Only when we reached London did I realise what my mother meant.'

Devlin felt sick with rage. What kind of parent would send an innocent young daughter into the clutches of a man like Farley? It was unconscionable.

'In any event,' she went on, her voice curiously devoid of the hot emotions firing off in him, 'it was not long after that Lord Farley showed me my obituary in *The Times*.'

'Your obituary?'

'My parents fabricated my death. Farley told me there was a grave marked by a stone with my name upon it.'

'Damn them all.'

Devlin tried to convey some semblance of calm, but inside rage burned. Damn them all. They had taken a fresh, headstrong, spirited girl, robbed her of her life, and sent her into hell.

And he had left her there, all alone, when she had been only fifteen. He should have sent her to Serena or one of his sisters. Their kind hearts would have understood how to help her. Instead he had walked away, content to consign the pleasure of her company to fond memory.

Without speaking more of the matter, they walked through the park to their apartments. Madeleine busied herself with housework, while Devlin, still feeling the burden of abandoning Madeleine, turned the pages of the book for Linette, showing her the pictures of horses. His mind simmered. He did not make his afternoon call to Miss Duprey as had been expected. He did not attend Mrs Drummond-Burrell's musical evening that was touted the event of the season. Instead, he took a long walk in the drizzle and chill.

When he returned, Madeleine was in her own bed. He came to her side and her eyes fluttered open. In the light of the candle he carried, her eyes looked red and puffy. He blew out the candle, picked her up, and carried her to his bed.

His room was plunged in darkness. Wordlessly, they made love. The darkness and silence heightened the sense of melancholy in their lovemaking. Devlin felt rather than saw her and heard nothing but her breathing and the sounds of their bodies coming together. It was as if she had half-disappeared already and he was desperately clinging to what was left of her. When both were sated, he held her against him, his fingers combing her hair off her face, wet with tears. He still could not speak, but simply tightly held on to her until sleep finally came to him.

When morning came, Madeleine carefully manoeuvred herself out of the bed so as not to disturb Devlin. She found her nightdress in a heap on the floor and, as she donned it, gazed at the sleeping man. His handsome face was relaxed and peaceful, as it had not been since that fateful meeting with her mother and sister. At this moment he looked so much like Linette no one would doubt his paternity. She no longer doubted it, but accepted it as another of the painful paradoxes of her life. Like loving him and, therefore, having to lose him.

The foreboding sense that their idyllic interlude would soon speed to its end had lingered with her since the bookshop, and, thus, this day seemed grave indeed.

The feeling did not leave her when she busied herself preparing Linette's breakfast, accompanied by the child's irrepressible chatter. It was unusual for her to rise before Bart and Sophie, but perhaps the newly married couple were beginning their day in a happier mood than she.

Madeleine cooked coddled eggs and toast. When first Devlin brought them here, she could do nothing so useful; now she had learned so many skills. She could cook simple meals, scrub a floor, dust furniture and do simple sewing. She knew how to shop and how to bargain with shopkeepers. There was no doubting it. She was prepared to leave.

Bart came into the room, his face pinched with worry.
'What is it, Bart?'

'Sophie is feeling very poorly.' His voice was stressed.

'Shall I go to her?' Madeleine wiped her hands.

Bart nodded, giving her an agonised look.

Bart's room was spare but as orderly as Devlin's was disordered. Sophie lay on the bed, each breath coming with effort. Her face was nearly as pale as the linens she lay upon and dark circles showed under her eyes. She woke as Madeleine came to her side and gave a wan smile.

'We shall get the doctor for you, I think,' Madeleine said.

'Oh, no,' rasped Sophie, her voice thin and weak. 'There is no need. I shall be all right directly.'

'Indeed, you shall.' Madeleine patted her reassuringly. 'I will bring you some tea. Would you like that?'

Her waiflike friend nodded and wearily closed her eyes.

Madeleine returned to Bart in haste. 'Fetch the doctor. I cannot like the way she breathes.'

Bart immediately grabbed his coat and hat, hanging on a hook by the back door. 'I thought so, as well. I will get the man right now.' He let the door slam behind him as he rushed out.

Not long after, Devlin came into the kitchen.

'Deddy!' Linette squealed, scattering her wooden horses with a clatter as she bounded into his arms.

Her heart lurching as it always did at such tender scenes, Madeleine asked, 'May I prepare you some food, Devlin?'

He gave Linette a hug and a kiss and set her back on the floor. She happily returned to the corner where her horses lay. 'No, I must be off…a…a piece of business that must not be delayed.'

Madeleine faced him. She'd been about to tell him of Sophie, but changed her mind. No need to add to the stress evident in his countenance.

'Very well,' she said, trying to keep her voice even.

His mouth was set in a firm determined line. He held her gaze for a moment before he turned on his heel and left.

Madeleine squeezed her eyes shut and took long steadying breaths. Linette banged her horses on the wooden floor, saying, 'Gallump. Gallump,' as they galloped around her. Before Madeleine allowed herself further thoughts of Devlin, she hurried to check on Sophie.

His first piece of business complete, Devlin proceeded to Mayfair, knowing the hour was early for calls, but he had no wish to postpone this meeting. Best to dispense with it.

The Duprey butler ushered him into the parlour. Devlin paced the room where he'd spent several exceedingly boring afternoons.

The door opened and Emily Duprey crept in, glancing furtively behind her.

'Lord Devlin.' She cast him an anxious glance and shut the door.

'Miss Duprey, forgive the early hour. I wished to speak with your father.'

'As I understand. But if I could have a moment...' She regarded him with a worried expression.

He had no idea how to act with her. Since learning she was Madeleine's sister, dealing with her seemed an impossibility.

Suddenly he realised what had attracted him to her. The tilt of her head, the gesture of her hand, the shape of her brow and chin were Madeleine's. It was his attachment to Madeleine that led him to this woman, who at present was wringing her hands and regarding him anxiously.

He had wronged Emily Duprey. Led her to expect from him an offer now repugnant to him. According to her brother, the family considered it a settled matter, and it was for this sole reason he had returned to this house.

'Miss Duprey, I must beg your forgiveness, but after yesterday, you must realise that any further—'

'Never mind that, sir.' She cast him a pleading glance. 'My sister—'

Before she could continue, the butler arrived to escort him to Lord Duprey's study. He bowed to Miss Duprey, who wore a stricken expression on her face.

Lord Duprey, sitting behind a large desk, rose when Devlin entered the room. Lean and sallow-skinned, with a shock of white hair framing an aristocratic face, he approached Devlin. As he came close, Devlin recognised eyes of the same shade of blue as Madeleine's, except in this man bloodshot red surrounded the blue, and his lids were half closed in an expression of dissipation.

'Lord Devlin,' the man said formally, 'please sit down.' He gestured to a chair next to a table, where he poured them both generous glasses of sherry. Duprey, not waiting for his guest, took a long sip of the nut-brown liquid.

Devlin remained standing. 'I am very conscious of the early hour and have no wish to detain you beyond a moment.'

Duprey peered at him through the slits in his eyes. 'On the contrary. I am pleased that you have come. We have business to transact.'

'We have no business to transact. I came to make that clear to you.'

The older man walked back behind the desk and sat, taking another sip of his drink. 'You have singled out my daughter for your attentions in a way no one could dispute. It is time for you to honour this declaration you have implied so strongly.'

Devlin blanched. Surely this man had heard of the events of the previous day. 'I dispute your words, sir. I have shown no partiality, as anyone on the town knows. I have no intentions toward your daughter Emily, and I wish to make that clear.'

Lord Duprey's eyebrows lifted in a mocking expression. 'And I wish to make clear to you that you will honour your obligations to my daughter. You have been sniffing around her all Season, like some mongrel around a bitch. You will come up to scratch, or else.'

Devlin bristled under the crude threat, but he was determined not to lose his temper. He sent Duprey an equally mocking, but menacing look. 'Of which daughter do you speak?'

Duprey drained the contents of his glass and poured himself another from a decanter on the desk. 'So the chit told you, eh?' He laughed, a dry mirthless sound. 'Well, you will marry Emily Duprey and make this family an honourable connection to Heronvale's fortune. I care not a whit how much you bed that little whore.'

Devlin dove across the desk, grabbing Duprey by the knot in his neckcloth and scattering the desk's contents to the floor. The man's cheeks turned red as he sputtered for breath.

'You dare speak of her that way again and I will kill you.' Devlin released him and Duprey fell back into his chair.

When Duprey regained his breath, he smiled sardonically. 'I wonder what story she concocted for you, Steele. Probably some nonsense. I tell you, my luck was with me when she could not keep her skirts down for Farley—or, should I say, she could not keep her breeches up? Let me tell you, she was quite a sight in those clothes. Wished she wasn't my daughter once or twice.'

Devlin clenched his fists. Duprey again laughed, the racking sound repellent. 'Yes, indeed, her lustiness quite settled my debts. Got rid of the expense of another useless daughter, as well.'

'Do you mean you gave her to Farley in payment of gaming debts?'

Duprey drained another glass of sherry. 'Glad of it. Kept me from ruin.'

'Damn you, Duprey,' Devlin said through clenched teeth.

The smile remained frozen on the older man's face. 'Well, damn *you*, Steele, because you are going to marry Emily or suffer the scandal. Your brother dislikes scandal, I'll wager.'

'The scandal is on your head, Duprey. No one will receive any member of your family after I tell them what you did to Madeleine.'

'If they would believe you. My youngest daughter died, you see. There is a grave to prove it.'

'An empty grave.'

'Oh, it is not empty. I purchased a suitable corpse as soon as it became available.'

Bile rose in Devlin's throat.

Duprey raised the ante. 'So you would only expose the chit to much sordid attention.'

Devlin gaped at the malevolent man seated so casually. Surely he was bluffing, a gamester playing the cards the only way possible when the deal was a poor one.

This wager, however, involved not cards, but the reputations of the people Devlin held most dear. What effect on them if he played the game poorly?

Devlin spun on his heel and left the suffocating atmosphere of the Duprey town house. Inhaling fresh air into his lungs. Devlin hurried to call upon his brother, only to discover he and Serena had left early for Heronvale. He begged paper and pen from Barclay and then rushed to his brother's stable.

Jem was inside.

'Jem, thank God you are here. I need your help,' Devlin said, not bothering with a greeting. 'Is there a mount to carry me to Heronvale?'

'Yes, my lord,' Jem responded. 'His lordship took the carriage with m'lady. How may I serve you?'

'Have someone get the horse ready immediately and you deliver this letter to my apartments.'

The doctor gestured for Madeleine and Bart to follow him out of the room where Sophie coughed softly as she lay abed.

The doctor spoke in hushed tones. 'She has a touch of consumption.'

Bart wrung his hands. 'Is there some palliative? A poultice?'

'I am afraid there is little I can do. Country air would be as good as any tonic I could concoct. Alas, this city...' The doctor shook his head. 'It is bad for the lungs.'

Bart gave Madeleine an agonised glance.

'Then she shall go to the country,' Madeleine said. 'Bart, you could take her, could you not?'

'It might be the very thing,' the doctor said.

Bart knitted his eyebrows. 'Perhaps I could take her to Heronvale. They would take us in. The Marquess said he was in my debt. I should ask Dev.'

Madeleine grabbed his arm. 'You must not wait, surely. He might be gone all day.'

'But what of you, Miss Maddy? I should not leave you.'

She smiled. 'You must. It is the only thing to do. I have become quite useful, you know. I am well able to care for things here. Do not give us a thought.'

Bart needed no more coaxing. As soon as the doctor took his leave, the worried new husband was off to hire a posting chaise for his ill wife. Madeleine set to the task of packing Sophie's belongings, refusing to listen to her friend's protests.

'Do not be nonsensical, Sophie,' Madeleine scolded. 'Devlin and I can manage very well.'

Sophie curled up on her cot, making herself even smaller. 'I cannot like being separated from you.'

Madeleine came to her side and put her arms around her. 'Please do not fret. Bart will care for you very well. He loves you, you know.'

Sophie's face took on a dreamy look. She nodded her head and lodged no further complaint.

Within two hours, Madeleine and Linette watched the chaise drive away, driven by four sturdy but otherwise unremarkable mis-matched horses. Linette, as always, was in raptures about the beasts, but whimpered to see the coach drive away. She hugged her mother's neck. Madeleine thought she might nap for a bit and took her upstairs.

She had no sooner put Linette down upon her small bed when she heard the knocker. Thinking perhaps Bart and Sophie had forgotten something, she rushed down the stairs and flung open the door.

Her sister Emily stood before her.

Chapter Twenty-One

Emily let out a gasp, her gloved hand flying up to cover her mouth. 'I had thought…I thought this Lord Devlin's residence.'

Madeleine eyed Emily warily. 'It is, but he is not here presently.' What could have induced her sister to come here? Surely their mother would not allow such an improper visit.

Emily twisted the cords of her reticule, looking even more discomposed. 'Oh, dear.' She glanced back at the street where a carriage drove out of sight. 'The hack has left.'

'Then you'd best come in.' Madeleine stepped aside, holding the door ajar so Emily could pass into the hallway. She continued to look anxious and confused.

Madeleine's heart beat with excitement. She had not spoken to a member of her family for almost four years.

Emily turned to her. 'I did not know you would be here. That is, I did not realise…' She gave a deep sigh. 'I do not understand any of this!'

Madeleine remembered her sister Emily, two years older, as far more knowledgeable and worldly than she. At this moment, however, she felt herself to be the wiser one. Among the jumble of feelings swirling around inside her was a strong desire to throw her arms around Emily in a sisterly embrace.

'Come into the parlour.' Madeleine led the way and closed the door behind them.

Emily spun around to her. 'Oh, Madeleine! I had no notion...' Tears welled in her eyes. 'I thought you were dead.'

Had news of Madeleine's fall from respectability been kept from Emily? Madeleine always assumed her sisters knew all about it and welcomed the ruse of her demise as her parents must have.

Emily continued, 'How came you to be with L...Lord Devlin? Oh, I do not understand any of it! And Mama would tell me nothing, and Papa said I was a fool and had better keep my mouth shut.'

'You did not know?' Madeleine still could not believe it. She took a tentative step toward her sister, who quickly closed the distance and gave her the embrace Madeleine had longed for.

'Madeleine, Madeleine.' Emily choked back sobs. 'I have felt so guilty. Jessame and I had teased you so, and then you disappeared. You were not found for ages. Papa said no one could see the...the body, because it had been outside so long... Although it could not have been, because you are here, so it must have all been a hoax.'

Madeleine patted her back. 'Now, do not cry, Emily. There is no need. Indeed, I am so sorry to have given you such a shock. Come, sit down and I will get us some tea.'

She persuaded Emily to sit on the settee until she brought the tea and, when they were seated together, gave her sister a somewhat amended version of the events that brought them both to the present moment. Among the details Madeleine neglected to mention were a precise description of the duties required of her by Farley, the exact nature of her relationship with Devlin, and, of course, the existence of Linette.

'So, you see, Lord Devlin has been so kind as to assist me, and when he comes into his fortune he will lend me the money to set up a...a dress shop.'

Perhaps this rose-colored version would help to preserve

Devlin's opportunity to marry Emily, if that were still his intent. To think he might become a part of the family Madeleine had lost, however, was very difficult to contemplate.

She changed the subject. 'Emily, why have you come here? You really should not have. This is a single gentleman's residence.'

'I know I should not have come, but I could not let Papa—' She grabbed Madeleine's arm. 'Papa means to force Lord Devlin to marry me. He threatens to send a notice to the *Gazette* that Lord Devlin has offered for me, but it is all untrue.'

'It is untrue?'

'Indeed.' Emily sighed heavily. 'I must stop him.'

Madeleine stared at her sister, fumbling at her words. 'But I thought…I thought Devlin did wish to marry you.'

'No, I do not think so.' Emily's brow furrowed. 'He courted the Season's Diamond as much as he did me, and I think she may have refused Greythorne for him…'

Madeleine's eyebrows lifted. Devlin courted a Diamond of the *ton*?

Emily continued. 'At least that is what they say. I am persuaded Lord Devlin never intended to marry me, no matter how much our brother Robert boasted of it all over town. Indeed, I tried to explain to Papa, but he would not listen.'

But Devlin said Emily had been his choice. Had that been untrue? Did he say that to cover up his wish to marry a Diamond?

'Why do you think Devlin would not marry you?'

Emily gave a little laugh. 'Oh, Madeleine, look at me. I am no beauty. There is nothing to distinguish me from other ladies. Certainly nothing to compete with the pick of the Season.'

Her sister looked well enough, Madeleine thought. Indeed, Emily's face seemed comfortably dear. Madeleine had not realised how much she'd missed this sister she'd thought never cared a fig for her.

A door slammed and halting footsteps sounded on the stairs. 'Mama! Mama!'

Madeleine froze. Emily stared at her, eyebrows raised.

Linette ran in, coming to a stop when she noticed the strange lady seated next to her mother. Her thumb went into her mouth.

Resigned, Madeleine said. 'It is all right, Linette. Come give a curtsy to Miss Duprey.'

Linette, still sucking on her thumb, wobbled on one leg as she tried to accomplish her mother's request.

'Your child?' Emily asked, her eyes wide.

Madeleine nodded.

'Lord Farley's?' she asked.

Madeleine shook her head.

Emily stared at the little girl who climbed into her mother's lap and laid her head against her mother's breast, rubbing her eyes.

Emily's gaze met Madeleine's and held there for several moments. 'She is Lord Devlin's.'

Madeleine nodded. She did not expect Emily to understand how wonderful it was for her to have Linette, to believe that Devlin was indeed Linette's father and that a part of him would always be with her in Linette.

Emily walked to the window. 'Why should Lord Devlin pretend to be courting me or any other lady while living here with you and…and this child? What game has he been playing?'

A game to win money, money enough to support her and their daughter, a coil Madeleine had forced upon him.

She could not tell her sister this. The best she could do was preserve Devlin's chances to marry whomever he wished.

'I am not fit to be his wife, Emily. Not after Lord Farley. I assure you, I was no more than a momentary indiscretion on Devlin's part, but he would not abandon us.'

Emily rubbed her brow. 'It is of no consequence, I suppose. Tell Lord Devlin he may resist Father's trickery. I will not place any damage to my reputation at Lord Devlin's door. He has no obligation to me, and so I will say to anyone. I'll threaten to expose what Father has done to you. That will stop him.'

It would also expose her family to terrible scandal. 'I do not wish for our family to be hurt—'

'Father, hurt? He would never take such a chance. Leave it to me.' Emily briskly retrieved her reticule from the side table and headed toward the door. 'I must leave.'

'No, not so soon,' cried Madeleine, jumping to her feet with Linette still in her arms. Please, allow her a little bit of family for a few minutes more.

Emily turned back to her, the pinched expression on her face softening. Gently she touched Madeleine's cheek. 'I was always so jealous of you, Madeleine, more reason for me to feel guilt when I thought you dead.'

'Jealous of me?'

'You are quite a dazzling beauty.' Emily smiled at her with a wistful expression. 'That year before you disappeared, you had grown so pretty, you cast Jessame and me into the shade. We were green with envy.' She gave a little sigh and kissed Madeleine's cheek. 'I am glad you are alive. Please thank Lord Devlin for being so kind to me. I have had the loveliest time this Season.'

Madeleine could think of nothing to say to this. Emily strode purposefully toward the door, pausing on the threshold. 'Madeleine?'

Madeleine rushed to her side. 'Yes?'

She gave a little laugh. 'I do not have the least notion how to get back home. Do you know where I can find a hack?'

Madeleine gave a tentative smile. 'Wait a moment. Linette and I will walk with you. There will be a hack near the shops.'

As they walked toward the shops, Madeleine begged for news about Jessame and Robert, thirstily drinking in each small tidbit of information Emily provided. Neither spoke of their parents. As they walked, a stylish phaeton came into view, the gentleman holding the ribbons doing an admirable job controlling a pair of spirited chestnuts.

'Oh, my goodness,' said Emily. 'It is Amanda Reynolds.'

The young lady seated next to the phaeton's driver was the loveliest creature Madeleine had ever seen, fair, delicate, with blonde curls peeping out of a modish bonnet. Her stylish fawn-coloured dress, topped by a matching spencer, adorned a perfect figure.

'Who is she?' she asked.

The two sisters paused to watch these passers-by.

'The Diamond I told you about,' Emily said. 'And I believe that is Devlin's friend with her. She does not like him above half. How shocking for them to be riding together with no more than a tiger for chaperon. What could it mean?'

Madeleine only half attended to these words. Her eyes were fixed on the Diamond, who looked beautiful even seated in silence next to the gentleman. Devlin's friend, another unknown piece of Devlin's life on the town.

Her knowledge of him was confined to their apartments and the few places he could take her. She could not have known he'd attracted this exquisite lady.

As the phaeton rolled past, the Diamond turned around and caught Madeleine's gaze.

Emily quickly covered her face with the brim of her bonnet. 'I must not let her see me.'

A hack pulled up at the end of the street, and Madeleine and Emily rushed over to it. After a swift hug, Madeleine bundled her sister into the vehicle and waved her goodbye, watching until the hack drove completely out of sight.

Lord Farley paced the pavement across the street from Devlin Steele's apartments, waiting. It had become his practice to spend some part of each day or night in this neighbourhood. He often caught a glimpse of Madeleine, but she was always accompanied by Steele, that brutish-looking man of his, or that insipid little maid.

He could hardly believe his good fortune when she bid goodbye to the female who walked out of the house with her. She was alone at last. The child did not matter. Farley crossed the street, timing it so that he placed himself between her and her door. She was as absorbed as ever in the child and did not attend to his approach.

He stepped directly in her path. She looked up and gave a strangled cry.

He smiled at her, his most winning smile, the one he'd used to attract her in the first place. 'Madeleine, my dear, it is my pleasure to see you.'

Her eyes darted to both sides and she protectively grasped her daughter's hand. 'Let me by, if you please.'

'I wish to speak to you.' He placed his hand on her shoulder. She wrenched away.

She picked up the child and tried to walk past him. 'I have no wish to speak to you.'

He blocked her way, putting his arm tightly around her waist so that she could not easily squirm away. She struggled nevertheless. He held her more tightly against his side. With his mouth tantalisingly close to her ear, he said, 'I want you back, Madeleine.' He did not resist the opportunity, but let his tongue lap the delicate skin of her earlobe.

The sharp heel of her walking boot pounded into his foot. Pain shot through him and he dropped his hold on her. She hurried away, but not quickly enough.

He caught her arm and held it vise-like, his lips again near her ear. 'You will return to me, Madeleine, or one dark night that pretty soldier of yours will find a knife in his back.'

'No!' She struggled. The child began to cry.

Farley wrapped his fingers with Linette's curls. 'I wonder how easy it would be to snatch this child? The chimney sweeps would pay a pretty price for her, I own. Or perhaps a gentleman might fancy some sport with her?'

'Do not touch her!' shrieked Madeleine.

'I repeat, Madeleine. Return to me or I will carry out my

threats. You will never know when I am about. I will get them, both of them, you may be sure.'

A man walked up to them with a swift step.

'Sir! Sir! Help me!'

The man faced Farley. 'Let the lady go.'

'This is not your affair,' Farley protested. 'It is only a trifling bit of spirit from my fancy piece here. Nothing to trouble you.'

'No, do not heed him,' Madeleine pleaded.

The man grabbed Farley by the back of his collar, pulling so forcefully, his breath was cut off.

'Unhand her,' the man growled.

Farley, gasping futilely for air, knew when the cards dealt could not be played. He acquiesced.

'Be gone.'

Farley brushed off his coat. Before he turned to leave, he bowed to Madeleine. 'Remember what I said, my dear. I will carry out my plans.'

Farley strolled off, taking care not to look nonplussed.

Madeleine clutched at Linette, whose little arms were tight around her neck and whose head was buried into her shoulder. 'I cannot thank you enough, sir. We are truly in your debt.'

The man bowed. 'Glad to be of service. May I escort you to your destination?'

Madeleine recognised the gentleman as the man who, moments before, had driven by with the Diamond. Devlin's friend.

'Thank you, but I am near my residence...' Madeleine glanced toward her door, just a few houses away.

The Diamond stood at the top of the steps at her door, watching her with interest. Madeleine could not avoid her, too afraid to go somewhere else until they drove off.

She allowed Devlin's friend to walk her to her door as Miss Reynolds watched. Madeleine halted. 'We are here. Thank you, sir.'

'Here?' he asked. 'These are Devlin Steele's apartments.'

As Miss Reynolds stood decorously, Madeleine said in a feeble voice, 'I...I am in his employ.'

'Indeed?' A smile, somewhat cynical, flashed across his face. Miss Reynolds looked shocked.

'Well,' said the gentleman agreeably. 'Let me make our introductions.' He gestured to the ethereal creature at his elbow. 'This is Miss Reynolds, and I am Captain Ramsford, a friend of Lord Devlin's.'

'Mama, I want Deddy!' whimpered Linette.

Ramsford's eyebrows shot up, and Miss Reynold's mouth fell open.

Blushing, Madeleine hurried to the door. 'I will see if Lord Devlin is at home.'

She rushed inside with Linette, caring not if they thought it rude to be kept waiting on the doorstep like tradesmen. Linette curled up on the stairs, still looking frightened. Madeleine called for Devlin, but there was no answer.

Before she stepped back outside she heard Lord Ramsford and Miss Reynolds through the crack in the door.

'Oh, my goodness,' Miss Reynolds cried.

'Compose yourself. You will see Devlin by and by.' He added in a mocking tone, 'In the meantime, you may depend on me.'

Noting Miss Reynolds used Devlin's given name, Madeleine stepped back outside. 'Lord Devlin is not at home.'

Ramsford peered at her quizzically. 'A pity.' He turned to Miss Reynolds. 'We have come on a fool's errand, as I predicted. Now, perhaps you will allow me to convey you home.'

Miss Reynolds gave him a scathing glance. Her forehead wrinkled, and she spoke to Madeleine. 'Who was that man who accosted you?'

Madeleine blinked. 'No one you should know, my lady.'

'Are you all right, Miss...?' Miss Reynolds lifted her eyebrows, obviously wanting Madeleine to reveal her name.

Madeleine lowered her eyes. 'I shall require no further assistance.' She ignored the other request. 'If you will forgive me, I must see to my daughter.'

Without a glance back, Madeleine rushed through the doorway, bolted the door, and went directly to Linette. 'Come, darling,' she said soothingly. 'The bad man will not scare us again.'

The afternoon crept by, spent soothing Linette, entertaining her and attempting to still her own agitation from the afternoon events. Madeleine longed for Devlin to return home. She had decided to warn him only about her father's trickery and Farley's threat. If he did not wish her to know of the Diamond, she would pretend ignorance. In any event, her future would be unchanged.

As time wore on, Madeleine grew more uneasy. When she peeked out the front windows, there always seemed to be some man loitering near the lamppost across the street. Not Farley, but familiar figures. His lackeys. He was having her watched.

Each minute Devlin did not return caused her increased agitation. She pictured him bleeding in some alleyway, a knife thrust into his back. And if that image were not disturbing enough, she envisioned him in the arms of the beautiful Diamond.

She jumped at a sharp knock on the door. With a pounding heart, she peered out the window. It was not Farley, nor one of his men, but a footman dressed in Heronvale livery. She opened the door. The footman handed her a note and left.

The note was addressed to her. With trembling fingers, she broke the seal and read: *My dearest Maddy. I am called away on urgent business. Everything will be settled upon my return. I will be gone only one night and will be home for dinner tomorrow. Explain to Bart. Kiss Linette for me. Yours, etc., D.S.*

She folded the paper again, her heart pounding in her chest. What urgent business was this? Did it involve the Diamond, perhaps? Well, at least Farley could not make good his threat. Devlin would not be killed in some alleyway this night.

Madeleine sat down again with her sewing, trying to calm herself. Linette played close by at her feet. Through the crack in the curtains, she watched two men conversing. They scrutinised the house. How long before they determined she and Linette were alone?

She pricked her finger with the needle and put her finger to her mouth to stop the bleeding.

She'd be damned if she would sit here and wait for Farley to come after her. Even if Farley captured her, he would still make good on his threats to Devlin and Linette. She knew Farley too well. Nothing would save the two people she loved as long as that man breathed life.

Madeleine's pricked finger remained poised in the air. Was that something she could do? She set her sewing on the side table and absorbed herself in thought. She could sneak back to Farley's establishment and wait for him. Surprise would be on her side. She could wait until he slept. Then she could kill him.

Almost without effort, the plan formed itself in her head. First, she would take Linette to the Marquess and Marchioness. They wanted to adopt her and would be very pleased to have her. Linette would receive every advantage under their care, and, if things went wrong, Farley would not dare to touch a child under the Marquess's protection.

But would Devlin be safe? The only way to be sure was to kill Farley. Devlin could then marry Miss Reynolds with no impediment. And have a happy life.

If she were caught, she would be hanged. If she escaped, she must disappear forever. If she failed…well, she must not fail.

Rushing over to the desk, she composed a farewell letter to Devlin. She had to write it several times before sealing the final effort. The bleakness of the task made her hand tremble.

How to tell him to forget her? How to tell him how much she loved him? How to explain this was the only thing to be done?

At dusk, Madeleine, donned yet another costume. With her newly acquired sewing skills, she altered some old clothes of Devlin's, stitching the trousers so that they fit her slim hips and came over her walking boots. She found an old cap of Bart's to cover her hair, and a caped coat. Shortened and its cuffs removed, the coat was large enough to hide Linette beneath and Devlin's sabre behind. Farley's lackeys would be watching the back door as well as the front, but the house shared an area with other residences, so a boy walking out the back would not arouse suspicion. She took the risk of leaving candles burning in the house to look as if they were at home.

She enlisted Linette's cooperation by promising her a visit to the Marquess, who would let her see his horses. She also promised that Linette would see Devlin soon, and that she would have a supreme adventure, but first she must be quiet and still, so the bad man would not discover them.

Linette played her role beautifully, as did Madeleine. A boy in a big coat sauntered down the street to no one's notice.

It was dark when Madeleine reached the Marquess's town house. She had no idea how to discover the servants' entrance, so she strode up to the front door. The huge brass knocker was removed. There was nothing to do but rap on the door with her knuckles.

The Heronvale butler opened the door and looked disapprovingly at her.

'Be gone, ruffian,' he ordered through a crack in the door.

'Please, sir, wait. It is Miss England. Do you remember me? I must see the Marquess. It will only take a moment.'

The elderly man's eyes grew huge as he gaped at her. 'The Marquess and Marchioness are not at home.'

The strap that she had devised to hold Linette dug into her

neck, but she dared not reveal the child's presence. 'May I wait for them, please?'

The man regarded her with a concerned look. 'His lordship and ladyship intend to spend an indefinite time at Heronvale.'

Heronvale?

Madeleine walked down the long steps to the street. This spoiled her plans to be rid of Farley and herself before Devlin returned. She must travel to Heronvale first.

She found her way to the Marquess's stable, where once she had come with Devlin for an early morning ride. She crept inside when the stable boy was not looking. It was not difficult to find a secluded corner in which to hide, nor to convince Linette to be very quiet so they could sleep next to the horses.

When the first rays of light shone through the stable windows, Madeleine rose and searched for the saddles. She was tightening the cinch when the stable door opened and the head groom walked in.

'See here!' he shouted, rushing over to her and grabbing her around the waist.

'Mama! Mama!' Linette shouted as she flung her arms around Madeleine's legs.

'What the devil...?' the groom exclaimed.

Madeleine recognised him as the man who had been with Devlin the night she had run away from the Marquess's town house.

'The Marchioness gave me permission. Do you recall me, sir? I am Lord Devlin's...friend.'

'Does he know you are here?' the man asked.

'No, Lord Devlin is away. That is why I must go to the Marquess. Lord Devlin told me I should.' Madeleine struggled for an explanation that would win his cooperation.

'Mama?' Linette gripped the cloth of Madeleine's trousers.

The groom straightened. 'Who is this?'

'My daughter.'

He regarded her, a thoughtful expression on his face. 'Why are you dressed like that?'

Madeleine thought wildly. 'I feared riding all that distance to Heronvale. It would not be safe as a woman. Please, let me borrow the horse. I promise to return it.'

He rubbed his chin. 'I do not think his lordship would like it if I let you ride off to Heronvale.'

'But you must!'

Already she was terribly delayed. It would have been so much better to have Linette safe and the deed accomplished by now. She needed to do this before Devlin returned. Before he stopped her.

The groom put his hands on his hips. 'I'll take you in the curricle. It will be faster and I think Lord Devlin would charge me to keep you safe.'

Madeleine thought she might kiss the man, so grateful was she. 'Thank you, sir.'

Farley fumed as his carriage sped along. The chit had hoodwinked him. It was late before his men realised that she had been alone in the house and, by the time he had given the order to break in, she and her child were gone.

It took more time to discover that Steele had hotfooted it to his brother's estate. Farley wagered that, somehow, Madeleine was headed there, as well. Farley and his men would reach the outskirts of Heronvale at dawn. He would send his men ahead to discover if she'd arrived there. If not, he would lie in wait for her.

She would not foil him again.

Chapter Twenty-Two

Devlin woke in his old room at Heronvale. For a moment he thought he was an invalid again and the past months merely one of his fevered dreams. A disquieting sense of unease lingered. It had nothing to do with the heated words he and his brother had exchanged. No, something more elusive.

He had confessed the whole to his brother, which had gone rather better than he could have expected, but they did not agree on the solution. Ned was in accord with Devlin about the impropriety of marriage to Emily Duprey, but did not agree that Devlin must marry Madeleine.

Ned's reasoning was sound, Devlin supposed. Ned had argued that Madeleine and the child deserved a peaceful life after all they had endured. As the wife of a Steele, she would be scrutinised. Would not some eager gossipmonger expose her past?

Who in society would trouble themselves with his business if he reactivated his commission in the army? Devlin had countered. Ned nearly turned apoplectic at that suggestion.

Devlin sat up in bed, stretching his limbs and trying to let the new day give perspective on the past one. In any event, Ned could not stop him from rejoining the army. Ned had, after all, given him the bank draft for Madeleine. It provided enough money to repurchase his commission. But how the deuce was he to silence Duprey?

At least Ned cared not a fig for the dust that would be kicked up if Duprey made good his threat, though Ned did not relish becoming the latest *on-dit* for the *ton*. Serena might suffer from it, he had said. Devlin had been surprised by the softness in his brother's expression when he spoke Serena's name. Come to think of it, Ned and Serena seemed unusually at ease with each other.

Devlin shrugged. Whatever the reason, he was glad of it.

He dressed quickly and headed for the stables. A hard ride would clear his mind and rid him of this sense of foreboding.

As he set the horse into a trot, he thought of Madeleine. What a race they could have if she were to ride the estate with him. They could explore all his childhood haunts, the special places he treasured from those simpler days.

The fields stretched ahead of him, some thick with crops, some fallow. He knew every inch of this land. Urging his horse into a gallop, he sped over them, jumping hedges, clearing fences, and letting the exhilaration replace all other thought.

Farley settled himself in the windowseat of the village's posting house. The ale was tolerable and the breakfast generous. More important, any traveller to Heronvale would by necessity pass directly in front of the window. His horse was kept ready, and he could depend on his own eyes if his lackeys failed to warn him if she came into view.

He regarded the innkeeper's daughter with an appraising eye. She was comely enough, but too common for his tastes. He wondered how many men had their first tumble with a tavern wench. It would make a fetching costume for Madeleine to wear. He could just see the simple dress dipping low, revealing her full breasts as she bent to pour a drink. Farley took a deep swig of his ale. He'd be damned if he'd share her this time.

This time she would be all his, to do with as he wished.

* * *

Devlin's ride was ill fated, a bad omen to be sure. After his horse threw a shoe, he led her home on foot, taking up precious time he needed to conclude matters with his brother. The sun was high in the sky when he delivered the horse to the head groom.

'What's amiss, m'lord?' the old retainer asked, having spied him walking with the horse.

'Threw a shoe,' Devlin replied, handing over the reins.

As the man examined the hoof, Devlin made the mistake of mentioning Jem to him. This launched the proud father into a long discourse about his son and how the Marquess was right to value Jem so highly, him being very much like his father. Devlin attended to the conversation with disguised impatience. He had not eaten a bite that day and had much to do before he could return to Madeleine.

'And I was saying to your man yesterday, how I wish the young'uns could live here in the country where the air is not carrying some disease or another, but Jem would not hear of it, nor that wife of his…'

'Saying to my man?'

'Yes, m'lord. Mr Bart. And what a poor little thing that new wife of his is, so sick and all, but she'll be well enough staying with Nurse. Nurse still knows just what should be done, though I'd wager she is five and seventy, if she is a day.'

Devlin grabbed the groom's arm. 'They are here?'

The old man gave him a puzzled look. 'They arrived soon after you.'

Not waiting a moment for the groom. Devlin threw a saddle on one of the other mounts and raced for Nurse's cottage.

She was in her front yard, leaning on her stick, a basket over her arm. She dropped the basket and threw a hand across her chest when he thundered toward her.

'Goodness! Master Devlin, I declare. 'Tis so good to see you. I'm about to make a nice posset for that dear little one.'

'Where are they?' He swung his leg over to dismount before the horse had quite stopped.

'I have the dear girl all right and tight, Master Devlin, never you fear, but you must take a care you don't break your neck. I've told you many a time—'

He ran inside with her limping behind him.

Devlin found Bart seated by the bedside where a pale Sophie lay. Bart's face was pinched with worry.

'My God, what happened?'

Bart glanced up in surprise. 'Dev!'

Nurse poked Devlin on the shoulder with her bony finger. 'You'll not go racketing in this house, m'lord, and waking the girl. She needs her rest. If you want to be talking, get into the other room and keep your voices down.'

Devlin did as he was told, Bart rising to go with him. They went into the main room in the cottage.

'Is Madeleine with you?' Devlin asked anxiously.

'No, but she thought... What are you doing here?'

'Never mind that now. What of Sophie?'

Bart rubbed his face and flopped into a chair. 'She could hardly breathe. The doctor said the only hope was country air. Dev, I would not have come had I known you would be absent.'

'Now, no fussing,' said Nurse, walking in. 'I told you she'd be right and tight. Sleeping like a baby, she is.' She limped over to the fire and busied herself with the posset.

Devlin placed his hand on Bart's shoulder. 'You were right to bring Sophie here. I promise you Nurse will know just what to do for her. I trust Madeleine and Linette have done very well, so do not worry on that side. I had sent word to her that I would be away, but to be prudent I will return to London immediately.'

'We should not have left her,' Bart said.

'Nonsense,' countered Devlin. 'It was my error, leaving as I did with only a note. I must not tarry.'

As he galloped back to the house, that sense of dread returned. Madeleine was alone and she knew no one who could help her if anything went amiss. He must reach her without delay. Devlin ordered a fresh mount, and hurried to inform his brother.

Madeleine pretended to be calm as she sat beside the chattering Linette, who was in transports over riding behind two horses and spying so many more along the way. Jem patiently answered Linette's endless questions about the beasts, at the same time asking no questions of Madeleine. She was grateful to him for that.

They passed through a small village. 'Not long now,' he said.

Not long before she would hug Linette for the last time; kiss her little cheek for the last time. Madeleine might have managed it well enough if she could have handed Linette over to the Marquess in London, before she'd had all these hours to contemplate never seeing her little girl again. With each mile her soul ebbed away, bit by painful bit.

After this wrenching deed was accomplished, the rest of it would seem easy. She would travel back to London, to the gaming hell where she would find Farley. She feared killing him, but only because she might be wicked enough to enjoy it. It should be a comfort to know that Devlin would have the life he deserved, with a beautiful wife who could be a credit to him instead of a mistress who placed his life in danger.

It was no comfort, however. Losing him would hurt as much as losing Linette.

Horses' hooves pounded behind them, and Jem steered the curricle to the side to give the riders room to pass. One rider came aside the curricle's team and grabbed the harness while others surrounded the vehicle, their horses whinnying and breathing hard.

'Get her!' someone shouted.

Madeleine immediately clutched Linette, holding the child tight while men grabbed at them both. The curricle came to an abrupt stop, Jem was on his feet, snapping at the men with his whip. Madeleine crouched on the seat, the shouts of the men harsh in her ears and the smell of horse sweat filling her nostrils. Jem's whip snapped and cracked above her head. A shot rang out, and Jem tumbled from the curricle.

Madeleine forced herself not to think of him. She tucked Linette beneath her feet and unsheathed Devlin's sabre, slashing it at her attackers as Devlin had demonstrated. She drove them back again. Through the din she could hear Jem moaning.

'Damn you, I said get the chit.' That was Farley's voice. He had come for her and to make good his threat toward Linette.

'Mama,' Linette cried, cowering at her feet.

'Cowards!' shouted Farley. 'Seize her now.'

The sabre sliced at the arm of one of the attackers. He fell back, cursing, blood spurting from his arm. Madeleine swung at another, but another man climbed on the curricle and grabbed her from behind. He squeezed her wrist until the sword clattered to the ground. Madeleine struggled against him. Farley rode near and plucked Linette from the vehicle.

'No!' Madeleine screamed.

She clawed at her captor's eyes and kicked him in the groin with all her might. With a cry of pain, he pushed her away. She lost her footing and fell hard on to the ground, the breath knocked out of her. With her cheek flat against the ground, she saw Jem writhing in pain, white-faced, blood staining his shoulder. The horses' stamping hooves sounded perilously close, the animals as panicked as she. The dirt they kicked up rained down on her. The horses bolted, sending Farley's man sprawling off the back in the wake of the curricle clattering down the road.

'Mama! Mama!' Linette's screams rose above the din.

Madeleine forced herself to rise. She groped for the sabre.

Farley dismounted, holding Linette as if she were a parcel of old rags. His men, one mounted, one not, circled around their comrades. The two on the ground were helped to their feet.

Ignoring that she was outnumbered, Madeleine took advantage of the distraction. She strode toward Farley, sabre in hand.

'Release my child.'

Farley laughed, the evil sound stilling Linette's cries. Gazing smugly at Madeleine, he held Linette in front of him, protecting his chest with her little body. 'Still wish to thrust your sword into me, my dear?'

'Let her go.' Her demand was useless, she knew. Two of his lackeys closed in on her again. She turned, slashing the sabre at them. Out of the corner of her eye a third man aimed a pistol at her.

'Do not damage her!' Farley ordered. 'Surround her. There are four of you and one of her.'

The men did as they were told. Madeleine spun around, turning to each of them as they jeered at her.

'Drop the sword, my dear,' Farley said, his voice sickly smooth. 'You and your child are mine now.'

Madeleine closed her eyes. Her heart despaired.

She heard a galloping horse and cries of surprise from Farley's men. Her eyes flew open, and she saw the horseman.

Devlin.

He had no weapon save savage cries and murder in his eyes. He charged straight toward the men surrounding Madeleine, grabbing one of them as the man attempted to run. Devlin lifted him by the collar of his coat and tossed him down again. Madeleine raised the sabre, and Devlin grabbed it out of her hand. He became someone she had not imagined before, a demon on horseback, who easily scattered Farley's men. One reached a horse, mounted and beat a hasty retreat. The others ran for the woods.

With only a glance toward Madeleine, Devlin dismounted and approached Farley, sabre menacing. 'Unhand the child, Farley.'

Farley took a step back. Before Devlin could reach him, Farley drew a silver-bladed knife from his belt and held it against Linette's tiny throat. Its blade flashed in the afternoon sun.

'I would drop the sword if I were you, Steele.' Farley's upper lip curled.

Devlin lowered his sword very slightly.

'I mean it,' growled Farley. He pressed the blade against the child's neck, drawing a trickle of blood. She shrieked.

'No,' pleaded Madeleine.

Devlin watched the blood drip over Farley's fingers to stain the front of Linette's dress. The child, her face chalky white, was rigid, terror bulging her eyes. His vision blurred, and, distinctly as if it were happening to him again, he felt each stab of the French cuirassier.

He shook his head clear, ignoring his old demons and the panic that accompanied them. 'Let the child go, Farley.' Devlin's voice was steady.

'I'll give you the brat.' Farley sneered. 'But I keep the mother.'

'No deals,' said Devlin, advancing.

'She's mine.' Farley's voice went up a pitch and he placed the point of the knife below Linette's chin. 'You stole her from me and now I want her back.'

Devlin halted. There was no way to disarm Farley or strike him before he cut deep into Linette's throat.

Panic rose again and again he pushed it away. Battle was much like a game, he reminded himself, a series of points and counterpoints. As in the card came they'd played not more than three months ago, Devlin must wait until Farley made a mistake.

'I did not steal her.' Devlin kept his voice deceptively calm. 'You offered her, remember? You lost at your own game.'

'Your play was dishonest!' Farley waved the knife.

'It was not, as you well know. You gambled and lost,' he continued reasonably.

'Now you lose!' Farley gave a mirthless laugh. He swung the knife dramatically back to Linette's throat. Devlin's grip hardened on the hilt of the sword.

Suddenly, Farley's gaze left Devlin's face and focused behind him, his jaw dropping open. Devlin turned.

Madeleine had mounted one of the horses. The agitated beast bucked and twisted and kicked. It huffed and blew, its eyes wild. Devlin fell back, away from its kicks. Farley gaped, eyes frozen on the out-of-control animal.

How was Madeleine able to remain in the saddle? Devlin had visions of her falling off and being trampled to death by the horse's hooves. Somehow she hung on. The horse leapt and vaulted ever closer to Farley, who gave a terrified cry. He dropped Linette to the ground, and covered his face against the lethal hooves of the approaching horse.

Devlin grabbed Linette, covering her with his body. Let the hooves kick at him. He would use his body to protect his child.

'Drop the knife, Farley.' Madeleine shouted from the rearing horse. Devlin glanced up.

The horse came under perfect control, advancing slowly toward Farley. White-faced, Farley sank to his knees.

Devlin stood, holding Linette, who had her small arms tightly wrapped around his neck.

'Is she all right?' Madeleine asked, her voice trembling as she backed up the horse.

'I think so,' Devlin replied. He gave her a half-grin. 'Excellent horsemanship.'

She shrugged.

With an enraged cry, Farley charged toward Devlin and Linette, his knife raised.

Madeleine kicked at the horse. The animal shot forward, rearing and whinnying. Its hooves came down on Farley, knocking him to the ground. Madeleine pulled the animal away and forced it back under control. Farley moaned and rolled over. The knife protruded from his chest. Blood soaked his clothing and pooled next to his now-still body.

Chapter Twenty-Three

Madeleine stared out the window. The setting sun cast a reddish glow over the impressive Heronvale park and the rolling countryside. A fire crackled in the ornate marble fireplace at the end of the room, but the cup of tea on the table beside her grew cold. She tucked her feet underneath her on the settee and tried to banish the image of Farley's death from her mind.

The door opened.

'There you are.' Devlin walked into the room.

She looked up at him for a moment and back to the window.

He sat beside her and put his hand gently under her chin, turning her face to him. 'Are you all right?'

Concern shone in his eyes. She could not bear it. She nodded.

He smiled at her, drinking her in with his gaze. 'I see Serena found a dress for you.'

'She has been kind.'

The Marchioness had taken Madeleine and Linette under her wing as soon as they reached Heronvale. They were cosseted and pampered, cleaned up, and dressed in clothes that were hurriedly found in attic trunks.

He put his arm around her and tucked her next to him. She rested her head on his shoulder. It was enticingly comfortable.

'Where is Linette?' he asked.

'I believe the Marquess and Marchioness took her to the stables.'

'Ah, that should please her.' He kissed the top of her head. 'Did you visit Sophie?'

'Yes.'

Sophie had burst into tears when she'd seen her. Madeleine held her and rocked her as if she had been Linette.

'Did you…settle things?' Madeleine asked.

There had been much commotion when they arrived at Heronvale. Devlin had carried the injured Jem on his horse. They had left Farley's body where it lay.

He snuggled her closer to him. 'All is set right, Maddy. Ned spoke to the magistrate, and no further enquiry will be required.'

She closed her eyes. 'I thought I would enjoy killing him.'

He stroked her hair. 'Death is not something to enjoy, but you did not kill him, my love. His own treachery did that.'

He should not call her his love, she thought. Did he now feel even more obligated to her? He should not.

She turned her gaze to the scene from the window. 'Heronvale is very beautiful,' she said.

'I am pleased you like it.'

His arm felt so strong around her and his body warmed hers. She wished she could remain in his warmth and strength forever, but it was time to settle the matters between them, as well.

'Perhaps Linette would be happy here.'

'Linette?'

Madeleine pulled away from him. He regarded her with a puzzled expression.

'I have decided that I should…should agree for Linette to be adopted by the Marquess.'

Devlin's brows lifted. 'Are you mad?'

'It would be best for her, do you not think?' She forced herself to speak casually.

'No, I do not think.' He scowled. 'Perhaps you had better tell me where this addled-brained idea came from.'

She rose from the settee and folded her arms across her chest. 'Well, they can offer her so much more than I. I am persuaded her life would have more advantages.' She walked toward the window. 'She would still see you from time to time, as well.'

He stood as well, matching her tone, but with an edge of sarcasm. 'And where will you be while Linette has this idyll?'

'Oh, I shall do well, I think. You needn't concern yourself.'

He gripped her by the shoulders. 'Tell me what this is about.'

She avoided his eyes. 'My sister Emily visited me—'

He interrupted her. 'And she said I was to marry her. Well, I am not.'

Madeleine tried to pull away from his grasp, but he would not release her. She tried to boldly meet his eye. 'She told me you did not court her, but another lady. The Diamond of the *ton*.'

He blinked in surprise. 'Amanda Reynolds? Not exactly so.'

'I met Miss Reynolds, Devlin,' Madeleine said, her voice soft. 'She would make you a lovely wife.'

'You met Amanda Reynolds as well?' His hand flew up in surprise. 'I was only absent a few hours.'

She continued earnestly. 'She is beautiful, Devlin. The catch of the Season, Emily said. And I thought she had such kind eyes…'

'Damn her eyes!' he barked. 'What do her eyes matter to me?' He grabbed her shoulders again. 'I am not going to marry Amanda Reynolds.'

She pulled back.

'Do you know why I came here, Maddy?' He spoke softly. She shook her head.

'It was to inform my brother that I would marry you.'

Her gaze shot up.

'You, Maddy. Not your sister. Not Amanda Reynolds. You. It is you I love.'

She stared at him, her eyes wide and wary.

He gazed at her with tenderness. 'I came to inform my brother that I would marry you. I did not ask his approval. I checked with my old regiment. If I rejoin the cavalry, I may be able to support you and Linette, if you can bear following the drum. Others have done it, Maddy. Perhaps we can, too.'

'Follow the drum,' she repeated.

'We may be sent to Canada, at best, although it might be Africa or India or some other ungodly place, but we would be together.'

'You cannot mean to rejoin the army. Not after Waterloo.'

He set his jaw firmly. 'I can master Waterloo.'

She reached up and stroked his cheek with the back of her soft hand. 'But what of your inheritance? Your estate?'

'What good is money to me, my love, if you and Linette are not with me?'

'Oh, Devlin,' she whispered, 'have we not always known we could not be together?'

'We must be together, Maddy.'

Laughter sounded in the hallway. Ned and Serena walked in the room, Ned carrying Linette on his shoulders. He leaned over and flipped her over, causing a squeal of delight.

'Mama!' Linette ran over to Madeleine and jumped into her arms. 'I saw a pony and Markiss let me ride her!'

'That is wonderful, sweetling.' Madeleine hugged her daughter for a moment before the child squirmed out of her arms, reaching for Devlin. He squatted down to her level, giving her his total attention, though she told him exactly what she'd told her mother.

Madeleine stared at them, trying to memorise the moment. It was so beautiful, it hurt.

The Marquess regarded her, his expression of concern much like his brother's. 'How do you go on, Miss England?'

She shot him a suspicious glance. 'I suspect you know that is not my name.'

He smiled at her. 'Madeleine, then, if I may?'

His wife took his arm, approval shining in her eyes.

'As you wish, my lord,' Madeleine murmured.

Devlin stood, facing his brother. 'I have asked Madeleine to marry me, Ned.'

'How lovely,' exclaimed Serena.

The Marquess, however, knit his brows.

'I have not accepted, my lord,' Madeleine was quick to add.

'Oh, dear,' said Serena.

Devlin put his arm around Madeleine.

The Marquess pursed his lips. 'It is not a wise course.'

'Oh, nonsense!' Serena broke in. 'It is plain as a pikestaff they are in love with each other.'

'Darling,' Ned said, his voice softening as he turned to his wife, 'there is more to marriage than love.'

'A contract? A business matter? A merging of two fortunes?' Devlin spoke with heat. 'That may have suited you, Ned, but not me. I am a younger son. I will not even reside in England. What can it signify who I marry?'

Ned's cheek twitched. 'This plan of yours to rejoin the army is unconscionable.'

'If it is the only way I may be with Maddy, it is worth it,' Devlin said.

'You will be with no one if you lie dead on some battlefield,' his brother shot back.

Devlin's teeth clenched. 'I love Maddy and I will do anything to stay with her. Loving her is the only thing that matters.'

'You have to stay alive, don't you?'

'Oh, please stop.' Madeleine cried. 'Stop arguing on my account.'

'Oh, pish. Of course love matters,' exclaimed Serena, her

eyes flashing at her husband. 'If you love Devlin, Ned, you ought to simply give him his estate and have done with it.' She placed her hands on her hips. 'More to marriage than love... Nonsense. Ned, you told me you loved me from our first meeting, as I have loved you. It has made all the difference.' She spun around to Madeleine. 'Tell me, Madeleine. Do you love Devlin?'

Madeleine gazed at Devlin. 'I love Devlin more than life itself, but he deserves a better wife than I can be.'

Devlin gave her a returning look of adoration.

Serena smiled at them. She turned to her husband. 'See?'

Ned shook his head. 'What I see is trouble ahead for them.'

'Did you know that Madeleine taught me how to love you, Ned?' Serena persisted. 'I went to Devlin's apartments and begged her to teach me what to do.'

Ned's jaw dropped.

'So, you can place our happiness at her door.' She placed her hand on her stomach. 'We would not have this baby if not for Madeleine.'

Both Madeleine and Devlin gaped in surprise.

A slow smile lit Ned's countenance. He moved toward his wife and took her in his arms, lifting her, and twirling her around. While Madeleine and Devlin watched in astonishment, Ned placed his lips on Serena's and held them there, deepening the kiss until it was clear they had forgotten there were witnesses in the room.

'Mama,' Linette piped up, 'Markiss kiss.'

Serena and Ned broke apart, red-faced.

'Um,' Ned mumbled. 'If you will pardon us...'

As Serena's laughter trilled, Ned took her arm, but paused, turning back to Devlin. 'We'll settle the estate papers and the bank draft later.' He escorted his wife out of the room.

Devlin stared at the door. He turned to Madeleine, amazement on his face. 'You are responsible for that?'

Madeleine felt her face grow hot. 'I told her only what you have taught me about love.'

He walked over to her and gently lifted her chin with his finger. 'I have not yet begun to teach you about love. Marry me. Come live with me at Edgeworth. We shall breed a stable of horses.'

'I cannot.' Her voiced cracked. 'My past.'

His arms encircled her. 'No one will know of your past. Your family will be ruined if they speak of it, and Farley is no longer a threat. No one else knows of you.'

'People will wonder.'

'Then we will give them a fiction to believe.' He held her close against him, her head resting on his chest. 'Perhaps you could become the daughter of a merchant or some such. We could say we secretly married years ago when I was on leave from Spain. Linette would be legitimate, then. How would that suit you?'

She relaxed against the steadiness of his heartbeat. 'Oh, I suppose. It is merely another mask, is it not? But not a shameful one.'

'I will give you the life you deserve.' Devlin took a deep breath and squeezed her tighter. Lifting her face to his, he placed his lips tenderly against hers.

'Deddy kiss!' Linette squealed, running over to them.

Laughing, Devlin and Madeleine lifted her up between them and kissed again.

Epilogue

The two magnificent horses raced over the countryside, neck and neck, clearing every fence and hedge. Their hooves beat the earth like thunder, until at the stone marker on the rise, their riders drew them to a halt.

'I won,' Devlin said. 'Arrived before you this time.'

'Oh, no, indeed,' said his wife. Her apparel gave her the appearance of a slim lad, but the cascade of mahogany-coloured hair down her back belied that impression. 'I won.'

From this high vantage point, Devlin surveyed the fields of his estate, thick and fragrant with hops. He gave silent thanks to his brother. For the first time in Ned's life, he had acted in a way their father would have disapproved. He had given Devlin Edgeworth, and his fortune, as well.

In the centre of this picturesque scene was the house, not as grand as nearby Heronvale, but more precious to Devlin because he shared it with his wife. In the distance Devlin watched their daughter, mounted on a white pony, jumping the low bars set up by Jem, as their best breeding mares grazed nearby. Unseen but also busy at work were his steward, Bart, who managed to recall every niggling task necessary to run the estate, and Sophie who, under much protest, had created Madeleine's unusual riding outfit.

'It is beautiful here,' sighed Madeleine. 'I never hoped for so much happiness.'

He grinned at her. 'Do not be so happy. I won this race, you know.'

She pursed her lips. 'Only because I have been a little tired of late.'

'Tired?' He gazed at her, worry furrowing his brow. 'Maddy, are you unwell? Perhaps you should not be riding today.'

'Not unwell precisely,' she said, turning her steed to make a more sedate way down the hill.

He rode beside her.

She sighed. 'I could not resist one more run. I shall not be free to do so again for some time.'

'What the deuce are you talking about?'

She grinned at him, a mischievous twinkle in her eye. 'I am due to give Linette a brother or sister next summer.'

He pulled his horse to a halt. 'What?'

Madeleine rode back to him. 'I am increasing, husband.'

'Good God! And you are racketing all over the countryside, hell for leather? I ought to throttle you!'

'Not throttle,' she said, coming along beside him, the two horses head-to-tail to each other. The sultry look on her face heated his loins. She smiled and leaned toward him. 'Kiss.'

Devlin Steele did as his wife bid him.

*　*　*　*　*

Chivalrous Captain, Rebel Mistress

DIANE GASTON

To my Uncle Bob, a veteran of World War II,
and my cousin Dick, who served in Vietnam.
They are heroes still.

Prologue

1812—Badajoz, Spain

The heavy footsteps of the marauding mob were close, so close Lieutenant Allan Landon smelled their sweaty bodies and the blood staining their uniforms. Allan and his captain, Gabriel Deane, hid in the shadows as the mob moved past, intent, no doubt, on more plundering, more rape, more slaying of innocent civilians.

Was there anything more loathsome than men gone amok, egging each other on to more violence and destruction?

Fire ravaged a tall stone building and illuminated the rabble from behind. Brandishing clubs and bayonets, they rumbled past Allan, whose muscles were taut with outrage. These were not the enemy, but Allan's own countrymen, British soldiers, lost to all decency, all morality, in the throes of madness.

After the bloody siege of Badajoz, leaving thousands of their comrades dead, a rumour swept through the troops that Wellington had authorised three hours of plunder. It had been like a spark to tinder.

As the marauders disappeared around the corner, Allan and Gabriel Deane stepped back on to the street.

'Wellington should hang them all,' Allan said.

Gabe shook his head. 'Too many of them. We need them to fight the French.'

The loud crack of a pistol firing made them both jump back, but it was too distant to be a threat.

Gabe muttered, 'We're going to get ourselves killed and all for damned Tranville.'

Edwin Tranville.

Edwin's father, Brigadier General Lionel Tranville, had ordered them into this cauldron of violence. His son, who was also his aide-de-camp, was missing, and Allan and Deane were to find him and return him safely to camp.

'We have our orders.' Allan's tone sounded fatalistic even to himself, but, like it or not, his duty was to obey his superior officers. The rioting crowd had forgotten that duty.

Two men burst from an alleyway and ran past them, their boots beating sharply against the stones.

From that alleyway came a woman's cry. *'Non!'*

Women's screams had filled their ears all night, cutting through Allan's gut like a knife, always too distant for Allan and Gabe to aid them. This cry, however, sounded near. They ran towards it, through the alley and into a small courtyard, expecting to rescue a woman in distress.

Instead the woman held a knife, ready to plunge its blade into the back of a whining and cowering red-coated British soldier.

Gabe seized the woman from behind and disarmed her. 'Oh, no, you don't, *señora.*'

The British soldier, bloody hands covering his face, tried to stand. 'She tried to kill me!' he wailed before collapsing in an insensible heap on the cobblestones.

Nearby Allan noticed the body of a French soldier lying in a puddle of blood.

Deane gripped the woman's arms. 'You'll have to come with us, *señora*.'

'Captain—' Allan gestured to the body.

Another British soldier stepped into the light 'Wait.'

Allan whirled, his pistol raised.

The man held up both hands. 'I am Ensign Vernon of the East Essex.' He pointed to the British soldier collapsed face down on the ground. 'He was trying to kill the boy and rape the woman. I saw it. He and two others. The others ran.'

'What boy?' Gabe glanced around.

Something moved in the shadows, and Allan turned and almost fired.

Vernon stopped him. 'Don't shoot. It is the boy.'

Still gripping the woman, Deane dragged her over to the inert figure of the man she'd been ready to kill.

Deane rolled him over with his foot and looked up at Allan. 'Good God, Landon, do you see who this is?'

'Edwin Tranville,' the ensign answered, loathing in his voice. 'General Tranville's son.' Allan grew cold with anger.

They had found Edwin Tranville, not a victim, but an attempted rapist and possibly a murderer. Allan glanced at Ensign Vernon and saw his own revulsion reflected in the man's eyes.

'You jest. What the devil is going on here?' Allan scanned the scene.

The ensign pointed to Edwin, sharing Allan's disdain. 'He tried to choke the boy and she defended him with the knife. He is drunk.'

The boy, no more than twelve years old, ran to the Frenchman's body. *'Papa!'*

'Non, non, non, Claude,' the woman cried.

'Deuce, they are French.' Deane knelt next to the body to check for a pulse. 'He's dead.'

A French family caught in the carnage, Allan surmised, a man merely trying to get his wife and child to safety. Allan turned back to Tranville, tasting bile in his throat. Had Edwin murdered the Frenchman in front of the boy and his mother and then tried to rape the woman?

The woman said, *'Mon mari.'* Her husband.

Gabe suddenly rose and strode back to Tranville. He swung his leg as if to kick him, but stopped himself. Then he pointed to the dead Frenchman and asked the ensign, 'Did Tranville kill him?'

Vernon shook his head. 'I did not see.'

Gabe gazed back at the woman with great concern. 'Deuce. What will happen to her now?' A moment earlier he'd been ready to arrest her.

Footsteps sounded and there were shouts nearby.

Gabe straightened. 'We must get them out of here.' He signalled to Allan. 'Landon, take Tranville back to camp. Ensign, I'll need your help.'

To camp, not to the brig?

Allan stepped over to him. 'You do not intend to turn her in!' It was Edwin who should be turned in.

'Of course not,' Deane snapped. 'I'm going to find her a safe place to stay. Maybe a church. Or somewhere.' He gave both Allan and the ensign pointed looks. 'We say nothing of this. Agreed?'

Say nothing? Allan could not stomach it. 'He ought to hang for this.'

'He is the general's son,' Gabe shot back. 'If we report his crime, the general will have *our* necks, not his son's.' He gazed towards the woman. 'He may even come after her and the boy.' Gabe looked down at Tranville, curled up like a baby on the ground. 'This bastard is so drunk he may not even know what he did.'

'Drink is no excuse.' Allan could not believe Gabe would let Edwin go unpunished.

Allan had learned to look the other way when the soldiers in his company emptied a dead Frenchman's pockets, or gambled away their meagre pay on the roll of dice, or drank themselves into a stupor. These were men from the rookeries of London, the distant hills of Scotland, the poverty of Ireland, but no man, least of all an officer with an education and advantages in life, should get away with what Edwin had done this night. The proper thing to do was report him and let him hang. Damn the consequences.

Allan gazed at the woman comforting her son. His shoulders sagged. Allan was willing to risk his own neck for justice, but had no right to risk an already victimised mother and child.

His jaw flexed. 'Very well. We say nothing.'

Gabe turned to the ensign. 'Do I have your word, Ensign?'

'You do, sir,' he answered.

Glass shattered and the roof of the burning building collapsed, shooting sparks high into the air.

Allan pulled Edwin to a sitting position and hoisted him over his shoulder.

'Take care,' Gabe said to him.

With a curt nod, Allan trudged off in the same direction they had come. He almost hoped to be set upon by the mob if it meant the end of Edwin Tranville, but the streets he walked had been so thoroughly sacked that the mauraders had abandoned them. Allan carried Edwin to the place where the Royal Scots were billeted, the sounds of Badajoz growing fainter with each step.

He reached the general's billet and knocked on the door. The general's batman answered, and the scent of cooked meat filled Allan's nostrils.

'I have him,' Allan said.

The general rose from a chair, a napkin tucked into his shirt collar. 'What is this? What happened to him?'

Allan clenched his jaw before answering, 'He is as we found him.' He dropped Edwin on to a cot in the room and only then saw that his face was cut from his ear to the corner of his mouth.

'He is injured!' His father shouted. He waved to his batman. 'Quick! Summon the surgeon.' He leaned over his drunk son. 'I had no idea he'd been injured in the battle.'

The wound was too fresh to have been from the battle and Allan wagered the general knew it as well.

Edwin Tranville would bear a visible scar of this night, which was at least some punishment for his crimes. Edwin whimpered and rolled over, looking more like a child than a murderer and rapist.

The general paced back and forth. Allan waited, hoping to be dismissed, hoping he would not be required to provide more details.

But the general seemed deep in thought. Suddenly, he stopped pacing and faced Allan. 'He was injured in the siege, I am certain of it. He was not supposed to be in the fighting.' He started pacing again. 'I suppose he could not resist.'

He was convincing himself, Allan thought. 'Sir,' he responded, not really in assent.

The general gave Allan a piercing gaze. 'He was injured in the siege. Do you comprehend me?'

Allan indeed comprehended. This was the story the general expected him to tell. He stood at attention. 'I comprehend, sir.'

A Latin quotation from his school days sprang to mind. Was it from Tacitus? *That cannot be safe which is not honourable.*

Allan shivered with trepidation. No good could come from disguising the true nature of Edwin Tranville's injury or his character, he was certain of it, but he'd given his word to his captain and the fate of too many people rested on his keeping it.

Allan hoped there was at least some honour in that.

Chapter One

June 18th, 1815—Waterloo

Marian Pallant's lungs burned and her legs ached. She ran as if the devil himself were at her heels.

Perhaps he was, if the devil was named Napoleon Bonaparte. Napoleon had escaped from Elba and was again on the march, heading straight for Waterloo and a clash with Wellington's army, and Marian was in the middle of it.

Already she heard the random cracking of musket fire behind her and the sound of thousands of boots pounding into the muddy ground to the drum beat of the French *pas de charge*. Somewhere ahead were the British.

She hoped.

The muddy fingers of the earth, still soaked from the night's torrential rains, grabbed at her half-boots. The field's tall rye whipped at her hands and legs. She glimpsed a farm in the distance and ran towards it. If nothing else, perhaps she could hide there.

Only three days earlier she and Domina had been dancing at the Duchess of Richmond's ball when Wellington arrived with news that Napoleon's army was making its way to Brussels. The officers made haste to leave, but, during a tearful goodbye, Domina had learned from her *most passionate love,* Lieutenant Harry Oliver, that, unless the Allies were victorious at a place called Quatre Bras, the Duke expected to defend Brussels near Waterloo. Domina spent two days begging Marian to come with her to find Ollie's regiment. Domina was determined to see the battle and be nearby in case Ollie needed her.

Finally Marian relented, but only to keep Domina from making the journey alone. Marian thought of them dressing in Domina's brother's clothes so it would not be so obvious they were two women alone. They'd ridden together on Domina's brother's horse for hours and hours in darkness and pouring rain, hopelessly lost until they finally heard men's voices.

Speaking French.

Domina had panicked, kicking the horse into a gallop so frenzied that Marian flew off and hit the ground hard, the breath knocked out of her. Afraid to shout lest the French hear her, Marian watched Domina and the horse disappear into the rainy night. She huddled against a nearby tree in the darkness and pouring rain, hoping for Domina to return.

She never did.

Marian spent the night full of fear that Domina had been captured by the French. What would French soldiers do to an English girl? But when daylight came, she shoved worries about Domina from her mind. The French columns had started to march directly towards her.

The farm was her only chance for safety.

A wooded area partially surrounded the farm buildings, and Marian had to cross a field of fragrant rye to reach it. The crop would certainly be ruined when the soldiers trampled on it, but for now the tall grass hid her from Napoleon's army.

Still, she heard them, coming closer.

Her foot caught in a hole and she fell. For a moment she lay there, her cheek against the cool wet earth, too tired to move, but suddenly the ground vibrated with the unmistakable pounding of a horse's hooves.

Domina?

She struggled to her feet.

Too late. The huffing steed, too large to be Domina's, thundered directly for her. Her boots slipped in the mud as she tried to jump aside. She threw her arms over her face and prepared to be trampled.

Instead a strong hand seized her coat collar and hoisted her up on to the saddle as if she weighed nothing more than a mere satchel.

'Here, boy. What are you doing in this field?' An English voice.

Thank God.

She opened her eyes and caught a glimpse of a red uniform. 'I want to go to that farm.' She pointed towards the group of buildings surrounded by a wall.

'You're English?' He slowed his horse. 'I am headed there. To Hougoumont.'

Was that the name of the farm? Marian did not care. She was grateful to be off her weary feet and to be with a British soldier and not a French one.

The horse quickly reached the patch of woods whose green leaves sprinkled them with leftover raindrops. A low branch snagged Marian's cap, snatching it from her head, and her blonde hair tumbled down her back.

'Good God. You're a woman.' He pulled on the reins and his horse turned round in a circle. 'What the devil are you doing here?'

Marian turned to get a proper look at him. Her eyes widened. She'd seen him before. She and Domina had whispered about the tall and handsome officer they'd spied during a stroll through the Parc of Brussels. His angular face looked strong, his bow-shaped lips firm and decisive, his eyes a piercing hazel.

'I am lost,' she said.

'Do you not know there is about to be a battle?'

She did not wish to debate the matter. 'I was trying to reach somewhere safe.'

'Nowhere is safe,' he snapped. Instead of turning towards the farm, he rode back to where her cap hung on the tree branch, looking as if it had been placed on a peg by the garden door. He snatched it and thrust it into her hands. 'Put the cap back on. Do not let on that you are a woman.'

Did he think she was doltish? She repinned her hair as best she could and covered it with the cap. Behind them came the sounds of men entering the wood. A musketball whizzed past Marian's ear.

'Skirmishers.' The officer set his horse into a gallop so swift the trees suddenly became a blur of brown and green.

They reached Hougoumont gate. 'Captain Landon with a message for Colonel MacDonnell,' he announced.

Marian made a mental note of his name. *Captain Landon.*

The gate opened. 'There are skirmishers in the wood,' he told the men.

'We see them!' one soldier responded, gesturing to a wall where other men were preparing to fire through loopholes. A company of soldiers filed past them out of the gate, undoubtedly to engage the French in the wood.

The soldier took hold of Captain Landon's horse and pointed. 'That's the colonel over there.'

The colonel paced through the yard, watching the men and barking orders. Some of them wore the red coats of the British; others wore a green foreign uniform.

'Stay with me,' Captain Landon told her.

He dismounted and reached up to help her off the horse. Then he gripped her arm as if afraid she might run off and held on to her even when handing the message to the colonel and waiting for him to read it.

The colonel closed the note. 'I want you to wait here a bit

until we see what these Frenchies are up to. Then I'll send back my response.' He pointed to Marian. 'Who's the boy?'

'An English lad caught in the thick of things.' Landon squeezed Marian's arm, a warning, she presumed, to go along with his story.

MacDonnell looked at her suspiciously. 'Are you with the army, boy?'

Marian made her voice low. 'No, sir. From Brussels. I wanted to see the battle.'

The colonel laughed. 'Well, you will see a battle, all right. What's your name?'

Marian's mind whirled, trying to think of a name she might remember to answer to. 'Fenton,' she finally said. 'Marion Fenton.' Her given name could be for a boy, and Fenton was Domina's surname. If anything happened to her, God forbid, perhaps Domina's family would be alerted. No one else knew she'd come to Brussels.

Captain Landon said, 'I'll come back to fetch him after the battle and see he is returned to his family. Where should I put him in the meantime?'

The colonel inclined his head towards the large brick house. 'The château should do. Find him a corner to sit in.'

The captain marched Marian into the château. Green uniformed soldiers filled the hall and adjacent rooms, some gazing out of the windows.

'Why are they in green?' she whispered.

The captain answered, 'They are German. Nassauers.'

The soldiers looked frightened. Marian thought them very young, mere boys, certainly younger than she at nearly twenty-one.

'English boy,' the captain told them, pointing to her. 'English.'

An officer approached them. 'I speak English.'

Captain Landon turned to him. 'This boy is lost. He needs a safe place to stay during the battle.'

'Any room,' replied the officer, his accent heavy. 'Avay from vindow.'

The captain nodded. 'Would you tell your men sh—he's English.'

The officer nodded and spoke to his troops in his Germanic tongue.

Captain Landon led Marian away. They walked through the house, searching, she supposed, for a room without a window.

'I can find my own hiding place, Captain,' she said. 'You must return to your duties.'

'I need to talk to you first.' His voice was low and angry.

She supposed she was in for more scolding. She deserved it, after all.

They walked through a hallway into what must have been a formal drawing room, although its furniture was covered in white cloth.

Captain Landon finally removed his grip and uncovered a small chair, carrying it back to the hallway. 'You will be safest here, I think.' He gave her a fierce look and gestured for her to sit.

She was more than happy to sit. Her legs ached and her feet felt raw from running in wet boots.

He looked down on her, his elbows akimbo. 'Now. Who are you and what the devil are you doing in the middle of a battlefield?'

She met his gaze with defiance. 'I did not intend to be in the middle of the battlefield.'

He merely glared, as if waiting for a better answer.

She took off her cap and plucked the pins from her hair. 'I am Miss Marian Pallant—'

'Not Fenton?' He sounded confused.

She could not blame him. She quickly put her hair in a plait while his eyes bore into her.

'I gave that name in case—in case something happened

to me. I was with my friend Domina Fenton, but we became separated in the night.'

'Your friend was with you? What could have brought you out here?' he demanded.

She pinned the plait to the top of her head. 'Domina is Sir Roger Fenton's daughter. She is secretly betrothed to one of the officers and she wanted to be near him during the battle.' It sounded so foolish now. 'I was afraid for her to come alone.'

His eyes widened. 'You are respectable young ladies?'

She did not like the tone of surprise in his voice. 'Of course we are.'

He pursed his lips. 'Respectable young ladies do not dress up as boys and ride out in the middle of the night.'

She covered her hair again with her cap. 'Dressing as boys was preferable to showing ourselves as women.'

He rubbed his face. 'I dare say you are correct in that matter.'

She glanced away. 'I am so worried about Domina.' Turning back, she gestured dismissively. 'I quite agree with you that it was a foolish idea. We became lost, and our horse almost wandered into a French camp. I fell off when we galloped away.' Her stomach twisted in worry. 'I do not know what happened to Domina.'

He gazed at her a long time with those intense hazel eyes. Finally he said, 'Surely your parents and Domina's must be very worried about you by now.'

She gave a wan smile. 'My parents died a long time ago.'

Allan Landon took in a quick breath as his gaze rested upon her. At this moment Marian Pallant looked nothing like a boy. He could only see a vulnerable and beautiful young woman. Even though her wealth of blonde hair was now hidden, he could not forget the brief moment the locks had framed her face like a golden halo.

'Your parents are dead?' he asked inanely.

She nodded. 'They died of fever in India when I was nine.'

He noticed her voice catch, even though she was obviously trying to disguise any emotion. It reminded him anew that she was a vulnerable young woman, one trying valiantly to keep her wits about her.

'Is Sir Roger Fenton your guardian, then?' he asked.

'No.' She glanced away. 'My guardian does not trouble himself about me overmuch. He leaves my care to his man of business, who knew I was a guest of the Fentons, so I suppose you could say, at the moment, I am in Domina's father's charge.' Her worried look returned. 'I should have talked Domina out of this silly scheme instead of accompanying her. I am so afraid for her.'

She seemed more concerned for her friend than for herself. He could give no reassurance, however. The French were not known to be gentle with captives, especially female ones—although Allan well remembered one instance when British soldiers were as brutal.

'I suspect the Fentons are frantic over the fate of both of you, then.'

She nodded, looking contrite.

He felt a wave of sympathy for her, even though she'd brought this on herself with her reckless behaviour.

Again her blue eyes sought his. 'Do you have anyone frantic over your fate, Captain?'

Odd that his thoughts skipped over his mother and older brother at home on the family estate in Nottinghamshire and went directly to his father, who had been so proud to have a son in uniform and who would have cheered his son's success, his advance from lieutenant to captain and other battle commendations.

His father had been gone these four years, his life violently snatched away. He had not lived to celebrate his son's victories in battle, to lament the horrors he'd endured, nor to shudder at the times he'd narrowly escaped death himself.

Miss Pallant's brows rose. 'Is it so difficult to think of someone who might worry over you?'

He cocked his head. 'My mother and brother would worry, I suppose.'

She gave him a quizzical look, making him wonder if his grief over his father's death showed too clearly in his eyes. It was his turn to shutter his emotions.

She glanced away again. 'It must be hard for them.'

Was it hard on them? he wondered. He'd always imagined they were used to him being far away. He'd been gone longer than his father.

A German voice shouted what could only have been an order. The tramping of feet and cacophony of men's voices suggested to Allan that the French must be closing in on the farm.

'What does it mean?' she asked, her voice breathless.

He tried to appease her alarm. 'I suspect the Nassauers have been ordered out of the château. That is all.'

Her eyes flashed like a cornered fox. 'That does not sound good. I wish I had stayed in Brussels.' Her expression turned ironical. 'It is too late to be remorseful, is it not?'

'My father used to say it is better to do what one is supposed to do now than to be remorseful later.'

She kept her eyes upon him, and he realised he had brought up the subject he most wanted to avoid.

'A wise man,' she said.

'He was.' The pain of his father's loss struck him anew.

She regarded him with sympathy. 'He is deceased?'

'He was killed.' He cleared his throat. 'You heard, no doubt, of the Luddite riots in Nottinghamshire a few years ago?'

She nodded.

'My father was the local magistrate. The rioters broke into our house and killed him.'

Her expression seemed to mirror his pain. 'How terrible for you.'

Suddenly muskets cracked and shouts were raised, the sounds of a siege.

She paled. 'The French are attacking?'

He paced. 'Yes. And I must go.' He hated to leave her. 'Stay here, out of the way. You'll be safe. I'll come back for you after the battle. With any luck I can see you returned to Brussels. Perhaps news of this escapade will not spread and your reputation will be preserved.'

'My reputation.' She gave a dry laugh. 'What a trifle it seems now.' She gazed at him with a new intensity. 'You will take care, Captain?'

Allan thought he would carry the impact of her glittering blue eyes throughout the battle. 'Do not worry over me.'

More muskets cracked.

He turned in the sound's direction. 'I must hurry.'

'Yes, you must, Captain.' She put on a brave smile.

'I'll be back for you,' he vowed, as much for himself as for her.

She extended her hand and he wrapped his fingers around it for a brief moment.

'Godspeed,' she whispered.

Allan forced himself to leave her alone in the hallway. He retraced their steps through the house, angry that her foolish act placed her in such danger, and angrier still that he could not extricate her from it.

He had his duty, his orders. Orders must be obeyed.

Allan's duty was to be Generals Tranville and Picton's messenger during the battle. He was paired with Edwin Tranville, the general's son, and both were given the same messages to carry so that if one was shot down, the other might still make it through. Unfortunately, right after the first message was placed in their hands, Edwin disappeared, hiding no doubt.

Edwin had hid from battle countless times on the Peninsula. Afterward he would emerge with some plausible explanation of his whereabouts. This time, however, his cowardice meant that Allan alone must ensure Tranville and Picton's messages made it through.

The outcome of the battle could depend upon it.

So he had no choice. He had to leave Miss Pallant here at Hougoumont, which could well become the most dangerous place in the entire battle. The French would need to attack the farm to reach Wellington's right flank, and Wellington ordered Hougoumont held at all costs.

Allan reached the entrance of the château, Miss Pallant's clear blue eyes still haunting him. The mixture of courage and vulnerability within her pulled at his sensibilities, making him ache to stay to protect her.

But the soldier in him had orders to be elsewhere.

This was more blame to lay at Edwin's feet. If Edwin possessed even half of Miss Pallant's courage, Allan could trust him to carry the generals' messages, and seek permission to take her back to Brussels.

Outside the château Allan stopped one of the Coldstream Guardsmen, the British regiment defending Hougoumont. 'What is the situation?'

'Our men have been driven back from the wood. The enemy is close by.'

Allan ran to the wall and looked through a loophole while an infantryman reloaded.

The woods below teemed with the blue coats of the French, their cream trousers brown with mud. As they broke into the open, British soldiers, firing from the walls, mowed them down. Their bodies littered the grass.

Allan searched for Colonel MacDonnell and found him inside the farmhouse at an upper window that provided a good view of the fighting.

MacDonnell said, 'You'd better wait a bit, Landon.'

'I agree, sir.'

The sheer number of Frenchmen coming at the walls and falling from the musket fire was staggering. The enemy regiment was one commanded by Prince Jerome, Napoleon's brother, but the walls of the farm offered good protection. The French had no such advantage.

Allan turned to MacDonnell again. 'May I be of service in some way?'

The colonel looked proud. 'My men are doing all I could wish. I have no need of you.'

Allan could not merely sit around and watch. He returned to the yard and searched for any weakness in the defence. One soldier was shot in the forehead, the force of the ball throwing him back on to the ground. French ladders appeared at the gap created by the man's loss.

Allan seized the man's musket, powder and ammunition and took his place at the wall, firing through the loophole until the ladders and the men trying to climb them fell upon the ground already filled with dead and wounded.

'Look!' cried one of the guardsmen nearby. 'The captain knows how to load and fire a musket!'

Other guardsmen laughed, but soon forgot about him as another wave of blue-coated soldiers tried to reach the walls.

Allan lost track of time, so caught was he in the rhythm of loading and firing. Eventually the shots around him slowed.

'They are retreating!' a man cried.

The French were withdrawing, like a wave ebbing from the shore.

Allan put down the musket and left his place at the wall. He met MacDonnell near the stable.

'Get word to Wellington that we repelled the first attack, but if they keep coming we'll need more ammunition,' Mac-Donnell told him.

One of the soldiers brought out his horse and Allan mounted the steed. 'I'll get your message through.' He didn't know how to say what he most wanted MacDonnell to know. 'The boy is in the château, but have someone look out for him, will you?'

MacDonnell nodded, but one of his officers called him away at the same time.

Allan had to ride off without any assurance that MacDonnell would even remember the presence of the boy Miss Pallant pretended to be.

Chapter Two

The shouts of the soldiers and the crack of musket fire signalled a new attack. Marian's eyes flew open and she shook off the haze of sleep. Her exhaustion had overtaken her during the lull in fighting.

Now it was clear the French were attacking the farm again. The sounds were even louder and more alarming than before. So were the screams of the wounded horses and men.

She hugged her knees to her chest as the barrage continued. Had the captain made it through? With every shot in the first attack, she'd feared he'd been struck and now her fears for him were renewed. One thing she knew for certain. He was gone—either gone back to the British line or just...gone.

She cried out in frustration.

He must survive. To think that he would not just plunged her into more despair.

The hallway suddenly felt like a prison. Its walls might wrap her in relative safety, but each urgent shout, each agonised scream, cut into her like a sword thrust. To hear, but not see, the events made everything worse. She hated feeling alone and useless while men were dying.

She stood and paced.

This was absurd. Surely there was something she could do to assist. She'd promised Captain Landon that she would stay in the hallway, but he was not present to stop her, was he?

Marian left where the captain had placed her and made her way to the entrance hall.

The green-uniformed soldiers were gone, but several of the Coldstream Guards rushed past her. The sounds of the siege intensified now that she'd emerged from her cocoon of a hiding place.

The château's main door swung open and two men carried another man inside. Blood poured from a wound in his chest.

She rushed forwards. 'I can help. Tell me what to do.' She forgot to make her voice low.

They did not seem to notice. 'No help for this one, laddie,' one answered in a thick Scottish accent. They dumped the injured soldier in a corner and rushed out again.

Marian looked around her. Several wounded men leaned against the walls of the hall. The marble floor was smeared with their blood.

Her stomach rebelled at the sight.

She held her breath for a moment, determined not to be sick. 'I must do something,' she cried.

One of the men, blood oozing through the fingers he held against his arm, answered her. 'Find us some bandages, lad.'

Bandages. Where would she find bandages?

She ran back to the drawing room where the captain had found the chair for her. Pulling the covers off the furniture, she gathered as much of the white cloth as she could carry in her arms. She returned to the hall and dumped the cloth in a pile next to the man clutching his bleeding arm.

'I need a knife,' she said to him.

He shook his head, wincing in pain.

Another man whose face was covered in blood fumbled

through his coat. 'Here you go, lad.' He held out a small penknife.

Marian took the knife, still sticky with his blood, and used it to start a rent in the cloth so she could rip it into strips. She worked as quickly as she could, well aware that the man the soldiers had carried in was still moaning and coughing. Most of the other men suffered silently.

She knew nothing about tending to the injured. It stood to reason, though, that bleeding wounds needed to be bandaged, as the wounded soldier had suggested.

Marian grabbed a fistful of the strips of cloth and turned to him. 'I'll tend that other man first, then you, sir.' She gestured to the moaning man who'd been so swiftly left to die. 'And you,' she told the man who'd given her the knife.

'Do that, lad. I'm not so bad off.' His voice was taut with pain.

Marian touched his arm in sympathy and started for the gravely wounded soldier.

Her courage flagged as she reached him. Never had she seen such grievous injuries. Steeling herself, she gripped the bandages and forced herself to kneel at his side.

He was so young! Not much older than Domina's brother. Blood gurgled from a hole in his abdomen. Her hand trembling, she used some of the cloth to sponge it away. The dark pink of his innards became visible, and Marian recoiled, thinking she would surely be sick.

He seized her arm, gripping her hard. 'My mum,' he rasped. 'My mum.' His glassy eyes regarded her with alarm, and his breathing rattled like a rusty gate. 'My mum.'

She clasped his other hand, tears stinging her eyes. 'Your mum will be so proud of you.' It was not enough to say, not when this young man would die without ever seeing his mother again.

The young man's eyes widened and he rose up, still gripping her. With one deep breath he collapsed and air slowly left his lungs as his eyes turned blank.

'No,' she cried. The faces of her mother and father when death had taken them flashed before her. 'No.'

The room turned black and sound echoed. She was going to faint and the dead young man's hand was still in hers.

The door opened and two more men staggered in. She forced her eyes open and took several deep breaths.

More wounds. More blood. More men in need.

She released the young soldier's hand and gingerly closed his eyes. 'God keep you,' she whispered.

Marian grabbed her clean cloth and returned to the man who had told her to get bandages. 'You are next,' she said with a bravado she didn't feel inside.

He gestured to the soldier who had given her the knife. 'Tend him first.'

She nodded and kneeled on the floor, wiping away the blood on the soldier's head so she could see the wound. His skin was split right above his hairline. Swallowing hard, Marian pressed the wound closed with her fingers and wrapped a bandage tightly around his head.

'Thank you, lad,' the man said.

She moved to the first man and wrapped his wounded arm. Not taking time to think, she scuttled over to the next man, discovering yet another horrifying sight. She took a deep breath and tended that man's wound as well. One by one she dressed all the soldiers' wounds.

When she'd finished, one of the soldiers caught her arm. 'Can y'fetch us some water, lad?'

Water. Of course. They must be very thirsty. She was thirsty, as a matter of fact. She went in search of the kitchen, but found its pump dry. There was a well in the middle of the courtyard, near the stables, she remembered. She found a fairly clean bucket and ladle on the kitchen shelf and hurried back to the hall.

'I'll bring you water,' she told the wounded men as she crossed the room to the château's entrance.

When she stepped outside, the courtyard was filled with

soldiers. Men at the walls fired and reloaded their muskets, others repositioned themselves or moved the wounded away. The fighting was right outside the gate. She could hear it. French musket balls might find their way into the courtyard, she feared.

Gathering all her courage, Marian started for the well. Before she reached it, a man shouted, 'They're coming in the gate!'

To her horror a huge French soldier, wielding an ax, hewed his way into the courtyard followed by others. It was a frightening sight as they hacked their way toward the château. Several Guardsmen set upon them. The huge Frenchman was knocked to the ground, and one of the Guards plunged a bayonet into his back.

'Close the gate! Close the gate!'

Men pushed against the wooden gate as more French soldiers strained to get in. Without thinking, Marian dropped her bucket and added her slight strength to the effort to force the gates closed. Finally they secured it, but the fighting was still fierce between the British soldiers and the few Frenchmen who had made it inside.

Marian picked her way through the fighting and returned to the well. She pumped water into the bucket, her heart pounding at the carnage around her. When the bucket was full, one of the Guardsmen shoved a boy towards her, a French drummer boy, his drum still strapped to his chest.

'Take him,' the Guardsman said. 'Keep him out of harm's way.'

She took the boy's hand and pulled him back to the château with her.

'*Restez ici,*' she ordered. *Remain here.*

The drummer boy sat immediately, hugging his drum, his eyes as huge as saucers.

Marian passed the water to the men and told them about the gate closing and about the drummer boy. A moment later, more men entered the château, needing tending.

Eventually the musket fire became sporadic, and she heard a man shout, 'They're retreating.'

She paused for a moment in thankful relief.

'It is not over yet, lad,' one of the wounded men told her. 'D'you hear the guns?' The pounding of artillery had started an hour ago. 'We're not rid of Boney yet. I wager you could see what is happening on the battlefield from the upper floors.'

'Do you think so?' Marian responded.

'Go. Take a look-see.' The man gestured to the stairway. 'I'll watch the drummer.'

She could not resist. She climbed the stairs to the highest floor. In each of the rooms Guardsmen manned the windows. One soldier turned towards her when Marian peeked into the room.

'Where did you come from, lad?' the man asked.

She remembered to lower her voice this time. 'Brussels, sir. I came to see the battle.'

He laughed and gestured for her to approach. 'Well, come see, then.'

The sight was terrifying. On one side thousands of French soldiers marched twenty-four-men deep and one hundred and fifty wide. The rhythmic beating of the French *pas de charge* wafted up to the château's top windows. On the Allied Army side a regiment of Belgian soldiers fled the field. In between a red-coated soldier galloped across the ridge in full view of the French columns. Was it Captain Landon? Her throat constricted in anxiety.

Please let him be safe, she prayed.

'Where are the English?' There were no other soldiers in sight. Just the lone rider she imagined to be the captain.

'Wellington's got 'em hiding, I expect.' The soldier pointed out of the window. 'See those hedges?'

She nodded.

'Our boys are behind there, I'd wager.'

As the columns moved by the hedge, the crack of firearms could be heard. 'Rifles,' the soldier explained.

The columns edged away from the rifle fire and lost their formation. Suddenly a line of English soldiers rose up and fired upon them. Countless French soldiers fell as if they were in a game of skittles, but still others advanced until meeting the British line. The two sides began fighting hand to hand.

Marian turned away from the sight. 'Napoleon has too many men.'

'The Cuirassiers are coming.' Anxiety sounded in the soldier's voice. Cuirassiers were the French cavalry.

Marian felt like weeping, but she turned to watch the Cuirassiers on their powerful horses charging toward the English soldiers while the French drums still beat, over and over.

A battle was not glorious to watch, she thought, closing her eyes again. It was all about men wounded and men dying, not at all what she and Domina had imagined.

'They're breaking!' the soldier said.

Marian could not bear to see her countrymen running away like the French had run from Hougoumont. Her chin trembled and her throat constricted with unspent tears.

'I'll be damned.' The soldier whistled. 'If that is not a sight.'

Marian opened her eyes.

The French, not the British, had broken from their lines and were running away. 'I don't understand. Why did they run?'

'Who can tell?' The soldier laughed. 'Let's be grateful they did.'

She was indeed grateful, but by now she knew not to ask if the battle was over. The French would try again and Napoleon was known to pull victory from the jaws of defeat.

Marian took a breath and mentally braced herself for whatever came next.

Allan rode the ridge. After taking MacDonnell's message to Wellington, he searched for Picton, who seemed nowhere to be found. He'd settle for Tranville, then, for new orders.

From the distance he'd seen the second siege of Hougoumont and gave a cheer when the French had again been repelled.

He reached his regiment, the Royal Scots, just as the French attacked. Artillery pummelled the French columns, but still men in the front ranks fought hard in hand-to-hand combat. Allan unsheathed his sword and rode into the thick of it.

The fighting was fierce and bloody. Fists flew and bayonets jabbed and the air filled with the thud of bodies slamming into each other, of grunts and growls and cries of pain. Allan slashed at the French soldiers, more than once slicing into their flesh as they were about to kill. They came at him, trying to pull him from his horse. He managed to keep both his horse and himself in one piece, but blood and mud splattered on to his clothing. By the time the French retreated his arm was leaden with fatigue, and he breathed hard from the effort of the battle.

For a mere moment he indulged in the relief of still being alive, but only for a moment. He quickly resumed his search for Picton and Tranville, but spied Gabriel Deane instead. He headed towards his friend. Gabe, too, would have fought without heed to his own survival and Allan said a silent prayer of thanks that he appeared unscathed. General Tranville had been always been unfair to Gabe, denying him promotion because Gabe's father was in trade.

'Gabe!' he called. 'Have you seen Picton?'

Gabe rode up to him. 'Picton is dead. Shot right after he gave the order to attack.'

Allan bowed his head. 'I am sorry to hear of it.' The eccentric old soldier might have retired after this. 'Where is Tranville, then?'

'Struck down as well,' Gabe answered.

'Dead?' Allan would not so strongly grieve if Tranville was lost.

Gabe shook his head. 'I do not know. I saw him fall and I've not seen him since.'

Orders came for the cavalry to advance upon the retreating

French. Allan and Gabe grew silent as they watched the Scots Greys ride out, like magnificent waves of the ocean on their great grey horses.

'Perhaps we will win this after all,' Gabe said.

They *must* win, Allan thought as they watched the cavalry pursue the French all the way to the line of their artillery. The Allies were on the side of all that was right. Napoleon had broken the peace, and too many men had already died to feed his vanity.

Gabe struck Allan on the arm and pointed to where French lancers approached from the side. 'This cannot be good.'

'Sound the retreat!' Wellington's order carried all the way to Allan and Gabe's ears.

The bugler played the staccato rhythm that signalled an order to retreat, but it was too late. The cavalry were too far away to hear and too caught up in the excitement of routing the French infantry.

Allan and Gabe watched in horror as those gallant men were cut down by the lancers, whose fresh steeds outmatched the British cavalry's blown ones.

'Perhaps I spoke too soon of victory.' Gabe's voice turned low. He rode off to prepare his men for whatever came next.

Allan asked several other soldiers if they had seen Tranville. No one could confirm his death or his survival. He found the officer who had assumed Picton's command.

'I have messengers aplenty, Landon,' the man said. 'Make yourself useful wherever you see fit.'

Allan glanced towards Hougoumont, now being pounded by cannon fire. Dare he go there? See to the safety of one foolish woman over the needs of the many? He frowned. Cannon fire made Hougoumont even more dangerous, but perhaps if she stayed put as he'd asked she'd stay safe.

The cannon were also firing upon the infantry, and Wellington ordered them to move back behind the ridge and to lie down. Allan spied a whole regiment of Belgian troops deserting the field.

The cowards. Could they not see? The battle was far from over. Victory was still possible. The British had already captured thousands of French soldiers and were marching them toward Brussels.

Allan turned back again to Hougoumont, still being battered relentlessly.

Heading to the château became instantly impossible. A shout passed quickly through the ranks. 'Form square! Form square!'

A battalion of men stood two to four ranks deep, forming the shape of a square and presenting bayonets. Cavalry horses would not charge into bayonets, so, as long as the square did not break in panic, cavalry were powerless against them.

Allan rode to the crest of the ridge to see what prompted the order. Masses of French soldiers rode towards him, their horses shoulder to shoulder, advancing at a steadily increasing pace.

What was Napoleon thinking? There was no infantry marching in support of the cavalry. This was insanity.

But it was very real. The French advance was so massive, it shook the ground like thunder. The vision of a thousand horses and men was as awe inspiring as it was foolish. Allan stood rapt at the sight. He almost waited too late to gallop to the nearest square.

The square opened like a hinged door to allow him inside.

Another officer rode up to him. 'Captain Landon, good to see you in one piece.'

It was Lieutenant Vernon, whom he'd first met that ill-fated day at Badajoz. Vernon had been a mere ensign then. He had also been in the fighting at Quatre Bras two days ago. Gabe and Allan had run into him afterwards.

'Same to you, Vernon,' Allan said.

The roar of the French cavalry grew louder and shouts of *'Vive l'Empereur!'* reached their ears. A moment later the plumes of the Cuirassier helmets became visible at the crest of the ridge.

'Prepare to receive cavalry,' the British officers shouted.

Horses and riders poured over the crest, some slipping in the mud or falling into the ditch below, but countless numbers of them galloped straight for the squares. The men in the front line crouched with bayonets thrust forwards; the back line stood ready to fire a volley.

All depended upon the men remaining steady in the face of the massed charge.

Allan rode to one side of the square. 'Steady, men,' he told them. 'They cannot break you. Steady.'

The riders might have been willing to ride into the square, but the horses balked at the sight of the bayonets pointed towards them. They turned and galloped past, the men on their backs only able to fire a single pistol shot each.

The British infantry raked them with a barrage of musket fire, and the British cannon fire was unceasing. Smoke was everywhere, and through it the cries of wounded men.

Finally the cavalry retreated, but it was a short respite. They reformed and attacked again.

The squares held.

After the second attack, Allan left the square to ride to the ridge to reconnoitre. His attention riveted not on the French cavalry regrouping, but on Hougoumont.

The château at Hougoumont was on fire, the château he'd forbidden Miss Pallant to leave.

He immediately urged his horse into full gallop, risking interception from the French. He was hell-bent on reaching Hougoumont, praying he had not forced Miss Pallant into a nightmare from which she could not escape.

The gate did not open to him, even though there were only a few Frenchmen firing at the men on the walls.

'How can I get in?' he called as soon as he was close enough.

One of the soldiers pointed to another entrance, well protected by muskets.

He rode into heat and smoke. The barn was afire as well as the château and some soldiers had run in to pull the horses to safety. One of the animals broke free and ran back into the fire.

Allan tied his horse to a post and went to the door of the château, sure that during the rigours of battle the *boy* he'd brought there would have been forgotten. He prayed the fire had not yet consumed the hallway.

As he reached the door, he almost collided with someone dragging a man out. Someone dressed in boy's clothes.

'Miss Pallant!' he cried, forgetting her disguise.

She glanced at him as she struggled to get the man, too injured and weak to walk, out of the door, away from the fire. 'Help me, Captain.'

He took one of the man's arms and pulled him outside to the middle of the courtyard. As soon as she let go of the man, she started for the château's entrance again.

He caught her arm. 'What are you doing?'

She wrenched it away. 'There are more men in there.' She dashed inside again.

Allan followed her straight into an inferno. She ran to a corner and pulled a man by the collar of his coat, sliding him across the hall. Allan glanced up. The fire swirled above them and pieces of ceiling fell, one narrowly missing her. She paid no heed. Allan hurried through and found another man trying to crawl away from the flames. He flung the man over his shoulder and helped pull Miss Pallant's soldier at the same time. 'Hurry!' he cried. 'Now!'

They made it out of the door just as the ceiling collapsed.

'No!' She turned and tried to rush back in.

Still holding the wounded man, he caught her arm. 'You cannot go in there.' He gripped her hard. 'Now get the man you have saved to the courtyard.'

She nodded and pulled her charge away from the burning building, while the agonised screams of the trapped men pierced Allan's very soul. As soon as he lowered his injured soldier to the ground near the other men she had saved, Miss Pallant ran towards the château again. He tore after her, catching her around the waist before she charged into the inferno.

She struggled. 'There are men in there. Can't you hear them?'

He held her tight, his mouth by her ear. 'I hear them, but there is nothing we can do to save them.'

She twisted around and buried her face into his chest, only to pull away again. 'The little boy! The drummer boy! Is he still in there?'

One of the men on the ground answered her, 'He escaped, lad. I saw him. He's unharmed.'

Allan pulled her back into his arms and she collapsed against him.

'How many did you pull out of there?' he asked her.

'Only seven.' Her voice cracked.

Seven men? How had she mustered the strength? The courage? 'Those seven men are alive because of you.'

She shook her head. 'It was not enough. There are more.'

'They are gone.' He backed her away from the château where the flames were so close and hot that he feared they would combust like the château's walls. 'Come take some water.'

The well was busy with men drawing water to fight the fire and Allan had to wait to draw water to drink. She cupped her hands and scooped water from the well's bucket. Allan drank as well. One of the soldiers held out his shako and Allan filled it, passing it around to the rescued men. Allan's horse, tethered nearby, pulled at its reins, its eyes white with fear.

While the fire raged the French infantry attacked Hougoumont again. Colonel MacDonnell shouted orders to the men at the walls to keep firing. He and his officers moved through the area alert for weaknesses, ordering them reinforced.

Allan sat Miss Pallant on the ground, forcing her to rest. He lowered himself beside her.

'Will it never end?' she whispered, echoing Allan's own thoughts. As the sounds of the siege surrounded them, she glanced at him as if noticing him for the first time. 'Why are you here, Captain? You said you would come when it was over.'

He rubbed his face. 'No one had need of me. General Picton is dead and Tranville, too, most likely—'

Her eyes widened in surprise. 'Tranville!'

'General Lord Tranville. My superior officer.' What did she know of Tranville?

'Surely he did not return to the army?' Her voice rose.

'Are you acquainted with him?'

She pressed her hand against her forehead. 'He is my late aunt's husband. And my guardian.'

'Your guardian!'

'I—I have had no direct contact with him since my aunt died.' She averted her gaze. 'I never imagined he would return to the army, not since he inherited his title.'

Tranville had become a baron before the Allies left Spain. Both he and his son Edwin returned to England then and did not rejoin the regiment until Napoleon escaped from Elba a few months ago.

She bowed her head. 'He is dead?'

Allan put his hand on hers in sympathy. 'It appears so. Several of his men saw him struck down. No one has seen him since.'

She paused before speaking. 'You must know my cousin Edwin. Is—is he still alive?'

Of course Edwin was alive, safely hiding out of harm's way. 'I suspect he is. I've not heard otherwise.'

She put on a brave face, but clearly she was battling her

emotions. 'Well. I have rested enough. I must see if the wounded need attending.' She rose.

Allan rose with her and gripped her arm. 'No. It has become too dangerous for you here.'

The buildings still burned, but the Coldstream Guards, the Nassauers and the others had again set the French into retreat. How many more times could the French be repelled, though?

'I'm getting you out now.' Allan's duty was clear to him now. The army did not immediately need him, but this woman, the ward of his superior officer, did.

'But the wounded—' she protested.

'You've saved them. You have done enough.' Besides, he did not know how much more she could stand. She looked as if she might keel over from exhaustion at any moment.

She allowed him to lead her away. Allan took her to his horse, still skittish from the fire around them.

He lifted her on to the horse's back and called to one of the soldiers. 'Which way out?'

The man pointed. 'The south gate.'

At the gate Allan mounted behind her and spoke to the soldier who opened it for them. 'Tell MacDonnell I am taking the boy out of here now.'

Once through the gate Allan headed towards the Allied line, determined to at least get her beyond where the fighting would take place. The smoke from Hougoumont obscured his vision, thinning a bit as they proceeded through the orchard.

Suddenly pain shot through his shoulder, followed by the crack of rifle fire. He jerked back and his shako flew from his head. It was all he could do to stay in the saddle.

He pushed Miss Pallant down on the neck of his horse and covered her with his body. 'Snipers! Stay down.' He hung on with all his strength. 'I am hit.'

Chapter Three

Marian felt the captain's weight upon her back and sensed his sudden unsteadiness. The horse fled the orchard and galloped across a field towards a ridge where a line of cannons stood. Just as they came near the cannons fired, each with a spew of flames and white smoke and a deafening boom.

The horse made a high-pitched squeal and galloped even faster, away from the sound and the smoke, plunging into a field of tall rye grass, its shoots whipping against their arms and legs.

'Captain!' Marian worried over his wounds.

'Hold on.' Pain filled his voice. 'Cannot stop her.'

'Are you much hurt?' she yelled.

He did not answer at first. 'Yes,' he finally said.

Marian closed her eyes and pressed her face against the horse's neck, praying the captain had not received a fatal shot.

The horse found a dry, narrow path through the field and raced down its winding length, following its twists and turns until Marian had no idea how they would find their way out. The explosions of the cannon faded into some vague direction behind them until finally the horse slowed to an exhausted walk.

'We're safe, at least,' the captain said, sitting up again.

She turned to look at him. Blood stained the left side of his chest and he swayed in the saddle.

'You need tending,' she cried.

'First place we find.' His words were laboured.

They wandered aimlessly through farm fields that seemed to have no end. The sounds of the battle grew even fainter.

Finally Marian spied a thin column of smoke. She pointed to it. 'Look, Captain.'

It led to a small hut and barn, at the moment looking as grand as a fine country estate.

Marian called out, 'Hello? Help us!'

No one responded.

She tried saying it in French. *'Au secours.'*

Nothing but the distant sounds of the battle.

She turned around. Captain Landon swayed in the saddle. 'I must see to your wounds, Captain. We must stop here.'

The door to the hut opened and a little girl, no more than four years old, peered out.

'There is someone here!' Marian dismounted and carefully approached the little girl, who watched her with curiosity as she reached the door.

'Where are your parents?' she asked the child.

The little girl popped a thumb in her mouth and returned a blank stare.

Marian tried French, but the child's expression did not change. Thumb still in her mouth, the little girl rattled off some words, pointing towards a dirt road that led away from the hut.

It was not a language Marian understood. Flemish, most likely.

'This isn't going to be easy,' she muttered. 'We each of us cannot make ourselves understood.' She crouched to the child's level. 'Your mama? Mama?'

'Mama!' The child smiled and pointed to the road, chattering again.

Marian turned from the doorway to Captain Landon. 'Her mother cannot be far or I think she'd be in distress. She's not at all worried.' Perhaps her mother had merely gone to the fields for a moment. 'We need to stay. At least long enough for me to look at you.'

Allan winced. 'I agree.'

He started to dismount on his own, nearly losing his balance. Marian ran to him, ready to catch him if he fell, but he held on to the horse for support.

He made a weak gesture to the barn. 'In there. Won't see us right away. Just in case.'

'Just in case what?'

His brows knit. 'In case French soldiers come by.'

The sounds of battle had disappeared completely, but they did not know which side would be the victor.

He led the horse into the barn.

It was larger than the hut, with three stalls. In one a milk cow contentedly chewed her cud. The other stalls had no animals, but were piled with fresh-smelling hay. A shared trough was filled with clean-looking water. The captain's horse went immediately to the water and drank.

Holding on to the walls, the captain made his way to one of the empty stalls. He lowered himself on to the soft hay, his back leaning against the wood that separated this stall from the other, and groaned in pain.

'I need more light if I am to see your wound.' The sun was low in the sky and the barn was too dark for her to examine him. She glanced around and found an oil lantern. 'I can light it from the fireplace in the hut. I'll be right back.'

The little girl had stepped outside the hut, her thumb back in her mouth. Marian gestured with the lantern and the child chattered at her some more, but Marian could only smile and nod at her as she walked inside.

The hut was nothing more than one big room with a dirt

floor, a table and chairs and a big fireplace with a small fire smouldering beneath a big iron pot. Curtains hid where the beds must be. Marian found a taper by the fireplace and used it to light the lantern.

Back in the barn, Marian hung the lantern on a nearby peg and knelt beside the captain. He was wet with blood. 'We must remove your coat.'

He nodded, pulling off his shoulder belt and trying to work his buttons.

'I'll do that.' Marian unbuttoned his coat.

He leaned forwards and she pulled off the sleeve from his right arm first. There was as much blood soaking the back of his coat as the front. He uttered a pained sound as she pulled the sleeve off of his left arm. 'I am sorry,' she whispered.

She reached for his shirt but he stopped her. 'Not proper.'

Proper? She nearly laughed. 'Do not be tiresome, Captain.' She quickly took his shirt off too.

The wound, a hole in his shoulder the size of a gold sovereign, still oozed blood, and there was a corresponding one in his back that was only slightly smaller.

'The ball passed through you,' she said in relief. She would not have relished attempting to remove a ball from a man's flesh. 'I need a cloth to clean it.'

'In my pocket.'

There was a clean handkerchief in the right pocket. She dipped it in the water trough and used it to clean the wound.

Even as she worked Marian could not fail to notice his broad shoulders and the sculpted contours of his chest. Beneath her hand his muscles were firm. She and Domina had admired his appearance in uniform what seemed an age ago when they'd first glimpsed him in the Parc. *You should see him naked, Domina,* she said silently to herself.

Marian had stuffed rolls of bandage in her pockets before the fire. She pulled them out and wrapped his wound.

'Where did you learn to tend wounds?' he asked.

She smiled. 'At Hougoumont.'

He looked shocked. 'At Hougoumont?'

'It was all I could do.' The sounds and smell and heat of the fires at Hougoumont returned. Tears stung her eyes as she again heard the cries of men trapped inside.

She forced herself to stop thinking of it. 'I really have been a gently bred young lady.' At least since leaving India, she had been. In India she remembered running free.

She tied off the bandages. 'How does that feel, Captain?'

'Good.' His voice was tight.

She made a face. 'I know it hurts like the devil.'

His lips twitched into a smile that vanished into a spasm of pain. 'We should be on our way.' He tried to stand, but swayed and fell against the stall. 'Ahhhh!' he cried.

She jumped to her feet and caught him before he slipped to the ground. 'You cannot ride.'

His face was very pale. 'Must get you to Brussels.'

'Or die trying? I won't have it!' She pointed to his horse, now munching hay, coat damp with sweat and muscles trembling. 'Your horse is exhausted and you have lost a great deal of blood.'

Captain Landon tried to pull out of her supporting arm to go towards his horse. 'She needs tending. Rubbing down.'

She held him tight. 'You sit. I will look after your horse.'

He frowned. 'You cannot—'

'I can indeed. I know how to tend a horse.' This was a complete falsehood, of course, but he would not know she never paid much attention to horses except to ride them.

With her help, he sat down again and she found a horse blanket clean enough to wrap around him. A further search located a piece of sackcloth that she used to wipe off the horse's sweaty coat. She removed the horse's saddle and carried it and the saddlebags over to the captain.

His eyes seemed to have trouble focusing on her. 'Is there some water?'

Water. She could suddenly smell it from the trough, and

became aware of her own thirst. Surely there must be somewhere to get water without sharing it with the animals. 'I'll find some.'

There was a noise at the doorway. The little girl was watching them.

Marian gestured to her, pointing to the water and making a motion like a pump. *'L'eau?'*

The child popped her thumb into her mouth again and stared.

Marian rubbed her brow. 'I wish I knew how to say *water.'*

'Water?' The child blinked.

'Yes, yes.' Marian nodded. 'Water.'

The little girl led her to a pump behind the hut. Marian filled a nearby bucket and cupped her hands, drinking her fill. The child left her, but soon returned with a tin cup and handed it to her.

'Thank you,' she said.

The girl smiled. *'Dank u. Dank u. Dank u.'*

Marian carried the bucket and cup to the barn. The captain opened his eyes when she came near.

'Water.' She smiled, lifting the bucket to show him. She set it down and filled the cup for him.

His hand shook as he lifted the cup to his lips, but he swallowed eagerly. Afterwards he rested against the stall again.

And looked worse by the minute.

'When Valour is rested, we'll start out again.' Even his voice was weaker.

'Valour?'

'Valour.' He swallowed. 'My horse.'

She laughed. 'But she was not valorous! She bolted away from the cannons.'

He rose to the horse's defence. 'The fire frightened her. She's used to cannon.'

Then it must have been the flash of flame from the cannonade that had set the horse on her terrified gallop.

And brought them to this place.

She sat next to him, suddenly weary herself.

He seemed to be having difficulty keeping his eyes open. 'The cannon stopped. It is over.' He took a breath. 'I wonder who won.'

'We shall learn that tomorrow.' Marian tried to infuse her voice with a confidence she did not feel. Back in England one day had always seemed much like the last, but here, who knew what tomorrow would bring?

The captain coughed and cried out with the pain it created. It frightened Marian how pale he looked and how much it hurt him to simply take a breath. Soon his eyes closed and his breathing relaxed.

Let him sleep, she told herself, even though she felt very alone without his company. Memories of the day flooded her mind. The face of the dying soldier. The fire.

Eventually even those images could not keep her eyes from becoming very heavy. She'd just begun to doze when she heard voices outside. The parents returning?

She shot to her feet and peeked out of the door.

A man and a woman in peasant garb led a heavily laden mule. The little girl ran out to meet them. She pointed towards the barn.

Marian stepped outside. The man and woman both dropped their chins in surprise. She supposed she looked a fright, black with soot, clothing torn and stained with the captain's blood and the blood of other men she'd tended. She was dressed as a boy, she must recall. They would think her a boy.

'Bonjour,' she began and tried explaining her presence in French.

Their blank stares matched their little daughter's.

She sighed. *'Anglais?'*

They shook their heads.

There was no reason to expect peasants to speak anything but their own language. What use would they have for French or English? At least Marian knew one word of Flemish now. *Water.* She almost laughed.

Her gaze drifted to the mule. She expected to see it carrying hay or harvested crops or something, but its cargo was nothing so mundane. The mule was burdened with French cavalry helmets and bundles of red cloth.

Loot from the battlefield. Marian felt the blood drain from her face. They had been stripping the dead.

Bile rose into her throat, but she swallowed it back and gestured for them to follow her into the barn.

She pointed to Captain Landon. 'English,' she said. 'Injured.' Maybe they would understand something if she happened upon another word their languages had in common. 'Help us.' She fished in the pocket of her pantaloons and found a Belgian coin. She handed it to the man, who turned it over in his hand and nodded with approval.

He and his wife went outside and engaged in a lively discussion, which Marian hoped did not include a plan to kill them in their sleep. People who could strip the dead might be capable of anything. As a precaution she went through the captain's things and found his pistol. Hoping it was loaded and primed, she stuck it in her pocket.

Finally the man stepped back in. He nodded and gestured about the stall. She understood. They were to remain in the barn.

'Food?' she asked.

His brows knit.

'Nourriture,' she tried, making as if she were eating. 'Bread.'

He grinned and nodded. *'Brood.'*

'Yes. Yes. *Brood.'*

He gestured for her to wait.

She sank down next to the captain. 'We will have bread anyway.' Her brow furrowed. 'At least I hope *brood* is bread.'

The captain opened his eyes briefly, but closed them again.

He needed sleep, she was certain, but it made her feel very alone.

First the mule was unloaded and returned to the barn, then the wife brought Marian bread and another blanket. After eating, Marian piled as much straw as possible beneath her and Captain Landon. She pulled off his boots and extinguished the lantern. Lying down next to him, she covered them both with a blanket. With the pistol at her side, she finally fell into an exhausted sleep.

Pain. Searing pain. A throbbing that pulsated up his neck and down the length of his arm.

Allan could make sense of nothing else. Not the sounds, the smells, the lumpy surface upon which he lay. He didn't wish to open his eyes, to face more pain.

He tried to remember where he had been, what had happened. He remembered pulling Miss Pallant from the burning château. He remembered being shot and Valour running amok.

Valour nickered. He opened his eyes.

'Miss Pallant?' His throat was parched and speaking intensified the pain.

She had fallen asleep next to him. 'Captain?'

Her face, smudged with soot, was close, framed by a tangle of blonde hair. Her blue eyes dazzled.

He caught a lock of her hair between his fingers. 'Where is your cap?'

She looked around and found it on the floor. He watched her plait her hair and cover it.

Sunlight shone through cracks in the wood. He frowned. 'How long have we slept?'

She stretched. 'All night, I suppose.'

'All night!' He sat up straighter and the room spun around.

'The child's parents returned.' Her voice seemed tense. 'I gave them a coin so we could stay in here.'

A stab of pain hit his shoulder again. He held his breath until it faded. 'Did they know who won the battle?'

'Perhaps, but they could not tell me.' She grasped her knees to her chest. 'They speak Flemish. I don't suppose you speak Flemish, do you?'

'No.' But he knew many Belgians were on the side of the French and despised the Allies.

The door to the barn opened and the peasant farmer walked in. Allan noticed Marian pick up his pistol and put it in her pocket.

The peasant's expression was as guarded as Marian's. He nodded. *'Goedemorgen.'*

'Good morning,' she responded in a tight voice.

The man lifted a pail and spoke again, but this time Allan could not decipher the words. The farmer walked over to another stall and began milking the cow. The smell of fresh milk filled the barn. He was hungry, Allan realised.

'Brood?' Marian walked over to the peasant and showed him a coin from her pocket.

The man nodded and pointed to the door.

She placed the pistol next to Allan and covered it with the blanket. From a basket she handed him a small piece of bread. 'This is from last night. I am going to get some more for us. Take care. I do not entirely trust these people.'

Allan silently applauded her cleverness.

She left and the man finished milking his cow. When he walked past Allan carrying the bucket of milk, he paused. Turning back, he picked up the tin cup and dipped it into the milk, handing the cup to Allan. *'Drink de melk.'* The peasant gestured, and Allan easily understood him.

'Thank you.' He took the cup, cream swimming at the top and sipped. His hunger urged him to gulp it all down, but he knew better.

'The battle?' he tried asking the peasant. 'England or France?'

The man tapped his temple and shook his head. Did he

not know the battle's outcome or did he not understand the question? The man shrugged and walked out.

To be unable to converse was a frustration. To not know who won the battle was worse.

Had Wellington won?

It seemed essential to know. Had Napoleon been vanquished at last or were his victorious soldiers now pillaging the countryside? Was Miss Pallant safe here? Should he return her to the safety of her friends or was Brussels under Napoleon's control?

Allan tried to take stock of his injuries. It seemed a good thing that the ball had passed through his shoulder, although it burned and ached like the very devil.

He flexed his fingers. Despite a sharp pain that radiated down his arm, they worked well. More good news.

He rested his head against the stable wall, exhausted from the mild exertion. He felt hot and dizzy. Feverish, God forbid. He needed to regain his strength so they could ride out of here. He broke off a piece of the stale bread and dipped it in the milk, making it easier to eat. Even chewing exhausted him, but he slowly managed to finish it.

The door opened again, and Miss Pallant came to his side.

She sat by him. 'I have some more bread.'

'In a minute.' He handed her the cup of milk. 'Have some. It is very much like ambrosia, I think.'

She laughed. 'I do not know when I have been so hungry.'

He waited for her to finish drinking. 'Tell me why you do not trust our host.'

She tore off a piece of bread. 'I think they went to the battlefield and robbed the dead.'

He gritted his teeth. It happened after every battle. Oftentimes the very men who'd fought beside the dead returned to deface their final rest. Most of the officers turned a blind eye to the practice. In fact, most of them were not averse to purchasing some interesting piece of booty. A Frenchman's sword, perhaps. Or a fine gold watch.

'But they have fed us and didn't kill us during the night,' she added. 'That is something in their favour.' She nibbled on a crust.

'We must leave today.' Allan ignored the dizziness that intensified and his increasing difficulty breathing.

She regarded him intently and placed her fingers against his forehead. She felt cool. 'You have a fever, Captain.'

He feared as much. 'It is nothing of consequence. I just need a moment and we can go on our way.'

She watched him, arms crossed over her chest. He needed to prove he could do it.

'Help me stand.' If he could get to his feet, he'd be able to ride, he was certain of it.

She helped him struggle to his feet, pain blasting through his chest and down his arm. He lost his footing and she caught him, his bandaged and naked chest pressing against her as if in an embrace.

Allan cursed his weakness, cursed that he had placed her in this uncomfortable situation. To undress a strange man. To bind his gruesome wounds. To learn one of the horrid secrets of war.

He gained his balance and leaned against the stable wall.

Marian did not remove her hands from the skin beneath his arms. 'You are too weak for this.'

It seemed an obvious observation, but he made a dismissive gesture. 'Saddle Valour. We can ride to Brussels. It cannot be far.'

She did not move, but, instead, stared at him. His eyes betrayed him as surely as his body. No matter how hard he tried, he could not keep her in focus.

Finally she said, 'You cannot ride to Brussels.'

'You cannot go alone.' He managed to disguise the extent of his pain and his growing disorientation.

She nodded. 'I agree. I do not know what these people would do to you if I left you here alone.'

That was not what he meant. He meant a woman could not wander alone through a countryside that might be teeming with French soldiers.

She glanced away, but finally she met his gaze again. 'We must stay here until you are well enough to ride. I have your pistol and your sword in case these people try to hurt us and I have some coins to pay them for food. We shall just have to take care.'

His strength had failed him. He might have started the previous day as her protector, but at the moment she was acting as if she was his.

He could not allow it. 'I can ride.'

She gazed at him firmly. 'No, Captain. You must lie down again. Let me help you.' She moved to his side, wrapping one of his arms around her shoulder so that he could lean on her while she lowered him to the floor.

'No.' He wrenched away. 'Cannot do it. Must get you to safety.' He tried to ignore the pain and the spinning in his head. He could endure a few hours on a horse.

He took a step, keeping one hand on the stable wall.

'Captain,' her voice pleaded.

'I will saddle the horse.' He stepped out of the stall. His horse walked up to him. He grabbed her mane to steady himself.

But the room turned black.

The last thing Allan felt was the hard surface of the barn floor.

Chapter Four

'Captain!' Marian rushed to his side.

He opened his eyes. 'I passed out.'

'Now will you listen to reason? Please. We must stay here until you are well.' With all the strength she could muster, she helped him up again and settled him back on to the bed of hay. She made a pillow of his saddle by covering it with one of the blankets.

His breathing had turned laboured. 'I am sorry, Miss Pallant. I cannot get you out of here.'

'Considering I am the reason you were shot, I should apologise to you.' She tucked another blanket around him.

'A Frenchman shot me, not you,' he said.

She brushed damp hair off his face. 'Remain still, Captain. Rest.' His determination to take her back to Brussels was foolish. He was too ill.

He gave a wan smile. 'I seem to have little choice.'

She knelt next to him, tucking a blanket around him. 'I thought soldiers were realistic.'

He laughed. 'I do not know where you would get that

notion. If we were realistic, we would never march into battle or try to storm a fortress.'

'You do have a point.'

He closed his eyes, and she was free to watch him for a moment. A fine sheen of perspiration tinged his face, evidence of his fever, but he looked as if he wished to fight it, as he might fight the enemy. She would wager by the afternoon he would tell her he was ready to ride, even if his fever had worsened.

When her father had contracted the fever in India, he'd merely sunk into despair, lamenting that he'd brought the illness upon his household. His wife. Even at nine years old, Marian knew her father had simply given up. Her mother was dead and a daughter was apparently not enough to live for.

'Do not leave me, Captain,' she whispered.

He opened his eyes. 'I will not leave you. We both shall ride out of here this afternoon.'

She smiled and blinked away tears. *God keep him alive,* she prayed.

Valour whinnied and blew out a noisy breath.

Marian rose. 'She heard you, I expect, and thinks you meant now.' She released Valour from her stall and the mare immediately found the captain, lowering her head to nuzzle his arm.

'Ow, Valour, stop.' He shuddered from the pain, but stroked Valour's neck. 'Nothing to fret over.'

Marian smiled. 'She is trying to tend you.'

He returned her gaze. 'I already have an excellent nurse.'

She could only hope she would be good enough to pull him through. Marian led Valour away. 'I will feed her.' She found the feed and Valour soon forgot about her master.

Marian glanced around the barn. The door was open, providing plenty of light and fresh air, but living with animals and wearing dirty clothes still assaulted the nostrils. She took a broom from against the wall and performed a task she had never done before in her life—she swept the barn.

'What are you doing?' The captain could not see her.

'Sweeping out the dirty hay,' she responded.

'You should not have to perform such a task.' He sounded breathless and disapproving.

It stung. She very much wanted him to admire her, to value the fact that she was not missish or helpless.

She swept over to where he could see her. 'I prefer this work to the smell.'

'I should be doing the task,' he rasped.

Perhaps he merely felt guilty. That would certainly be like him.

'It is a simple enough task,' she remarked.

He looked up at her. 'You do whatever needs to be done, do you not, Miss Pallant?'

She felt herself go warm all over, as if the sun had chosen to shine only on her. 'As do you, Captain.' She held his gaze for a special moment. How alike they were in some ways. 'Your turn will come when you are better.'

He nodded and closed his eyes again.

Marian hummed as she finished the task, sweeping the dirty hay from the floor to the outside. Two chickens pecked at the soil around the hut. She glimpsed the farmer and his wife in the side yard sorting through the bundles they'd brought in the day before.

Their bounty from the dead.

Her good spirits fled, and she remembered that men had died in the battle, some in her arms.

Death had robbed her of almost everyone she cared about. Her parents. Her Indian amah. Her aunt. All she had left was her cousin Edwin and Domina, and she did not know if Domina had survived.

She glanced back at the captain, the light from the door shining on him. He would not die, she vowed, not as long as she drew breath. She turned back to see what else needed doing in the barn.

* * *

Marian was pitching fresh hay into the horse's stall when the farmer walked in and glanced all around. *'Wat is dit?'*

She could guess what he asked. 'I cleaned it.'

He raised his brows and tapped his head.

'I know.' She sighed. 'You do not understand.'

But he looked pleased and she felt a surge of pride that her work had been appreciated. He smiled. *'Brood?'*

She almost laughed. *'Brood.'* She nodded. Bread was to be her reward. 'Thank you.'

He looked down at the captain and frowned. *'Slaapt hij?'*

'Sleeping?' Her smile turned wan. 'Yes.' A feverish sleep. She fished into her pocket and held out a coin to the peasant. She pulled at her dirty coat. 'Clean clothes?'

He stared.

She repeated, this time pointing to the stains on the captain's trousers, as well.

'Ah.' The man nodded vigorously.

A few minutes later he brought back a basket of bread and cheese and an armful of folded clothes.

'Thank you,' she cried.

After he left, she set the food aside for later and examined the clothes. There were two sets consisting of shirts, coats and trousers. One set was very large, for the captain; one smaller, for her. She held one of the shirts up to her nose and smelled the bitter odour of gunpowder.

The peasant had brought her plundered clothing. The large trousers were white, like the trousers of the French soldiers who had stormed the gate at Hougoumont. These were pristine, however, obviously tucked away in some poor Frenchman's pack.

A wave of grief for the poor fellow washed over her. It seemed dishonourable to don his clothing and be glad of its cleanliness, but what choice did she have?

They would wear these garments only until she could wash

and dry their own. And she would say a prayer for the poor men who died to clothe them even temporarily.

Marian carried the bucket to the well to draw clean water, which she brought back to bathe the captain as best she could. She supposed a lady ought to try to get the farmer to undress the captain, but she was pretending to be a boy.

She knelt beside him. 'Captain, I have clean clothes for you, but first I must bathe you.' He was already shirtless, so there was nothing to do but remove his trousers. It should be no more difficult to pull off his trousers than to undress a doll.

He opened his eyes. 'Bathe?'

'Yes. It will cool you, as well.' She dipped the cloth in the water and wrung it out.

She started with his face, wiping off soot and dirt. Rinsing the cloth, she wiped his hair and rinsed again. She cleaned around his bandages, careful not to get them wet.

'I should not let you...' he murmured.

She made a face at him. 'I know. I know. My reputation and all that is proper.' She moved the cloth across his nipple and felt a strange surge of sensation inside her. She lifted the cloth, then rinsed it again, trying to regain composure. 'I suspect if you were feeling better you would give me a lecture.'

A wan smile formed on his lips. 'Indeed, I would.'

'Would it not be ridiculous for me to leave you dirty in soiled clothing merely because I am an unmarried miss?' Perhaps if she kept talking the fluttering inside her would cease. 'It would be nonsensical. Much of what one must do to preserve one's reputation is nonsensical, is it not?'

'Nonsensical,' he murmured.

'Yes...like—like being alone with a man. A few minutes alone and one's parents or guardian force a betrothal even if the gentleman and lady despise each other. Ridiculous.'

He leaned forwards and she washed off his back.

'Sometimes men are not to be trusted.' He spoke with difficulty.

It pained her. 'I know that.'

The teachers at the school she and Domina had attended explained such things very carefully, how men could behave if alone with a woman. 'But surely there are exceptions.' Such as one finding herself in the middle of a battle and a man saving her.

'Now I must remove your trousers,' she said, as if that were the most natural thing in the world. She reached for the buttons fastening them.

The captain put his hand over hers. 'That seems too much—'

She looked him straight in the eye. 'Blood has soaked through your trousers and, I expect, through your drawers as well. It is beginning to smell.' She exaggerated about the smelly part, but she wanted his co-operation.

His eyes were still feverish. 'I'll do it. Step away.'

She stepped out of his sight, but watched as he removed his trousers and drawers, just in case he needed her. With some effort he wiped his skin with the cloth.

This was her first glimpse of a totally naked man, she realised. She and Domina used to wonder how they would ever see a naked man. Never would they have guessed it would be under these circumstances. Marian's eyes were riveted upon his masculine parts, so different from those on the statues of Roman gods she'd seen in elegant houses in Bath and London. His was living flesh, warm and vari-coloured, more fascinating than attractive. She tilted her head as she examined him.

Once, when she and Domina were pressing one of the maids for some forbidden information, the woman described how men's parts grew bigger during lovemaking. Gazing at the captain, Marian's heart raced. *Bigger?*

She remembered the maid's description of lovemaking. What would it be like to do that with a man? With the captain?

She shook off her hoydenish thoughts and turned to hand him the French soldier's drawers.

The captain covered himself with the blanket and looked exhausted. 'The clothing?'

'You must let me help,' she insisted. 'Do not fuss.'

She put the drawers on his legs and pulled them up as far as she could, her hands under the blanket and very near his male parts. For a moment her gaze caught his and the fluttering inside her returned. His hands touched hers as he took the waistband of the drawers from her grip and pulled them up the rest of the way. Next she did the same with the trousers.

She cleared her throat. 'I will get the shirt.'

He leaned back against his saddle, pressing his hand against his wound.

She set the shirt aside and knelt down. 'Let me see your wound.' She moved his hand aside and carefully pulled the bandage away from his skin.

It looked inflamed and swollen and smelled of infection. The layers of cloth closest to the wound were moist with pus.

'You need a clean bandage,' she told him, but how she would ask the peasants for a bandage, she did not know. 'Lean forwards.' His back wound was not as nasty.

'Leave off the shirt,' he said, touching her arm. 'A new bandage would be good.'

'I'll get some clean water, then change my clothes. I'll see to it quickly.' She hurried out of the barn.

At the water pump she rinsed the bucket and the piece of cloth he'd used as a wash rag. She refilled the bucket with clean water and returned to the barn. Choosing the empty stall next to where the captain lay, she quickly removed the bloodstained clothing she'd worn for almost two days straight. She unwrapped the long scarf she'd used to bind her breasts to disguise that she was a woman. Bare from the waist up, Marian bent down to the bucket and scrubbed the blood from the fabric. She hung it over the wall of the stall, hoping it would dry a little before she had to put it back on. Using the cloth she rubbed her skin clean of blood and grime. No steaming hot bath in a copper tub with French-milled soap had ever felt as wonderful.

Eager to feel clean all over, she removed her breeches. Completely naked now, she turned and saw his face through a gap in the wood that separated the two stalls. Had he been watching her? She could not tell. Every nerve in her body sparked.

Heart pounding, she grabbed the clean shirt and held it against her chest. 'Captain?'

'I am still here,' he replied.

She quickly donned the clean trousers and reached for the scarf to begin rewrapping her breasts.

A sound made her turn.

The peasant woman stood at the opening to the stall, gaping open-mouthed. *'U bent een vrouw.'*

Marian could guess what the woman said. 'Yes. A woman.'

She quickly pulled on the shirt, her mind racing to provide an explanation, something the woman would accept and understand. Her vocabulary of fewer than five words was insufficient to explain why she was in the company of a wounded soldier.

She pointed to Captain Landon. 'I am his wife.'

'Wat?' The woman did not comprehend.

'Wife,' Marian repeated. She pointed to Landon. 'Husband.'

The woman shook her head.

'Married. Spouse,' she tried.

'She does not understand you,' the Captain said. *'Épouse. Mari.'*

Marian pointed to Landon again and hugged herself, making kissing sounds. She tapped her ring finger, which, of course, had no ring.

'Gehuwd!' The woman broke into a smile.

'Yes!' She nodded. Whatever *gehuwd* meant, it caused the peasant woman to smile.

Marian pointed to the door, then put her finger to her lips. 'Shh.' She gestured to herself. 'Shh.'

The peasant woman nodded. 'Shh,' she repeated. She walked over to Marian and clasped her hand.

A friend, Marian thought. At least for the moment.

She walked her new friend over to the captain. 'I want to show her your wound.'

'Excellent idea.' There was a catch in his voice. 'Maybe she will have bandages.'

Marian pointed to his bandage and pulled it away. She touched the bandages again. 'New bandages. Clean.'

The woman leaned down and examined the wound for herself. *'Zeer slecht.'*

'Zeer slecht?' Marian repeated. That did not sound good.

'Ja.' The woman nodded. She patted Marian's arm reassuringly and uttered a whole string of words Marian could not understand. She raised a finger as if to say 'wait a moment' and walked out the door.

After she left Marian sank to the floor next to the captain. 'I hope she understood.'

He touched her hand. 'We'll find out soon enough.'

'How are you feeling?' She felt his forehead.

'Better,' he said.

He looked worse, flushed and out of breath. She dipped the cloth in the water and wiped his brow.

He released a breath. 'That feels uncommonly good.'

'I'm worried your fever grows worse.' She dipped the cloth again and held it against his forehead.

'It is nothing.' He coughed and winced in pain, but managed to smile. 'So you are my wife now.'

Surely it was a harmless lie. 'I wanted her to approve of us.'

'Clever.' His voice rattled. 'Worked a charm.'

She beamed under the compliment. 'We must remain in their good graces. We are totally dependent on them.'

'Food. Clothing. Shelter,' he agreed.

She pulled at her shirt. 'I try to remember we would not have clean clothes if they had not stolen from the dead soldiers, much as I detest the thought. They are poor. It was generous of them to share what little they have with us.'

'And you gave them some coins,' he said.

She smiled. 'Yes.'

The peasant wife bustled in, bandages and folded towels in one hand and a small pot in the other. She knelt down at the captain's side, chattering and gesturing for Marian to unwind his old bandage. The captain tried to cooperate.

The woman dipped a cloth into the water and bathed around the wound. That done, she opened the pot. The scent of honey filled the air.

'Honey?' His eyes widened.

'Ja.' The woman nodded. *'Honing.'*

Honing. Another word for Marian to learn, but why?

The woman poured the honey directly into his wound and he trembled at its touch. After placing a cloth compress over it, she gestured for Marian to help him lean forwards. She dressed the exit wound in the same manner. Then she wrapped the cloth bandage around him to keep everything in place. She smiled and chattered at them both.

Marian helped him into his shirt. 'Honey.'

'Let us hope she knows more about healing than we do.' The captain glanced at the farmer's wife. 'Thank you, *madame.*'

Marian had been moved by the tenderness of the woman's care.

When the woman stood to leave Marian walked her to the door. She pointed to herself. 'Marian.'

The woman grinned and tapped her own chest. 'Karel.'

The two women embraced. Marian wiped away tears. She had an ally.

* * *

The rest of the day proved that comfort was fleeting.

The farmer left with the mule laden with plunder. Marian had neither the means nor the opportunity to ask him to carry a message to someone—anyone—English.

Captain Landon's fever steadily worsened and he slept a great deal of the time.

Marian busied herself by washing their soiled clothes, which dried quickly in the warm afternoon sun. She spent the rest of the time at the captain's side, talking when he wished to talk, bathing his face to cool him, or merely just sitting next to him.

Late in the afternoon he became even more fitful. The little girl carried in another basket of bread and cheese, this time with the addition of a tankard of ale.

The girl stared wide-eyed at the captain while Marian took the food and drink from her tiny arms.

'Fetch your mama,' Marian asked her. 'Mama.'

The little girl ran off and her mother showed up soon afterwards kneeling down to check the captain. She clucked her tongue and furrowed her brow and said…something. She rushed off again.

Several minutes went by before she returned with a pot of some sort of tea, leaves and pieces of bark floating in the liquid. She handed Marian a spoon and gestured for her to give the tea to the captain.

'Thank you, Karel,' Marian said.

She spooned the tea into the captain's mouth.

He roused. 'What is this?'

'Tea,' she responded. 'To make you feel better.'

By the time darkness fell, he was sleeping uneasily, their old clothes were dry and folded, and the farmer had still not returned. Marian surmised wherever he'd gone had been too far to return in a day.

She continued her ministrations as the moon rose in the

sky, lighting the stable with a soft glow that gave her enough light to see by. The captain mumbled and moved restlessly.

Exhausted, Marian fell asleep at his side, the wet cloth still in her hand.

'No!' the captain cried.

She woke with a start.

He rose to a sitting position. 'You bloody bastard. You ought to be hanged.'

He swung a fist at an imaginary enemy. His eyes flashed in the moonlight and he tried to rise.

'Captain, stay down!' Marian held him from behind and tried to keep him still.

'I ought to kill you myself.' His voice was low and dangerous and frightening.

'You are dreaming, Captain,' she told him. 'There is no one here but you and me. I am Marian Pallant. Remember me?'

He reached around and easily wrenched her off his back. Suddenly he held her in front of him, her legs straddling his, his face contorted in anger. 'I ought to kill you myself for what you did.'

Marian trembled with fear. While he still held her, she managed to cup his face between her hands and to keep his head steady enough to look at her. 'I'm Marian, Captain. You are dreaming. You are sick. You must lie down again.'

Her hair came loose and tumbled down her back. His face changed, but he seized her hair and with it drew her close so that her face was inches from his. 'Foolish woman,' he murmured, his other hand feeling her bound chest. 'Not a boy at all. A foolish woman.'

Her fear took a new turn, her heart beating so hard she thought it would burst inside her. Forcing him to look at her again, she made her voice steady and firm although she felt neither inside. 'Yes, I am foolish, but you are very sick and you are hurting me. Release me and lie back down this instant.'

For a brief moment he seemed to really see her, then his eyes drifted from her like a boat that had lost its sail.

He released her and collapsed against the saddle, shivering so hard his whole body convulsed. 'Cold,' he murmured. 'So cold.'

She gathered up all the blankets and wrapped them around him. Then she moved to the other side of the stable, watchful lest he would again mistake her for whomever he wished to kill. Or to seduce.

A rooster crowed.

Allan lifted his eyelids, seeing first the weathered grey wood of the barn stall, then the hay, the light from the window and finally Miss Marian Pallant.

She sat against the wall opposite him, her hair cascading on to her shoulders, her eyes closed. He examined her sleeping face.

How could she have thought such features would pass for a boy's? Her complexion was like fresh cream, her brows delicately arched, lips full and pink and turned up at the corners. Even with her hair loose and in a man's shirt and breeches, she looked as if she belonged in the finest ballroom, not sleeping in a peasant's barn.

He struggled to sit, but pain shot through his shoulder. Pressing his hand against his wound, he felt a bandage securely in place. It was damp with sweat.

No wonder. Blankets were piled at his feet. He kicked them away and made another effort to sit, trying to bear the pain. A cry escaped. 'Ah!'

Miss Pallant jumped and seemed to recoil from him. 'Captain?'

She looked at him as if he were the bogeyman himself while she plaited her hair.

His cry must have alarmed her. 'Forgive me. I put too much strain on my shoulder.' He rubbed his face. 'Is it afternoon?'

'No, morning.' Her wariness did not abate.

'Morning? Do you mean I slept all of yesterday?'

'You were very feverish,' she responded in a defensive tone. 'And, yes, you did sleep on and off. Do you not remember any of it?'

Bits and pieces of the previous day returned. Miss Pallant undressing him, stroking him with a cool cloth. Miss Pallant naked, her skin glowing and smooth against the dark rough wood of the stable, like a goddess thrust off Mount Olympus.

He glanced away from her. 'I remember some of it.'

'You were feverish all day,' she said. 'And all night.'

He touched his forehead. 'I feel better today. I hope I did not cause you any distress because of it.'

Her voice rose. 'No distress, Captain.'

She was like a skittish colt. What had happened?

She stood. 'Are you thirsty?'

He was very thirsty, come to think of it, but he shook his head. 'I am determined to no longer be a burden to you. I will get the water today. Tell me where to go.' Surely he could rise to his feet today.

'You will do no such thing.' She gave him a scolding look. 'Karel left some ale.' She handed him the tankard. 'Drink it if you are thirsty.'

It was reddish brown in colour, tasted both sweet and tart, and Allan thought it was quite the most delicious ale he'd ever consumed.

He drank half the contents. 'Karel is the wife's name?'

Miss Pallant nodded, still watching him as if he were a wildcat about to pounce.

He touched his shoulder. 'I remember. She dressed my wound.' The pain was finally fading.

'Are you hungry?' She reached for a basket and placed it near him. 'There is bread and cheese.'

He chose only one piece of bread and one square of cheese and handed the basket back to her. 'You must eat as well.'

She hesitated before taking the basket from his hand. What had caused this reticence towards him? A battle, a fire, and an escape had not robbed her of courage. What had? 'Miss Pallant, when I was feverish, did I do something to hurt you or frighten you?'

'Not at all.' Her response was clipped. 'You merely had a nightmare.'

There was more to it, he was certain, but it seemed she didn't want him to pursue it. 'The farmer packed up the plunder and left us yesterday, I remember. Did he return?'

She tore off a piece of bread and chewed it before answering, 'He has not.'

He wanted to ask her more, but even the minor exertion of sitting up and eating had greatly fatigued him. He could not even finish his bread. 'If you give me the basket again, I'll wrap this up.'

She reached for the bread instead. 'I will do it.'

Their fingers touched, and her gaze flew to his face. He could not find words, but tried to show his regret for whatever he had put her through.

Her expression softened.

He leaned back and tried not to show how much he enjoyed merely gazing upon her.

She rose. 'I believe I will sweep the barn.'

He remembered her doing so the day before. He tried to stand. 'Perhaps I can do it today.'

He made it to his feet, but his legs felt like rubber. She rushed over to lend her shoulder for support. She smelled of hay and a scent all her own, a combination that was pleasant to his nostrils.

The door to the barn swung open and the farmer's wife walked in, a little girl trailing her. *'Goedemorgen.'*

'Good morning, Karel,' Miss Pallant responded.

The woman broke into a smile and put her palms to her cheeks when she saw Allan and Miss Pallant with arms around each other. She immediately began talking and advanced on Allan, touching his face and gesturing that she wanted to check his bandage. Miss Pallant backed away and he braced himself against the stable wall.

The farmer's wife lifted his shirt and examined the wounds under the bandages. She turned to Miss Pallant and nodded approvingly. Still talking, she walked over to the cow and milked the animal while the little girl watched. Miss Pallant took the broom and began to sweep.

Allan refused to do nothing while the women worked. Using the wall for support, he made his way to Valour's stall.

The mare's eyes brightened and she huffed and nickered in excitement. 'Ready to ride, girl?' he murmured.

Valour moved her head up and down.

He smiled. 'I am eager to be off as well.' He found a brush with which to groom her.

Miss Pallant, still holding her broom, rushed over. 'You mustn't do that. You need to rest, Captain.'

'I need to regain my strength,' he countered.

They needed to leave this place. They needed to discover what had happened in the battle, whether it was safe for him to return her to her friends in Brussels. If possible, he would like to get her back to Brussels today. Each day away meant more damage to her reputation.

From outside the barn came a man's voice. *'Engels! Waar ben je?'*

'Jakob?' The farmer's wife stood up so fast the milk stool clattered on to the floor. She left her bucket and ran out of the barn, her little daughter at her heels.

'Toon jezelf, Engels!' Apparently the farmer had returned.

'Help me to the door,' Allan demanded.

Leaning on Miss Pallant, he reached the barn's door.

Gesturing for Marian to remain behind him, he stepped into the light.

The farmer, his eyes blazing, pointed to him. *'Engels, bah!*

U won—' He ranted on, and Allan caught both Wellington's and Napoleon's names in the foreign diatribe.

Two words stood out. *U won.* The Allies won. Wellington had done it, by God!

But this peasant farmer did not cheer about it. He carried an axe and shook it in the air.

His wife seized his arm and tugged on it. *'Nee!'* she pleaded. The little girl clung to her skirts and wailed.

Allan was no match for this man, not in his debilitated state.

The farmer, face crimson with anger, advanced, raising the axe high.

Chapter Five

'Stop!' Miss Pallant cried.

She emerged from the barn, Allan's pistol in her hand. *Smart girl,* he said to himself.

She aimed it at the farmer. 'Back away.'

The farmer halted and pointed at her. *'Een vrouw?'*

'Back!' Miss Pallant repeated.

The farmer gripped the axe even tighter.

'Marian, nee.' His wife started towards her.

'No, Karel!' Miss Pallant's voice turned pleading. 'Stay back.' Her expression turned firm again as she pointed the pistol at the husband and glanced nervously at Allan. 'What now, Captain?'

His mind worked quickly. 'Give the pistol to me.' He extended his hand. 'We leave now. Can you saddle the horse?'

'I can.' Her voice was determined. She inched towards him and gave him the pistol.

The farmer cast a worried look to his wife. They exchanged several tense words. Planning to overpower him, perhaps? If they guessed how close his legs were to buckling beneath him, they might succeed. Allan held the pistol with both hands, supporting his weary arms against his body.

The farmer and his wife continued their argument, the man pointing towards the mule bucolically watching this scene unfold. Was the man worried they might report him for stealing from the dead? The French would not have cared; the French army survived on plunder, but Wellington might not be so forgiving. If the farmer killed them, no one would ever know. They would simply have disappeared.

'Mama!' The little girl pulled at her mother's skirts as the woman tried to shield the child with her body.

Allan would not kill a child. He was not Edwin Tranville.

His long-standing anger at Edwin strengthened Allan's arms. He lifted the pistol higher, but sweat dripped from his brow. Miss Pallant had better hurry.

He heard her moving around behind him, and Valour's hooves stamping the ground, as if as impatient as he.

'Your boots, Captain?' she called to him.

'Bring them. I'll don them later.'

Marian led the horse to him, saddled and with his boots sticking out from the bags slung across the horse's back.

'Hold the pistol while I mount.' He handed the pistol to her, and prayed for the strength to seat himself on the horse. His wound now throbbed in agony and the muscles in his legs were trembling with the effort of standing so long.

He grabbed the pommel and put his stockinged foot in the stirrup. Taking a deep breath, he swung his leg over the horse.

And cried out with pain.

But he made it into the saddle, even though his vision momentarily turned black.

'Farewell, Karel,' Miss Pallant cried as she mounted the horse. She clutched Allan's arm with one hand and held the pistol in the other. 'Go now.'

Valour sped off as if she'd understood the need to hurry.

The farmer ran after them, shouting and swinging the axe, but Valour galloped faster, down the same path on which the farmer had undoubtedly just arrived. Allan gave Valour her head until they were a safe distance away and the path opened on to a larger road. He slowed the mare before she was blown.

They passed fields and wood, all blurring into shades of green and brown. Allan's muscles ached and his wound throbbed, but he hung on. Miss Pallant, seated behind him, clung to his back.

The road on which they travelled showed no signs of leading anywhere. Allan tried to keep them heading in a north-easterly direction, surmising they would either find a road that led to Brussels or they'd reach the Dutch border. Either way they would be travelling away from France and would be unlikely to encounter a retreating French army.

'We should stop, Captain,' Miss Pallant said to him.

'Not yet,' he managed. He swayed in the saddle.

'Captain—'

'I am well enough.' The day was not far advanced. They might reach a town soon if he held on a little longer.

The road twisted to follow a stream flowing alongside. Valour turned toward the water.

'She is thirsty, Captain. Let her drink.'

'Very well.' He could not argue, even though he had no assurance he'd have the strength to mount the horse again once off her back.

Miss Pallant slipped off, landing on her feet. Allan's legs nearly gave out on him when he dismounted.

Marian had guessed he'd been holding on by a thin tether. She'd felt the tension in the muscles of his back as he rode.

'You must rest, too,' she insisted.

'We are too exposed here,' he said. 'I do not think the farmer would pursue us, but if I am wrong—' He glanced around and pointed to some thick bushes across a very narrow section of the stream. 'Come. We can hide over there.'

She helped him cross the stream to the shelter of the foliage before returning to lead Valour over. The sanctuary was ideal. There was even a pool of water perfect for Valour to drink unseen.

The Captain collapsed to the ground and leaned against a tree trunk, his eyes closed, breathing hard from the walk. How had he managed to ride so far? she wondered. Only the day before she'd feared he would die.

Marian reached into the saddlebags and pulled out the tin cup she'd packed along with their clothing. Walking a bit upstream from where Valour stood she filled the cup and drank, then refilled it and carried it to the captain. 'Drink this.'

He returned a grateful look as he wrapped his fingers around the cup.

His stockings were shredded from the stirrup. 'It is time you put on your boots.'

He lowered the cup. 'My feet will welcome them.'

It was the closest he'd come to complaining throughout this ordeal. She retrieved his clean stockings and boots from the saddlebags. 'Shall I put them on for you?'

'My stockings, if you do not mind. The boots I must do myself.' His voice was weary, though he seemed to be making an effort to disguise it.

She took his foot in her hand, brushing off the leaves and removing the torn stockings. She gently slipped on the clean one, pulling it up and smoothing out the wrinkles. She glanced at his face.

He gazed at her with an expression that made her go warm all over. She quickly turned her attention to his other foot.

When she finished, he said, 'Thank you, Miss Pallant.' His voice, low and raspy, seemed to reach deep inside her, making her want—something.

'Has your fever returned?' She moved closer to place her palm on his forehead. 'You feel cool.'

'On the mend.' He smiled. His hand closed around hers. 'I hope to give you no more trouble, Miss Pallant. You have endured enough already. You have done extremely well.'

Her heart swelled at his praise, although she suspected it was his courage that fed her own. 'I am not about to complain of the need to tend you. Where would I be without you?'

He laughed. 'Shall we take turns admiring each other?'

He admired her? Her insides fluttered at the thought.

'Sit and rest, Miss Pallant. You were right to make us stop. We should be safe enough here.'

She leaned against the same tree trunk as he, her shoulder touching his. 'Surely the farmer will not come after us.'

'I think not.' He paused. 'Did you hear him? I believe he said the Allies won the battle.'

'How very glad I am of it.' She sighed. 'Was that what angered him, do you think? Was he angry that Napoleon lost? I heard talk in Brussels that some of the Belgians preferred Napoleon.'

'Perhaps that was the reason.' His voice had a hard edge. 'Or he feared we would charge him with theft.'

She faced him. 'You will not do that, will you? You will not charge him with theft? They were so poor. His wife was kind to us. You might not have survived without the help she rendered.'

His eyes softened. 'I will say nothing.'

She reached for him, but withdrew her hand and sat back again.

'I do not know what awaits you in Brussels, though.' His voice turned low.

'Do you mean about Domina?' A wave of guilt washed over her. She had forgotten that Domina might not have encountered a chivalrous man like the captain.

'Your friend, as well, but I was primarily thinking of your reputation.'

She felt like laughing. 'Really, Captain, I am grateful to be alive. Nothing else seems as important.' Except, perhaps, knowing he also was alive.

Their conversation fell away and soon his breathing slowed to the even cadence of sleep. Valour contentedly chewed on a patch of grass. The air was warm, and the sound of the trickling stream and the rustling leaves lulled Marian until her eyes, too, closed and sleep overtook her.

She woke to a touch on her shoulder. The Captain stood over her, boots on. 'We should be off.'

She quickly stood. 'How long did I sleep?'

'Two hours. Perhaps a bit more, I would guess.' He glanced at the sun, which had dipped lower in the sky. 'But we need to make the most of daylight.'

They mounted Valour again and returned to the road.

The landscape did not change for miles but as the sun dipped low in the sky the spire of a church steeple came in sight.

'A village, Captain,' she cried.

He turned his head. 'At last, Miss Pallant.'

It was near dark when they reached the village streets and found an inn. They left Valour to the care of the stable workers and entered the inn.

The innkeeper's brows rose at their appearance. They must have looked strange, indeed, in their plundered clothing, wearing shirts and no coats, and looking weary from all they'd been through.

'Do you speak English?' the captain asked.

The innkeeper straightened. *'Français, monsieur.'*

Marian tapped the captain on the arm. 'We have very few coins left.'

The captain spoke French to the innkeeper, negotiating the price of the room and board. At this point Marian would have been happy to sleep in the stable with Valour. She'd become used to stables.

The captain procured the room and ordered a hot meal to be brought to them. The arrangements complete, the innkeeper grabbed a lighted candle and led them up a stairway.

Captain Landon leaned down to her ear. 'I was afraid we would not have enough for two rooms.'

She nodded. 'I am certain we do not.'

He faltered on the step and clapped his hand against his wound. She offered her shoulder, but he shook his head. They had another flight to climb and a long hallway before finally being escorted into a very small room with a tiny window and only enough space for the bed and a small table and chair.

The innkeeper lit a candle on the table from the one he carried. He inclined his head very slightly and spoke in French. 'Your meal will be delivered directly.'

When the door closed behind him, Captain Landon clasped the bedpost.

Marian hurried to his side. 'You must lie down, Captain.'

'The chair will suffice.'

She would not hear of it. 'Nonsense.' She gently manoeuvred him to the bed, and he gave no further argument.

He sat with numb acceptance as she pulled off his boots. 'Lie down for a bit,' she murmured.

He moaned as he lowered himself against the pillows. She had no wish to disturb him further, either by helping him remove his shirt or trousers or even by covering him.

Wanting nothing more than to lie next to him, she instead busied herself with unpacking their own clothing from the saddlebags. She hung the clothes in layers over the chair, hoping the wrinkles would fall out. When she finished, a knock on the door brought their food.

A maid carried in the tray and already the scent of the food made Marian's mouth water. There were two large bowls of stew, and a dish piled with potatoes cut into long rectangles. As soon as the maid left, Marian picked up one of the potato pieces. It tasted fried on the outside but soft and full of flavour on the inside.

She glanced to the captain, too deeply asleep for even the scent of the food to wake him. She was tempted to eat the whole plate of potatoes without him.

Shaking her head in dismay over her selfishness, she turned to him. 'Captain?'

He did not rouse.

'Captain?' She touched his unwounded shoulder.

His eyes opened, softening into a look that made her knees turn to melted wax.

'Our food is here,' she told him.

He sat on the bed and she on the chair as they ate, too hungry for conversation. Along with the stew and potatoes were large tankards of beer. Marian drank the entire contents of one. By the time they had finished their dishes were almost as clean as if scrubbed by a scullery maid. She felt calmer than she'd felt in days, even since before the Duchess of Richmond's Ball.

She was also very sleepy.

She stacked the dishes on the tray and set them outside the door. When she came back in the room, the Captain pointed to the clothing hanging on the chair. 'Are those clean?'

She nodded.

'I believe I would prefer sleeping in clean clothing than in these.' He looked down at himself.

Now that he mentioned it, Marian could well agree. She was also anxious to remove the clothing of the dead soldiers.

'I will help you.' She separated her clothing from his.

His gaze caught hers. 'I will be grateful.'

Her body flooded with sensation again and this time she understood it had nothing to do with tending to an injured soldier, but everything to do with him being a man. She pulled off his shirt, dusty from the road, and helped him on with the laundered one, which sported a tattered hole where the musket ball had torn through. She reached for the buttons on his trousers.

He stopped her. 'I will manage this part.'

She turned away.

When she turned back he lay against the pillows, eyes already closed. She sat in the chair and rested her head on the table, using her arms for a pillow.

'Miss Pallant.' His voice intruded. She'd almost fallen asleep. 'Share the bed or I'll insist we change places.'

She glanced over at him. His eyes were still closed. She should not sleep with him, but the chair was so hard and the bed so temptingly soft. She and Domina had shared a bed on occasion when travelling with Domina's family, and she and the captain had slept in the same stall the past two nights, after all. And he was not delirious.

She pushed the chair away from the table and pulled off her cap, removing the pins and setting them carefully aside. Again lamenting the lack of a comb, she redid her plait and quickly changed back into Domina's brother's clothes.

One last moment of decision. She hesitated only a second longer before climbing under the covers next to him. Even though careful not to touch him, she felt the warmth of his body nearby. He faced her and she watched him in repose, the pain gone from his features, his strong face softened and shadowed with a three-day growth of whiskers. She was tempted to touch his beard, to discover how it felt. Soft like the hair on his head? She slid her hand towards him, but made herself roll over away from him instead.

Sleep eluded her. He moved closer and took her in his arms, spooning her against him. She ought to be shocked. She ought to push away and return to the chair.

Instead she nestled against him and instantly fell asleep.

Marian woke to the morning sun warming her face. The captain faced her, one of his arms resting across her shoulder. The other lay over her hair, now loose and splayed over the pillows.

She gasped and tried to edge away.

His eyes fluttered open and gazed into hers. His lips widened into a sleepy smile. 'Good morning, Miss Pallant.'

'Morning,' she managed.

He smoothed her hair off her face. 'We seem to be still in one piece.'

His stroking hand sent waves of sensation all through her. 'One piece,' she repeated.

She'd danced with gentlemen and even had kisses stolen by one or two, but never had she felt the nearness of a man more acutely than this. She felt naked next to him, even though they were both fully clothed. At the same time she felt completely at ease with him.

His expression sobered and his hand rested against the back of her neck. 'I am glad you are here.'

She opened her mouth to tell him she, too, was glad they were safe in the inn, but he drew her forwards until their bodies touched. His lips were so close she tasted his breath the moment before his lips met hers. His kiss, so gentle at first, seemed to reach down to the most female part of her. A needful sound escaped and she pressed against him.

His arms tightened around her and she felt the firm shape of him beneath his trousers. Remembering how close her fingers had come to touching him there, she sighed, and his tongue slipped into her mouth.

This was a completely surprising experience, but she lost herself in the pleasure of such a kiss from this man. The pleasure that radiated throughout her body and made her desire so much more from him.

She suddenly understood how men and women needed to couple, to join together in that carnal way. She understood it because she felt it with Captain Landon.

His hand reached under her shirt and rubbed against her breasts, though they were still bound up by her scarf. He might as well have been touching her bare flesh, the sensation was so acute. She wanted to cry out.

She writhed against him, feeling the evidence of his male

member. It had grown bigger, just like the maid described. What harm would there be in letting him bed her? Her reputation was already likely in tatters. Why resist this—this promise of unknown delights? They were already connected by their shared ordeal—why not be connected in flesh?

His hand journeyed lower. She covered it with her own and directed his hand lower still to the place between her legs where she was needing him to touch her. He complied, bringing intense sensation. As if a part of him, her body moved against his fingers. The sensation grew into exquisite rapture, supreme joy and suddenly, exploding pleasure.

She seized his shoulders to steady herself.

He cried out and rolled away from her, grasping his shoulder.

She'd touched his wound.

'I am sorry. I am sorry.' She sat up and reached for him, fearful she'd done some irreparable damage.

He covered the wound with his hand. 'Do not touch it!' he cried. Breathing heavily as if he'd run a league, he made a mollifying gesture with his hand. 'Give me a moment.'

Pain had thrust Allan back to reason.

By God, he'd been about to make love to her! He'd already touched her in ways a gentleman would never touch a respectable female who was not his wife. What was he thinking?

He had not been thinking, merely feeling, revelling in her beauty, her nearness and his need. He'd taken advantage of her in the most abominable way.

The pain subsided enough for him to sit next to her. 'It is I who should apologise,' he rasped. 'I took advantage.' He shook his head. After all she had done for him, he'd engaged in selfish indulgence. 'It will not happen again.'

'You are sorry that happened between us?' Her question was asked in a tone he could only interpret as dismay. She turned away from him and straightened her clothing.

How could he explain it to her? He had aroused her, seduced

her so well that she would have easily allowed him to deflower her. How did he admit to this valiant woman who had saved his life that he had been selfish enough to abandon all propriety with her?

As he watched her, his senses merely flamed anew and he could think only of tasting her lips again or feeling her convulse against his fingers. He was in danger of repeating his behaviour and more. He spun away, got up and walked to the window.

The window faced the stable and the scent of horse, leather and hay wafted the great distance to their third-floor room. The scent reminded him of the peasant's stable, of Miss Pallant bringing him water and food and tending his wound, of her aiming a pistol at a huge man with an axe a man who could have cut her down as easily as chopping wood for winter.

And he would repay her with dishonour.

Her half-boots sounded against the wooden floor. 'I will go below and see to some food and clean bandages for your wound.'

'Wait,' he cried, intending to tell her he alone was at fault, intending to ask her forgiveness. Instead, below he spied a man.

A man in a red coat.

A red uniform.

He turned to her, so quickly that pain shot through his shoulder again. He clutched it and laboured to speak. 'There are English soldiers down there.' Three men in red coats entered the stable. 'I can get you back to Brussels at last.'

Chapter Six

By late afternoon they were on the road to Brussels, a wide, flat, well-travelled road very unlike the ones they'd ridden the previous day. They rode in a carriage and Valour remained at the village stable. The English soldiers had lent them the money for the trip and for stabling Valour. Captain Landon had given them his vowel, although Marian was determined to pay for all of it.

She glanced out of the carriage window and watched wounded soldiers, in wagons and on foot, head towards Brussels. Even three days after the battle there were still great numbers of wounded on the road.

She turned to Captain Landon. His eyes were closed and his head rested against the side of the carriage. He was still weak, but insisted upon escorting her back to Brussels.

It would have been much easier if he would have allowed her to make the journey alone. Then their goodbyes would have already been spoken, and she could make him a memory or perhaps forget altogether that he regretted nearly making love to her.

She knew that men needed to bed women. The teachers at

the boarding school had explained that to her and Domina. They'd explained that men visited brothels and kept mistresses and seduced maids because men must bed women. Men's urges were very strong. Once aroused, they must be satisfied.

This was the reason a young lady must never be alone with a man and must never titillate his carnal desires. Alarming tales reinforced this lesson, tales of respectable girls bearing babies out of wedlock, being tossed out of their homes and winding up as women of the street.

Marian understood perfectly now.

At the time she had listened to these lessons with an arched brow. Certainly *she* would be able to handle any man who dared make unwanted advances towards her.

What she had not understood was that she, too, could be overpowered by irresistible urges. And that one man could arouse them.

Captain Landon.

Marian flushed with shame at the memory of what happened between them, Yet at the same time she yearned to repeat the experience.

She sighed. It was all too confusing.

'What is it?' His eyes were open and gazing at her.

'Nothing.' Surely he could not read her mind. 'Why do you ask?'

'You sighed.'

She turned back to the window so he could not see her pink cheeks. 'I was looking at all the wounded soldiers. Why are they still on the road? Why are they not cared for?'

'They said at the inn there were many casualties.' He glanced out the window and swore softly. 'Good God.'

'They have been on the road for miles. So many of them,' she whispered.

He leaned further out of the window. 'I can see Brussels ahead.'

'We are near?' They had been on the road for five hours,

but she was still not ready. She looked into his eyes. 'Then we will be saying goodbye soon.'

His expression sobered. 'As soon as you are safely returned to your friends.'

Her friends? She could hardly remember them. 'It will seem odd.'

'To be with your friends again?'

'No.' Her throat tightened. 'To not be with you.'

His eyes darkened. 'Indeed.'

Tears pricked her eyes. 'Perhaps we can see each other? In Brussels, I mean?'

He averted his gaze. 'That may not be advisable.'

She felt crushed. Had her wanton behaviour caused so great a dislike he wished to avoid her? Then why had he not simply sent her back to Brussels alone?

'I see.' Her voice came out sharp.

He turned back to her. 'Maybe news of your escapade can be kept quiet. At Hougoumont and at the village you were disguised as a boy. No one knew you. You may be able to return with your reputation intact.'

'My reputation.' She thought of the previous night. 'Perhaps my wanton behaviour deserves a bad reputation.'

He took her hand. 'That was my fault. My dishonor. I ought to offer—'

'No!' She pulled her hand away. 'I will not make you pay for what was my fault. It was all my fault. I came to the battle-field. I joined you in bed. I—I made you touch me.'

He shook his head. 'It is just that right now. I have nothing to give you. No wealth. Nothing.'

Did he think she cared about such things? No, she cared about love. She'd seen marriage without love and wanted none of it.

The Captain went on. 'We stopped before we went too far. If we can protect your reputation, it will be as if this whole time did not happen.' He lowered his gaze. 'If not, I will offer—'

She waved a hand. 'Enough, Captain. You are not obligated to marry me. Take me back to the Fentons. We will both of us act as if nothing happened.'

Outwardly she might be able to pretend that her life was unchanged, but truly her time with Captain Landon had changed everything inside her. All the frivolity that had consumed her and Domina before—the routs, the balls, the latest ladies' fashions—seemed meaningless to her now.

They soon entered the city. Soldiers were everywhere, sitting on the pavement or leaning against buildings, all wounded, all looking as if they needed a bed and much doctoring.

'Look at them.' Marian cried in alarm. 'Is there no shelter for them? No care for them?'

The captain, too, looked affected by the sight. 'There must be too many.'

'You have a room, though, do you not, Captain?' she asked. 'You have a place to stay in Brussels?'

'Not in Brussels,' he responded. 'I will go back to the village inn where we were last night. I have to get Valour, after all. And when I am a bit more healed, I must return to the regiment.'

She glanced out the window again at the numbers of homeless soldiers. 'But the coachman said he will return there *tomorrow*, not tonight.'

He gave a not-too-reassuring smile. 'I'll find something for tonight.'

'Where?' she cried. If there were rooms available, no men would be on the streets. 'Do you have friends in Brussels?'

He shrugged. 'Likely not. My regiment is probably already on the march.'

Marian felt distraught. She would stay on the street with him, to care for him, rather than have him be alone.

'Do not worry about me.'

The carriage entered the more fashionable part of the city, where London society had chosen housing. Even on these familiar streets, soldiers were languishing.

The Fentons' rooms were nearby. Marian took a breath against a sudden pang of anxiety. 'We are almost there.' She could not leave him without knowing he had a place to stay.

The carriage stopped.

'Is this the place?' he asked.

They were practically in front of the Fentons' door. 'Yes,' she murmured.

Climbing from the carriage caused him pain, but the captain insisted upon helping her out.

He spoke to the driver. 'Where will I find you?'

The coachman named the stable where he would refresh the horses. 'I'll take whatever passengers I can find and leave tomorrow morning by eight.'

'Thank you,' the Captain replied.

As the carriage rolled away, he glanced at Marian. 'Which door?'

She pointed. 'This one.'

He did not move, instead stood looking down upon her.

'Oh, Captain,' she whispered. 'I cannot bear for us to be parted.'

He enfolded her in his arms and she buried her face against his chest, feeling the bandage beneath his clothing.

'Nor I,' he murmured, holding her even tighter. 'We will meet again some day.'

Marian wished she could believe him, but it felt like she would be parted from him for ever.

He released her slowly, caressing her face before knocking upon the Fentons' door.

A manservant opened it.

'Captain Landon escorting Miss Pallant,' the captain said.

The manservant gaped first at the captain, then Marian. She looked down at herself, still in Domina's brother's clothes, now torn and shabby. The captain's coat was ripped where the musket ball had pierced it.

'Come in.' The manservant stepped aside. 'I'll announce you.'

He left them waiting in the hall. The captain pressed his hand to his shoulder again and pain flitted across his face.

At least they had had shelter in the Belgian farmer's stable—where would the captain be this night, before returning to the inn and Valour?

She glanced around the hall, at the marble table holding a vase of flowers, at the silver tray, now empty, that had once held piles of invitations. There was no chair for the captain. She'd never noticed the lack of a chair before.

A quarter of an hour passed before the servant returned to escort them above stairs to the Fentons' drawing room. When they entered, both Sir Roger and Lady Fenton were present.

Lady Fenton glared at Marian. 'You have some nerve returning here big-as-you-please.'

Marian's face burned as if it had been slapped. She had not expected a warm welcome, but this was no welcome at all.

Captain Landon stepped forward. 'Allow me to explain—'

Sir Roger raised his quizzing glass to his eye. 'Who are you?'

'Captain Landon, sir,' he responded. 'Miss Pallant has been through a great deal. She deserves your every consideration.'

Lady Fenton laughed. 'Consideration? She has dishonoured us! Acted totally against anything we could wish—'

Marian broke in. 'Is Domina safe?'

'Domina?' the lady huffed. 'Safe from your bad influence, I can tell you. She told us you ran off during the night—off to be with some soldier, we could guess.' Lady Fenton turned to Captain Landon. 'You, sir? Did she run off with you?'

The captain's eyes turned flinty. 'You misunderstand.'

Sir Roger pursed his lips. He turned away from Marian and

addressed himself to the captain. 'Our son's horse came back, obviously having been ridden hard. Some of our son's clothing was missing.' He gestured to Marian. 'Domina eventually admitted Marian had run off.'

Lady Fenton added, 'At first our daughter would not tell us where she had gone. We soon wore her down—'

Sir Roger went on. 'Our daughter said Marian wished to witness the battle, but we do not credit that.'

'What well-bred young lady would even think to witness a battle?' His wife shook her head. 'Not that she is as well bred as she pretends, born in India and all that. This behaviour is hoydenish in the extreme.'

'Domina is unhurt?' All the abuse of her character washed over Marian for the moment. None of it mattered if her friend had come home in one piece.

Lady Fenton shot daggers at her. 'She is vastly hurt by your behaviour and by how you abused her friendship and took advantage of us all.'

The captain straightened. 'You have been misled. Miss Pallant did not—'

Lady Fenton held up a hand. 'Do not say a word. I will not believe it.'

It finally dawned on Marian that Domina had blamed the entire escapade on her. She swallowed. 'Leave it, Captain. They will not hear you.'

Lady Fenton glared at her. 'Your trunk is packed. Take it now or send instructions where to deliver it.'

The captain stepped forwards. 'Wait a moment. You accepted responsibility for this young lady. You are still responsible for her.'

Lady Fenton laughed in his face. 'It seems *you* have accepted responsibility for her. It is you who have dishonoured her, is it not, sir?'

His eyes blazed at the woman. 'Miss Pallant has done nothing that requires apology.'

Marian felt her face burn. He was wrong and he knew it. 'I do not wish to stay here. I will go back in the carriage.'

The captain turned to her. 'You will not leave. These people brought you to Brussels and they will not abandon you now.'

'She will go,' Sir Roger said.

The Fentons had been like a mother and father to her. Domina had been like a sister. Or so she'd thought.

How easily they turned her out.

'It is near dark.' The captain spoke in a firm voice. 'There is no guarantee of finding accommodations so late.'

Not for him either, she thought.

'Tomorrow I will make other arrangements for her,' he went on. 'Tonight she stays with you or a story will soon circulate about how respectable young women cannot trust you to chaperon them.'

'You would not dare speak against us.' Lady Fenton looked as if she would explode.

The captain glared.

'Very well.' Lady Fenton's shoulders slumped. 'She must confine herself to her room. I do not wish to set eyes on her again.'

He nodded and turned to Marian, reaching over to steady himself on the back of a chair. 'I'll come for you in the morning.'

She could not help but feel relief. She would be parted from him for only a night.

Her brows knit. 'But you have no place to stay tonight.' She turned to the Fentons. 'There is room in this house. He must stay here.'

'I will not hear of it!' cried Lady Fenton.

The captain looked directly into Marian's eyes. 'I will manage. It is only one night.' With a fortifying breath he released his grip on the chair and bowed to Sir Roger and Lady Fenton. 'I will call for Miss Pallant in the morning.'

He walked to the door, but needed to hold on to the door-jamb a moment before proceeding to the stairs.

'Captain!' Marian ran after him.

From the top of the stairs she watched his descent. The manservant waited at the bottom step.

The captain faltered. Seizing the banister, he bent slightly as if seized with pain.

'Captain!' Marian hurried to him, but the manservant reached him first and assisted him the rest of the way.

Sir Roger and Lady Fenton came to the top of the stairs.

Marian looked back at them. 'You heartless people. Can you not see he is wounded? A Frenchman's musket ball went through him, and still he helped me return to you. He said he'd return me safely *home*.' She choked back an angry sob.

She turned to the manservant. 'He has no place to stay.'

The man's expression was sympathetic.

The captain waved them off. 'I am quite back to rights again.'

Marian glared at the Fentons. 'He must stay here as well. Otherwise he will be on the streets like the others.'

'It is not our concern,' said Lady Fenton.

'Now, dear…' Sir Roger looked uncertain.

The manservant spoke up. 'If I may be so bold, sir. This soldier may use my bed and I'll make up a cot for myself.'

'Very well.' Sir Roger looked relieved. 'Take him below. He may stay.'

The Captain did not protest when the man offered his shoulder to assist him. Marian watched them make their way to the door down to the servants' quarters. The manservant glanced back at her. 'Do not fret, miss. I'll see he is well tended.'

She waited until they closed the door behind them before climbing the stairs to the room where she once so happily spent her nights. When she passed Sir Roger and Lady Fenton on the first landing, she refused to even look at them. Her room was one flight up, but she deliberately set a slow pace.

Let them not see the distress burning inside her. When she reached the room, she still did not hurry.

After she closed the door behind her she leaned against it for a moment. By God, she would not give in to tears now, not even angry ones.

With a groan of frustration she removed her half-boots, all scratched and worn, and tore off the cap that had hidden her hair. At least she would finally be able to brush out its tangles.

There was a faint knock at the door. Domina's maid peeked in. 'I came to help you, if you wish, miss.' Becky was young, but aspired to be a fine lady's maid some day.

At least her face was friendly. 'Oh, Becky, I do not wish to get you in trouble.'

The maid shrugged. 'We won't tell them, then, will we?' She picked up the cap and jacket off the floor. 'What happened to you, miss?'

Marian glanced away. 'I wound up in the middle of the battle for a while, and have since been trying to get back.' She lifted her gaze to the girl. 'Miss Fenton told them I went alone, but that was not the truth. She must have found her way back; I do thank God for that.'

'I think she came in before dawn,' Becky admitted, folding the jacket. 'But there is time to talk of that later. What might I do for you now?'

'I do not know what to request.' She put her hand in her hair. 'All I really want is to wash myself and my hair, but I dare not request a bath.'

Becky smiled. 'Let's get you out of the rest of those clothes and into a wrapper. We'll sneak you down to the kitchen for a bath. Lady Fenton will never know.'

Marian hugged her. 'I cannot think of anything that would be more generous.'

'I'll come back for you when the water is ready,' Becky said.

Marian shed the rest of her clothing and nearly cheered

aloud when she freed herself from the scarf binding her chest. She rolled the garments into a ball, intending to burn them. She'd send Domina's brother new ones.

Standing in the room naked felt better than wearing those clothes. She could still smell the blood and smoke of Hougoumont upon them even though she'd tried to scrub them clean.

She turned to the trunk and opened it, searching through to find her nightrail and her brush and comb. She wrapped the robe around her, tied the sash, and sat in the chair in front of her dressing table. Starting from the ends, she combed the tangles from her hair.

Half an hour had gone by before she could pass the comb through without it catching on a knot.

Becky returned. 'We can sneak you down to the kitchen now. We've set up a tub in the scullery. It will be quite private there.'

Marian followed her down the servants' staircase to the area below stairs where, as well as the kitchen, the house-keeper's and the manservant's rooms were located. Marian had never been in this part of the house.

When they entered the kitchen, Captain Landon was the first person she saw. He sat at the table, a huge plate of food in front of him. Also in a robe, he was clean-shaven and his wet brown hair gleamed almost black. He'd obviously also been offered a bath.

She warmed at the idea he'd been so well tended. 'Captain, they appear to be taking good care of you.'

'They are indeed.' His gaze flickered over her.

She wrapped her nightrail tighter and touched her hair, wishing she had tied it back with a ribbon.

'Enjoy your bath,' he said.

She might have, except with every stroke of the wash cloth against her skin, she thought of his hand stroking her. The look he had just given her when gazing on her dishabille had been unreadable.

* * *

When she finished her bath, he was no longer in the kitchen, but the cook insisted she eat a meal. Not nearly as hungry as she thought she might be, she ate enough to show Cook how grateful she was for the kindness. Afterwards she climbed the servants' stairs to her room with no one to see her.

She entered her room and found Domina sitting on the bed.

Domina jumped off. 'Oh, Marian! I've been waiting ages for you.'

Marian felt cold. 'Domina.'

The short auburn curls that framed Domina's round face bobbed as she hurried towards Marian. 'I expect you are angry because of what I said to Mama and Papa, but I had to do it. They were so angry.' Her eyes filled with fat tears. 'Marian, it is so dreadful. So terribly dreadful.' She threw her arms around Marian and sobbed. 'Ollie is dead! His name was on a list. He was killed in the battle.'

Lieutenant Harry Oliver had proudly worn the uniform and gleaming Grecian helmet of the Inniskilling Dragoons, and Domina had fallen head over ears in love with him. She and Ollie were secretly betrothed, because Ollie had no title and Domina's mother would never have approved the match, but they were in *love*.

Now Ollie, the reason they'd ridden off to be near the battle, was dead.

Marian set her anger aside. 'I am so sorry, Domina.' She held her grieving friend.

Domina sniffled. 'Mama and Papa do not understand. But you do, don't you, Marian?'

Marian had never understood Domina's infatuation with the rather ordinary Harry Oliver, but she did understand loss and now she knew the horror of a soldier's death.

She coaxed her friend back to the bed and sat next to her. 'I am so sad for you.'

Domina went into great detail about how devastated she

was, how perfect a man Ollie had been, and how her life was over. 'And…and the worst of it is—' tears streamed down her cheeks '—I have not had my monthly courses.'

'What?' Marian gaped at her.

Domina blew her nose into a soggy handkerchief. 'I may have Ollie's child inside me.'

'Do not say you bedded him, Domina.' Marian shook her head.

Domina sighed. 'How could I resist? We had such a passion for each other.' She collapsed against the pillow with fresh sobs.

Marian lifted her so Domina was forced to look at her. 'Do your parents know?'

Domina's eyes widened as if she thought Marian had lost her wits. 'Certainly not.'

Marian held her firmly. 'You must tell them. If you are increasing, they will have to make plans—'

'I will never give up Ollie's baby!' Domina cried.

Marian shook her. 'Then you had better tell your parents so they can make plans for both of you. Your reputation and your child's future are at stake.'

Domina sobered. 'My child's future. Yes, you are right.' She gave Marian a quick hug and hopped off the bed. 'I will tell them directly.' Her curls danced as if she were still a carefree débutante as she ran to the door. She turned to wave at Marian before she fled into the hallway, never once asking about Marian's health or about what had happened after Marian fell off the horse.

Soon the sound of raised voices reached Marian's ears, Lady Fenton's shrill cries, Sir Roger's booming tones and Domina's strident wails.

Domina had taken her advice.

Marian donned her nightdress and crawled into bed and fell asleep quickly in spite of the verbal battle being waged. She slept soundly until a knock on the door woke her.

Becky entered carrying a candle. 'Miss Pallant, I came to tell you we are leaving as soon as it is light.'

'Leaving?' Marian sat up.

Becky nodded. 'Sir Roger and Lady Fenton have ordered a carriage. We are to return to England posthaste, but you are not to come with us.' The candle illuminated the maid's worried face. 'What will you do, miss?'

The Fentons had already planned to abandon her, so this came as no great surprise.

'Do not worry over me.' The Captain would not desert her, that much she knew.

'Then, goodbye, miss.' Becky turned to leave.

Marian rose from the bed. 'Wait a moment.'

She ran to her trunk and rummaged through it until she found her coin purse. She dropped several coins into the maid's hands.

Becky stared at the money. 'Oh, miss, it is too much.'

Marian gave her a quick embrace. 'Your kindness deserves reward. If you ever need any assistance at all, you must find me.'

The girl stared at her hand again before curtsying and rushing out of the room.

Marian sat upon the edge of the bed to wait until dawn and the Fentons' departure. After that, she and the Captain would decide what to do.

Glad as she was to delay saying goodbye to him, she knew it was only a matter of time.

Perhaps he would find her a way to return to England. Or maybe he would locate her cousin Edwin and place her in Edwin's care. Edwin would want to return to England. He would inherit his father's title and estate and there would be much for him to arrange.

Marian had almost forgotten that her Uncle Tranville had also lost his life at Waterloo. She had never been close to him, so it was difficult to feel grief. He had rarely been in her company. If he hadn't been away at war, he had been with his mistress, breaking her aunt's heart and, Marian believed, hastening her death.

Marian remembered seeing Uncle Tranville once in Bath, strolling in the square with the woman who'd been his mistress for years. Her uncle had touched the woman as if to remove a bit of lint from her spencer. The woman had pressed his hand against her breast.

Another memory flashed through her mind, one more painful, a memory of her father. In India she'd been out in the market with her *amah* when she glimpsed her father in a carriage, his arms around an exotic creature draped in colourful silks. The woman slipped on to her father's lap and put her lips on her father's mouth.

Later when her parents became sick with the fever, her mother accused her father of catching it from *that woman.* Marian, though a child, somehow she knew who her mother meant, just as she knew *that woman,* and later her Uncle Tranville's mistress, had chosen to be carnal with a man.

Marian gave a cry and lay back on the bed, covering her face with her hands.

She'd never understood before what would drive a woman to abandon all morality and be carnal with a man not her husband.

Not until now. Not until Captain Landon.

Chapter Seven

'Captain!'

The man's voice roused Allan from a sleep so deep and welcome he did not wish to leave it.

'Captain, wake up.' He recognised the voice as Johnson's, the manservant who had given up his bed for him.

Allan opened his eyes to the man's Spartan room.

Johnson stood over him. 'I must leave, Captain. We depart within the hour.'

Allan sat up. 'Depart?'

'For England, sir. Sir Roger and Lady Fenton decided quite abruptly. The Belgian cook and housemaids remain, but the rest of us travel with the family.' He stepped forwards. 'If you rise now, I have time to change your bandage and assist with your dress.'

'What of Miss Pallant?' Returning to England would be best for her. He must see her, though, before she departed.

'She is not to travel with us.'

Allan rose from the bed. This was outrageous. 'They would leave her here? What sort of people are they?'

The man frowned. 'It is not my place to criticise my employers, sir.'

Allan lifted a hand. 'Forgive me. I did not mean for you to speak against them.'

The manservant untied the bandage.

Allan asked, 'Why the haste in leaving? Are you able to tell me that much?'

'I do not know, sir,' the man admitted. 'It came after heated words with their daughter.'

About Miss Pallant? Allan wondered. Perhaps the daughter had told the truth, but, if so, how could these people leave Miss Pallant alone in Brussels? It was unconscionable no matter what she had done.

He sat still as Johnson re-bandaged his wounds. There was still the problem of finding someone to take charge of Miss Pallant before irreparable damage was done to her reputation.

The bandaging completed, the manservant brought Allan's clothes, freshly laundered and brushed. Mended, as well. There were no longer holes in his shirt and coat, no stains on his trousers.

'This is indeed a kindness.' Allan fingered the mended area of his coat. Even his wounds felt on the mend. After Johnson helped him dress, Allan spoke. 'I want to show you my appreciation, but I have no money with me.'

The manservant looked embarrassed. 'No need, sir.' He handed Allan his boots, polished to gleaming black. 'I must be off, sir. I'll be needed by now.'

None the less, Allan would not forget this kind man. As soon as he could arrange it, a token of his gratitude would be sent to him. 'I am very grateful to you.'

The servant bowed his head. 'We are all grateful to *you*, sir, and to the rest of our soldiers.' He hurried out.

After donning his boots and buttoning his coat, Allan climbed the stairs and watched from the recesses of the hall as the Fentons' trunks and bandboxes were carried out the door. Lastly Sir Roger, Lady Fenton and a young woman Allan presumed was their daughter bustled down the stairway, followed by a grumbling boy of about fourteen years.

'I still do not see why we have to leave,' the boy complained.

The family reached the front door. Only the daughter, her face shrouded by a hooded cape, turned back and glanced towards the top of the stairs.

As soon as the door closed behind them, Allan stepped out into the hall. He, too, glanced to the top of the stairs.

Miss Pallant stood there.

Gone was the scruffy lad or the dishevelled nurse or the alluring creature dressed in nothing but a robe. All were replaced by a woman who ought to have been decorating London's finest drawing rooms. Her blonde hair was pulled on top of her head with curls framing her flawless complexion. Her lips were full and her cheeks tinged with pink. She wore a filmy white gown, like an angel might wear, and her shoulders were draped with a colourful shawl.

'Captain.' To his surprise, her voice was excited and her sapphire-blue eyes sparkled. 'I have a wonderful notion.' She started down the stairs, and he felt riveted to the spot waiting for her. 'The Fentons have left for England, but I know they paid for these rooms for another month, at least. We can use the house for the injured soldiers.'

And he'd expected her to lament being abandoned.

'You can stay here, as well. You need a place to recuperate.' She reached the bottom step. 'Have you eaten? Come to the kitchen. If we can convince the cook and the maids to stay, we should be able to offer good care to a great many of them.'

He held up a hand. 'One moment, Miss Pallant—'

But she continued past him. 'I will need your help, because I have no idea who to contact or which of the soldiers are most in need. There are several rooms here. And if we could find extra bedding—'

He seized her arm. 'You cannot do this!'

She lifted her chin. 'After the manner in which Sir Roger and Lady Fenton treated me, I have no qualms about using rooms for which they have already paid.'

'That is not what I meant.' Allan felt like shaking her. 'You cannot care for wounded soldiers.'

She gaped at him. 'Why not? I have cared for you, have I not? And the men at Hougoumont?' Her voice cracked and he realised her high spirits hid more painful emotions.

He suddenly had the urge to hold her, to comfort her for all she had seen and endured.

But he did not. 'Can you not see?' he said instead. 'I gave you no other choice. Besides, you were disguised as a boy then. No one knew you were a respectable young lady. In Brussels your identity will become known. You must consider your reputation—'

'Oh, do not prose on about my reputation again.' She pulled away with a scornful laugh. 'Am I to pit my reputation against their suffering? Do not be nonsensical, Captain.' She walked towards the servants' staircase.

He followed her. 'I do not dispute that using this house would be a great service to those men, only that you should not provide their care.'

She stopped and again pain flitted through her eyes. 'My chaperons have abandoned me, Captain. I do not know anyone who might take me in. Indeed, I know of no one but you upon whom I may depend. Let me be of some use.' Her expression turned pleading. 'I will ask Cook and the maids. If they do not object to helping the soldiers, then neither should we.'

The cook and the maids, all women with grey hair and lined faces, spoke enough French and English that Miss Pallant was able to communicate her plan. While Cook fed them breakfast, Miss Pallant explained to them, 'I will pay you and pay for the food and other supplies the soldiers will need.'

'Can you afford such an expense?' Allan asked her.

She made a dismissive gesture. 'I have wealth enough. My

father made a great deal of money in the East India Company. Neither Lord Tranville nor his man of business bothered overmuch with the amounts I drew out, so I have plenty with me to pay for what we need.'

She had wealth? A woman with wealth had excellent prospects—if she preserved her good name.

The cook and two maids enthusiastically agreed to help care for the wounded soldiers. Apparently these women were not among the Belgians supporting the French.

Miss Pallant gazed at him from across the kitchen table. 'Will you help, Captain? You must know where to go or who to speak to about this.'

He knew her well enough now to be certain she could not be persuaded to abandon this idea. 'I will assist only if you agree not to personally provide care to the men.'

Her gaze did not waver. 'I will do what is required.'

Blast her. Her stubborn streak had already created more trouble for her than she deserved.

He stood. 'Miss Pallant, would you be so good as to speak with me above stairs.'

Allan walked out, hearing with relief her footsteps behind him. He climbed the stairs to the drawing room, the room where the Fentons had so cruelly turned her away. He held the door open for her and caught the scent of roses as she walked by him.

She whirled on him as he closed the door. 'You are going to try to talk me out of this.'

He felt no need to apologise. 'I certainly am. Will you sit?'

She merely walked over to the window and looked out, arms crossed over her chest.

He cleared his throat. 'Very well. Do not sit.' He walked over to stand behind her, wanting to put his hands on her shoulders, remembering how soft and warm she'd felt in his arms when they'd shared the bed—

He dared not think of that. 'Consider this carefully. It is generous of you to pay for the care of the soldiers, and I've certainly no objection to using this house, but you cannot be a lone woman caring for men.'

'The cook and the maids will be helping,' she responded defensively.

'But they are not proper chaperons for you. We must find you a respectable place to stay.' He was distracted by the graceful shape of her neck and by the golden tendrils that caressed its nape.

She turned and was inches from him. 'Where, Captain? I have no friends here who were not friends of the Fentons. My guardian is dead and my cousin, if he is alive, surely is in no position to help me at the moment. Why would anyone take me in when Sir Roger and Lady Fenton have cast me off?'

Her gaze reached his eyes and he forgot for a moment to breathe.

'Perhaps they have said nothing to their friends,' he managed, though his voice turned husky. 'To speak of it would reveal their failure to properly chaperon you, and, do not forget, everyone would have been preoccupied by the battle. We can invent a story to protect your reputation.'

'Do I deserve the protection, Captain?' she whispered. 'Have I not demonstrated all the wanton behaviour of which I have been accused? Should you, of all people, not know how little I deserve a good name?' Her eyes filled with tears, but she ruthlessly blinked them away.

Not before one fell on to her cheek.

Allan brushed it away with the pad of his thumb. 'My fault,' he murmured. He leaned down, closer, so close he felt her breath on his lips.

She made a tiny, yearning sound, tilting her head up to his.

No! He had hurt her enough with his seduction.

He moved away. 'Heed me.' He was unable to more than glance at the surprised expression on her face. 'If we say nothing, no one will know you and I shared the—the time together.'

She turned back to the window, but her breathing quickened. 'I am already lost. Let me at least stay busy. Do some good. After it is all done, perhaps Edwin will be free to take me back to England.'

Edwin.

Allan would be damned if he put her in the care of such a man. She could not know the despicable behaviour of which Edwin was capable.

But Allan's own behaviour deserved censure, as well, did it not? Guilt tore at his insides. He had not forced her, perhaps, but he certainly had taken advantage of her.

And almost did so again in this room.

He straightened. 'I will go to the Place Royale and see if there is someone else with whom you can stay. I must go there and report in, in any event.' He started for the door but turned back. 'I will inform the authorities that there are accommodations for several soldiers at this address.'

She looked over her shoulder. 'Thank you, Captain.' Her voice seemed sad. 'I doubt you will find anyone willing to accept me, but would you also enquire of my cousin Edwin? I should like to know if he is alive and how I might contact him to inform him I am here?'

He nodded, but enquiring of her cousin did not mean he would ever put her into Edwin's care.

The walk to the Place Royale tired Allan more than he expected, and the sheer number and condition of the wounded on the streets tore at his emotions.

The Place Royale was all chaos. There was no question of finding an English family in Brussels who might offer Miss Pallant their hospitality. He could find no one even willing to discuss the matter. Most English families, it seemed, had fled to Antwerp and those who remained apparently had been prevailed upon to house wounded soldiers. News of another house available for the wounded was welcomed, however. He was told to expect arrivals that very day.

Allan reported to the regimental office, another place fraught with confusion. He was able to report in and be listed as wounded. He gave the Fentons' house as his direction.

He also learned that the battle cost about forty thousand lives, both Allies and French. The men in the office were too busy for him to ask about Edwin Tranville or, more importantly, whether Gabe and his other friends had survived. He was too exhausted to pore through the lists posted of all the dead and wounded officers. The regiment had already marched for France and, until he was well enough to rejoin it, he would not discover how many of the soldiers had survived, men who'd fought at his side throughout Spain and France and now Waterloo.

He walked into the square.

Forty thousand men lost. The battlefield must have been thick with bodies. At least Miss Pallant had been spared that sight.

In the square vendors were selling the casualty list. Allan used one of his last coins to purchase a copy to peruse later when he was alone. He'd discover then who among his friends he must grieve.

As he crossed the square, the faces of his men flashed through his mind. He stopped to catch his breath and looked around him. Soldiers slept on the pavement, others sat on the benches, still others sat with their backs against the stone walls. They all stared vacantly.

You are right, Marian, he said to himself, using her given name for the first time. *You are right to help them.*

He spied a uniform of the Royal Scots, a man lying on a spot of grass. With one hand clasped to his wounded shoulder, he hurried over.

It was a corporal from his old company. 'Reilly!'

The man's uniform sleeve was stained with blood and his face was flushed with fever.

He opened his eyes. 'Captain?'

Allan crouched down. 'Can you stand, Reilly? I'm taking you with me.'

Allan helped him to his feet, his own wound aching with the effort. Had Allan been stronger, he would have carried Reilly, but, taking frequent rests, they hobbled back to the Fentons' house. Allan knocked upon the door.

Marian—he'd turned a corner; she was no longer Miss Pallant in his mind—answered the door, her arms laden with bed linens. She dropped them to the floor.

'Oh, my!' She rushed to assist him.

'This is Corporal Reilly from my regiment,' he said as the three of them stepped into the hall. 'I could not pass him by.'

'Ma'am.' Reilly inclined his head to her.

'Can we get you above stairs, Corporal Reilly?' She turned to Allan. 'We can put him in one of the bedrooms.'

With Marian on one side and Allan on the other they struggled up the stairs and led the corporal into the first bedroom they came upon.

'This was Lady Fenton's room,' Marian told Allan in a conspiratorial tone.

He nodded. Lady Fenton would certainly suffer a fit of vapours if she knew her bed was to be occupied by a simple soldier.

They sat Reilly upon the mattress.

'Do not worry, Captain,' she said with a smile. 'I changed the linens.'

He laughed, but was stifled by a spasm of pain. He grasped the bedpost.

Her forehead furrowed. 'Sit, Captain. You have overtaxed yourself.'

He did not protest, lowering himself into a nearby cushioned chair.

She turned to Reilly. 'Now, Corporal, I am going to unbutton your coat and pull off your boots, and you certainly may lie down, but I must send one of the servants to undress you and tend your wounds.' She glanced towards Allan. 'Your captain will not allow me to do more.'

'Thank you, ma'am,' Reilly mumbled.

When she was done, Allan accompanied her below stairs, all the way to the kitchen where she found one of the maids.

'I will go, *tout de suite*,' the maid responded, bustling out, looking as eager as Marian to tend their first patient.

'Now you, Captain,' Marian said. 'You must rest.' She helped him to the manservant's room where he'd spent the night.

He sat on the bed. His shoulder ached and his legs felt like rubber. She knelt and pulled off his boots, then, placing herself between his legs, reached up to unbutton his coat. What had seemed businesslike and efficient, when performed for Reilly, now was nothing but erotic to his senses. He wanted to press his exhausted body against hers, to savour her softness and her strength.

Instead he touched her hand.

She paused for only a moment. 'I will help you remove your coat.' She gave him a look that suggested she knew precisely what he had been feeling. 'Just your coat and your shirt. I want to check your wound.'

He tried to remain very still while she unbuttoned his coat and pulled it off him. He controlled himself when she lifted his shirt over his head.

She looked beneath his bandage. 'It looks black and blue. Does it pain you?'

He took her hand in his and held it against his heart. 'Not so much now.' His nostrils filled with her rose scent; he savoured her nearness.

He leaned forwards and touched his lips to hers. The kiss grew in intensity. Her arms encircled his neck and she pressed herself against him, powerfully arousing him.

And forcing himself to his senses. 'Enough, Marian.'

She blinked and her cheeks flushed pink.

He averted his gaze. 'I have crossed the bounds of propriety again.'

Her smile was tight. 'Calling me by my given name is hardly a serious breach of propriety.'

His gaze touched hers. 'You know what I mean.'

She whispered, 'I like it…you calling me Marian, that is.'

He touched her cheek and desire grew in her expressive eyes. Now he had aroused her. The idea both thrilled him and made him angry at himself.

He turned away. 'Go now,' he said in a harsh voice.

She hurried out.

Marian ran all the way up the stairs to the hallway, grabbing the linens she'd dropped earlier. She busied herself with making beds, anything to keep her from dwelling upon her body's reaction to the captain.

She feared she'd go mad thinking about him and re-experiencing her body's reaction to him, an aching that was both pleasurable and terribly unsettling.

The Fentons had labelled her lost to all propriety. They were correct. Her reaction to the captain was proof.

She could not be ashamed of it, though, nor was she ashamed of her efforts to help the soldiers. Both seemed right, as if destiny had decreed she act in such a manner.

It mattered only that the captain again regretted her wanton response to him. Had his voice not been harsh after she ground herself against him, after she had almost induced him to lay with her again?

More wounded soldiers arrived and soon she was busy directing where each should sleep, what each needed in order to be comfortable, who was most in need of care. The most severely injured received beds, and the others cots on the floor or a sofa. Eleven men came to them and they filled every room, fed them all and, thanks to some old trunks in the attic, made certain all had clean nightclothes to wear while their clothing was laundered and mended.

The captain slept through all this activity. Marian checked on him whenever she could, fearful the exertions of the day might bring back his fever, but his forehead was always cool to her touch. He was merely exhausted.

When night fell and everyone had gone to their beds, Marian made her way to the kitchen. It was quiet and peaceful as she fixed herself a pot of tea by the light of the embers in the oven and a single candle. As she waited for the tea to steep she lay her head down on the table, feeling a satisfied weariness.

'Marian?'

She glanced up. The captain was framed in the doorway.

'You are awake.' She tried not to sound as tired as she felt. 'Are you feeling unwell?'

'Not at all.' He strolled in and took a seat in the chair opposite her at the bare wooden table. 'Very rested, however.' He smiled, and it felt like butterflies were set free inside her.

'Are you hungry?' she asked.

His smile widened. 'Starving.'

She rose and found some cold meat and cheese for him to eat. She poured him a cup of tea.

He took an eager bite of the cheese. She enjoyed watching him eat, so ordinary and comfortable an event, so unlike the anxious times they'd spent together.

'How did you fare while I slept the day away?' he asked between bites.

She smiled proudly. 'We have eleven more patients.'

As he ate, she told him all they'd done that day to make the men comfortable.

'I did not dress wounds,' she added, pouring him more tea.

He nodded in approval and sipped from his cup. 'It must be very late. Why are you in the kitchen?'

'After midnight?' She yawned. 'Cook has given me her room. She will sleep on the sofa in the drawing room so she will hear the soldiers if they need her. The maids are on the third floor.'

'And we are on this level,' he said, his warm eyes resting on her like a caress.

Her heart skipped. 'Yes.'

He stared down into his tea. 'I owe you an apology.'

She felt a pang of disappointment at losing that warm gaze. 'For what?'

His eyes lifted. 'When I walked to the Place Royale, there were wounded soldiers everywhere. You were right. How could we not help them?'

She smiled. He'd said *we*.

He went on. 'I was not able to enquire for your cousin. There was no opportunity.'

'Later, then.' She hoped Edwin was alive, but what if he wanted her to leave Brussels now, when so much needed to be done?

Marian gazed at Captain Landon through her lashes.

She did not wish to leave. She was precisely where she wanted to be at the moment.

As he finished his meal and she, her tea, they chatted about practical things. Supplies they needed. How to feed all the men. How the tasks should be divided.

He walked her to the cook's room, and carried the candle inside to light the one next to her bed. She stayed near the door, fearful that her wantonness would overtake her again. As he passed her to leave, he stopped and stared down at her.

Marian felt a spiral of sensation twirl through her. With his free hand he tilted her face to his and touched his lips to hers. She seized the cloth of his shirt and clenched it in her fists, her body meeting his as if she had no control.

He stepped away. 'Goodnight, Marian.'

And was gone.

Chapter Eight

The next few days formed a routine that almost gave Allan an incongruous sense of peace. Marian, the cook and the maids were kept busy seeing every man was well tended and well fed. One of the maids, a widow who'd borne and reared many children, proved very skilled at tending the men's wounds. The other maid learned fast. Cook was kept busy feeding them all.

Marian did whatever else was needed, and, like the colonel of the regiment, she kept everyone organised and on task.

If Marian was the colonel, Allan was the quartermaster. He made certain they had all necessary supplies, going out each day to procure something with Marian's seemingly unlimited funds. It was a good task for him, helping him regain his strength and his stamina.

He'd been able to access some of his pay and immediately sent for Valour to be stabled nearby. He'd just visited the stable to make certain the horse was properly tended, and had purchased a bag of flour for Cook. He placed it on the table for her.

'*Merci, Capitaine,*' Cook said, clapping her hands in appreciation.

He asked, '*Où est Madamoiselle Pallant?*' Marian would want to know Valour had arrived safely.

'*Votre chambre,*' Cook replied.

His room? He hurried down the corridor and found her seated on the bed, a large piece of paper in one hand and a feather duster in the other. Her expression was distressed.

He forgot about Valour. 'What is it?'

She blinked up at him. 'A list of the casualties from the battle. I found it under the bed.'

Where he had tossed it after reading it. Too many good men were dead. Too many maimed. Some survived at least. Gabe, for one. Allan was grateful Gabe had survived.

'Domina's betrothed is listed.' Her voice wobbled.

They had not discussed the man for whom her friend had convinced her to run off to a battlefield. In fact, they had discussed nothing about the battle at all. Waterloo had sometimes seemed more like a former nightmare than a memory.

'Was he killed?' he asked.

She looked down at the piece of paper and nodded. 'Domina told me so that first night, but it seems real to see his name on a list.'

Perhaps that explained the Fentons' quick departure from Brussels. It made him slightly more sympathetic towards them.

'I remember some of the others listed as well.' Her voice went up a pitch as if she were battling emotion. 'We attended many of the same social events.'

'I am sorry for them.' He was sorry any of them were lost.

She turned the list over. 'At least Edwin is not listed.'

Allan felt a twinge of guilt. 'I never asked about him for you.' Possibly because he did not want Edwin near her.

She waved a dismissive hand. 'I confess to having forgotten about him as well. I hope this means he is unharmed.' She looked down at the piece of paper again. 'It lists my guardian as missing.'

Allan had never searched the list for Tranville's name. 'Missing?' Perhaps his body was never found. It happened sometimes. 'This list was printed soon after the battle. It may not be accurate.'

She dropped the paper on to the bed. 'I should not have read it. It brings back how horrible it all was.'

He sat next to her and put his arms around her. 'Let us hope Waterloo was the last big battle.'

She pressed her face against his chest and it was all he could do to keep from pulling her on to his lap and tasting her lips once again. He just held her close, trying to content himself with as much.

She pulled away. 'Enough feeling sorry for myself.'

He brushed a stray strand of hair away from her face. 'Would you like for me to enquire about your cousin today? I can go out again.'

She gently touched his wounded shoulder. 'You have already been out today. You mustn't do too much.'

He took her hand and squeezed it. 'I am feeling rather fit.'

She sighed. 'I would like to know if Edwin is in Brussels. I just do not want him to take me away before our soldiers are well.'

'Then we will not allow him to do so.' He rubbed the palm of her hand with his thumb.

Her eyes darkened and her lips parted slightly, pulling him towards her.

He caught himself. 'I'll go directly.'

Without another word or another glance back at her, he walked out of the room and back outdoors, making his way to the Place Royale.

He had walked too fast across the Parc of Brussels and was winded by the time he entered the regimental offices.

'Are you fit to rejoin the regiment?' the officer in charge asked him.

If he became winded by a walk through the streets of Brussels, he doubted he would be able to join a march. 'Not as yet.' Besides, he did not wish to leave Brussels yet.

The man eyed him sceptically.

'I am looking for one of the Royal Scots' officers,' Allan told him.

The man looked down at his papers. 'Who?'

'Captain Edwin Tranville.'

The officer's brows rose. 'The General's son? Why?'

'I enquire for a friend.' That was as much as he wished to explain. 'Is he in Brussels?'

The man laughed. 'Search the taverns. You will find him.'

Allan frowned. 'Where is he staying?'

He jabbed his finger on a stack of papers. 'I will have to go through this whole pile before finding that answer. Just search the taverns. It will be faster.'

Allan started with taverns nearest the Place Royale. The officer was correct. He found Edwin in the third place he entered, a nearby inn.

'Oh, Lawd.' Edwin looked up as Allan approached the table where he sat alone. 'I heard you were dead.'

Allan's greeting was just as friendly. 'I, on the other hand, knew you would make it through without a scratch. Tell me, where did you go after we were dispatched with that first message?'

Edwin smirked. 'My horse went lame. I had no choice but to withdraw to the rear.'

It was one of Edwin's typical excuses and they both knew it.

Edwin waved his hand. 'Well, sit down. It hurts my neck to look up at you.' His words were slurred. 'Have some beer. Belgian beer.' He laughed and rubbed the scar on his face, the one he'd received at Badajoz. 'It is not half bad.'

Allan sat, but ordered nothing. 'I have been searching for you.'

Edwin put his tankard down with a loud clap. His jaw dropped. 'Gawd. Do not tell me my father sent you.'

Allan straightened. 'Your father?'

Edwin took another swig. 'Just like him to send you, all *sober* and everything.'

'But—your father was killed in the battle.' He gripped the edge of the table.

Edwin lifted the tankard again and his voice echoed. 'Not killed. Wounded. What do they say? *Fallen in battle.*' He gulped down more beer. 'Seems he was picked up again. Literally. He's rusticating at the Hôtel de Flandres under the care of his loving mistress, a woman I despise, by the way. Her son, whom I also despise, was the big hero. Carried my father off the battlefield. Curse him! He's been a thorn in my side since we were boys. Probably did it to keep me from inheriting.'

Allan could not believe his ears. 'Your father is alive and in Brussels?'

'I believe I just said that.' He wagged a finger at Allan. 'Perhaps you are not as sober as I thought.'

'What happened to him?'

'You require details?' Edwin rolled his eyes. 'He was struck down from his horse, his leg broken from a musket ball. He was quickly covered over, under other bodies, I suppose. Why that damned fellow went looking for him is beyond me.'

Allan glared at him. 'You were disappointed he did not die?'

Edwin laughed and touched his scar again. 'Oh, I did not wish my father dead, I assure you. I merely dislike seeing him in the clutches of that woman and her son. She'll squeeze more money out of him, you mark my words.'

Edwin Tranville sickened him. He'd be damned if he told this drunken coward about Marian now.

There was no need. His father, her guardian, was alive.

Allan stood. 'Are you also staying at the Hôtel de Flandres? In case I need to find you again.'

Edwin pointed to the ceiling. 'I have a room in this very inn. Handy, I admit.'

Allan had enough. He gave Edwin a curt nod, before striding away.

Edwin's voice followed him. 'Wait! You did not tell me why you were looking for me!'

Allan left the inn and made his way across the Parc.

General Tranville was alive? This changed everything. He might be able to avoid informing Edwin of Marian's presence in Brussels, but he could not hide it from her guardian.

General Tranville was legally responsible for Marian's welfare. Most importantly, he could provide the protection Marian needed. Tranville could prevent any damage to her reputation.

The longer Allan remained under the same roof with her, the closer he came to completely compromising her. And even if he kept his hands off her, each day she risked it becoming known by some member of society that she was living unprotected in a household of men.

This might be her only opportunity to erase any harm their time together could cost her.

Even though it meant leaving her in the care of a man Allan despised.

The more Marian thought about it, the more she decided that Edwin had probably already left for England. It had been over two weeks since the battle. Certainly he would have tied up his army affairs in that time.

She was glad. If she were required to travel to England with him, it would stop her from seeing her soldiers recovered.

And would part her from the captain.

Their parting was inevitable, though. He grew stronger every day. Soon he would be required to return to his regiment. She dreaded the thought of it.

She climbed the stairway to the upper floors and knocked upon Corporal Reilly's bedroom door.

'Come in,' he responded.

He sat by the window in a patch of sunlight, his arm bandaged and in a sling.

'How good to see you up, Corporal.' She smiled at him.

He struggled to his feet. 'Good afternoon, Miss Pallant.'

She gestured for him to sit. 'I've come with fresh linens.'

He lowered himself in the chair again, a frown on his face. 'Doesn't seem fitting for a lady such as yourself to be making beds.'

She pulled off the old linens. 'Now you are sounding like Captain Landon.'

Reilly grinned. 'He is a stickler for what's proper.'

She laughed. 'Indeed.'

He sobered again. 'He is a good 'un, though. Brave as they come.'

She covered the mattress with a clean sheet and thought of him carrying a soldier out of the burning château and covering her with his body after he was shot. 'Indeed,' she repeated more softly.

'I've known him since he was a green lad. Didn't know the first thing about being an officer. He learned quick, though. Has lots of pluck, that one.'

She tucked in the corners of the sheet.

Reilly went on, 'I remember when General Tranville ordered Landon and Captain Deane into Badajoz during the pillaging. His son was lost and the general thought he'd gone into the town.' He paused and so did she. 'Any road, a sane man would have removed himself from Tranville's sight for a couple hours rather than enter those streets. Soldiers were deranged in there.' He shook his head. 'But, no, before you know it, here comes Captain Landon, carrying the general's son over his shoulder.'

She finished smoothing the blankets. 'That is quite a story.'

One the captain had never told her. She patted the bed. 'There. Clean linens. Is there anything else you need?'

He stood and bowed his head. 'I'm pampered enough. I thank you, Miss Pallant.'

Marian walked out of the room.

The captain had rescued her cousin? Another brave and wonderful thing to add to a list of many. Filled with pride for him, she hummed as she walked down the stairs. When she reached the hall, the front door opened.

The captain walked in.

Marian felt her whole body come alive. 'Captain!'

His gaze rose to her. His expression was grim.

'What is it?' She turned cold. 'Is it Edwin?' Do not say her last blood relative was dead.

'Where can we talk?' Even his tone was grim.

She could think of nowhere to be private but his bed chamber. When they entered the room, he signalled her to sit and he closed the door.

Her heart raced painfully. 'Tell me, please, Captain, is Edwin dead?'

He raised his hand as if to stop her. 'He is unharmed, do not fear. He is here in Brussels. I spoke to him.'

'Thank God.' She pressed her hand against her chest. 'I was so frightened.'

'That is not what I must tell you.'

Her eyes widened. 'What then?'

'Listen to me.' He swallowed. 'Your uncle. He is alive. He wasn't lost, Marian. He is alive.'

'Uncle Tranville?' Her heart started racing again.

He paced in front of her. 'He was found alive and carried off the battlefield after the battle was over.' He frowned. 'I do not know all the details. Someone known to him carried him out. He broke a leg.' He waved a hand as if these details were of no consequence. 'He is here in Brussels, recuperating.'

'In Brussels?' Marian's mind whirled.

She must be glad his life was spared, mustn't she? Even if

she had no familial affection for him. She just did not want him here. She wanted nothing to interfere with her caring for her soldiers.

But, then, how likely was it that Uncle Tranville would trouble himself over her?

'Perhaps you could call upon him,' she said to the captain. 'I should like to know if he is recuperating well or if he is in need of anything I could provide.'

His pacing ceased. '*You* must call upon him, Marian.'

'I do not want him to know I am here.'

His brows rose. 'He is your guardian. He must know you are here. He is responsible for you.'

She stood. 'He cares nothing for me. For my aunt's sake, I would like to know if he needs my help, but otherwise I prefer to have nothing to do with him.'

He gave her an even look. 'He is *legally* responsible for you.'

She tossed her head. 'What do I care for that? I am well able to take care of myself.'

He grasped her arms. 'You do not comprehend. You are no longer a stranded orphan needing protection. You have a guardian who can assume your care.'

She tilted her head back so she could look him in the eye. 'You do not comprehend, Captain. I want nothing to do with my uncle.'

He brusquely released her. 'I must insist upon this. You must go to him. Place yourself in his charge.'

It shocked her that he would send her away. 'I am needed here, Captain. We have men to tend, whose health and well-being are in our hands. I cannot leave them. Not for *him*.'

'Marian, it is not for him. It is for you. If you are under the care of your guardian and his party, there can be no taint to your character.' He spoke in an earnest tone. 'Only the members of this household know what you have been doing and none of them will besmirch you. This is your only chance.'

Her insides twisted. 'You cannot make me go.'

He pierced her with his gaze. 'I must.'

'Why?' She felt close to tears. 'Because he is your superior officer?'

Something flickered in his eyes. 'No. Because this is the only way to preserve your good name and your future. No other reason.'

It still felt like betrayal. 'You will give me no choice. You will force me.'

His eyes hardened again. 'Yes.'

The captain took her that very afternoon.

The beauty of the Parc was lost on Marian as they walked through it to reach her uncle's hotel. The tension between them clouded her vision to the green shrubbery, white statues and colourful flowers. All she saw were more injured soldiers sitting upon benches and resting beneath trees. Could they not take more men into their care?

Could the captain not see that she needed to take care of the soldiers? It angered and disappointed her that he considered the needs of the men less important than the preservation of her reputation.

Even more painful, being forced to stay with her uncle meant being parted from the captain. Each day she'd shared with him made it more like he was the very air she must breathe, essential to life. She knew eventually his duties to his regiment would take him away, but even a few more weeks, a few more days, would be more precious than the finest jewels.

In her daydreams they would meet again away from war, somewhere in England where he was free to choose being with her rather than feeling it an obligation. There he would court her and perhaps they could kiss without her feeling she had seduced him into it.

Perhaps then he would not find anything about her of which to disapprove.

Her mind filled with all the ways he disapproved of her as they continued across the Parc. It helped fuel her anger.

And dampen the pain of parting with him.

Too quickly they arrived at the elegant Hôtel de Flandres, and the captain enquired after her uncle Tranville. The hotel's attendant showed them into a small drawing room to wait while he announced their arrival.

After a brief time a lovely woman entered the room. 'Miss Pallant? Captain Landon?' She extended her hand to them.

Marian did not miss the stunned expression on Allan's face at the sight of this chestnut-haired beauty. She felt inexplicably jealous.

'I am Ariana Blane,' the captivating creature said.

'Ariana Blane?' Marian's eyes widened in surprise.

Ariana Blane was the actress who had posed as Cleopatra in a scandalous painting that had been engraved and widely printed to publicise the play. When Marian left for Brussels, all of London had been clamouring for tickets to the performance.

'I saw you play Juliet at Drury Lane,' she told Miss Blane.

'That seems a long time ago.' Miss Blane looked wistful. 'I am afraid we did not know of your presence in Brussels, Miss Pallant, or we would have sent word about your uncle. I will take you to him right away.'

As she led them out of the drawing room and up the stairway, the Captain asked, 'Miss Blane, what connection do you have with Lord Tranville?'

She gave him a coy look. 'I might ask the same question of your connection to Miss Pallant.'

His eyes narrowed. 'I am her escort.'

She laughed. 'My connection is not so simple.' She paused on the stairs. 'I am betrothed to a man whose mother is a friend of Lord Tranville. When we learned Lord Tranville had been injured, she assumed his care.'

The captain seemed to relax.

'How bad are his injuries?' Marian asked, hating herself for hoping they were severe enough that he could not bother with her.

They continued up the stairs.

'He has a badly broken leg and has just recovered from fever and an infection of the lungs,' Miss Blane said. 'He is weak, but much improved, certainly well enough to receive you.'

Marian felt a pang of disappointment.

They walked down a hallway and Miss Blane knocked upon a door. 'Are you ready for us?' she called.

The door was opened by a manservant, a man who looked familiar to Marian, but she could not work out why.

Her uncle was propped up in a large bed, wrapped in a colourful banyan. He looked smaller than she recalled and pale, but alert. His hair had turned white in the two years since she'd last seen him, just after her aunt died.

An older woman approached. 'Miss Pallant, I do not know if you know me—'

This was another surprise. 'Mrs Vernon! I remember you. From Bath.'

Mrs Vernon had been the mistress Marian's aunt had so despised, the woman her aunt had said lured her uncle away. The manservant had then been in her employ.

'Oh, my goodness.' Marian turned back to Miss Blane. 'Jack Vernon! Is Jack Vernon your betrothed?'

Jack was Mrs Vernon's son. When they'd been children, Edwin used to pick fights with Jack, and Marian would try to stop him. Otherwise Edwin would come home with a black eye and a bloody nose, and his father would bellow at him for being a ninny.

'He is indeed.' Miss Blane smiled.

'Jack Vernon?' The captain looked equally incredulous. 'Lieutenant Jack Vernon of the East Essex?'

Mrs Vernon answered him. 'That is my son. Do you know him?'

'I do.' The captain sounded surprised.

The connections made Marian's mind swirl. The captain was connected to her uncle and cousin and to Jack Vernon, as well.

'You just missed him,' Miss Blane said. 'Jack left to rejoin his regiment yesterday.'

Marian nearly forgot her manners. 'Mrs Vernon, allow me to present Captain Landon.'

'Landon!' Her uncle's voiced boomed from the bed, feeling neglected, Marian thought. 'Attend me.'

The captain stiffened before approaching her uncle's bedside. 'Yes, sir.'

'Why are you not with the regiment?'

Marian hurried over. 'He was injured, Uncle.'

'Injured?' Her uncle huffed. 'I was not informed of this.'

'Sir.' The captain's voice had a hard edge. 'We only today learned of your presence in Brussels.'

'*We?* What do you mean by *we*, Landon?' His expression was contemptuous. 'What do you have to do with my niece?' He turned to Marian. 'What the devil are you doing in Brussels, girl? You have no call to be here.'

She fought to hold her temper. 'I came with Sir Roger and Lady Fenton. You do recall their daughter is a great friend of mine.'

'Sir Roger brought you?' He looked indignant. 'I gave no such permission.'

Marian met his eye. 'Your man of business gave permission for me to stay with the Fentons.' As if his man of business cared any more than her guardian did where she went or what she did. 'Did you not put him in charge of me?'

He leaned forwards in bed. 'Do not be impertinent.'

Impertinent? Marian had no intention of allowing her uncle to intimidate her.

He turned back to the captain. 'What is your part in this, Landon?'

Marian held her breath, hoping the Captain would lie, hoping he would see now how awful her uncle could be.

Hoping he would not leave her.

The captain straightened. 'I am recuperating in the house Sir Roger leased in this city.'

Marian could have kissed him. He had not lied, precisely; merely withheld the whole truth. *Well done, Captain!* She applauded silently.

'I've a mind to ring a peal over Sir Roger's head, bringing my niece here. Damned fools, all these English flocking to Brussels when Napoleon was about to attack.'

Miss Blane rolled her eyes and Mrs Vernon lowered hers. These two English women, of course, had flocked to Brussels and had probably nursed him back to health.

Tranville pointed at Marian. 'You, girl, you tell Sir Roger I wish him to call upon me posthaste.'

Marian kept her voice steady. 'I will inform him of your request the next time I see him.'

She heard a breath escape the captain's mouth.

Please keep quiet, Captain.

Her uncle turned his attention back to him. 'What news of the regiment, Landon?'

'I know little, except they were bound for France,' he responded.

'Has Edwin gone with them?' he asked.

A muscle in the captain's jaw tensed. 'No, sir.'

Mrs Vernon came to Tranville's side and took his hand. 'Remember, Lionel? Edwin is staying nearby until you are well.'

'Fool,' he huffed. 'His duty is to the regiment.' He pointed to the captain. 'I told him to befriend you. Said he could learn a thing or two from you. But Edwin never did anything I told him to do—' His voice broke off into a fit of coughing.

Marian felt angry on Edwin's behalf. He'd accepted a commission in the army to please his father even though Edwin had been totally unsuited to it.

Her uncle's coughing subsided and he leaned back against the pillow, looking weak and tired.

Unfortunately he roused again. 'Landon, you should have insisted Sir Roger or his wife accompany my niece. This is family business, not regimental business. It is not your affair.'

Marian spoke before the captain could respond. 'Captain Landon came at my request, Uncle,' she replied sharply. 'You have no call to scold him for it—'

Her uncle's eyes bulged. 'See here, girl!'

She kept on. 'He was being a gentleman, which is more than I can say for—'

The captain put a hand on her arm. 'Enough, Marian.'

She glanced at him in alarm and mouthed, 'No.'

He turned to her uncle. 'I will tell you why I have escorted your niece.'

'Go on.' Her uncle gave her a smug look.

Marian felt ill.

The captain set his chin. 'Sir Roger and Lady Fenton left for England several days ago. Your niece remained and opened the house for wounded soldiers.'

'What?' Uncle Tranville sat upright. 'She is acting as a nurse? Shameful. That is only for lowlife.'

'We are acting as your nurses,' Miss Blane muttered, but Uncle Tranville seemed to take no notice.

Marian lifted her chin. 'It is true Sir Roger left and I stayed behind. And it is true Captain Landon is one of the soldiers in my care, the only officer, which is why I chose him to escort me. I have not acted the nurse, however. Those tasks have been performed by the Fentons' Belgian servants. I have merely managed the house.'

'Managed the house,' her uncle muttered in disdain. 'You make it sound like a brothel.' His thoughts seemed to drift for a moment, then caught on some idea. He peered at the Captain and spoke in the most matter-of-fact tone. 'You spent the night under the same roof with my niece without a proper chaperon?'

Captain Landon straightened and held her uncle's gaze. 'Yes, sir. She kept me alive.'

Her uncle waved those words away as if Captain Landon's life was of no consequence. 'That is very improper. Very improper indeed.'

When had her uncle ever cared about where she went or what she did? 'You are being nonsensical, Uncle.'

He tapped his fingers on his mouth. 'He compromised a decent young lady.'

'He did not compromise me,' Marian cried. It would be more accurate to say that she had compromised him. 'Besides, you are not one to pass judgement, Uncle.'

When had he ever acted with propriety? He'd never taken any steps to conceal his relationship with Mrs Vernon. All of Bath knew. Marian's aunt had been greatly shamed by it. He'd not even remained faithful to Mrs Vernon, which caused even more talk.

'Perhaps this is not the best time to discuss this,' Miss Blane broke in. 'Are you not becoming fatigued, Lord Tranville?'

'I am as fit as you are.' His eyes shot daggers at her.

Miss Blane seemed unaffected.

'Listen.' The captain stepped forwards. 'I can resolve this—'

'Indeed you can, Landon!' Her uncle laughed as if in triumph. 'You can marry her.'

'Marry me!' Marian cried.

'Marry her.' The older man's expression turned smug. 'It is the perfect solution. He compromised her; he must marry her.'

'He did not compromise me!'

Her uncle paid her no heed. 'I must admit, I once thought that I'd marry you to Edwin, but now that Edwin will be a baron one day he needs to look a great deal higher. Landon will be perfect, though. He's a younger son, perfectly respectable, but needing to marry a fortune. You, my girl, have an excellent fortune.'

None of Marian's fantasies of how a gentleman might propose marriage had ever included her uncle. She would not go along with this no matter what. She'd already refused when the captain tried to propose out of duty; she certainly would not accept when the proposal came through her uncle. She was speechless with rage. How dared he?

The captain wore a thunderous expression. Mrs Vernon looked as if she might cry. Miss Blane looked disgusted.

'Sir.' The captain's voice was taut. 'It is not your place to propose—'

'Of course it is my place to propose,' her uncle interrupted. 'I am her guardian. I am supposed to see her married. This way I am saved the trouble of finding someone to bring her out into society.'

'I had my come-out in Bath with Domina,' Marian said to no avail.

Her uncle was beyond listening. 'I am correct that you have no fortune, am I not?' he demanded of the captain.

Allan was consumed with rage. Of all the manipulative, self-centred things Tranville had done, this was the pinnacle.

'I have no fortune,' he admitted stiffly. 'But that is of no consequence. You have no right to force—'

'Oh, I do not *force*.' Tranville's self-congratulatory tone turned threatening. 'I insist. If you do not do right by my niece, I will ruin your career in the army. I will make certain the parents of every marriageable young lady in the *ton* learn you are a callous seducer of respectable women.'

'You will do nothing of the sort!' cried Marian.

Tranville turned his malevolent gaze on her. 'Will I not, you ungrateful wretch!'

Allan could endure this no longer. He surged forwards, ready to put his face into Tranville's and tell him exactly what he thought of him.

Miss Blane pulled him back.

Tranville continued to address Marian. 'If you do not do what I say, young lady, you will not get a penny of your money until you inherit. How will you live then, eh? You'll be in the first man's bed who will have you. By the time you inherit, no decent man will want you.'

Allan pulled away from Miss Blane. 'This is beyond everything. Apologise this instant!'

Tranville was unstoppable. 'Is it not a bit late to play the champion, Landon? You have been sharing quarters with her for days.'

'Say and do what you want about me,' Allan seethed, 'but your niece has done nothing to deserve these high-handed threats. Her behaviour is to be admired, not punished.'

The General's eyes narrowed. 'You know what I am capable of, Landon. If you value your army career, your good name and your future, you will do as I say.' He tilted his head towards Marian. 'And if you defy my wishes, she will be ruined.'

'Lionel—' Mrs Vernon pleaded.

His head whipped around to her. 'Stay out of this, woman!'

Allan held up his hands. 'Enough!' He turned from Tranville to Marian. 'We will marry. Even though I detest your uncle's interference in the matter, marriage has always been the only honourable option.'

'No,' she rasped, so low only Allan could hear.

Tranville laughed like a demon. 'I knew he would agree the moment I said you were rich.'

Allan glared at him, his fingers curled into fists. It was all he could do not to strangle the life out of him.

'Let us leave now, Marian.' He took her arm and backed away from the bed. 'We can discuss this as we walk back.'

They started towards the door.

'Not so hasty, girl,' her uncle called after her.

Now what?

'You are not going back to perform menial tasks to a house full of men. You stay here.'

'No!' she cried.

Allan could not leave her with Tranville. Not after this. 'If you say I've already compromised her, what does it matter? She comes with me.'

'Do not add arrest to the list of things I might do to you, Landon,' Tranville countered. 'I am her legal guardian. She must do as I tell her and I tell her she is to stay here.'

'She can share my room,' Miss Blane offered. 'Come. I'll accompany you both out. You can have her things sent here later, Captain.'

'You see she returns, Ariana,' Tranville shouted.

Miss Blane hurried them out of the door.

When they were out of earshot, she stopped them both. 'Retreat was necessary. It is sometimes, is it not, Captain?'

He did not answer her.

'He is horrible,' Marian cried. 'I refuse to do as he says. I do not care what he does to me.'

Miss Blane raised a finger. 'Ah, but you do care what he does to Captain Landon.'

Marian averted her face.

'Let him do what he wants to me.' Allan touched Marian's hand. 'I will not let him hurt her.'

Sympathy warmed Miss Blane's eyes. 'The more you defy him, the worse he will become. Do you not know this to be true, Captain?'

'Yes,' he had to admit.

Miss Blane went on, 'Idleness is bringing out the worst in him. I suggest you act as if you intend to do as he says. Give it a little time. You will be able to do as you wish once he has something else to think about.'

'You sound as if you know him well,' Marian said.

She smiled. 'Jack and I have been targets of his manipulation, but Jack made threats of his own. Tranville heeded them. We will renew those threats on your behalf, if necessary.'

'I do not fear a confrontation with him,' Allan said, his anger still blazing too hot to allow her to douse the flames.

'I am certain you fear nothing, Captain,' she responded. She shooed them to the stairway. 'Talk together privately, but do not do anything hasty.' She turned to Marian. 'I will wait for you in the drawing room. Rest assured, you will be away from Lord Tranville's company in my room.'

The Captain nodded in gratitude. 'Come outside with me,' he said to Marian, taking her arm.

They descended the stairs and continued through the hall out the front door of the hotel.

Outside the Hôtel de Flandres, he faced her. 'Forgive me, Marian. I was wrong to bring you here.'

She clutched the sleeves of his coat. 'Take me home, Captain. I do not want to stay here. I want to be with you and our soldiers.'

He shook his head. 'I cannot. The cost to you is too great. We must do as Miss Blane suggests. Retreat for the moment and allow emotions to calm down.'

'He cannot make us marry.' Her face filled with anger again.

'When do you inherit?' he asked.

She looked at him suspiciously. 'In a little more than a year's time, when I turn twenty-one.'

'Twenty-one?' He was surprised. Most heiresses did not receive their inheritance until at least twenty-five.

'I know it is unusual,' she said. 'But that was how my father wrote the will. Why do you ask?'

'I propose we become betrothed, but we postpone marriage until after you are twenty-one. Once you have inherited, you can decide to cry off if you wish.' This way they could play Tranville's game and win.

Her brow furrowed. 'You propose to become betrothed only to thwart my uncle's manipulations?'

He still believed that marrying her was the only honourable thing he could do, but he could not tolerate her thinking he had done so to appease Tranville. Indeed, he could not quite imagine life without her. He believed that fate had brought them together. All they had to do was the right thing, the honourable thing and all would work out well.

He cupped his hand against her cheek. 'There is so much we have endured together that was not under our control. Let us put the issue of whether we marry or not into our hands and no one else's.'

She nodded and flew into his embrace, her arms wrapped around his neck, her face against his heart. 'This is not the proposal of which I have dreamed. I do not know if you want to marry me or want to be released from the obligation.'

He held her. 'I know you do not want to marry me. You have said so more than once, but one thing I do know.'

'What is that?' she murmured against his chest.

He released her and lifted her chin with his finger. 'My proposal is vastly superior to General Tranville's.'

A laugh escaped her. 'Do not jest.'

He held her against him again. 'Be betrothed to me. For now. Perhaps even before I must leave Brussels we will be free to know our own minds.'

'I do not want to stay here.' She pulled away from him. 'I want to be with our soldiers.'

'I know.' He glanced towards the hotel. 'Avoid Tranville, but if you must see him, avoid a confrontation.'

She gave him a steady gaze. 'I promise to avoid him.'

He smiled. 'And I promise to see that your soldiers receive the best care possible.'

Her eyes glistened with tears. 'Deep in the left-hand corner of my trunk is a purse. Keep its contents to pay for food and

the servants' wages and for Valour, if you need it. I am very
fond of Valour.'

His smile faded. 'I will see to it.' He had no intention of
using her money for Valour, though. Only for the others. 'I
will send your trunk.'

She nodded.

'We should say goodbye,' he murmured.

She ran into his arms again. 'Goodbye, Captain.'

He squeezed her as tightly as he could. 'I will call upon
you as soon as I can.'

With a quick brush of his lips against hers, Allan backed
away and turned to walk from her.

Chapter Nine

Edwin Tranville lounged on a bench, trying to muster enough energy to wander back to the inn that had become his home in Brussels, the one with the excellent Belgian beer. He'd come from there to the Hôtel de Flandres, shamed by Landon into the notion that he owed his father a visit.

Thank God he had talked himself out of it before crossing the threshold. He glanced over at the hotel's entrance.

A British officer stood there with a woman. The two were engaged in an intense conversation and lots of intimate embraces. Lawd. It was probably some doxie trying to squeeze out more coin by making him more ruttish.

Would the man fall for her trick? The army seemed to breed men who were easily duped into paying a princely sum for a common whore.

'Do not heed her,' he said aloud, as if the officer was close enough to hear. 'Do not pay a penny more than she's worth.'

He peered at them again. The woman seemed to be dressed in a fashionable frock and there was something familiar about the man. Edwin rose from the bench and edged closer.

Lawd. It was Landon.

Landon, that paragon of perfection, was attempting to purchase a woman's services. How very amusing.

The woman lifted her face and the sun illuminated her features.

It was his cousin!

Marian was in Brussels? How delightful she was here. Edwin greatly needed a friendly smile and some support and sympathy, just the sort Marian could provide.

He took an eager step forwards, but stopped. Why was she with Landon? Why this *intimate* conversation with him?

Landon kissed her on the lips and set off towards the Parc, a stern look on his face.

Edwin fumed.

Was everything in his life to be a competition with Landon? His father already relentlessly compared his skills as an officer to Landon's and, of course, Landon was never the one found wanting. He should not have to compete for Marian's attention too. Marian was not like other women. She was clever and had been the only woman who truly understood him.

She was his cousin, after all. He'd even thought that some day he might marry her, if he had to…. Some day, when he was ready. Good God, would he now be required to *romance* her better than Landon?

Marian stood at the doorway of the hotel for a long time, watching Landon walk away. Suddenly, she pulled open the door and went inside as if Landon had upset her. That was good.

Edwin rubbed his scar. What ought he to do next? Go in the hotel and see Marian? Or chase after Landon and discover what had transpired between them?

He decided to chase after Landon.

It was easy to spy him striding across one of the paths in the Parc. Edwin ran to catch up to him.

'Landon!'

Landon turned and scowled, but waited.

Edwin panted so hard he could barely speak. 'Where are you going in such haste?'

'Back to my rooms, if it is any of your concern.' Landon started walking again.

'I saw you with a lady just now.' He stopped to catch his breath. Lawd, he needed a brandy. Or more Belgian beer.

Landon glared at him.

Edwin straightened his spine. 'You were with my cousin and I demand to know what business you have with her.'

Landon stared down into Edwin's face. 'If you wish to know, ask her.' He turned away again.

Edwin seized his arm and pulled him back. 'I am asking you, sir.'

Landon winced and placed a hand on his shoulder. When he spoke his eyes glittered with acrimony. 'I am betrothed to her.' He pushed Edwin aside and strode away.

Edwin's jaw fell.

Betrothed? Marian was betrothed to Landon?

This was a matter not to be endured.

He headed back to the inn where he lodged. No beer this time. He needed brandy to calm his nerves.

He scratched his scar. Brandy first, then he'd return to his father's hotel and get to the bottom of this loathsome betrothal.

When Allan reached the Fentons' rooms a missive was waiting for him, asking him to report to the regimental office at the Place Royale the next day. They wanted him to rejoin the regiment in France as soon as possible.

He crumbled the paper in his fist.

He needed more time, time with Marian to sort out the mess he'd created by taking her to Tranville.

He wanted to marry her. It was, simply, the right thing to do. Tranville's interference and threats had tainted what should be something wonderful between them.

It was a good plan for them to wait. Allan needed to make

something of himself before marrying her. He could not just live on her fortune. He had to bring something to their marriage. He had to *be* something.

With Napoleon's defeat at Waterloo, war was probably over and a future in the army was not likely. Besides, Allan had enough of battle.

He needed something. Some direction in life. Something to bring to a marriage with Marian.

He crumpled the missive from the regimental office in his hand and went off to tell the servants and the soldiers that Marian would not be back.

Edwin was very careful not to drink too much brandy. Marian had always been able to tell when he'd imbibed too much. He drank only enough to steady his shaking hand and settle his nerves before returning to the Hôtel de Flandres.

He supposed he must call upon his father before seeking out Marian, always a depressing prospect and one he'd almost totally avoided. Why pretend a filial affection he neither felt nor received? Landon had been right about one thing. Edwin would have been delighted if his father had died on the battle-field. Jack Vernon did him no favour by acting the hero.

At least his father's illness provided him the excuse of remaining in Brussels. Edwin was perfectly willing to pretend concern for his father in order to avoid marching to France with the regiment. He had already called upon his father once soon after Jack brought him back to Brussels. His father had been feverish and smelly and the detestable Mrs Vernon had hovered over him.

At this moment, though, it was expedient to make another visit to the sickbed and play the dutiful, concerned son. It was what Marian would expect of him.

He entered the hotel and walked up the stairway to his father's room.

He lifted his hand to knock on the door. 'Lawd, I hope that woman is not in there.' He hated encountering Mary

Vernon, or any of the Vernons. He took a breath and rapped on the door.

Mrs Vernon's manservant opened the door.

'I came to see my father,' he snapped at the man.

'He is sleeping, sir,' the servant said. 'I would not suggest waking him.'

Thank God. Perhaps his luck was improving. 'Very well. I will call upon my cousin, then. Which room is hers?'

The man hesitated before responding, 'If you would be so good as to wait in the drawing room off the hall of the hotel, I will seek out Miss Pallant and send her to you.'

This servant was Mrs Vernon's man. He had no right to dictate to Edwin. 'Direct me to Miss Pallant's room.'

The servant stood his ground. 'I cannot. It is not my place to do so. Be so good as to wait below stairs.'

Edwin gave the servant a withering look, but turned and sauntered away. He descended the stairs and stopped the hotel attendant. 'Bring me a carafe of claret and two glasses, and put it on Lord Tranville's account.' At least if he must wait for Marian, his father could provide the refreshment.

The drawing room was reasonably comfortable and the attendant was prompt in delivering the wine. Edwin lowered himself into a chair and poured a glass, downing it in one gulp. He poured another.

No sooner had he done so than his cousin entered the room.

'Marian!' He stood and held out his hands.

She allowed a quick kiss on the cheek. 'I am happy to see you, Edwin.' No smile creased her face. 'I hope you are well.'

'I am,' he exclaimed, then thought better of it. 'As well as a man can be who has endured a battle.'

She sat in one of the chairs. 'Were you injured?'

'No.' He stroked his scar. 'At least nothing to signify.'

She gazed at him with some sympathy. Let her think him the worse for wear.

'So you were in the battle?' she asked.

He sat in a chair opposite her. Next to the table holding the claret. 'I carried messages for General Picton and for Father.' He lowered his eyes as if a pang of grief assailed him. 'That is, until Picton fell and Father was lost.'

'You carried messages?' She seemed to brighten. 'What a coincidence—' She waved a hand. 'Never mind.'

He narrowed his eyes. Landon had probably told her the same thing. At least it seemed Landon had not mentioned his absence in the battle.

'I understand Uncle Tranville had a very dramatic rescue.' She seemed to be making conversation with effort.

'Yes.' Edwin did not elaborate. He had no intention of glorifying Jack Vernon. 'Would you like a glass of claret? I took the trouble of ordering it, thinking it would please you.'

She nodded. 'That was kind of you.'

He poured claret into the empty glass and handed it to her.

He took a big drink from his own glass, wishing the claret were as warming and numbing as brandy or as smooth as the Belgian beer. 'I just learned today you were in Brussels.'

She barely sipped hers. 'I came with Domina and her family, but they have gone back to England now.'

'Domina.' He rolled his eyes. Marian's tedious friend.

'We came in late May,' she added.

None of this explained how she had become betrothed to Landon. 'I suppose you attended many parties.'

She nodded again and took another sip of wine, but glanced down at her lap, seemingly lost in thoughts that did not involve him.

He drained his glass of claret and poured himself another. Nothing for it but to be direct. 'I happened to meet up with Allan Landon earlier today—'

Her head rose.

He went on, 'He told me—'

'—that we are betrothed.' Her eyes flashed as if the idea made her angry.

He leaned forwards and grasped one of her hands. 'Why, Marian? I did not even know you were acquainted with him. Are you really going to marry him?'

She looked away. 'Oh, Edwin. It is very complicated.'

He donned an expression of devoted interest. 'I am at liberty to listen.'

She looked angry again. 'I do not wish to talk about it. Can you understand? It was a very sudden thing and not at all a certainty. It is too much to explain.'

Not a certainty? That was encouraging.

He squeezed her hand. 'I always thought you would marry me, Marian.' He tried not to sound resentful. 'I thought you knew that.'

She pulled out of his grasp. 'Oh, Edwin.' She looked at him with dismay. 'We are much too close to be married. It is simply not possible.'

He was offended by her tone. 'Many cousins marry. The whole aristocracy is one inbred mess.'

She shook her head. 'But you and I grew up like brother and sister. I could never think of you any other way.'

But she could think that way of Landon? He poured himself the last of the claret.

She looked at his glass disapprovingly. 'Besides, you never said one word to me about marriage. Ever.'

'How could I? I was stuck in the army.' He drank his wine and damned her disapproval.

She made an exasperated sound. 'I have had enough of proposals, Edwin. Do not tease me about this further. You are my cousin and I love you as such. But that is all.' She stood. 'I must go back to my room now.'

He stood as well. 'Do not leave yet, Marian!'

'I must. I simply cannot talk about this any longer.' She started for the door.

He went after her. 'Tell me one thing, then.'

She stopped.

'Do you want to marry Landon?'

Her eyes were pained. 'Call on me tomorrow, Edwin.' She started for the door. 'Perhaps I will be better company.'

He pushed ahead of her and blocked the doorway. 'Do you want to marry Landon?' he demanded.

'I do not know,' she finally answered.

He stepped aside and she fled up the stairs.

Edwin returned to his chair and picked up his glass, draining it of its contents. Then he finished hers, as well.

Lawd, if Marian married Landon, Edwin's father would be comparing him to Landon from now until doomsday.

He slammed down the glass and stormed out of the room, back to the inn and the tavern that offered sweet oblivion.

The next day Allan called upon Marian and paced the drawing room, waiting for her. It was not long before she appeared, Miss Blane at her side.

'Good day to you, Captain,' Miss Blane said from the doorway. 'Do not fear, I have no intention of remaining in the room. It is too soon to speak to Lord Tranville again, by the way, so I would not advise you attempting it.' She closed the door behind her.

'Marian,' Allan whispered.

He had missed her. If possible she looked more beautiful than ever. Her dress was pale green, making the blue of her eyes even more vibrant. Her blonde hair was skilfully arranged, a dark green ribbon threaded through it. He could not take his eyes off her.

She walked gracefully towards him, reminding him of the swans on the Thames. 'Why are you staring at me?'

He blinked. 'I am having difficulty believing anyone ever mistook you for a boy.'

Her face reddened. 'Had I been a boy, we would not be in such a fix.'

'It is not a fix, Marian.'

She averted her gaze. 'I suppose you are going to ask me to call you Allan.'

'Not if you do not wish to.' It only mattered a little that she did not wish this intimacy with him.

'Good.' She still sounded unhappy. 'I am not certain I can give up calling you Captain.' She glanced at him again. 'How are our soldiers?'

'All are doing well.' He added, 'They send their regards to you.'

Her expression softened. 'Please tell them all they are constantly in my thoughts.'

He nodded.

He ought to invite her to sit, but instead took a step closer to her. 'I am ordered back to the regiment.'

She looked surprised. 'When?'

'Tomorrow. Or the next day, if I find some excuse.' He lowered his voice. 'It gives us no time.'

She made a sound deep in her throat. 'Oh.' She took a breath. 'Well, there is nothing we must do.'

'I thought I might convince Tranville to remove his threats, but Miss Blane is right. It is too soon, and now I will be unable to attempt it.'

She lifted a hand to her brow. 'I think talking to him makes matters worse.'

He took her hands in his. 'You are likely correct and I am regretful that I ever forced you into it. Now I am sorry I cannot be here to protect you from him.'

She glanced away. 'I plan to avoid him.'

He lifted her hands to his lips. 'We will sort this out, Marian, I promise you.'

She looked him in the eyes. 'I just feel this horrible sense of doom. It frightens me more than the French or the fire or the farmer's axe.'

His insides constricted in pain. He embraced her. 'No, Marian. We will find our way. You will know if you want to truly accept my real proposal of marriage. You and I will freely decide what we want.'

The door opened.

'There you are!' Edwin Tranville walked in.

Damned Edwin.

They stepped apart.

Edwin put on a sardonic expression. 'I am interrupting.'

Marian said, 'Yes, Edwin. You are interrupting. The captain and I are saying goodbye.'

Edwin brightened. 'You are leaving, Landon?'

'To rejoin the regiment,' Allan's voice turned sour. 'Are you not ordered to France, as well?'

Edwin smirked. 'Alas, no,' he drawled. 'I am to remain with my father. To render him whatever assistance he requires.'

Allan stiffened. Edwin had been drinking. 'Perhaps your father needs some assistance right this moment.'

Edwin slid into a chair, even though Marian was still standing. 'I've just come from him.'

'Did you want something, Edwin?' She sounded annoyed.

'Nothing at all.' He sighed. 'Except to see you.'

'This is not a good time,' she responded. 'Would you come back later?'

His eyes flashed. 'Very well.' He made no move to leave.

She waved an impatient hand. 'Edwin! Do not be tedious. Leave now.'

His expression hardened, but he got up and sauntered out of the door.

Allan was glad of his leaving, but Edwin's brief presence had already changed the mood between them.

'Are you fond of your cousin?' he asked her.

'We grew up together,' she said noncommittally. 'Do you dislike him?'

He clenched his jaw before answering, 'Yes. Very much.'

Allan needed to warn her about her cousin, especially since Edwin would remain in Brussels after Allan left. But how much could he tell her without speaking of matters he'd promised to keep in confidence? 'He drinks heavily.'

She sighed. 'I know it.'

He held her by her arms. 'Promise me to take care around him.'

She tried to pull away. 'You are acting like a husband. Telling me what to do—'

He held firm. 'That is not the point. I've seen Edwin when drinking. He is not safe to be around.'

'Not safe?' Her brows rose.

'I cannot say more, but I am serious. Promise me you will avoid him at such times.'

She lifted her eyes to his. 'Edwin does not concern me. I have always been able to handle him.'

Her gaze made him think only of the pain of leaving her, and his hands slid to caress her neck. There was so much more he wanted to tell her, if he could only work out how to put his emotions into words. How, in spite of Tranville's interference and his complete lack of fortune, he still desired her with every part of him, as strongly as that night when they'd shared the same bed.

He leaned down to take possession of her lips.

She made a sound deep in her throat and wound her arms around him, deepening the kiss into something more erotic than he'd dared dream. He held her firmly against him, wanting more, needing more.

She pulled away. 'I cannot—' She backed away from him.

He reached out to touch her again, but withdrew his hand.

She wrapped her own arms around herself. 'Perhaps we should say goodbye now.'

Now? He was not ready.

'Please, Captain?' Her voice rose to a higher pitch. 'I must do this in a hurry. It is too painful.'

It heartened him that parting from him was painful to her. It convinced him she was as attached to him as he was to her.

'As you wish.' Allan could not make himself move, however.

Her eyes creased and her voice turned low. 'Goodbye, then, Captain.'

'Goodbye, Marian,' he murmured in reply.

He bowed and forced himself to walk to the door.

'Captain!' She ran to him.

He opened his arms and caught her in a tight embrace. He held her as if he would never release her, never lose the scent of roses that surrounded her, or the softness of her curves, or her courage and resourcefulness.

'I am so used to being with you,' she murmured against him. 'I do not know how to go on without you.'

He held her close. 'I do not know how I will go along without you, either.'

She pushed away from him again. 'Go, please. I am all right now.'

'I will write to you.' It seemed like not enough to say.

'Yes. Yes. Just leave now.' Her voice cracked. 'Please?'

He leaned down and kissed her on the cheek.

She looked up into his eyes. 'Godspeed, Captain,' she whispered. 'Godspeed.'

Chapter Ten

A week later Marian felt pushed to the limits of her endurance. How ironic that a week at the Hôtel de Flandres had been harder to bear than all the danger and hardship she'd shared with the captain. Her nerves were frayed to ragged threads, and she wished only to scream and hurl breakable objects about the room.

She missed him.

It made no sense that his absence should create such a void. They'd known each other for so short a time.

It did not help that her uncle had insisted upon her presence so he could bully her and order her about. She hated being controlled by him.

He'd discovered that she'd offered to help care for the injured soldiers recuperating in the hotel. 'It is not seemly for a young lady and well you should know it,' he'd snapped at her. He'd also refused to allow her to visit the soldiers at the Fentons' house.

She'd barely existed to her uncle before this, but now she was someone to command, the only person he could command. He was too dependent upon Mrs Vernon to order her about, and her servants took orders only from her.

Miss Blane simply ignored him and did whatever she wanted. She was an intriguing person, very confident and secure in her betrothal to Mrs Vernon's son. If it weren't for Ariana Blane's connection to Uncle Tranville and the Vernons, Marian might have wished to make her a friend.

Marian's feelings about Mrs Vernon were very muddled. She could not forgive the older woman for the injury to her aunt, but, at the same time, Marian pitied her for remaining attached to a man such as her uncle.

Edwin was irritating, but a distraction. He called frequently and seemed to fall into his childhood habit of depending upon her for companionship. Poor Edwin! He'd inherited the worst from his parents. He was as weak as his mother and as selfish as his father. And he had no desire to improve himself or to help anyone else.

Edwin certainly made no effort to help with the battle's casualties. He did nothing useful as far as Marian could tell. The only useful task Edwin performed was to deliver his father's mail.

Each day he visited the regimental office and picked up any mail that came for his father in the regimental packets from London or Paris where the regiment was currently stationed. Then he returned to the office with whatever mail his father wished to send.

This day, Edwin brought his father a letter. Because Mrs Vernon was out on an errand, Uncle Tranville sent for Marian to write his reply.

It was an ordeal. If she asked her uncle to repeat a word, he protested that she should pay better attention. If she asked him to speak slowly, he shouted for her to write faster.

When the silly letter was completed, signed and sealed, he turned to Edwin. 'This goes back today, do you hear? I want it in the next packet to London.'

Edwin gave him a withering look. 'Do not be tedious, Father. There won't be another packet until tomorrow.'

Uncle Tranville sat up in the bed. 'I want it at the regimental office, *today.*'

'Very well.' Edwin's manner made it seem as if this was an onerous task instead of a short walk across the Parc.

'Do you have more need of me?' Marian kept her voice civil with effort.

'No. Go.' He waved her away. 'You've already wearied me excessively.'

She walked out with Edwin. When they were in the hallway, he asked, 'Would you like to share a glass of claret with me in the drawing room?'

'I would much prefer to be outside.' She was feeling like a tethered falcon. All she wanted was to stretch her wings. 'May I walk with you to the Place Royale?'

'Can we have some claret first?' His voice rose in dismay.

'No, indeed. You drink too much as it is,' she scolded. 'Let us leave now.'

She fetched her hat and shawl, and they were off. Soldiers still lounged on the benches, but for the fresh air, not because they were forced to live out of doors. It heartened her that the men were recovering, that they were not abandoned.

Edwin also glanced at the benches. 'They should order them out of the park. These men have no rank. What if we wanted to sit down?'

'Edwin, have some compassion!' She pushed him.

He glowered, but Marian enjoyed the scent of the grass and swish of trees and being away from her uncle.

Edwin paused and regarded her with a weary expression. 'I almost forgot.' He reached in his coat. 'I have a letter for you, too. It was sent in care of Father in the packet from Paris. It's from Landon.'

'From the captain?' She snatched it out of Edwin's hands

and gazed at the captain's clear, confident script on the envelope. 'I am going to walk back. I want to read it.'

'Read it here.' Edwin said. 'I'll make these fellows leave the bench.'

'No, you will not,' she responded. 'I'm not taking their seat.'

He lolled his head, like he always did when he thought she'd made a ridiculous statement. He pointed. 'There's an empty bench.'

Marian walked quickly across the path to reach it. She sat and immediately broke the seal of the letter. Then she began to read.

'Aren't you going to read it out loud?' Edwin asked in a sarcastic tone.

She poked him gently. 'Stop jesting. Be quiet so I can read.'

'This is a bore,' he complained.

Dear Marian, the letter said. *I have only a short time to write this note to inform you that I have successfully rejoined my regiment. We are in Paris, but there is no danger here. I believe the French are as weary of war as we are. There is much beauty in this city. Perhaps I will be lucky enough to have time to visit the museums and sights. I would be even luckier if I could bring you here with me some day. Yours, Allan Landon. P.S. Valour quite misses you, as do I.*

Why did it make her want to cry?

Perhaps because it sounded like him. It sounded so *dutiful.* So perfectly correct.

Except for the whimsical postscript.

'Let me read it.' Edwin reached for it.

'No!' Marian folded it up and, having no pockets, slipped it down her dress. Next to her heart.

Edwin rolled his eyes. 'I suppose it is all maudlin and full of declarations of love.'

Is that what she wished? Once she and Domina talked of such things.

She stood. 'If it were, I would not tell you. Let us be on our way.' She started towards the Place Royal.

He hurried after her. 'You never kept secrets from me before, you know.'

Oh, yes, she had. She had never confided in him. In fact, he had never been very curious to know what she was thinking or feeling. Or doing.

'Edwin, just stop it! You are making me cross.' She walked on.

He kept pace with her and kept his lips pressed shut.

They reached the regimental offices.

Edwin opened the door for her. 'Tell me one thing, Marian.' He looked angry. 'Are you going to write back to him?'

She could feel the paper of the letter crackling against her chest. 'Yes, I am going to write back and I want you to put it with the other mail going to the regiment.'

He glowered at her, but did not refuse.

She decided to give herself a day to think about a reply. At this moment she felt too agitated to know what to say to the Captain. The joy of hearing from him was great, but she still did not know if he wrote out of duty or true regard. She knew he cared about her. Everything in his behaviour told her so. She knew she could make him desire her in that physical way, but did he love her?

Tomorrow her thoughts would be calmer.

With that meagre comfort, she waited until Edwin gave Uncle Tranville's letter to the proper person.

When Marian's letter arrived, Allan was more excited than he would dare admit. The fact that she'd written back to him so quickly was some evidence of her attachment. Perhaps they could make theirs a real betrothal. Each day away from her persuaded Allan that he desired that above all things.

Her handwriting was as graceful and as beautiful as she was herself.

Dear Captain, she wrote.

I am very pleased to hear that you arrived in Paris without mishap and that the city offers some enjoyment for you. I remain in good health, but am quite ready to return to England. My uncle insists that I wait until he is able to travel.

She sounded so cold, so impersonal. His spirits sank dismally. He read on.

On the pretext of an errand Miss Blane and I went to check on our soldiers without my uncle's knowing of it. I am happy to report that they are all doing very well. Five of them have returned to duty. The others await passage home.

Bless Miss Blane. He was glad Marian had an ally in her, even though the actress was, he suspected, as defiant as Marian.

The letter continued. *Please tend to your own health, as well. I remain your friend, Marian Pallant.*

He rubbed his face. *Friend.* This was a dreadful letter.

There was a postscript, however. *P.S. Please tell Valour that she has quite spoiled me for other horses. Although I do hope she enjoys trotting around France, I wish she will not forget me.*

Allan smiled.

He immediately sought out pen and ink and sat down to compose a reply.

In the beginning half of this letter, he wrote the barest news of his activities with the regiment and asked dutiful questions about her health and the health of those around her. In the postscript, however, he let Valour tell of the various sights of Paris from a horse's point of view, of missing her, of wishing they were together.

Over the next few weeks several letters passed between them, the postscripts becoming longer and longer, teeming with humour and hopeful emotions that they might happily see each other again.

This was a new side of Marian to discover. Playful and

fanciful, and brave in its own way. Through Valour she more openly expressed her emotions, including worries that 'Valour' would tire of her some day, or that 'Valour' might feel duty bound to provide her a ride, merely because Marian had cared for her at the peasant's farm.

Allan-as-Valour wrote back, reassuring her that Valour's fondest wish was to carry both Allan and Marian on her back again.

Allan could hardly attend to his regimental duties and he bemoaned the free time he had, which seemed more and more difficult to fill. He passed the time by visiting the city's sights.

And writing about them to Marian.

Edwin Tranville rubbed the scar on his face as he paced the drawing room waiting for Marian. She rarely cared about seeing him these days. She merely wanted to either send a letter to Landon or see if he had sent her one.

She would not even talk about the letters with him. Hadn't read him a single one. He'd taken to intercepting them when he could, and had quite perfected the means to unseal and reseal them without her noticing the tampering.

The letters turned sillier as the weeks went on. They made him want to down gallons of Belgian beer. Talking through a horse, indeed. He'd never thought Marian could be so ridiculous.

He had to do something and quick.

There was no enduring having her marry Landon. Even now his father used Landon's name to jab at him. 'Landon knows his duty,' his father repeated often. 'He is a capital officer. Knows his duty to your cousin, as well…' Then his father would congratulate himself on his cleverness at so easily marrying Marian off, then he would lament that Edwin was not dutiful, brave or clever.'

Edwin was not greatly disappointed at Marian's refusal to marry him. She had become much too bossy and he had no wish to hear her proselytise about the evils of drink every day of his life. He'd formed a plan, though, to erase Landon from the scene, a brilliant plan, if he said so himself. He had no doubt he could pull it off and that she would fall for it.

The attendant brought a decanter of claret and Edwin downed two glasses right away.

Marian finally entered the hotel's drawing room. 'Hello, Edwin.' She smiled brightly. 'Any letters today?'

He seethed at her greeting, the only way she greeted him these days.

'No letter, I'm afraid.' He put on a serious face.

Her shoulders sagged.

'Do not tell me you are fretting.' He tried to sound concerned for her.

'I am not fretting.' Her voice turned low. 'There is no trouble in Paris, is there? What are they saying at the regimental office?'

He made himself grimace and turn away.

She ran to him and clutched at his arm. 'What has happened, Edwin? You know something. Is the captain ill? Has he been injured?'

He gave her a sarcastic smile. 'He is, in fact, very well indeed.'

She looked puzzled. 'Then what is it?'

He cocked his head. 'I am not certain I should tell you.'

She faced him. 'Tell me what?'

He turned away.

'Tell me what, Edwin?' Her voice had become frantic.

'Very well, but do not be angry at me.' He gave her a direct look. 'I heard something today.'

'About the captain?'

Edwin cringed inside. Landon was all she cared about.

'Yes.' He paused. He must make it seem as if he did not want to tell her.

'Edwin.' She raised her voice. 'I am losing my patience!'

'Very well,' he snapped.

Her eyes flashed at him. 'Go on.'

He donned his most sympathetic expression. 'Some of the fellows at the regimental offices were talking about him.' He could not help but relish this next part. 'Landon has apparently developed a *tendre* for a Frenchwoman. She consumes his time, and they are living as—' he smirked 'as man and wife.'

Her eyes widened and she stared at him a long time, so long that he began to wonder if she'd seen through him. He poured another glass of claret.

She spun away and stared at one of the walls as if there were something on it to fascinate, something besides a tedious Flemish landscape.

Finally she spoke. 'I cannot believe this. It is not like him.'

'Marian, how well do you really know Landon? I've served with him in the same regiment for years. I tell you, he is not always the person he pretends to be.'

She sank into a chair.

'I could have warned you, Marian,' Edwin said. 'But I didn't think you were seriously going to marry him. He is not the sort to let a mere betrothal bar him from the pleasures of a willing Frenchwoman.'

'It cannot be true,' she rasped.

He thought she would believe it more easily than this. He rubbed his scar and drank more claret. Realising he ought to share, he poured her a glass and carried it over to her.

He tried again. 'It is said Landon has boasted about marrying an heiress and becoming wealthy. He is spending freely.'

'He would not say such a thing.' She placed the glass upon the table without even looking at it.

Edwin sat in a nearby chair, drumming on its arm with his fingers.

Time to be bold.

'If you do not believe me,' he said. 'I'll take you to the

regimental office. You can ask the fellows there. More than one heard the tale in their correspondence.'

He gambled that she would not take him up on the offer.

She just stared at him, looking very unhappy indeed.

It was quite gratifying.

'No need for that,' she said in almost a whisper. 'But I would like you to wait while I write a letter. Do you mind? I'd like you to take it to the regimental office today to be included in the next packet.'

He pretended to be put out. 'Very well. I suppose I shall have to call upon Father anyway. See to his mail. Send word when your letter is ready.'

She stood and, without another look at him, walked out of the room with a determined step.

His victory was not entirely sweet. She had not fallen into his arms for comfort, but at least she had believed him.

He rose and finished the rest of the claret.

Allan eagerly opened this latest letter from Marian. He was in the stable, ready to give Valour a nice run. It seemed the best place and time to read it.

Besides, it had just been placed in his hands a few minutes before.

He stood in a ray of sunlight in Valour's stall and unfolded the paper.

He read:

Dear Captain,

I have given our situation a great deal of thought and have no wish to stand in your way. I know my own mind and have decided we will not suit.

Do not fear that my uncle will carry out his threats to you. His interest in managing my life has waned as his health improves. When he returns to England I am confident he will forget me and the betrothal.

This decision is a final one. You are herewith released from any obligation to me.

Wishing you continued health and future happiness,

Marian Pallant

P.S. Please do not write to me. Your duty to me is done.

'What?' he said aloud. He read the letter again. 'No!'

It was as if she'd run him through with a sword. The letter made no sense. It came without warning. Without explanation. What did *'stand in your way'* mean? What did any of it mean?

It must be a mistake.

He checked the date, thinking this might have been written before their friendly, flirtatious discourse, but, no, it was dated three days ago.

Valour whinnied.

Allan patted her neck. She was saddled and ready, but he could not think of anything but returning to his rooms and writing to Marian.

Over the next two weeks he wrote her three letters. Each was returned unopened. After the last one was returned, he heard that Tranville had travelled back to England. He had to think Marian had gone with him and his party.

It was dusk when he heard this news. Instead of returning to his rooms he walked along the Seine in the shadow of Notre Dame, the stone of its towers glowing gold in the setting sun. Boats of all sizes floated in the river as Allan imagined they'd done even before the old cathedral had had its first stone laid.

He walked until his thoughts were clear and his emotions quieted. It had been his duty to offer marriage, but it had always been her right to refuse him. A lady always had that right.

Allan would never know what might have happened between them had he not involved Tranville. He was convinced Tranville's interference had sounded the death knell to his future with Marian.

His only choice now was to withdraw like a gentleman and try to plan what next to do with his life.

Knowing she would not be in it.

Chapter Eleven

April 1817—London

Marian sat behind the desk in the small library of her townhouse near Portman Square.

She tapped at the papers the man had shown her. 'Are we truly going to make this happen, Mr Yost?'

The slim man, hair greying at his temples, cocked his head. 'There is a great deal of interest. Soldiers from all over the country are willing to march, and many others are willing to sign the petition. We have only to say the word to set the plan in motion.'

She needed this Soldiers' March. She needed something to occupy her mind and her passion.

The restlessness that had been her constant companion since leaving Brussels had been somewhat assuaged by plotting for this march. She had financed and organised it with the assistance of Mr Yost.

Marian had left Brussels almost two years ago. She'd returned to Bath to occupy her aunt's house where she and Edwin had been reared. Ariana Blane had returned to London.

Edwin, her uncle and Mrs Vernon had gone on to her uncle's country estate in Dorset, the one he'd inherited when he become a baron.

As Marian had predicted, her uncle lost interest in her as soon as they reached the shores of England and he could look forward to more interesting matters, like lording it over an entire estate and the surrounding countryside. No more was ever said about the betrothal.

Mrs Vernon wrote to her that she and Uncle Tranville had married, and that he and Edwin had sold their commissions in the army. Marian sent her a dutiful letter in return and waited out the time until her twenty-first birthday.

While in Bath she'd read with great concern about the plight of the soldiers returning from the war. Mr Yost's essays about the Napoleonic war veterans in the radical newspaper, *The Political Register,* had made a great impression on her. When she moved to London, to her surprise the town house she purchased in Mayfair wound up being next door to Mr Yost.

He was also a friend of the liberal orator Henry Hunt. In early December she'd read of Mr Hunt's involvement in the demonstration at Spa Fields where ten thousand had gathered to protest high prices and to advocate parliamentary reform. Unfortunately the meeting had turned into a riot, something that must not happen in her demonstration.

'What does Mr Hunt say?' she asked Yost.

Hunt was still a powerful figure in the movement for reform. Since the Spa Fields riots, though, Mr Hunt had withdrawn from taking any active role in protests against the government. Still, his support and advice would be invaluable.

Mr Yost regarded her with a serious expression. 'He believes your plan can be implemented if done carefully.'

A *frisson* of excitement raced up Marian's spine. This felt so right, as if it had been her destiny to see first-hand the courage and sacrifice of the British soldiers, so she would understand their plight and have the passion to do something about it.

She sat back in her chair. 'Oh, Mr Yost. Ever since I came to live in London, it has greatly pained me to see our Waterloo veterans begging on the streets in their tattered uniforms. I am determined to assist them all.'

The soldiers had come back from war to the high prices created by the Corn Laws and few opportunities for employment. The government, it seemed, had simply abandoned them.

But Marian would not. She knew first-hand what they had endured. She'd bandaged their wounds and quenched their thirst.

And watched them die.

And had fallen in love with one of them.

'Hunt advises us to be careful,' Mr Yost said. 'The Seditious Meeting Act makes it illegal—'

Marian pulled herself back to the present. '—for a meeting of more than fifty people,' she finished for him. 'We must be very clever and lawful and peaceful.'

'The Spa Fields meetings were supposed to have been peaceful,' he reminded her.

She averted her gaze. 'I know.' She would never forgive herself if she led the soldiers into more violence and injury, as had occurred at Spa Fields.

Her idea was to craft their demonstration after that of the Blanketeers, weavers and spinners who, a month before, had been organised into a march from Manchester to London. They marched in groups of ten, precisely following the law. Unfortunately, their plan was thwarted before the marchers could reach London and later Parliament passed the Sedition Meeting Act making it even more difficult to carry out a demonstration, even a peaceful one.

She and Mr Yost would need to be even more clever.

He regarded her. 'In any event, Mr Hunt approves. What say you, Miss Pallant?'

'We proceed.' She handed the papers back to him.

The door opened and Marian's lady companion entered. Mr Yost glanced towards her and his colour heightened.

A smile flitted across her companion's face.

Marian smiled at the flirtation between Blanche and Mr Yost. 'Come in, Blanche. We are finished.'

'I came to warn you of the time. We need to leave soon if we are to arrive at your friend's house as expected.' Blanche lowered her eyes. 'How do you do, Mr Yost?'

'I am splendid, Mrs Nunn.' His voice turned rough.

Marian felt like applauding. This quiet romance blooming beneath her feet was delightful.

Blanche had sailed on the same boat back from Belgium as Marian. Her husband, a cavalry officer heavily in debt, had been killed at Waterloo, and the despondent Blanche had been attempting to jump overboard when Marian pulled her off the boat's railing. She offered Blanche employment as her companion. Uncle Tranville had approved, perhaps because hiring a companion gave him an excuse to leave her in Bath and forget about her.

Whatever the reason, Marian was delighted Blanche had accepted the employment and was now sharing careful pleasantries with Mr Yost.

Marian rose from behind the desk. 'I'll leave you two and fetch my hat and gloves.'

Mr Yost looked at her as if he'd forgotten she was there. He probably had. 'I ought to offer to escort you ladies, but I fear it would not be wise for Miss Pallant to be seen with me on the streets of Mayfair.'

Marian assured him, 'Reilly will walk with us.'

Reilly was the corporal from Captain Landon's regiment, their first patient in Brussels. He'd come to the servants' door, begging for work, and Marian had instantly recognised him. She'd insisted he come in to be fed and, before he'd eaten his fill, she'd hired him to work for her. Reilly was now Marian's butler and most loyal retainer.

All Marian's servants had some connection to the war.

Her cook and housemaids were soldiers' widows. Toby, her footman, had lost a leg at Waterloo. He had been one of the soldiers she'd pulled from the burning chateau at Hougoumont and though there were many tasks his impediment prevented him from performing, he was a tenacious worker otherwise.

Because of their connections to Waterloo, none of Marian's servants would ever betray her. They were in support of the demonstration. Reilly and Toby both would take an active part in it.

Mr Yost reluctantly bade his farewell to Blanche—and to Marian—and returned to his house. Then Marian, Reilly and Blanche started out for Mount Street.

'It is a pity Mr Yost could not walk with us, is it not?' Marian remarked to Blanche.

Her companion blushed. 'Indeed. His company would have been most agreeable.'

Marian smiled. 'Most agreeable.'

The day was sunny, but so breezy they often had to grab hold of their hats to keep them on their heads. The wind echoed a return of Marian's restlessness. She chastised herself. She was happy and free and her life had purpose. She had even received this invitation to again mix in society, something she'd done in only a limited way in Bath. She'd had her come-out in Bath, but never a London Season. That once had been a bitter disappointment, but since Waterloo mixing in society and wearing the latest fashions seemed unimportant.

Still, she could not refuse this first invitation to call upon Lady Ullman.

Her old friend Domina.

Domina's life could not have taken a more opposite turn than Marian's. Within a fortnight of arriving back in London from Brussels, Domina had married the widower Earl Ullman. Seven months later the new Lady Ullman gave birth. Marian read the birth announcement in the *Morning Post*. The Earl Ullman had a son by his new wife.

Marian had written a note of congratulations, and when

she and Blanche moved to London, she sent another letter informing Domina of her new lodgings. She pitied Domina. Her marriage seemed even more tragic than Marian's might have been.

But Marian would not think of that, *could* not think of Captain Landon. She refused to do so. In fact, he rarely crossed her mind now. She rarely wondered where he was, if his wounds had healed.

If he had remained with that Frenchwoman.

'You've turned quiet, Marian,' Blanche remarked.

'Have I?' She blinked in surprise. 'I must have been woolgathering.'

'Are you concerned about this visit?'

Marian's brows knitted. 'I suppose I am. Domina and I did not part under the best of circumstances.'

'Indeed,' responded the companion.

Marian had already told Blanche about their escapade in Belgium, the plan to reunite Domina with Ollie before the battle and what had happened to Marian when they'd become separated. Marian had told Blanche everything except about Domina's pregnancy.

And about Captain Landon.

Marian walked on. 'I confess I am intensely curious about Domina. How she could marry so quickly.'

'I must own some of that curiosity, as well,' Blanche admitted. 'I could not have married so soon after losing my husband.'

Marian slanted her a knowing look. 'Ah, but time heals, does it not?'

Blanche blushed.

They reached Earl Ullman's townhouse on Mount Street. It was a great deal finer than Marian's snug little one.

'Domina has done well.' Marian craned her neck to see to the top floors.

Reilly sounded the knocker. 'I will wait for you nearby, miss.'

Her brows rose. 'Are you certain? Someone might offer you some refreshment if you come in.'

'I'm hungrier for the fine day.' He glanced at the sky. The April breeze had blown away the haze, revealing a rare peek at blue sky.

'Do as you wish,' she told him. 'We should not be long.'

Reilly stepped back as a footman in pristine livery opened the door and ushered them in to a marble-floored hall decorated with jardinières of daffodils and classical-themed paintings.

'How lovely the flowers are,' Marian whispered to Blanche.

The footman helped them off with their coats and passed the garments to a waiting maid. After leading them up an elegant marble staircase he crossed through a doorway framed in gilded moulding to announce them.

Domina bounced up from a pale-pink brocade sofa and rushed over to Marian, her arms extended. 'Oh, I cannot believe you are here! I have missed you so.'

'You look wonderful, Domina.' Marian meant it.

Domina's eyes sparkled, her skin glowed with health and her red curls were bright as ever. As she grasped both of Marian's hands, the skirt of her peach gown swirled around her ankles. The gown looked as new and fresh as its wearer.

Marian had expected to see evidence of suffering on Domina's face, some indications she had endured the death of a lover, the birth of his child and marriage to a stranger.

Her friend looked perfectly radiant.

'I am splendid now you are here.' She squeezed Marian's hands as fondly as if she had never betrayed her and allowed her to be abandoned in Brussels.

'Let me present my companion…' Marian turned to Blanche and introduced her to the new Lady Ullman. Marian briefly answered Domina's polite questions about her situation. That she and Blanche lived on Bryanston Street. That they managed to keep themselves busy. 'Although I cannot say what we do,' she added truthfully.

'We must do something about your social life, mustn't we? I will see you get invitations from Ullie's friends.'

Marian started. '*Ollie*'s friends?'

Domina's smile faltered for a brief moment. '*Ullie*'s. Lord Ullman, but I call him Ullie. He likes it excessively.' She gestured for them to sit down. 'I've ordered tea. I have so much to tell you...'

Where Marian had been brief, Domina indulged in great detail, telling all about meeting Lord Ullman within days after she and her parents came to London directly after leaving Belgium. He had proposed quickly.

'After Ollie, of course, I felt I never could fall in love again, but, you know, Marian, he looks a lot like Ollie—' The tea arrived, but Domina did not even stop to take a breath. 'Ullie is older, as you might expect, but that is not a bad thing.'

'How old is he?' Marian managed to break in.

'Forty-two, but he is quite robust. And he dotes on the baby, even though he has two children by his late wife.' She leaned forwards and whispered to Marian, 'It is fortunate that the baby looks just like him.'

Marian ought not to be shocked that Lord Ullman did not know the truth about the baby's paternity; it was a protection for both mother and child, after all. Still, she suddenly felt very sorry for Harry Oliver's parents. They would never know that a part of their son lived on.

'You have had a baby?' Blanche asked. Blanche loved children and lamented that she had never conceived by her husband.

'A son!' Domina said brightly. She avoided Marian's eyes. 'He is with his nurse, of course, but we miss him terribly. Nurse wrote to us that he is walking now.' She paused. 'We named him Harry.'

Marian felt another pang of sadness. Perhaps Domina was not as blissful as she wished to pretend.

There was no further indication of it as Domina chattered on. 'Little Harry is third in line for the title. Ullie is excessively wealthy so he shall have every advantage—'

Domina had done the very best she could for Harry Oliver's child. What right had Marian to judge her?

Domina went on to talk about Lord Ullman's money, his influence, his country estates, the dresses being made for her, the ball she planned during the Season. Marian and Blanche could only listen and sip their tea.

Marian occupied her mind with trying to invent a polite way to take their leave. Finally the door opened, and Domina stopped mid-sentence. A portly, balding man entered the room, and Domina leapt from her seat and into his arms. Another man stood behind him, but his face was obscured by the loving couple's reunion.

'Ullie,' Domina cried. 'Come meet my dearest friend in the whole world!'

'Delighted, my dear,' he said. 'My nephew is with me. We may both be presented.'

Lord Ullman stepped aside to reveal his nephew. Marian stood, stunned.

It was Captain Landon. *Her* Captain Landon.

She was too astounded to speak when Domina presented Lord Ullman to her and Blanche, but Domina took no notice. 'And this is Ullie's nephew, Mr Landon.'

'Captain,' Marian whispered.

He nodded stiffly. 'Miss Pallant.'

Gone was the mended red coat of his uniform. Instead he wore a deep blue coat of fine wool. His linen was pristine white, and buckskin trousers hugged his muscular thighs.

'Do you know each other?' Domina cried. 'How can that be?'

Marian answered. 'The captain was in Brussels, Domina.'

'Domina?' The captain looked astounded.

Domina put her hands to her cheeks. 'Oh, my. I remember now! We saw him in the Parc!' She tittered. 'I thought you were familiar when we met, Allan, but it was such a brief meeting I had no time to remember where I had seen you. In Brussels! And now you are a relation!' Before he could comment, she turned to Marian. 'But we were not introduced to him, Marian.'

Domina's parents apparently had not told her of meeting the captain in Brussels, nor of their sordid imaginings of what had transpired between them.

'I met him afterwards,' she explained.

Domina giggled. 'And here we all are now. What a coincidence.' She waved her hands. 'Do sit, everyone. I'll send for more tea.'

Her husband stopped her. 'Do not trouble yourself, my dear. Rest. Allan would prefer brandy, I am certain.'

'As you please,' the captain murmured. His eyes sought Marian again. 'I trust you are in good health, Miss Pallant.' They both remained standing.

'I am well enough, Captain.' Marian fought to keep her gaze steady and her nerves calm. Her whole body had responded to him just as if she'd this moment crawled into bed with him. She had to get away. 'We must leave, I am afraid. It is late.'

'Oh, no,' Domina cried. 'You just arrived!'

Even Blanche looked surprised.

'I assure you, we must go.' She turned to Domina's husband. 'It was such a pleasure to meet you, Lord Ullman. I look forward to a further acquaintance, but we must bid you good day.'

He held a glass of brandy in each hand. 'Do not hurry off.'

'We must,' she insisted. 'I—I have an appointment. I regret not having more time. Come, Blanche.'

Blanche was on her feet.

'I'll ring for the footman to show you out,' Domina rose to cross the room to the bell pull.

'Do not trouble yourself,' Marian said. 'We will find our way out. Please continue your visit with the captain.'

Marian walked briskly to the doorway, Blanche following.

Domina called after her. 'Come back soon, Marian. I will see you receive some invitations!'

Once in the hall it seemed to take forever for the maid to bring their coats and for the footman to help put them on.

They had almost made their escape when the captain appeared. 'I will walk you home, Marian.'

'No need,' she replied in a bright tone. 'My butler waits outside for us.'

'I wish to speak with you.' His eyes pierced her. 'Wait a moment for me.'

She could not flee from what was inevitable. If he was in London, she might see him again, somewhere, some time.

'Very well, Captain.' She turned to Blanche. 'You and Reilly may go on ahead. I will follow soon.'

She could tell Blanche was bursting with questions about this impressive-looking man and why he sought Marian's company, but Blanche simply said, 'Good day…Captain', and left.

Marian's heart was beating as if she were running a foot-race. In her mind she'd convinced herself he was gone, as her parents were gone, as her aunt was gone, as the soldiers who died in her arms and those taken by the fire were gone.

She'd almost succeeded.

But now he was here, looking as handsome and intense as ever. Even in a gentleman's clothes everything about him was familiar, even the scent of him. It was as if almost two years had vanished.

Neither of them spoke while they waited for the footman to bring the captain's hat and topcoat. When finally they stepped out into the street, the breeze had calmed and the blue skies were already replaced with grey.

'I live near Portman Square,' she told him. 'Do you know where that is?'

'I am not a stranger to London, Marian,' he answered, his voice low.

She'd offended him. It ought not to matter. After all, he had offended her very deeply with his easy infidelity. She started walking and did not take his arm.

'I did not know Lord Tranville's town house was near Portman Square.' His voice turned more conciliatory.

'I do not live with Lord Tranville,' she responded. 'I am free of him, which does not matter to him one whit.'

Their arms brushed as they walked together, silent again. The silence lasted until Marian could stand it no longer. 'You obviously did not tell Domina that you knew me.'

His pace slowed. 'I had no notion my uncle's wife was Domina until you spoke her name. I only met her once, very briefly. Uncle Ullman never used her given name.' He slanted a glance at her. 'Did you know Ullman was my uncle?'

'I did not.' Indeed, what had she known of the captain? Almost nothing, as Edwin had said.

They walked on.

He added, as if it were an afterthought, 'Our former association seems largely unknown to anyone.'

True. The gossip and scandal the Fentons feared and that had so concerned the captain had never materialised. 'So I cannot imagine why you would wish to speak with me, Captain.'

'I am no longer a captain. I sold my commission.'

He had long ceased being *her* Captain—why did this news disappoint her?

'A decade of war was sufficient for me,' he added.

One day of war had been enough for Marian.

But that one day of war had also changed everything for her, and he had been a part of it. No matter how she tried to deceive herself, he would always return to her, whenever she saw a soldier, whenever anyone mentioned Waterloo.

If only they had parted like they'd met. In an instant. First here, then gone. How much better that would have been than the pain of the marriage proposal and its aftermath. Her chest hurt from it this very moment. No wonder it was called a *broken* heart.

She gave herself a mental shake. This kind of thinking was ridiculous. Any romance between them had existed in her own mind. They'd become attached because of the circumstances, nothing more.

'What happened, Marian?' he said suddenly, his voice deep with emotion.

'Happened?' She blinked, thinking for a moment he could read her thoughts.

'Your last letter,' he said. 'I wrote back for an explanation, but you returned my letters unopened.'

Her throat tightened. She had no wish to go through this again. 'Surely there was no mystery, Captain. I was very clear.' Tears pricked her eyes. 'I explained it to you. I told you Uncle Tranville was no longer a threat. I told you I had made my decision.'

He still looked confounded. 'But, why?'

She could bear no more of this. 'Listen to me, Captain. My uncle had affairs right under my aunt's nose. I saw what it did to her.' Her father's infidelity had done worse, bringing illness into their house, leaving her an orphan. 'It was not the sort of marriage I desired.'

The line between his eyes deepened. 'What have your uncle's affairs to do with me?'

Her eyes flashed at him. 'Do not play me for a fool.'

They reached Grosvenor Square, the most fashionable square in Mayfair. He extended his hand towards Hyde Park, only two streets away. 'Let us cross through the park.'

His long quick strides gave her no choice but to follow, although it was difficult to keep up. He did not slow until they crossed through Grosvenor Gate and reached one of the walking paths.

Soon the carriages and curricles would crowd the park, but the afternoon was still early enough that the fashionable world had not yet arrived. At the moment, she and the captain were alone.

'Now answer my question,' he demanded. 'What did your uncle's affairs have to do with me?'

She made herself meet his gaze. 'I know about the Frenchwoman.'

'The Frenchwoman.' His forehead creased. 'What Frenchwoman?'

She gaped at him. '*The* Frenchwoman. Your mistress. Your *paramour.*'

He shook his head. 'Marian, I have no *paramour.*'

'But you did. In Paris.' Marian put her hands on her hips. 'Did you think I would not discover it?'

He stepped back. 'There was nothing to discover. I had no mistress. Not then. Not now.' His expression was earnest. 'Who told you this tale?'

'Edwin told me.'

'Edwin!' He spat out the name like a piece of rancid meat.

She straightened. 'Edwin heard it at the regimental offices in Brussels.'

He seized her arms and drew her so close she felt his breath on her lips. 'Impossible.' Just as suddenly he released her, only to dip down to her again with a disparaging laugh. 'It is not true. Edwin did not hear about it at the regimental offices, because it did not happen. Edwin lied to you.'

She rubbed her arms where his fingers had touched. 'Why would he lie to me?' She breathed.

She felt sick inside. Edwin must have lied. Why had he done such a terrible thing to her?

The captain held her again, more gently this time, so that there were only inches between them. His scent made her feel as if she'd downed too many glasses of wine, and her senses flared as they'd not done since he'd held her in Belgium.

'You believed him.' His eyes bore into her. 'How could

you think me capable of such a thing? I considered myself betrothed to you. I wanted no other woman.'

She tried to remain rational, but her emotions warred within her, wanting him to hold her, wanting to run away.

She steeled herself. 'How could I not think that of you? You were forced by my uncle into offering for me.'

'You forget I offered marriage before your uncle stuck his nose in it.'

'Out of duty,' she reminded him.

His grip tightened. 'After what we endured together—after how I behaved—it *was* my duty, even if your uncle had not threatened us. But did I not also say I *wanted* to be betrothed to you? That I would wait until you were free to accept or reject me? Does this sound like a man who would take a mistress?'

He was so close their breath mingled. She remembered the taste of him, remembered his hands caressing her. Why had she believed him capable of keeping a French mistress?

Men need women to bed, her teachers had instructed.

'It is what men do,' she cried.

A memory flashed through her mind—her father being kissed by the Indian woman. Her mother screaming at him before both fell ill and died. The pain returned.

She wrested her thoughts back to the present. 'Why should I think you any different?'

He drew her even closer. 'Because we spent time together in the most intimate of ways.'

Her knees turned weak. She wanted to melt into his arms and be comforted by him.

She pulled away. 'You were either ill or we were running from danger. That is not a courtship.'

'It ought to have been enough to take the measure of my character.' He turned from her and started on the path again.

She had to run to keep up with him.

She'd been blind to that simple reasoning. Edwin had

chosen the one falsehood to which she was so vulnerable. Infidelity killed her parents and killed her aunt's spirit. There was nothing he could have said about Captain Landon that could have fed into worse fears.

Her body was awash with arousal and rage.

And regret.

What might have happened between her and the captain had her uncle and cousin not so cruelly interfered?

She followed the captain through Cumberland Gate.

He abruptly stopped. 'Which street is yours?'

'Not far. Bryanston Street.' She was surprised she could even speak.

They crossed Oxford Street and walked the short distance to tiny Bryanston Street, giving her time to calm herself.

'I know this street.' His tone changed completely. 'John Yost lives here.'

Her nerves went on alert. 'Mr Yost?'

'Are you acquainted with him?' His expression was intense.

She stopped in front of her town house and tried to casually point to the one next to it. 'He lives next door.'

Edwin had been right about one thing. She did not know very much about the captain. She did not know if he was Whig or Tory, if he believed in reform or if he thought it right for the government to favour the rich and neglect the needy.

Her heart pounded with this new concern. 'Why do you ask about Mr Yost?'

Chapter Twelve

Allan gazed down upon Marian, too many emotions battling inside him to make his thinking clear. Why had he asked about John Yost? What did he care about Yost at a time like this?

He suspected his mind forced the distraction upon him to keep him sane. His confusion and anger, his raw desire for her, he'd thought buried with his work.

Damned Edwin Tranville! Allan should have known Edwin was behind all this.

What did it say about Marian's regard for him that she believed Edwin so easily? Was her opinion of him so low that she could entertain such a lie? She had not even given him a chance to defend himself.

Marian looked accusingly at him now. 'Why did you ask about Mr Yost?'

He'd already forgotten about Yost.

Allan rubbed his forehead. 'No reason. His name came up in my work, is all.'

'Your work?' Her voice rose a pitch.

'I am employed by Lord Sidmouth.'

Her eyes widened. 'Lord Sidmouth?'

'The Home Secretary.'

'I know who Lord Sidmouth is.' She tucked an errant lock of hair back under her bonnet. 'Why does the Home Secretary speak about my neighbour? Does Mr Yost pose some danger to me?'

'No danger.' Allan regretted even mentioning the man. 'Yost is merely known as a liberal thinker who has written on various radical topics. It makes him of interest to the Home Secretary.'

She did not quite meet his eye. 'What work do you do for Lord Sidmouth?'

He shrugged. 'I attempt to uncover possible treasonable offences, such as if someone is inciting unrest or rioting or some such activity.'

She took a quick intake of breath. 'And Mr Yost? Is he inciting unrest and rioting?'

'Not that I know of.'

There had been talk, though, that Mr Yost had met with Henry Hunt recently. Sidmouth believed something could be afoot between the two men.

But Allan did not want to talk about this. 'Who lives here with you?' Another man, he meant?

She seemed distracted. 'Who lives here? Mrs Nunn, who is my companion, and our servants. Why do you ask me that?'

Their conversation had become even more stilted and difficult than when they'd been talking of the past.

'No reason,' he quickly countered. He was not about to admit he was worried that she'd taken a lover.

The door was opened by a looming manservant with the aura of a bodyguard.

The man laughed. 'Captain!'

Allan looked into his face. 'Reilly?' He could hardly believe his eyes.

Reilly made a congenial, if exaggerated, bow. 'Good day to you, Captain Landon.'

'He is no longer a captain, Reilly.' Marian entered the house and glanced back at Allan. 'Mr Reilly is my butler.'

Without thinking, Allan followed her inside, his hand extended to clasp Reilly's. 'By God, Reilly. I am astounded, but it is good to see you.' He asked Reilly about his wounds and listened to Reilly explain how Marian had taken him in and trained him to be her butler.

'In fact, we all have a connection to Waterloo here,' Reilly told him. 'Toby, our footman, lost a leg at Hougoumont. Mrs Nunn, Cook and the maids are all Waterloo widows.'

'Indeed?' Allan was impressed. He turned to Marian. 'You hired them because of Waterloo?'

She nodded. She remained by the door, her fingers clasping the doorknob.

'How did you find—?' He lifted his hand. 'I beg your pardon. I am intruding, and you indicated an appointment you must keep.' He stepped back towards the door. 'I am glad to see you looking so fit, Reilly.' His glance went from Reilly to Marian. 'Good day to you, Miss Pallant.'

She leaned against the door. 'Good day, Captain.'

He walked out remembering their companionship in the house in Brussels. Her door now closed behind him, and he felt as empty as he had felt when reading her final letter.

Allan walked the streets with his head and emotions awhirl. He had half a mind to report Edwin's crimes at Badajoz to the Colonel-in-Chief of the regiment.

Except he'd given his word not to speak of it to anyone.

What would be the use anyway? Exacting revenge against Edwin would change nothing with Marian.

He passed a flower vendor with a large basket. She sang, 'Buy my fine roses… Buy my fine roses.'

The flowers' scent reminded him of Marian. He shook his head and walked on.

He crossed Oxford Street and walked past Hanover Square to enter the Coach and Horses Inn on Conduit Street, choosing a seat in a dark corner of the taproom. He'd done a fair amount of ale drinking in taverns and inns since working for Sidmouth, keeping his ears open for hints of sedition, but other than complaints about high prices and concerns about the numbers of unemployed in the streets, he'd heard nothing of impending discord.

At the moment, though, the conversations around him held no interest. He wanted to ease his own unrest.

Caused by Marian Pallant, the woman who had not believed in him, who had not wished to marry him.

He cursed Edwin Tranville once more.

After Paris, Allan had poured his energies into building a new future for himself. He still had the drive to make something of his life, even if it no longer was to be worthy of marrying her. He strived for something big—he wanted to run for a seat in the House of Commons. But first he needed to prove himself worthy and knowledgeable.

Allan was a second son and, though his family was well known in Nottinghamshire, he had few connections in London besides his uncle. Uncle Ullman had introduced him to Lord Sidmouth, and Lord Sidmouth had offered him employment. What could be a better situation for him than to work for the Home Office?

Allan believed passionately in Sidmouth's work. His father had been killed when a protesting mob had run amok. At Badajoz Allan had witnessed first hand the violence and destruction of men out of control.

Each day he worked to prevent a protest march or rioting in the streets was a day he avenged his father's death. And atoned for what his fellow soldiers, including Edwin, had done at Badajoz.

If this were not enough, his work also served to replace the passion he'd felt for Marian.

Almost.

Seeing her again brought it all back. She looked more beautiful than ever, and there was a new fire of determination in her eyes that made her even more tantalising.

The tavern maid delivered a tankard of ale. Allan wrapped his fingers around it and drank deeply, remembering the ale Marian had given him after his fever broke. He drained the tankard of its contents and ordered another one.

Maybe one more—or three more—would wash away his anger and regret.

Three days later Allan saw Marian again.

His uncle had arranged for him to be invited to Lady Doncaster's musicale, where many of society's influential people would be in attendance. As Allan walked from his rooms near St James's Square to Duke Street, mere streets away from where Marian lived, it occurred to him she might be there.

As soon as he entered the Doncaster town house and greeted his hostess, his gaze found Marian, standing with his uncle and Lady Ullman. Like a moth to flame, he crossed the room to them.

'Uncle, Lady Ullman, good evening.' He bowed.

'Allan!' cried Domina. 'You must call me Domina. We are family.' She turned to her friend. 'I have brought Marian with us.'

Allan bowed to Marian. 'Good evening, Miss Pallant.'

'Capt—' she began, then caught herself. 'Mr Landon.' She dropped into a curtsy.

She was easily the loveliest woman in the room. A bit taller than was fashionable, but her hair gleamed like spun gold. Her gown was some gossamer confection as angel-white as the first gown he'd seen her in, its only decoration a simple edging of gold ribbon.

The memory of her dressed in boys' clothing dragging injured soldiers from a burning house flashed through his mind. He smiled.

The colour rose in her face, making her even lovelier.

Lord Ullman seized his wife's arm. 'Someone you must meet, my dear.' He whisked her away, leaving Allan with Marian.

Marian's eyes flickered with irritation as they so callously left her.

'Domina has abandoned you again, it seems,' he remarked.

Her lips pursed. 'And she knew this was my first real foray into society since Brussels. I know hardly anyone.'

Because Tranville had not bothered to see her properly introduced.

'Chin up, Marian,' he said quietly. 'You faced the French. Surely a few lords and their ladies cannot daunt you.'

Her eyes rose to his. 'I feel out of place.'

Out of place? Because she outshone them, perhaps.

Across the room a woman glanced towards her, then whispered something to a lady next to her. Both continued to gaze at her.

She sighed. 'I have not escaped gossip, it seems.'

'Perhaps they are merely envious of your gown,' Allan said.

She rolled her eyes, not even heeding his compliment. 'More likely they are saying I am woefully out of fashion. Everyone else is festooned with lace and frills.' Her voice turned to a whisper. 'Or perhaps it is you who have captured their interest.'

'Me?' He was surprised.

'An eligible man, surely women would notice.' She averted her gaze. 'Forgive me—for all I know, you may no longer be eligible.'

He spoke in a low tone. 'I am not married, if that is what you mean, Marian. I am not betrothed.'

Her eyes rose to his and that sense of connection they'd shared so often in Brussels returned.

She quickly looked away. 'Perhaps Domina has gossiped about me.'

He felt the distance between them again. 'Surely she would not have spoken about Brussels.'

She waved a hand. 'Not about Brussels, but she is very

capable of chattering on about me living independently. The *ton* is not likely to favour that.'

He'd had the same thought. An independent woman was by definition suspect, unless she was a widow or an aged spinster. He wondered what those ladies might think of her if they knew she'd run into a burning building or swept out a barn.

He was about to make that remark when Lord Sidmouth approached.

'Good evening, Landon.' Sidmouth gave Marian a speculative look.

Allan obligingly presented Sidmouth to her.

Her eyes widened at the mention of his name. 'You are Home Secretary.'

'Am indeed, Miss Pallant.' Sidmouth nodded towards Allan. 'Landon works for me. Good assistant.'

'Yes, he told me.' Something in her manner changed and that glint of determination returned to her eyes.

'Mark my words. Landon will rise high. He's that sort.'

She slanted a glance toward Allan. 'Rise high?'

'My hope, Miss Pallant,' Allan explained, 'is to sit in the House of Commons some day.'

'Is it?' Her voice turned more sarcastic than impressed.

'Will succeed, too. Mark my words.' Sidmouth walked away.

The butler announced that the music was about to begin. Everyone made their way to the ballroom, which was set up with rows of chairs.

Allan caught sight of his uncle helping Domina into a seat next to another couple. 'Would you do the honour of sitting with me, Miss Pallant?'

She also had noticed her friend had seemingly forgotten her. 'Thank you, Mr Landon. That is kind of you.'

Kind? To sit with anyone else would feel unnatural.

Cards detailing the programme had been placed on each chair. An Italian soprano, Giuditta Pasta, would sing from *Figaro*, and a pianist would play some of John Field's works.

They settled in seats towards the back of the room. The performers were soon ready.

The first selection, one of John Field's nocturnes, had a certain sweetness and delicacy yet depth of mood that seemed to perfectly reflect Allan's companion. At first Marian sat very still and listened intently to the music. Eventually her gaze drifted, and Allan sensed her thoughts had travelled elsewhere, somewhere beyond this room, beyond the music and his company.

The Italian soprano was next. She walked into the room dressed in breeches. Her role in *Figaro* was Cherubino, an adolescent page always played by a soprano.

Allan exchanged glances with Marian, and knew she, too, was reminded of her own disguise as an adolescent boy.

The soprano began to sing. Allan's Italian was limited, but he was able to translate the first line:

You, who know what love is, see if I have it in my heart.

The line ran through his mind during the rest of the musical evening. Seated next to Marian, Allan felt more attuned to her than to the music. He knew when she listened and when she drifted away. He wished he could drift away with her.

When the music concluded, the audience clapped, but immediately stood, ready to seek out the refreshments, which would be served in another room. Allan and Marian did not rise immediately. It took Allan a few moments to remember they were in the Doncaster ballroom.

When they entered the room with the refreshments, Marian's friend Domina rushed up to them. 'Marian! I thought I had lost you, but I was excessively grateful to know you were with Allan. I knew I need not worry at all. Have you enjoyed the performance?'

'I did enjoy it,' Marian said.

Allan wanted to deliver a set-down to Domina for abandoning her friend. Again.

'That is splendid.' Domina clapped her hands. 'Ullie has introduced me to so many wonderful people, people we would never have met in Bath. I shan't ever recall all their names, but it has been quite exciting.' She glanced over to where her husband kept an eye on her. 'I would ask you to join us, but there are no chairs.'

'You should—' He was about to tell her that she and his uncle should choose a table to include Marian, but Domina was off, her skirts sailing behind her. 'Your friend angers me,' he muttered.

Marian sighed. 'She angers me, too.'

They joined some people with whom Allan was mildly acquainted and talked of the music. It was an entirely pleasant time.

When Domina decided she wanted to leave, she sent a footman to alert Marian. Allan escorted her out of the town house to where his uncle and Domina, and others, waited for their carriages to reach the front of the queue. It had rained earlier in the day, but the night was fine, and Allan did not mind that the wait for the Ullman carriage dragged on.

Marian looked impatient. 'I could walk home faster than this.'

Allan was the only one close enough to hear her. 'I will escort you, if you wish.'

She glanced around. 'Will anyone remark upon it, I wonder?'

'We have darkness on our side. I will inform my uncle. If he has no objection, we can slip away.'

A minute later, they were crossing Oxford Street.

'Thank you for taking me home, Captain.'

He smiled. It felt good to hear her call him 'Captain' again. 'I enjoy the walk.'

'I did learn one thing this evening,' she said.

'What was that?' He liked this sudden camaraderie with her. It reminded him of better times.

'I have little need to mix in society.'

They walked side by side again, but he wished he could thread her arm through his. 'Are you certain? You cannot isolate yourself.'

She looked pensive. 'I no longer belong in such company.'

He could not believe it. 'You look as if you have always graced the fashionable world.'

It was her turn to look surprised. 'Why, thank you, Captain.' She shook her head. 'No matter. It holds little interest to me.'

He frowned. 'Because of Belgium?'

She slanted a glance. 'Yes. It changed me.'

He looked into her face. 'It changed me, too.'

Her lips trembled and he was lost again in a haze of wanting her, needing her, unable to conceive of being apart from her.

They stood on the Mayfair street, gazing upon each other. For Allan the moment stretched until he lost how long they remained there. Slowly he bent down, bringing his lips closer to hers.

She turned away and started walking again. The moment passed and they began to talk of the musicale and the people there, about Domina's total self-absorption.

They reached her street and walked up to her door.

'Thank you again, Captain.' She extended her hand.

He took it and, wanting so much more, pulled her close enough to place a kiss upon her forehead. 'I enjoyed your company.'

She looked up at him, her eyes large.

Before he lost the thin tether on his restraint, he sounded her knocker. Reilly almost instantly opened the door and Marian rushed inside.

Allan nodded to Reilly and stepped away. 'Goodnight, Miss Pallant.'

From just within the threshold, she turned back to him. 'Godspeed, Captain.'

Allan had hoped to see her at other entertainments over the next few days but, even though his uncle and Domina were present, Marian was not a member of their party. He began to worry about her. Was she ill? Was some man not of his uncle's set entertaining her? Or was she merely turning her back on a society in which she felt she no longer belonged?

He told himself not to think of her, to concentrate on work instead. He filled his time checking in with Sidmouth's sources, reading newspapers, visiting taverns and coffee houses.

This day he was in the office, seated at his desk, perusing a Nottingham newspaper. Some familiar names dotted the pages, making him wonder how they went on. Between the lines he read of much distress from lost jobs and high prices. It was like that throughout Great Britain.

Lord Sidmouth rapped on his door.

Allan lowered the newspaper and stood. 'Come in, sir.'

'Well? What have you found?' Sidmouth sat in a nearby chair.

'Nothing specific.' Allan folded the paper. 'Something has changed in the last week. I can sense it, although I've heard nothing and read nothing specific.'

'Have the same feeling,' Sidmouth said. 'What of Mr Yost?'

Allan shrugged. 'His name recurs, but in the context of people wondering if he will dare write another essay.'

Sidmouth pounded his knee. 'He's our key. Bet a pony on it.' He leaned towards Allan. 'I have an idea.'

'What is it?'

He leaned back again, lounging in the chair. 'You are acquainted with his neighbour. Pretty girl. Met her with you at Lady Doncaster's.'

Allan held his gaze steady.

'Miss Pallant,' Sidmouth went on. 'That's the name. Size-able fortune. Father was with the East India Company. Lord Tranville's niece by marriage. Had some sort of falling out with him. Been living on her own since inheriting.'

Allan was appalled. 'You investigated her?'

A corner of the lord's mouth turned up. 'Asked a few questions here and there.'

Allan's fingers curled into a fist.

'Unconventional sort. Lives with a companion. Controls her own funds. Went to Brussels with Sir Roger and his wife. Something happened there. Don't know what it is yet.'

Good God.

Allan's eyes narrowed. 'What has this to do with Yost?' Why was Sidmouth digging into Marian's past? Did he know that Allan had been with her?

'Had this idea.' Sidmouth grinned in delight. 'Call upon her. Court her, even. Makes sense for you to court an heiress.'

Now he was sounding like Tranville.

'Court Miss Pallant?'

Sidmouth cocked his head. 'Only for show, if you like. Too uncommon for an MP's wife, I'd say. Look for a peer's daughter for that. Real reason is to get information about Yost. Watch his house. See what she knows, what her servants know. Servants talk, see everything.'

By God, this was callous.

Allan gripped the arm of his chair. 'You want me to use Miss Pallant in order to spy on John Yost.'

'That's the right of it.' Sidmouth grinned. 'Inspired idea, is it not?'

Allan stood. 'It is a detestable idea! Toying with a young lady's affections merely for information. It is dishonourable.'

Sidmouth's expression darkened. 'Then do not court her. Just call upon her. You are a friend of hers, are you not?'

Sidmouth had a way of manipulating people for his own

ends. He apparently had no qualms about manipulating Marian.

Allan gave Sidmouth a direct stare. 'I want no part of this.'

Sidmouth rose and sauntered to the door, but he turned back. 'This is not a request, Landon. This is the job you agreed to perform when I employed you. If you care about your future and the future of your country, you'll befriend your Miss Pallant, court her, sleep with her, anything necessary to get information that prevents sedition. Do as I say and persist until you have something on Yost to bring to me.' He strolled out of the room.

Allan sank in the chair and ran his hand through his hair.

To do his job, to serve his country, to avenge his father, he had to take advantage of Marian.

Chapter Thirteen

Marian sat at her desk and riffled through the latest set of invitations. Domina had been true to her word. Invitations arrived every day to various events and Domina often penned notes offering to include her in their party. Marian found excuses to refuse, although each time she wondered if *he* would be attending.

He consumed her thoughts much too often, her *Captain*, but it was essential she stay away from him. He worked for the Home Secretary. His job was to thwart everything she was working hard to bring about.

She dropped the invitations on the desk and pulled out a sheet of paper to pen a conciliatory note to Domina, refusing yet another offer to accompany her to a breakfast, but promising to call upon her soon.

Blanche walked in. 'Do you need to speak with Mr Yost today?'

Marian put down her pen. 'I do not think so. Why?'

She blushed. 'I just met him outside when I was coming from the shops. He invited me to walk with him in the park.'

Marian hid her amusement, wondering how long Mr Yost stood at his window watching for Blanche to return. 'If he needs to speak with me, he certainly may, but otherwise, enjoy the day.'

'You do not mind?' Blanche took her duties as companion so seriously she felt guilty ever leaving Marian alone.

'I do not mind,' Marian assured her. 'I have letters to write and much to keep me occupied.'

Blanche grinned at her. 'Thank you, Marian.' She started for the door.

Marian called after her. 'Invite Mr Yost to dinner, if you like.'

Blanche stopped. 'Indeed?'

'Of course. It will be pleasant.'

Blanche returned a grateful look. 'I will, then.'

'Tell Cook,' Marian added.

Blanche nodded and swept out of the room looking blissfully happy, the way a woman in love ought to look.

Marian rested her chin on her hand. Blanche renewed Marian's faith in romance. Mr Yost was a good man with a solid independent income. Both he and Blanche deserved happiness.

Something that eluded Marian.

Her own fault. What might have happened if she'd even considered that Edwin had lied to her? What if she had opened one of the captain's letters instead of returning them?

Perhaps she would be wed to him and sharing his bed at night. She couldn't deny the fact that her body still yearned for him.

As did her soul.

She forced herself to pick up her pen, dip it in the inkpot and resume writing her letter.

One thing was certain, she would not be planning a soldiers' march if her husband worked for the Home Secretary. How then would the soldiers' voices be heard? She was determined to give them that voice. There was nothing more important to her.

She easily finished her correspondence and stood, stretching the stiffness from her muscles. She walked out to the hall just as someone sounded the knocker.

'I'll get it, Reilly,' she called out. 'I'm right here.' She opened the door.

The captain stood at the threshold.

'Captain!' She felt herself flush.

He removed his hat. 'I did not expect you to answer the door. Domina said you have refused several invitations—'

Now she understood. 'Domina sent you? I am sorry you have been put to so much inconvenience.'

He shook his head. 'She did not send me.'

He had come of his own volition? She flushed again, too instantly aware of him.

She stepped aside. 'Do come in.'

Reilly appeared, all smiles when he saw who it was. 'Captain! May I take your things?'

He handed Reilly his hat and gloves. 'How do you fare today?' he asked the butler.

A pleased expression lit Reilly's face. 'In good health, sir.'

'Well—' Marian clasped her hands together '—come to the drawing room, will you? Reilly, bring us tea.'

'Yes, miss,' he said.

She led the captain to the small drawing room on the first floor, the one that faced the front of the house. 'Do sit, Captain, and tell me why you have come.'

He stood until she lowered herself in a chair. 'I merely was in the neighbourhood and thought to see how you went on.'

'Why?' There must be more to it than that.

'Do I need more reason than the concern of a friend?'

They could never be friends, not even if they were not political enemies.

'Everything is splendid here.' She did not wish to be the topic of conversation. 'How is the Home Office?'

His eyes flickered. 'No Blanketeers at the city gates as yet.'

Had he been a part of thwarting the Blanketeers' march?

Marian tried to keep her voice even. 'Ah, but did not one of the Blanketeers make it through? The newspapers said he delivered his petition.'

'One man is not a riot,' he countered.

This irritated her. 'Not every protest is a riot. The papers said the men marched peacefully in small groups.'

The captain countered, 'Ah, but the intent was for them all to meet in a large gathering. When numbers are large, there is always the danger of riot.'

Her brows rose. 'Cannot large numbers of men gather and behave in organised, disciplined ways?'

'It only takes one spark to set a fire. One man, one mistake, and a riot might result.' His fingers tapped the arm of the chair.

She smiled stiffly. 'I was not thinking of marches upon Parliament. I was thinking of soldiers. Are soldiers not disciplined, even though their numbers are large?'

'Even soldiers can run amok.' His tone turned bleak and pain filled his eyes.

He witnessed such a thing, she realised. *In the war.*

She wanted to comfort him, to soothe away the pain of whatever it was he'd endured.

Would he want her comfort if he knew she was planning a soldiers' march? Her march would be different, however. *Her* soldiers would maintain discipline. There would be no arrests, no injuries. They would make the government pay attention, to recognise that if their needs were neglected they could indeed be a force to be reckoned with.

Reilly entered with the tea tray. After he left Marian was silent as she fixed the captain's tea, remembering from Brussels exactly how he liked it.

He took a sip and closed his eyes, as if savouring the taste. 'I have learned how to appreciate this luxury.'

Marian knew instantly what he meant. 'Yes. There is so much I no longer take for granted.' She handed him the plate of biscuits.

'Good food,' he said, taking a bite of a biscuit.

She touched her gown. 'Clean clothing.'

He seemed to be thinking for a minute. 'Absence of pain.'

That pierced her heart. 'No one brandishing axes.'

'Or shooting at us.'

'Dry shoes and stockings,' she added.

He lifted a finger. 'Speaking English.'

She smiled and patted her chair. 'Furniture.'

He smiled in return. 'A bed.'

Their gazes caught and held and he was slow to glance away. She remembered the night she had shared his bed, remembered the lovemaking they shared, remembered how she urged him to do more.

She stared into her teacup.

He spoke quietly. 'I only regret the suffering you endured.'

She glanced up at him. 'I do not regret even that.'

Marian regretted nothing between them, except the interference of her uncle and cousin. That she greatly regretted.

'It made me realise what is important,' she told him. 'It made me realise I can be strong.'

He looked at her. 'You were remarkably strong, Marian. To that I owe my life.'

She felt her cheeks burn. 'Say no more. You deserve equal credit.' She brushed a lock of hair off her forehead and latched on to a safer subject. 'We should give equal credit to Valour, you know. She saved us a time or two.'

He smiled. 'Indeed.'

'Where is Valour?' She would like to see the horse again,

stroke her muzzle and whisper her thanks. 'Do you have her in London?'

'I do.' He took another sip of tea. 'I may have to send her to my uncle's country house, though. It is expensive to keep her here and I have little time to ride her.'

Marian lowered her gaze, reminded of his limited finances. 'She will not like being parted from you.'

'But she will enjoy galloping through the fields and breathing the fresh country air.'

The door opened and Blanche walked in, followed by Mr Yost. 'We are back.' Blanche saw the Captain. 'Oh—forgive me. I did not know you had a caller.'

Allan stood. 'It is good to see you again, Mrs Nunn. I trust you are well.'

She curtsied. 'Very well, Mr Landon.' She turned to Mr Yost. 'Allow me to present our neighbour, Mr Yost. Mr Yost, this is Mr Landon, who was acquainted with Miss Pallant in Brussels.'

Marian's heart raced. She had not felt this level of anxiety since Waterloo. The captain was already suspicious of Mr Yost; he had said so that first day. He could make this meeting a very difficult one.

Instead he surprised her.

He strode forwards and extended his hand in a most gentlemanly manner.

Mr Yost shook it. 'You were in Brussels for the battle, then?'

'With the Royal Scots,' he explained.

'A momentous day in history,' responded Mr Yost.

Marian was still filled with anxiety. She needed to warn Yost. 'Captain Landon is now working for Lord Sidmouth at the Home Office.'

Mr Yost did not miss a beat. 'Are you, sir?'

'I am.' The captain smiled genially. 'I am no longer a captain, however, although Miss Pallant persists in calling me one.'

Marian doubted she could ever call him anything else.

She rose and walked towards the door. 'Do sit. I will ask Reilly for more tea.'

Once in the hallway, she leaned against the wall for a moment, trying to sort her disordered emotions.

She found Reilly nearby. 'You ought to have warned me Mr Yost was here, Reilly.'

He appeared chagrined. 'I could not, miss. Mrs Nunn asked where you were and I said the drawing room and she was already at the door with Mr Yost behind her.'

She pressed her fingers to her temple. 'Never mind. I suppose we need more tea. Can you bring some?'

When she walked back into the drawing room, the gentlemen started to rise, but she signalled them to remain seated.

As she returned to her chair, Mr Yost addressed the captain. 'Work for the Home Office, you say? I suspect you have heard my name spoken there.'

What was he doing?

'It has been mentioned,' the captain replied. 'I am afraid you have a reputation as a radical essayist.'

Yost was unapologetic. 'I dare say I have written what might be termed radical criticism of the government in my time. My views remain liberal, but the climate is too dangerous to publish them at the moment.' He leaned towards the captain. 'I am curious, sir, why you choose to work for the Home Office.'

The captain's eyes turned piercing. 'I know the carnage protesting mobs can do. I seek to stop it.'

Marian remembered. 'Your father,' she whispered, too low for anyone to hear. She was surprised she had not thought of it before. She raised her voice. 'The captain's father was killed by rioters.'

Yost lowered his head. 'My sympathies, Mr Landon. That is a great sadness to bear.' He raised his head again. 'Perhaps we can agree that violence helps no one's cause.'

The captain lifted his tea cup to his lips. 'On that we can agree.'

The tense moment passed and the two men continued discussing their differences, but in a quite civil manner.

Reilly, looking abashed, entered with the tea tray. 'Cook says dinner will be ready in an hour.' He hurried out.

Marian bit her lip, wishing she had not snapped at him.

The captain rose. 'I have overstayed my welcome, I fear.'

'Oh!' Blanche exclaimed. 'Right in the middle of your debate.'

He smiled at her. 'We are not likely to resolve anything no matter how long I stay.'

'But it is interesting,' Blanche went on. 'I should think you could talk even through dinner.' Her eyes brightened. 'Marian, might we ask Mr Landon to join us for dinner?'

Marian could not compose an answer. Had Blanche's wits gone begging?

Captain Landon glanced at her. 'I am not dressed for dinner.'

'Well, neither am I,' said Yost.

The captain's voice changed in tone. 'You are staying, sir?'

'Yes,' Blanche answered. 'You would make our numbers even and it would be like a party. Can we not include him, Marian?'

She was trapped. She turned to the captain. 'You are very welcome to stay to dinner, if you do not have another engagement.' Perhaps he would take the hint that she expected him to say no.

Instead he gazed into her eyes. 'I would be honoured to dine with you.' He smiled. 'I never take a good meal for granted.'

Marian felt herself flush. He was reminding her of their past hardships, hardships of which they'd so light-heartedly jested earlier.

'That is splendid, Mr Landon,' Blanche said.

Marian had never confided in Blanche about the exact nature of her acquaintance with the captain in Belgium, but surely Blanche knew not to keep the fox in with the chickens for longer than necessary.

More tea was poured and the conversation resumed, but about foods and favourite dinners, not politics.

Dinner was a lively affair and one Marian enjoyed more than she could have anticipated. Mr Yost and the captain listened attentively to each other and disagreed respectfully, much to Marian's relief and admiration. Both she and Blanche entered in the conversation, but Marian was careful to follow Yost's lead so she would not rouse Landon's suspicions. In many ways the captain's views were sympathetic to the people's suffering; he merely advocated different means to alleviate it.

'Change best happens within the boundaries of the law,' he said. 'If left to a mob, we risk the anarchy of the French Revolution.'

'But our government has been part of the problem,' Mr Yost countered. 'The Corn Laws, for example.'

The Corn Laws set high prices for grain and restricted its import. The laws protected the profits of large landowners, but also made bread, the staple food of the lower classes, very costly.

'Government makes bad decisions sometimes,' the captain responded. 'I am not saying the Corn Laws were bad. It is more complex than that. If the government makes too many mistakes, then one must elect a new government. That is working for change within the law.'

'You forget that only landowners can vote.' Yost stabbed the air with his fork. 'Who speaks then for those suffering souls who do not own land?'

'For that matter,' added Blanche, 'who speaks for women? We cannot vote no matter what.'

Captain Landon smiled at her. 'Do you advocate suffrage for women, Mrs Nunn? That is radical, indeed.'

She coloured. 'I meant only to make a point.'

Marian kept quiet. She strongly believed women should have the power to decide their own fate. Perhaps the captain would be shocked that she felt that way.

The captain speared a piece of meat with his fork. 'I believe that if good men are elected, they will do the right thing by everyone.'

The problem lay in recognising good. Marian gazed at the captain through lowered lashes. He was a man she'd once trusted with her life, yet now his job was to arrest organisers like herself and have them hanged for sedition. Would he see her hanged if he knew what she was about?

The discussion continued through the dessert and after-dinner tea, but Marian was more absorbed in observing the captain, yearning to be close to him again and at the same time wary lest she gave him cause to send her to the gallows.

The clock struck ten and the captain stopped mid-sentence. 'I had no idea of the time. Forgive me for staying so late.' He stood.

'I should go, too,' Yost said, but he made no effort to move.

'I'll walk you to the door, Captain.' Marian rose.

Their shoulders brushed as they walked to the hall. Marian could almost fantasise that they were companionable again.

The captain picked up his hat and gloves from the hall table. 'You did not need to walk me out, Marian.'

'Mr Yost and Blanche would have no time alone if I did not.'

His brows rose. 'He is courting her?'

She smiled. 'Oh, yes. It is quite a romance.'

He pulled on his gloves. 'I meant only to stay a civil fifteen minutes.' He glanced at her. 'But I much enjoyed dining with you.'

It had seemed right to her to see him seated across from her at the evening meal.

'I hope you did not think our neighbour too radical in his beliefs.' She meant she hoped he would not suspect Yost of more.

His expression turned serious. 'He was an interesting man. I liked him.'

She watched him adjust the fingers of the gloves and remembered when his bare hands had stroked her.

'I like him, too,' she replied. 'Which is a good thing, because of Blanche.'

He smiled.

She opened the door to a cool breeze that ruffled her skirt and cooled her face. He placed his hand on her arm and drew her closer. Her head tilted back and she closed her eyes.

Like before he placed a light kiss on her forehead and moved away slowly to step out of the doorway.

'Goodnight,' she managed, trembling with the need to be in his arms one more time.

He tipped his hat to her before placing it on his head and starting to walk away.

She hurried back to the drawing room and watched him through the window as he made his way down the street.

'To what do you owe that visit, Miss Pallant?' Yost asked, his voice grim.

'I do not know.' She was no longer able to see him.

Blanche leaned against the back of her chair. 'Well, I believe he has a *tendre* for you.'

Marian wrapped her arms around herself. 'I cannot think so.'

'He could be spying for the Home Office,' Yost said.

'I do not believe that!' Blanche cried.

Marian gave Yost a worried look. 'Do you think he suspects me?'

'I do not see how,' he replied. 'We keep your name out of everything. Likely he suspects me of something.'

'He is much too nice to be a spy,' Blanche insisted.

Yost laughed. 'Those are the kind one must worry about, my dear.'

Marian felt sombre. 'What shall we do?'

Yost lowered his brows in thought. 'It is best to act as if you have nothing at all to hide. That was my strategy tonight, and I think it worked well.' He tapped his chin. 'I suggest you accept his calls. In fact, accept some of the invitations your friend sends your way. No one will think a society lady is the organiser of a protest.'

She touched the cool window pane. In two weeks her soldiers would march and the entire event would be over. She did not know what would happen after that, how she would fill her time.

She did not know if Captain Landon would be a part of it.

The next day Lord Sidmouth summoned Allan as soon as he walked in to the Home Office.

'Well?' Sidmouth looked up from his desk as Allan entered. 'Did you call upon her?'

Allan scowled. 'I did.'

'And?' Sidmouth persisted.

Allan shrugged. 'I spent a pleasant evening. I even met John Yost. He was a guest of Miss Pallant's companion. Our conversation was lively and interesting.'

'Interesting, eh?' Sidmouth brightened. 'What did you learn?'

Allan gave him a direct look. 'Nothing we did not already know. Yost freely discussed his views, but said nothing to make me suspect him of sedition. He was a thoughtful, intelligent, reasoned man.'

Sidmouth made a derisive sound. 'Delighted you like the fellow. Go back. Keep digging. Keep your eyes and ears open.' He waved him off.

Allan started for the door, then turned. 'Sir, I cannot help but feel my continuing to call upon Miss Pallant is toying with her sensibilities—'

'I care nothing about her sensibilities!' Sidmouth replied. 'Your job is to gather information and this is the way it is done. Yost is the key, I tell you. I feel it.'

Allan left the room.

He waited two days before calling upon Marian again. A grey-haired maid answered the door this time, obviously one of Marian's war widows. She showed him into the drawing room and went to fetch her mistress from some other part of the house.

He heard the mumbling of voices. A door closed nearby and footsteps sounded in the hallway. A moment later she walked into the room.

'Captain,' she said with an edge to her voice. 'Good afternoon.'

He bowed to her. 'I hope I did not take you from something important. I had an impulse to call.' Less like an impulse and more like a command.

Still, a part of him gladdened to see her, to hear her voice again, to smell the scent of roses.

'I was finished,' she said, not explaining. 'Do sit. I've ordered tea again.'

They sat in the same chairs as the previous visit.

'This time I promise not to stay so long,' he said.

She averted her face.

He had difficulty dreaming up conversation. 'Where is Reilly today?'

'He and Toby—the footman—are doing errands for me.'

She did not seem inclined to elaborate so he had to come up with something else. 'And the lovebirds? Where are they?'

'Blanche and Mr Yost?' She glanced towards the door. 'Blanche went to the shops.' She paused briefly. 'I would not be surprised if Mr Yost also finds a sudden need to shop.'

'This sounds like a serious romance.' And also an opening for him to do Sidmouth's bidding.

She smiled. 'Yes. Is it not lovely?'

'As long as Yost's political beliefs do not cause him trouble.' He felt like a cad, but tried to cover it by matching her light tone.

Her smile fled and her expression turned serious. 'Will *you* cause Mr Yost trouble for his beliefs, Captain?'

'A man is still free to believe as he wishes.' He hated trying to pump her for information. 'But what he does must be within the law.'

'Within the law,' she repeated solemnly. 'I do not forget you work for Lord Sidmouth.'

Neither do I, he thought. 'I am sorry, Marian. I like Yost even if we disagree on some matters—'

He was about to ask her what she knew of Yost's activities when the knocker on the front door sounded and loud voices came from the hallway. Allan started for the door when it burst open revealing the maid.

'This man came in!' the woman cried. 'I opened the door and he came in and would not leave.'

Allan ran out of the room with Marian behind him.

A man was seated on the stairs, his head leaning against the banister. Allan rushed over and turned him around to see his face.

'Edwin!' Marian cried.

Chapter Fourteen

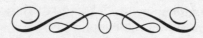

Marian stared down at her cousin. His clothes were rumpled and he smelled of spirits and vomit.

He opened his eyes, but they seemed unable to focus. 'Greetings, Marian!' he slurred.

She glared at him. 'You are drunk.'

He made a soundless laugh. 'Drunk as a wheelbarrow.'

'Get up.' The captain pulled Edwin off the stairs.

'Whoa!' Edwin pushed him away and grabbed for the banister. 'Can do it m'self.' Comprehension dawned on his face and he pointed at the captain. 'You! You are not 'sposed to be here.'

The captain seized Edwin's coat lapels and leaned close. 'Thought you were rid of me, did you?'

'Yes!' Edwin's reply was high-pitched.

The captain dragged him to the door.

'Leggo!' Edwin shoved the Captain away and staggered towards Marian. 'Marian, wanted to see you.'

'Not like this, Edwin!' She was furious at him. For coming to her house drunk. For lying to her about the captain, but she could not discuss it will him in such a state. 'You have to leave.'

The captain grabbed for his arm again, but Edwin twisted away.

'Can't make me go!' Edwin pointed to the captain again. 'Make him leave.'

'He is not drunk,' she retorted. 'You are. I want you out.'

His scarred face contorted. 'No! Want him out. I stay.'

He lunged at her and she cried out in alarm.

The captain seized him from behind and pulled him away from her. Edwin landed on the floor. His face contorted in anger and he rose up again, a frenzy of fists, wailing like a child. He groped for the captain's throat, but the captain shoved him away. Edwin staggered back, hitting the wall and falling against a table that shattered beneath him.

He lay still.

'Oh, my God!' Marian stared at him. 'Is he dead?'

The captain leaned down and felt for a pulse. 'Passed out.'

Marian sank down on the stairs. 'What am I going to do with him?'

The captain still laboured to catch his breath. 'I can put him in a hackney coach and send him home.'

'I have no idea where he is staying.' She had not even known Edwin was in London.

'Would he not be staying at your uncle's town house?'

'I cannot think he would be. He and my uncle had a big row.' Last she heard from the former Mrs Vernon, now Lady Tranville, was that Edwin was not welcome in any of his father's houses.

The captain straightened his coat. 'I could carry him into the park and leave him on a bench.'

'Surely not.'

He gave her a direct look. 'I'm quite serious.'

She was so angry at Edwin she could almost agree with this plan.

She stood. 'I am tempted to say yes, but something might happen and I would never forgive myself. I suppose he must stay here until he sobers up.'

The captain gave her a steady look. 'Marian, that is not wise.'

She waved a hand in exasperation. 'What choice do I have?'

'He cannot stay here.' His tone was insistent.

'No one could possibly object,' she went on. 'Edwin is a relation of mine. Besides, who would know? My servants will not talk of it.'

The captain rubbed his brow. 'That is not the point.' He crossed the hall and placed his hands on her shoulders, forcing her to look into his eyes. 'You cannot have him here because he is dangerous.'

'He's unconscious!'

His grip tightened. 'He might rouse at any moment. You saw him! And he could get much worse. The alcohol makes him out of his mind.'

She looked down at Edwin. 'I have seen him deep in his cups. He becomes silly or maudlin.'

The captain stared at her for a long time before speaking in a low voice. 'I have seen him become violent.' His fingers pressed into her shoulders. 'You must believe me.'

She remembered the captain had warned her of Edwin before. 'I believe you, Captain. But I have no choice. I cannot leave him in the park to attack someone else.'

He released a frustrated breath and let go of her. 'Post Reilly outside his door, then.'

She looked up at him with chagrin. 'Reilly is out of town and will not return until tomorrow.' Reilly was delivering messages about the march to their contacts outside the city. 'Toby, my footman, will be here, but he is a small man and he has only one leg.'

'That won't do.' Allan stared down at the floor before directing his gaze back at her. 'I will stay.'

'No—' she started to protest, but he placed his fingers on her lips.

'If Edwin's presence would remain unknown, then mine will, as well.' His gaze pierced into her. 'I will stay.'

His closeness made Marian light-headed, as giddy as if she'd been spun around. She inhaled deeply. 'Very well, Captain.'

He smiled at her.

Her eyes narrowed. 'Why are you smiling?' Had he noticed his effect on her?

'You persist in calling me Captain.'

'It is how I know you,' she murmured. It was how she preferred to think of him, not as a man doing Sidmouth's work. She cleared her throat. 'There is a spare bedroom above stairs, but how do we get him there?'

'I'll carry him.' He crouched down and hoisted Edwin over his shoulder as if he'd done such a thing before.

The maid peered around the corner. 'Has he gone?'

'No, but it is safe to come out, Hannah,' Marian told her.

The maid crept into the hall and saw the captain carrying Edwin up the stairs. 'Oh, my goodness!' she exclaimed.

'He is quite harmless now,' Marian assured her. 'He is my cousin and I'm afraid he must stay here to sleep off the drink. Run ahead, please, and put fresh linens on the bed in the spare bedroom.'

Hannah rushed past the captain, who'd reached the first flight of stairs. She'd managed to strip the old covers from the bed and tucked in a fresh sheet by the time Marian led the captain into the room to unceremoniously drop Edwin on to the bed.

'He smells foul.' Marian covered her nose with her hand. 'Can we take off his clothing?'

'I'll do it,' Captain Landon said.

Hannah put a hand on his arm. 'I'll help you, sir. After raising two boys of my own, I won't see anything I have not seen before.' Hannah had lost one of those sons to the war, in addition to losing her husband. The other son still marched to the drum.

'Thank you, Hannah,' the captain said.

'I'll find some nightclothes.' Marian would not intrude upon Reilly's or Toby's rooms without their permission, so she ran next door to Yost's house, even though she knew Yost was out.

She and Yost had been meeting to discuss the march when the captain called. At Mr Hunt's suggestion, Marian and Yost had organised the marchers into small groups. Yost, Hunt and Marian's household were the only ones who knew of her involvement. A few more men knew of Yost's, but they'd organised the groups in such a manner that, if betrayed, no man would have more than one or two names to provide. After leaving Marian, Yost intended to rendezvous with one of his contacts, who would spread the final information about the time, place and scope of the march.

After all that, Marian expected Yost to seek out Blanche.

Yost's valet was at home, however, and he agreed to lend Marian fresh nightclothes for Edwin.

In clean clothing and put to bed, Edwin curled up and slept like a baby. Until Toby returned, Marian felt obligated to sit with the captain in Edwin's room, where they talked quietly through the afternoon.

The Captain asked her about her life in India before her parents died. She told him about happy memories, such as when her *amah* took her into the market place with its colourful fruits and fragrant spices. Or to visit her *amah*'s relatives in tiny homes with much laughter and exotic cooking. Or to the silk shop, a fairy land of colourful, fluttering cloth.

'How did your parents become ill?' he asked her.

She again saw the woman kissing her father in the carriage, but that part was too painful to relate.

'My father came home with a fever, and soon nearly

everyone in the house died of it.' Her mother. Her father. Her *amah*.

She changed the subject. 'Tell me about your family.'

He told her about growing up in Nottinghamshire on his father's estate, of exploring the countryside as a boy or spending time in the nearby town with his childhood companions, getting into one scrape after another.

He laughed. 'My father would put his hands on his hips and ask me if I had windmills in my head. "Can you not just do what is right?" he would say. Those were wise words, but hard for a boy to heed.'

'I am sympathetic to you as a boy. How does one know what is right, especially if there are two sides to something?' His strong convictions about right and wrong made no sense to her. 'Is it not often a matter of one's point of view? For example, you are so certain the Spa Fields demonstrators and the Blanketeers were wrong, but surely if I'd asked them, they would have said you were wrong.'

His eyes narrowed. 'You are sounding like Mr Yost.'

She'd gone too far. He was the last person with whom she should debate politics.

'Oh, my!' she cried. 'I am repeating his views, am I not?' She tried to act as if the notion surprised her. 'But he is as convinced he is right as you are.'

'A man's opinions are never wrong, but what he *does* can be right or wrong. Those men at Spa Fields were right that there were many hardships that ought to be changed, they were wrong to break the law.' He paused and his expression turned even more serious. 'Do you think Yost puts his opinions in action?'

Her nerves flared. 'What do you mean?'

'Would he organise men to demonstrate or to march on London?'

'Surely he would not.' She took a breath. 'Would you see him arrested if he did?'

He frowned. 'I would be compelled to do so.'

Edwin stirred and mumbled something, instantly capturing their attention. He turned over and became quiet again.

Marian made certain they talked of other things thereafter and when Toby returned they locked Edwin's door and posted Toby in a chair outside the room with instructions to alert the captain if Edwin stirred. By dinnertime, Blanche and Yost had arrived from the shops and the four of them again shared a pleasant meal and evening together.

When the hour drew late Mr Yost took his leave. The Captain insisted Toby should go to bed and took up position in the chair outside Edwin's door. Marian brought him a footstool so he could prop his feet up.

The spare room was right across the hall from Marian's bed chamber, so the captain sat right outside her door. How was she to sleep knowing he was so near?

Their time together had been so companionable, almost like Brussels when they'd cared for the soldiers. She could almost pretend they could bridge the huge gap that had grown between them.

Until they began discussing Mr Yost and protests and arrests.

By the time the clock struck one, Edwin's snores rattled the windowpanes. Marian sat up in her bed.

It was not the cacophony coming from Edwin's throat that kept her awake, but the captain. Sleep was impossible when he was so near.

Exasperated with herself, she dangled her legs off the side of the bed. With sudden decision, she slipped off and padded to the fireplace. From one of the glowing coals she lit a taper and carried it to the door, opening it a crack to see if the captain was sleeping.

He immediately stood. 'Marian?'

She opened the door wider. 'I woke you. I am sorry.'

He rubbed his face. 'I was not asleep.'

A loud atonic sound, like blocks of wood scraping across a bare floor, came from behind the locked door.

'It is a wonder any of us can sleep,' Marian said. 'I never heard such snoring.'

'Even Blanche was awake.' He stifled a yawn.

She also covered her mouth with her hand. 'Blanche? Did you speak with her?'

'No. She may have thought me asleep. She hurried down the servants' stairs.'

'The servants' stairs?' That was odd. A drop of hot wax dripped on to Marian's finger. 'Oh!'

'You've burnt yourself.' The captain took the taper from her hand and used it to light a candle in a nearby sconce.

She placed her burnt finger to her mouth.

He pulled it away. 'Let me see.'

'It is nothing,' she said, suddenly finding it hard to breathe as he examined her finger.

Still holding her hand, he led her to the chair. 'Sit with me.'

She lowered herself on to the footstool.

He yawned again.

She glanced towards her bedchamber door. 'Would you like to lie down in my bed?'

His eyes grew wide. 'Share a bed again?'

A thrill shot through her, a thrill she dared not nourish. 'I meant that I would sit here and wake you if Edwin causes trouble.'

His lips turned up at one corner. 'I was hoping you meant we would share a bed like we did at the inn.'

'Hoping?' Her voice rose, remembering her moral lapse. 'I thought you disliked me for it.'

His brows rose. 'Disliked?'

She moved the stool away. 'Let us not discuss this.'

He leaned forwards and reached for her hand. 'I did not dislike what passed between us.'

She tucked her hands beneath her arms. 'You were appalled by it.'

'I was not.' He reached out again, holding her chin so she could not look away. 'I was appalled by my own weakness, Marian. I wanted nothing more than to—' He broke off.

'But that was because I made you.' She moved away again. 'I seduced you.'

She disliked remembering how wantonly she'd behaved, how much she'd wanted the captain to show her what could exist between a man and woman.

She wanted it even now.

'I had better go back to bed.' She fled into her room.

He followed her, catching her and spinning her around to face him. 'Marian? Do not be distressed.'

His arms encircled her and she buried her face in his coat, realising she had been desperate for his embrace. 'I am ashamed of how I behaved. Like a strumpet.'

She felt him laugh. 'A strumpet?' He continued to hold her and spoke in that low voice that might be her undoing if he did not stop. 'You'd guarded your emotions so long when we were in danger. The danger was past, and you...you needed comfort.'

His heart beat beneath her ear, soothing her. 'That does not explain my feelings now. I am in no danger now.'

He released her and lifted her chin. 'And you feel such urges now?'

She nodded.

'As do I.' His eyes darkened as he continued to stare down at her.

'Do not look at me,' she protested. 'I do not know what you are thinking.'

A slow smile creased his face. 'I am thinking of kissing you.'

His words set her body aflame. It was all she could do to wait while he slowly dipped his head until his lips touched hers. His kiss was gentle at first, then, like a fire that finally ignited, it flamed and devoured and demanded. Feeling as if her own passion might consume her, Marian kissed him back.

'Marian,' he murmured.

'Captain,' she whispered in response.

He swept her into his arms and carried her to her bed. Together they tumbled upon it. He kissed her again, playfully this time.

The wonder of it! She'd no idea there could be so many kinds of kisses. Playful, hungry, demanding. She tried another version, a kiss to tell him she did not want him to pull away this time. With that kiss the room blurred and sounds seemed to echo as if in a dream.

Boldly she pulled off her nightdress and knelt on the bed, letting his eyes savour her. She could hardly breathe.

His boots were already off and, with her eager help, he made quick work of the rest of his clothing. Feeling his bare skin against hers was both familiar and new. One moment she felt like the most experienced courtesan, knowing what she wanted, what she needed, and the next she marvelled at the experience, like the virgin she was.

He covered her with his body, dipping down to kiss her as she parted her legs and prayed he would not delay in fulfilling her desire for him. When the male part of him touched her most sensitive place she thought she might cry out. She wanted more, much more.

But he stopped.

She wanted to weep. Not again!

He looked her directly in the eye. 'Are you certain of this?'

'Yes. Yes,' she cried.

'Do you know what to do to prevent a baby?' he asked.

A baby could be prevented? She'd had no idea.

'Of course I know,' she lied.

Not even the risk of a baby would make her stop now.

She thought how glorious it would be if a baby grew inside

her from this. His baby. This might be her only chance. Tomorrow she could ask Blanche what women did to prevent babies.

She stared into his eyes. 'I am very certain of this.'

He stroked her skin until she felt like bursting with the pleasure of it. His hand closed on her breast and sensation shot straight to between her legs where the aching grew more intense. She gasped in delight.

He slid down her body and his tongue tasted her nipple, causing sensations she never could have imagined. She buried her hands in his hair and hoped he would not stop. Writhing beneath him, she heard sounds of pleasure escape her lips.

His hand flattened against her abdomen, and she remembered the magic his fingers created when he'd touched her most intimately. Part of her yearned for him to repeat that bliss, now—but even more she wanted to give him pleasure. Would a man find touching as thrilling as she did?

She decided to find out. 'Lie on your back,' she whispered.

He glanced at her in surprise, but complied.

'Your turn,' she murmured.

Her hand shook before she touched his skin and dared to explore him as he'd done to her. His skin was rough with the dark hair that peppered his chest and his arms and legs. She remembered how firm his muscles had felt beneath his skin and again savoured the strength they represented.

The light was dim in her bedchamber, coming only from the glow of coals in her fireplace and the flame of the sconce in the hall, but she could see what a beautiful man he was. She wanted to rejoice aloud that she was again feasting upon the sight of him, revelling in the feel of him, and that she was soon to be joined with him.

She felt giddy with excitement at what was to transpire between them. No longer afraid to be wanton, she relished each sensation. She was unafraid of offending him or seducing him. Let him prose on about duty this time; she would not listen to it.

She cared only that he said he wanted to make love with her. He said he'd hoped for it. He desired her, he said. She'd take him at his word, because she wanted this and wanted nothing to stop her from getting the pleasure he could bring.

She slipped her hand down the length of his chest to where his male member had grown large and hard for her. She clasped him in her palm and explored that most mysterious part of him.

He groaned. 'That is torture.'

'Oh!' She released him. 'I did not know it would hurt you.'

He took her hand and pressed her fingers around him again. 'I did not say to stop.'

So she did not stop until he took her hand away and turned her on her back. 'I cannot wait.'

'Then do not,' she murmured. Indeed, she was eager for what came next.

She parted her legs and his fingers slipped inside her and she began to understand what he'd meant about torture.

She, too, did not wish this torture to stop.

Suddenly he withdrew his fingers and was on top of her, ready to enter her. Her heart raced in panic or excitement, she didn't know which, as he pushed into her, little by little, gentle strokes that she somehow knew she didn't need or desire.

She lifted her hips and suddenly he pushed inside her, filling her completely.

Yes, she felt like saying. *At last,* but words were impossible in the moment.

He moved against her, and she marvelled at the new feeling, something else that had been beyond her imagination. She wanted it never to stop, this exquisite agony, this tormenting bliss.

Somehow she knew to move with him, and a rhythm formed between them, like a dance for which she'd never needed lessons. Their dance grew faster and faster and more and more frenzied, and her need grew as well, until it suddenly seemed unbearable.

She wanted to weep and wail that this almost-pain, almost-pleasure was too difficult to bear. She wanted it to stop, but was incapable of stopping.

Then, all of a sudden, there was an explosion of sensation, inconceivable waves of pleasure, leaving her gasping and writhing beneath him. He pushed into her even harder and she felt him shudder inside her, spilling his seed.

When his body relaxed he slid to her side, but still held her close. 'Marian,' he moaned.

She sat up on an elbow so she could look at him. 'Was that how it was supposed to be?'

'That was how it was supposed to be.' He was still breathing hard. 'But much, much better.'

She lay back with a satisfied sigh.

From the other room, Edwin's snores again reached their ears. They both burst into laughter.

'I dread him waking,' she murmured.

'I should resume my post before he does,' he said.

'No. Stay with me.' She snuggled against him, and he held her close.

Marian felt a lassitude that was again new and unexpected. Her eyes grew heavy and she felt at peace, but she fought sleep. She did not want to miss a moment of being next to him.

'Marian?' His voice rumbled in his chest.

'Mmm?' she responded.

'We must marry.'

She opened her eyes and looked at him. 'Not again.'

'I can explain my reasoning.'

She sat up and gathered the linens around her. 'I know your reasoning. You will say you have a duty to marry me because you made love to me, even though I freely chose to do so.' Could he not merely savour the experience? Must he spoil it?

The captain sat behind her, tucking her close against him and enfolding her in his arms. 'It is the right thing for us to do.'

'No, Captain.' Her voice cracked with emotion.

'Why not?' He nuzzled the sensitive skin of her neck.

She moved away and climbed out of bed. 'Too many reasons.' She groped for her nightdress and slipped it over her head.

'Name one of them.'

She walked to the window. The main reason was one she could not tell him. She was planning an act of sedition and it was his job to hang her for it.

She searched for another explanation. 'I have no wish to be the sort of conventional, society wife you will need if you wish to be an M.P.'

He was silent for a long moment and she knew he was forced to agree with her. 'Perhaps that will not matter so much,' he finally said.

She leaned her head against the cool glass of the window. This time there was no Edwin or Uncle Tranville to shatter their plans. This time it was Marian putting the sledgehammer to the glass.

'It is hopeless, Captain,' she whispered.

Allan embraced her from behind, treasuring the feel of her skin against his, even as he forced himself to listen to what she said. True, her unconventional, impulsive nature was not an asset in gaining a seat in Commons, but she was not a social pariah either. Voters would accept her. Perhaps they would even love her as he did.

She could not deny that they belonged together. Fate had brought them together because they completed each other, filled each other's empty spaces. Whatever else threatened to separate them, they would simply have to conquer, because, even if a battle raged around them, even if flaming roofs caved in on them or farmers threatened them with axes, they were better together.

This time he refused to give up. 'Allow me to court you, Marian. Let us see what happens.'

Before she could answer him, footsteps sounded on the street below. He leaned forwards to see out the window.

Two men approached Yost's door.

'What is this?' Why would men come to Yost's door in the middle of the night?

'I do not know,' she replied breathlessly, although he'd not meant to direct the question to her.

Allan's muscles tensed as he waited to see if the men would be admitted. He could only see the tops of their heads from this high vantage point, but he heard the door open and they seemed to converse with someone. They were admitted and, at the same time, a woman left the house.

'It is Blanche!' Marian whispered.

Allan moved away from the window and searched for his clothes. 'I am more concerned about the men entering his house than Blanche leaving it. Do you know of any reason he should have callers in the middle of the night?'

'Of course I do not know.' Her voice was clipped. 'He is merely a neighbour and dinner guest.'

Allan managed to don his trousers and shirt as he heard Blanche's footsteps on the servants' stairs. He stepped out into the hall to grab his boots.

Blanche appeared and froze when she saw him. 'I—I could not sleep. I was below stairs for a while.'

'You were at Yost's,' Allan said.

'Yes, I visited Mr Yost.' She averted her head.

Marian stood in the bedroom doorway.

'Am I discharged?' Blanche asked her.

Marian went to her. 'Oh, Blanche, of course you are not discharged! What should I do without you? If you and Mr Yost are lovers, I am certain that is a fine thing.'

'What do you know of his activities, Mrs Nunn?' Allan asked. 'Who were those men?'

She glanced at Marian before answering. 'I do not know what you mean. I do not know those men or why they knocked on his door.'

The sconce's candle illuminated her anxious expression.

He gave her an intent look. 'If Yost is involved in something nefarious, I would not like for you to be caught up in it.' This was true enough, just not his main motivation.

Blanche looked from him to Marian and back. 'Did you see the men from up here?'

Her implication was clear. She knew he had been in Marian's bedchamber, and, to judge by his present appearance, not entirely clothed at that.

The silence after her question was suddenly broken by the rattling of Edwin's doorknob.

'Hey, there,' Edwin called from within. 'Unlock this door.'

Chapter Fifteen

'Do not open the door,' Allan whispered. 'Talk to him first. See if the drink is worn off.'

The doorknob rattled again, more violently this time. 'Where am I?' Edwin cried. 'I heard voices. Open the door! Somebody open the door.'

Marian leaned against it. 'It is Marian. And I am not opening the door unless I know you are in your right senses.'

'Marian?' He sounded surprised. 'I'm sick, Marian. My head hurts like the devil.' He rattled the knob. 'Why is the door locked?'

She looked at Allan.

He shrugged. 'He slept a long time, and sounds safe enough.' He edged towards her room. 'Best he not see me.' Especially half undressed. 'I'll duck in here. I'm close enough to come to your aid, if need be.'

'One moment, Edwin,' she said through the door.

Allan stepped inside Marian's room and kept out of sight while he searched for his coat and waistcoat.

He heard Marian turn the key in the lock.

Edwin's voice became louder. 'Why did you lock me in there, Marian?'

'Because you came to my house out of your mind with drink, that's why,' Marian replied sharply. 'That was very bad of you, Edwin.'

'Stop yelling,' he whined. 'My head hurts. I need something to make it feel better. Do you have any brandy?'

'I am most certainly not giving you brandy!'

Blanche spoke up. 'Perhaps a little ale would do? A little watered-down ale used to help my husband the day after drinking. Shall I fetch some?'

Not too much, Allan thought. He found his neckcloth and just draped it around his neck. He donned his waistcoat and coat without bothering to button them.

'Very well,' Marian answered Blanche. Marian addressed Edwin again. 'Go into the room and sit. I'll be in as soon as I've put on a robe.'

'Do not lock me in again,' he demanded.

Allan stuffed his stockings inside his boots.

'I won't.' Marian told him. 'See? I'll leave the door open a crack. Go inside and light some candles from the fire.'

A moment later she slipped into her bedchamber.

Allan caught her arm. 'He seems controlled enough,' he whispered. 'I'm going to sneak out before he discovers I am here.' He wrapped his arms around her. 'I intend to court you, Marian. And marry you.'

'Captain—' she began in a warning tone.

'No argument.' He gave her a swift kiss.

Allan peered out of the door to make certain Edwin was not in the hallway, and gave Marian one more glance before slipping out of the room. Carrying his boots, he quickly made it to the servants' stairs he'd seen Blanche use earlier.

When he entered the hall, he encountered Blanche carrying the ale and a candle. He liked the woman and certainly did not wish to see her be hurt if her lover was a saboteur.

He nodded to her.

'Wait a moment, Mr Landon.' She placed the ale on the stairs. 'I will lock the door behind you.'

He lifted his boots to show her he needed time to put them on. He sat upon the stairs to do it.

She watched him silently.

He crossed the hall as quietly as he could and she opened the door for him.

'Take care, Mrs Nunn,' he said.

He started to leave, but she put a hand on his sleeve. 'Mr Landon, I will tell no one about you being in Marian's room.'

'Thank you.' He could at least promise not to tell Sidmouth she was Yost's lover.

When she closed the door behind him, he took a few steps and stopped in front of Yost's house. There was no sign from the front of a candle burning, no sign anyone was there. He decided to check the back. If he could get close enough, maybe he could see the faces of the men through a window.

He found the backs of the row of houses. Yost's house was the third from the end, Marian's, the second. All had walled gardens.

'In for a penny, in for a pound,' he said to himself, climbing the first wall.

Allan made it to the top. The easiest way to reach Yost's garden was to walk along the top of the walls. If anyone happened to be looking out their window at this hour, they'd easily see him.

He decided to try none the less.

Holding his arms out like a rope walker, he followed the narrow wall to the third garden and flattened himself on the top so he would be less visible. One window showed the glow of light.

He jumped down from the wall and a cat screeched. His heart nearly seized. Shrinking back into the shadows, he watched the lighted window to see if the curtains moved.

They were still. Releasing a tense breath, he picked his way to the back of the house.

The window was too high and there was nothing he could climb on to peer in. He hated to turn back now. He sidled to the back door and tested the knob.

It was unlocked.

Before he thought too much about it, he slipped inside the house and found his way to the first floor. Finding the room where Yost and the two men were talking was not difficult. Its door was slightly ajar and the voices carried into the hallway.

Allan recognised Yost's voice. 'So, you will meet the other organisers at the appointed place in two nights. The date is set.'

He heard chairs scrape against the floor. They were leaving! Allan ducked into a room across from this one. Its darkness concealed him. Yost carried a candle into the hallway, and Allan caught a glimpse of the two men's faces. They walked on to the stairway.

Allan waited as they descended. He could make out from the barest outline of a table and chairs that he stood in the dining room. Where Yost would take his meals. And serve invited guests.

Of which he was not one.

Allan had invaded another man's house, just as Luddites had once invaded his father's house. He felt sick.

Hearing Yost bid his guests farewell in the hall, Allan roused himself to make a dash for the back stairway, hurrying all the way to the ground floor and out the back door. He crept along the wall until finding a place to climb it. Then running, as if he were on the ground and not a surface the width of a brick, he retraced his steps. At the last house, he jumped down and brushed off his clothing.

At that moment, the two men turned the corner and Allan shrank into the shadows. They crossed Quebec Street and headed towards Oxford Street. Still feeling as if he ought to be hauled before a magistrate, Allan followed them.

They walked to a tavern in the North Bruton mews near Berkeley Square. Allan waited several minutes before following them inside. With luck he found a table nearby with a wooden barrier between so they could not see him. He ordered ale from the bar and carried it to his seat.

Much of the conversation between the two men was in tones so hushed Allan could not hear them. As they continued to drink, their voices became louder.

'The day is near,' one said. 'Let us drink to our success.'

'To our successful march!'

As he suspected: a march was planned.

They began to speculate as to who was the organising force behind the march, the real leader of it.

'It is not Yost, that is certain,' said one. 'He always speaks of someone else.'

His companion responded. 'Well, the leader is not Hunt. Hunt is staying out of it.'

'Has to be Yost,' the first man said firmly. 'Even though he denies it, he is it. Who else could it be?'

Indeed. Who else? Allan cupped his tankard of ale and stared into its contents. He didn't want to report Yost. He liked the man.

And he was Marian's friend, her companion's lover. How was he to turn in Yost? Would Marian ever understand? This would just be one more impediment to their being happy together. A huge one, if she saw her friend arrested for sedition.

Marian sat across from Edwin at the breakfast table. Hannah had laundered and brushed off his clothing, and Marian had badgered him to wash himself, so he looked— and smelled—a great deal better than the day before.

Still, he was ashen and his hand shook.

'Eat something, Edwin,' she demanded.

'Does it not look as if I am trying?' He lifted a piece of toast for her to see. 'Stop being so cross. It is very disagreeable.'

'I have reason to be cross.' She glared at him.

He rolled his eyes. 'Just because I had too much to drink—'

'Too much to drink!' she cried. 'You came to my house corned, pickled and salted. And you were rowdy, as well.'

He tossed off her words. 'Do not speak cant, Marian. It is most unbecoming. Besides, you cannot fault my coming here, because I did not even know I was doing it.'

'That makes it worse!' she retorted. 'You drink entirely too much, Edwin.'

He folded his arms over his chest. 'I do not need you to harangue me over it. I can handle myself very well without your scolding.'

Marian clamped her mouth shut. Edwin finished the piece of toast and held up another so she could see he was eating. A little colour returned to his face.

She chewed her lip, uncertain whether she should bring up the only topic she wanted to discuss with him. She took a breath. 'I have seen Captain Landon here in London, Edwin.'

He looked surprised, then resumed his cynical expression. 'Landon? Too bad.' He lifted his cup to his mouth.

'He told me there was no Frenchwoman in Paris.'

Edwin's hand stilled, the cup at his lips. 'Frenchwoman?' He placed the cup in its saucer and suddenly looked as if understanding dawned. 'Ah, the Frenchwoman. I had forgotten. Do you mean the woman in Paris was not French?'

'There was no woman, he said.'

Edwin laughed. 'As if he would admit such a thing. Do not tell me he is dangling after you again, although I suppose he still needs a wealthy wife.'

She averted her gaze. She had never once considered that the captain might be interested in her fortune.

No. She could not believe he was talking of the captain. The man who'd made love to her was not a fortune hunter.

She faced Edwin again. 'I am furious with you for making up that story. Did you do it to keep me from marrying the captain? Did you think that it would make me marry you?'

He gave her a withering glance. 'Do not insult me, Marian. After the set-down you gave me, I am not likely to propose to you again.'

She twisted the edge of the tablecloth with her fingers. Edwin was not behaving like a man telling a lie. What was she to think?

Edwin stood up again. 'You were correct. I do feel better for having eaten. I believe I shall try some of the ham.' As he stood at the sideboard his back to her, he said, 'I merely passed on information about Landon I received at the regimental offices, you know. I had no reason to doubt its veracity.'

She had to let the subject drop. She did not want to believe her cousin had lied to her about something so important. As weak in character as he was, he was still her only living blood relative.

She rubbed her forehead. 'Where are you staying?' Because he was certainly not welcome to stay with her. And she did not want him near if the captain called again.

Perhaps he would come to her tonight.

That thought filled her with excitement, even though she knew there was no future with him.

And Edwin brought doubt back again.

Edwin's back was to her. 'I'm staying at the Adelphi.'

She'd heard of it. Rooms popular with young gentlemen. 'What are your plans?'

He sat down again. 'Plans? What do I need with plans? I sold my commission when Father did. He gives me a good allowance. I can do whatever I wish.'

'You must have something useful to do.' She could not imagine the captain being so idle. 'Something other than drinking, that is.'

His eyes flashed. 'Do not start on that again, Marian.'

She glared at him. 'You were terrible, Edwin. You broke my table.'

His brows rose. 'I did? I cannot remember.'

'See? You should not drink like that.'

They went round about this again. Finally Marian said, 'Well, do not call upon me unless you are sober. I mean it, Edwin. I will turn you away.'

He pressed his temple with his fingers. 'Very well, Marian, but stop yelling. My head still aches.'

She let the subject drop and watched him drink his tea.

'What are you going to do today?' he asked between sips.

'I have an appointment this morning and this afternoon I have to call upon Domina.' And she hoped to see the captain that night.

'Domina.' He made a face. 'Lawd. Is she in London? She married Lord Ullman, I read. It should not surprise me. After he was jilted by Jack Vernon's sister, I suppose he had to settle for Domina.'

'He was jilted by Nancy Vernon?' This was new information.

'I was with him when he met her at the Egyptian Hall, of all places.' He gave a derisive laugh. 'She ran off with some penniless architect friend of Jack's.' He paused to rub his eyes. 'What a time that was. Such drama. Ariana Blane cuckolding Father and sleeping with Jack. You should have been there.'

Miss Blane and Uncle Tranville? Miss Blane never told her this when she and Marian shared a room in Brussels. She'd acted as if her connection to Uncle Tranville had been through Mrs Vernon.

Edwin laughed. 'I wonder if Domina knows she's got Nancy's leavings. It would be amusing to tell her.'

'Don't you dare!' Marian cried. 'She is actually quite happy, and I will not have you spoiling it.'

'Rich and titled. No wonder she is happy.' He continued eating. 'I believe I shall come with you.'

'To call upon Domina?' She wished he would not. 'Why?'

'I am that bored.' He bit into a piece of ham.

She tried to think of a reason to discourage him. There was no use in refusing. He would show up anyway, just to prove he could. 'You will have to change your clothing and return looking presentable. And *sober*.' She put emphasis on the word sober. 'And do not tell her about Jack's sister.'

He swallowed 'We'll see. Where is your appointment?'

'Here.'

'What is it about?' He spoke with his mouth full.

She narrowed her eyes. 'About *my* business, not yours, Edwin.' She rose from the table. 'I need to prepare, but do stay and eat as much as you wish.'

He nodded. 'What time will you call on Domina?'

'Perhaps around two.'

The visit was her attempt to improve her attendance at social events, as Yost had suggested, but Edwin coming along made it all the worse.

'I'll come back at two.' His voice was muffled with another mouthful of ham.

Allan walked into the Home Office in the late morning, still battling with guilt and indecision.

Sidmouth accosted him right away. 'I hope your tardiness means you have some information for me. Did you discover anything about Yost?'

Too much. But he was not ready to report it, even if his sworn duty to Sidmouth was to tell him what he knew.

'I have discovered nothing of consequence,' he said.

Except that the leader of the movement he was sworn to thwart was a friend of the woman whose bed he shared the night before, the woman he was determined to marry.

Sidmouth looked disapproving. 'Did you question Miss Pallant's servants?'

'I never had the opportunity,' he answered honestly. Good God. He did not want to involve Reilly in this.

Sidmouth frowned. 'Make opportunities, my boy. I have a new fellow in my employ who has discovered a great deal more than you have in half the time.'

'A new fellow?' This was a surprise to Allan. 'Who is it?'

'Hah!' Sidmouth laughed. 'A fellow who knows what he is about. Used him before. Makes things happen. Does what needs to be done and then some.' He clapped Allan on the shoulder. 'You need not know his name.'

Allan's eyes narrowed. Why keep the man's name from him?

He had heard the rumour that the man giving testimony about the Spa Field Riots had been a provocateur in Sidmouth's employ. He had not believed it at the time.

He'd accepted employment with Sidmouth because it meant protecting the government and enforcing the laws, but it seemed to him that much of what Sidmouth wished him to do skirted the boundaries of honourable behaviour. Spying on people, trespassing, betraying people who trusted him.

'Did you even see Yost last night?' Sidmouth demanded. 'Talk to him like before?'

'He was Miss Pallant's dinner guest, as was I,' Allan told him.

'Again?' Sidmouth leaned forwards in interest. 'What does this mean?'

Allan tried to maintain his composure. 'He is a single man in need of feeding.'

Sidmouth's face fell. 'That cannot be all.'

Allan's gaze remained steady. 'I believe Miss Pallant and her companion enjoy company and conversation at dinner.'

Sidmouth's brows rose. 'What do we know of this companion?'

'She is an impoverished widow quite grateful for employment.' And Allan could curse himself for even mentioning her to Sidmouth.

'A war widow? She could have connections.' Sidmouth stroked his chin.

'Or not.' Good God. Allan could not allow Sidmouth's suspicions to fall on Marian's companion.

'There's the pity, Landon.' Sidmouth clucked. 'You see only what people want you to see. You need to develop a more suspicious nature. Not going to succeed, if you do not. Remember, the crown depends upon this office to thwart any threats to the sovereignty and the peace of the citizenry.'

Allan believed in those duties of the Home Office whole-heartedly. He'd agreed to use the woman he loved to get information, had he not?

And now Sidmouth had hired someone who *does what needs to be done and then some.*

Allan flexed his fingers into a fist. 'What did this man of yours discover?'

Sidmouth gestured for Allan to come in to his office and have a seat. He lowered himself in the chair behind his desk and folded his hands in front of him. 'Someone—and I suspect Yost—is organising unemployed soldiers to march upon Parliament. The organisation is spreading around the country, and my man says it is imminent.'

'To what end? What are they seeking?' Allan asked. This all rang true. Yost had spoken of his concern for the plight of the soldiers.

'Jobs. Food. Compensation for their injuries in the war.' Sidmouth spoke as if these were unreasonable requests.

Of course his fellow soldiers needed such things. 'Are they advocating force?'

Sidmouth pursed his lips. 'Would you expect soldiers to be peaceful? Come on now. Been one yourself. Who else would take what they want by force?'

Allan gave him an even stare. 'Do you have evidence that they advocate violence against the Crown?'

Sidmouth restacked the papers on his desk. 'Not as yet, but I will.'

Edwin slouched in his chair, bored to tears with Domina's incessant chatter about Lady So-and-so's breakfast or ball or the latest play at Drury Lane. At least Ariana Blane—Vernon, he meant; she'd married Jack, for God's sake—was not performing. Word was she'd had a baby. Lawd.

He munched on a tray of raspberry tarts and sipped tea when his thirst demanded a more robust beverage.

Marian made a more successful show of appearing interested in Domina's drivel. In fact, she gave Domina a great deal more of her attention than she had him. Just because he'd arrived at her town house a little drunk.

Well, *very* drunk, he had to admit.

He touched his cheek. He often drank a great deal, but he did not often lose the ability to remember where he'd been and what he'd done. Like the time he'd awoken with a gash across his face. He'd gone into Badajoz during the sacking, his father had told him, and Landon had carried him out.

Landon.

He wondered if Landon had told Marian about Badajoz. He might not remember what happened in that city, but it would certainly make him look bad and Landon look good, if she were told he'd needed rescuing. Having Landon look good was nothing he could desire.

He detested that Landon was back. Courting her, no doubt. Edwin thought he'd convinced Marian to rebuff Landon entirely with the little story he'd created, but now she was wavering again, he could tell. He'd be damned if he let Landon make a fool of him.

Edwin gazed over at his cousin. The ladies had begun discussing gowns and that was enough to make Edwin wish for a pistol to shoot himself, the talk was so tedious. Having neglected to carry his firearm, Edwin regarded his cousin instead. She was a handsome enough woman, but more so, she could be depended upon to take care of him, no matter what. He liked the certainty of that. He did not want Landon around to change things. See how she'd cosseted him, even after he'd apparently broken her table in his drunken state.

He did not mind so much that she did not want to marry him as long as she did not marry Landon.

Just once he would like to show Marian, his father and everyone else that he could do better than Landon.

The door opened and Lord Ullman walked in.

'Ullie!' Domina cried, jumping up from her seat and into his arms.

Edwin almost choked on his tart. Finally Ullman recognised Marian and then him. 'Edwin, my boy, good to see you.'

Domina still held on to her husband's arm. 'Ullie, my love, would you mind entertaining Edwin for a while? I want to show Marian the new gowns you purchased for me.' She nuzzled Ullman's nose in apparent gratitude for his anticipated generosity.

'Of course, I do not mind, my dear.' He reached in his pocket and pulled out a velvet box. 'Show her this as well.'

Domina opened the box. Its contents sparkled with some kind of jewels. 'Ullie!' She wrapped her arms around him again, then skipped over to Marian. 'Look, Marian. Is it not the most beautiful thing you have ever seen?'

'Dazzling,' Marian said.

'Come!' Domina took her hand. 'I want to show you all the wonderful things Ullie has given me.'

The two ladies swept out of the room.

Ullman watched his wife's retreat. 'I love to indulge her.' He clapped his hands and turned to Edwin. 'How about some brandy, eh?'

'I would be delighted,' Edwin responded. Brandy was preferable to shooting himself in the head.

They chatted over various things, finishing one glass and pouring another. Edwin savoured how the brandy burned going down his throat, how it spread warmth even to his extremities.

'So tell me,' Ullman said, pouring Edwin a third glass. 'Is anything happening between my nephew and your cousin? I say, when last I saw them together, I was certain he would court her.'

Edwin pressed his fingers tightly around the stem of his glass. 'I know nothing of it.'

'Allan would be a good catch for her,' Ullman went on. 'My nephew is a man who can rise high. His work with Lord Sidmouth—'

'The Home Secretary?' This was news to Edwin. 'What the devil does he do for Sidmouth?'

'Important work.' Ullman beamed. 'He's investigating possible sedition. His job is to stop it before trouble erupts and to arrest those responsible for inciting riots.' He took a sip of his brandy. 'I dare say this will get him a seat in the Commons some day.'

'Lawd. Is that what he wants?' Such high aspirations. Some day Edwin would have to sit in the Lords, though he looked forward to that tedium as much as Domina's conversation. With his luck Landon would rise to be Prime Minister by that time and he'd still look bad.

Edwin no longer listened to Ullman. He was hatching a plan to call upon Lord Sidmouth and show everybody he could do the job a great deal better than Landon, whatever it was. Then he'd get the glory. Maybe he'd even stand for an election for M.P. instead of Landon.

This time he'd show them all.

Chapter Sixteen

Marian saw him from a distance.

She and Edwin strode down South Audley Street coming from their visit to Domina. He was standing there, waiting for them, and she could feel his eyes upon her even at this distance. She felt a flush of excitement and imagined her face was filled with colour, betraying some of the confused emotions inside her.

It was clear to her that she must not marry the captain, no matter how her body and soul yearned for him. She could not tolerate marriage to a man who worked to imprison men fighting for what was due them. Eventually he would imprison her spirit, if not herself, as well. She needed to be free to prevent suffering wherever she could. Who could not feel that way after witnessing men dying, burning in flames?

All her lofty ideals were vital to her, but ever since she'd confronted Edwin, what nagged at her the most was the matter of the Frenchwoman. She'd feel completely duped if the captain had lied to her about having a mistress in Paris. If she must ultimately part from him, she at least wanted to believe he was really the man she thought he was.

She'd stopped listening to the drone of Edwin's voice as her cousin approached him, closer and closer.

'Lawd,' Edwin muttered in a disgusted voice, when he, too, noticed who waited for them.

When they reached him, the captain removed his hat and bowed. 'Good afternoon, Marian.' His voice was warm, as if he, also, savoured the memory of their night together. He straightened again and nodded coldly to her cousin. 'Edwin.'

'Captain.' Marian's tone was shriller than she'd intended it to be.

The Captain ignored Edwin and spoke directly to Marian. 'I came to call upon you and learned you were at my uncle's.'

She had difficulty looking at him. 'We just came from there.'

'Dreadful bore,' Edwin drawled.

'Be quiet, Edwin,' Marian said sharply. She'd reached the limits of her patience with her cousin.

The captain frowned at Edwin. 'Have you been drinking?'

Edwin gave him a disdainful look. 'Is it any concern of yours?'

Marian answered for her cousin. 'Yes, he has been drinking. And he promised me he would not.'

One corner of Edwin's mouth lifted in an attempt at a smile. His scar merely made the effort look distorted. 'As I have explained to you, Marian, I promised I would not drink before calling upon Domina. I did not promise to refuse a drink when there. Ullman offered brandy and it would have been inhospitable to refuse.'

Marian turned away from him. This was what plagued her. Edwin's explanations always sounded reasonable, whether about his drinking or about the captain in Paris.

The captain spoke, 'May I speak with you alone, Marian?'

Edwin held up a hand. 'Have no fear of offending me,

Landon.' His tone was sarcastic. 'I actually have an important matter that requires my attention.'

Allan ignored him and waited for her answer.

She nodded and turned to her cousin. 'Do not come to my house if you have been drinking. I mean it. I will turn you away.'

Edwin made an exaggerated bow. 'I have learned from my one mistake.'

He sauntered away and the captain turned back to her. 'I am glad you remember my warning about his drinking.'

'Indeed,' she said stiffly.

Her disordered emotions about him made it difficult for her to even think.

He looked at her with concern. 'Marian, what distresses you?'

She wanted to believe in the captain, but both he and Edwin had been so convincing. 'Edwin has tried my patience. He has confused me, but I cannot discuss it now.' She forced herself to meet his gaze. 'What did you wish to say to me?'

She could see flecks of brown in his hazel eyes as he searched her face. Suddenly his expression relaxed and the ghost of a smile lit his lips.

'Do you have some time?' he asked.

She felt breathless. 'I am not expected anywhere, if that is what you mean.'

He took her hand. 'Come with me. I will take you to see an old friend.'

He led her to a line of hackney coaches on Oxford Street. He helped her into one and she heard him tell the jarvey to take them to somewhere on Knightsbridge Street. The hack left them off a short distance from Hyde Park Corner in front of a stable.

Marian seized his arm in excitement. 'You are taking me to see Valour!'

'An old friend, I said.' He smiled.

They walked into a large, well-kept stable with lines of stalls housing beautiful riding horses.

A stable lad greeted them. 'Saddle your horse, sir?'

'No need,' the captain replied. 'We are merely making a social call.'

The man gave him a bewildered look, but went on with his chores.

The captain led her to Valour's stall. The mare bobbed her head and shuffled in excitement.

'Oh, Valour!' Marian pressed her face against the horse's neck and stroked her. 'How I have missed you.'

For the moment all Marian's worries fled in the pleasure of seeing the horse again.

'There is a yard nearby,' the Captain said. 'We could give her a little walk.'

She beamed at him. 'Oh, yes. Let's do.'

He held the string to her bridle as they led her around the yard.

Marian turned to gaze at the mare. 'I feel sorry for her being so confined.'

The Captain nodded. 'I try to ride her as often as possible.'

'Do you ride in Hyde Park?' she asked, wanting desperately to merely enjoy the moment, the three of them together again.

'In the early morning mostly. Hyde Park gives her a good run.'

She felt wistful. 'I have never ridden much, but that sounds lovely.'

'You have not ridden much?' He sounded surprised.

'Not living in Bath.'

He continued to lead Valour around the small yard. 'You rode well enough in Belgium,' he remarked.

She shook her head. 'If I had been any kind of horsewoman, I would never have fallen off the horse I shared with Domina. I think Valour deserves most of the credit for me remaining on her back.' She lowered her gaze. 'Valour and you, of course. You held on to me.'

He glanced back at her. 'We made a good team, you, Valour and I.'

She almost smiled. 'We did.' She held back to pat Valour's muzzle.

Marian relished the memory of their days together, though they were fraught with hardship and danger. In many ways it had been as if no one else in the world existed but her, the captain and Valour. As they took another turn in the yard, the memories of Belgium returned. None of the memories fitted with Edwin's version of him in Paris.

She took a breath. 'I must ask you something, Captain.'

'Of course.'

All her distressed nerves returned. 'And you must tell me the truth.'

'I will.' He looked tentative, as if he was wary of what she would ask.

The clip-clop of Valour's hooves echoed in the yard before she could speak. 'Did you have an affair in Paris?'

He halted and it seemed as if his entire body tensed.

She went on, 'Because Edwin still claims you did, and I cannot determine which of you to believe.'

He seemed to glare at her. 'Are you asking me to prove it to you?'

She watched him, suddenly fearful of what he might say.

'I cannot prove it.' Pain flashed through his eyes. 'If I produced witnesses, Edwin would merely say they were lying for me. I can prove nothing.' His voice turned low. 'Upon my honour—' he touched her arm '—upon my *honour*, since meeting you there has been no other woman. I want to marry you, Marian. I want only you.'

She drew in a breath and felt tears sting her eyes. 'Oh, Captain.' It was the answer for which she'd hoped, but it only brought back the other barriers between them. Perhaps it would have been easier after all, if he'd been a man who'd deceived her all along.

'Believe me, Marian.' He touched her cheek and slid his fingers down to gently lift her chin.

Her heart pounded within her chest. Before she knew it, she closed the distance between them, twining her arms around his neck and pulling his head down into a kiss that overtook her senses, made her feel lighthearted, made her want more. He held her against him and she cared not one whit if someone walked into the yard and saw them.

Valour trotted up and nuzzled them, nickering low. They broke apart.

'Valour is jealous, I think,' he said.

Marian still clung to his arm. 'Come home with me.'

They returned a disappointed Valour to her stable and fussed over her a bit before Marian gave the horse one last goodbye hug.

'You will see her again, Marian,' Allan promised. 'In fact, you can ride her one morning.'

'I would like that.' But she knew that would never happen. She'd follow Yost's advice and continue to allow him to court her to deflect any suspicion of her, but after the march she must release him.

Arm in arm, they walked to Hyde Park Corner where they caught a hackney coach to carry them back to Marian's house. He held her as they rode.

'What saddens you?' he asked as the swaying of the coach and his arms lulled her.

'I am not sad,' she said.

He frowned and she knew she'd not convinced him.

The coach delivered them to her door, and Marian pulled her key from her reticule and handed it to him. She could make an excuse and bid him goodbye on her doorstep.

Instead she said, 'Reilly is still away and I suspect the other servants are busy.'

His eyes darkened. 'And Blanche?'

She whispered, 'With Mr Yost, of course.'

His expression changed for a moment, as if he'd had an upsetting thought, but he turned the key in the lock and swept her into an embrace as soon as they entered and closed the door behind them. His kiss sent her senses reeling and filled her with a desire she had no intention of denying.

He must have had the same thought, because he lifted her into his arms and carried her above stairs to her bedchamber. Before he even set her on her feet, she pulled off her hat and tossed it away. He sat her upon the bed and kissed her again as his hat, too, came off and he unbuttoned his coat.

As the captain stepped away to pull off his boots, Marian kicked off her shoes and took off her pelisse. She undid the bodice of her dress and slid the garment off, letting it fall to the floor. She turned her back to him, and without her asking, he loosened the laces of her corset.

Soon she was clad only in her shift and he in his shirt. She lifted the garment over her head and let the sunlight in the room reveal her nakedness.

He stilled and his eyes seemed to drink her in.

Perhaps if she were very lucky this would not be the last time with him. She could not be certain, however. She took a deep breath and resolved to remember every tiny detail. His glorious masculine body. The feel of his hands and lips against her skin. The incandescent pleasure she knew would come.

Allan let his gaze touch every part of her, from the luxurious blonde tresses escaping their pins, to her kiss-reddened lips, the graceful curve of her neck.

The fullness of her breasts.

Her skin was smooth as cream and seemed to shimmer from the sunlight pouring in the room. He was glad they made love in the light, as if there were no secrets between them.

He should have guessed her change in mood had been Edwin's doing. Would he always have to battle the doubt

Edwin seemed to know how to plant in her mind? If so, he would fight valiantly for her to believe him.

There was no woman but her for him.

His gaze continued, feeling reverent as he savoured her narrow waist and perfect navel. She remained boldly still, even when he took in the dark hair between her legs.

She became shy then, moving back upon the bed, lying against the pillows. He tore off his shirt and joined her, taking her head in his hands and leaning down to again taste her lips.

When he released her mouth, she sighed. 'I wish—' She broke off.

He tasted the tender skin beneath her ear. 'What do you wish?'

'You and I,' she murmured, not finishing her sentence.

He remembered then, the secrets he was hiding from her and felt ashamed after she'd exposed herself so openly to him.

He tensed. 'Marian, I have something to tell you—'

A tiny line formed between her brows. 'Then tell me later.' She reached for him and pulled him down upon her again.

He wanted to soothe her, to reassure her all would be well, but he knew his news of Yost would cause problems between them.

He stroked her skin, trying to calm her and himself, as well. He felt her desire grow under his touch. He kissed her again, one long, needful kiss, full of both promise and regret.

She opened to him and he entered her, savouring the warmth of her against him, of how they fit together with such perfection. To move inside her felt staggeringly wonderful. He moved slowly, wanting this sensation of joining with her to last as long as possible.

Desire overtook him and control fled. He drove into her with intense need. She met his pace, as if she responded to some inexplicable urgency. The sound of their joining and their breathing filled his ears until he was no longer able to compose a coherent thought. He was aware only of her. The pleasure of her. The intense need of her, a need that would never cease.

She cried out, and he felt her release spasm around him. She pushed him over the edge, shattering him with pleasure as he spilled his seed inside her.

She whimpered and tears shimmered in her eyes. He lifted his weight from her and rolled to her side. 'My God, did I hurt you?'

She covered her face with her arm. 'No. No. It was all I could desire.' She rose on an elbow and slid herself on top of him, her mouth finding his.

She quickly aroused him again with heated kisses and he showed her that he could enter her while she straddled him. She was a quick pupil because once more they moved in perfect accord, this time without the strange intensity of before. This time was quieter, a solace where before had been urgency. Together they again climbed to the pinnacle, slow and steady, until the end which was every bit a frenzy of bliss as before.

She collapsed on top of him and Allan felt awash in perfect contentment. Perfect union.

A cloud crossing in front of the sun darkened the room. Soon the servants and Blanche would return.

Their interlude had come to an end.

'I should dress,' Allan said, facing a reality he could not like.

'We both must.' She moved out of his arms and sat up. Her golden hair tumbled over her shoulders and more hairpins fell, joining others that now peppered the bed. 'Blanche will be home soon. She invited Mr Yost to dinner.'

Yost.

Allan could delay this no longer.

Marian rose from the bed and turned to him, before donning her shift. 'Would you like to stay for dinner?'

She would withdraw the invitation when he finished what he had to say to her.

He put on his shirt and trousers.

She sat at a dressing table and ran a brush through her hair. 'You did not answer. Would you like to stay for dinner?'

He walked over to stand behind her, meeting her gaze through the mirror that faced her. 'I have something of importance to tell you.'

She froze, brush poised in the air.

'I discovered something,' he began.

Her brows rose slightly.

He girded himself. 'I discovered that your neighbour, Mr Yost, is planning a march on London—a soldiers' march.'

She averted her gaze and continued to brush her hair. 'Do not be ridiculous.'

He looked down on her. 'It is true, Marian. I heard it myself, and Sidmouth knows as well.'

She gaped at him. 'You informed on Mr Yost?'

'No, another man did that.' An unscrupulous man, Allan feared.

She put her brush down with a trembling hand. 'Why do you tell me of this?'

He crouched down so he could look at her directly. 'Because he is your friend and Blanche's lover. And he is in danger of arrest.'

'You will arrest him?' Her eyes hardened.

'If the march takes place, or if there is some proof of his conspiracy, like a letter with his name on it, I may be forced to.' He touched her arm. 'The Seditious Meetings Act makes it a crime.'

'It is unjust.' Her eyes flashed at him. 'Besides, it sounds as if you only have rumours and speculation. You cannot arrest Yost on those grounds.'

'We do not need a reason to arrest him.' With the suspension of habeas corpus they could detain anyone they chose. 'Sidmouth will want to wait until he knows more before arresting Yost. Such as the time and place of the march and others who can be implicated in the planning of it.'

'And you think I can tell you who that is?' Her voice turned cold.

He jerked back. 'Not at all.' At least, not until this moment. His eyes narrowed. 'If you do know something, Marian, I would beg you to tell me.'

She lifted her chin. 'I would tell you nothing. If I knew something, that is.'

His mind was turning, calculating the timing of events. Yost's writings about the plight of the soldiers were printed months ago, yet the Home Office heard no rumours of Yost planning some demonstration until about a month ago.

Allan stood. 'How long have you been acquainted with Yost?'

Her face became like a mask. 'Are you interrogating me, Captain?'

He put his hands on his hips. 'Answer the question, Marian.'

'We met him after moving in, of course.'

That told him nothing except that she was being evasive. Why? He'd expected her to be upset at this news, but, by all signs, she'd not been surprised at it.

Allan's mind turned quickly. Besides the plight of the soldiers, Yost had written fervently about other radical issues, taking up the cause of the weavers, writing against the Corn Laws, all manner of topics. What had induced him to settle on the soldiers' problems? And how did he go from merely writing essays to becoming the leader of a soldiers' march?

Allan knew of only one person who so single-mindedly embraced the soldiers' cause. In fact, she would run into a burning building for them.

He stared down at her. 'You are in on this, are you not, Marian? You are in the thick of it with Yost.'

She shot to her feet. 'Now you *are* being ridiculous.'

He seized her arms. 'Good God, Marian. How deep in are you?'

She tried to pull away. 'Release me, Captain.'

He tightened his grip. 'First tell me! How deep?'

She met his eye with defiance. 'If I were involved, I would be a fool to tell you, would I not?'

He shook her. 'You risk arrest every bit as much as Yost. The penalty of sedition is death.'

Her face flushed with colour. 'Are you threatening me, Captain?'

'I am warning you, Marian.' He released her.

She glared at him. 'You accuse me of sedition. I accuse you of betraying men who fought and suffered at your side during the war. I cannot believe you are saying these things to me.'

'I am not betraying them.' He raised his voice. 'I am supporting the law.'

'A law that would put me to death for encouraging men to demand help?' She strode away from him, but turned back. 'It is said that Sidmouth hired provocateurs at Spa Fields and that *they* caused the violence, not the protesters. Is Sidmouth in danger of hanging, or would it merely be me?'

He looked her in the eye. 'He has hired men this time as well. You cannot go through with this. It is too dangerous.'

'I am no stranger to danger, am I, Captain?' She lifted her chin. 'Besides, I might have been speaking hypothetically. Will you arrest me for speaking hypothetically?'

Must he arrest her? She had all but admitted she had a part in this.

By God, no. He could never do such a thing. Her intent would never be criminal. Foolish, yes, but not criminal. Sidmouth would not care about that distinction, however. Allan could not stop Sidmouth from arresting her if he knew this much.

'Tell Yost to call off the march,' he demanded. 'It is too risky now. Stop it before it is too late for all of you.'

He turned away to stamp on his boots and don his waistcoat. He thrust his arms through the sleeves of his coat. The emotions between them filled the room like smoke from a blocked chimney.

Her voice was barely audible. 'Perhaps you ought not stay for dinner after all.'

Allan felt sick inside.

Marian laughed, but the sound was mournful. 'And again I free you from your obligation to marry me, Captain. I suspect that a threat to arrest and hang me is an indication we would not suit.'

'Marian,' he murmured, at a loss to say more.

She opened a drawer and pulled out a robe, wrapping it around her and walking to the door. 'Take what time you require to dress and then leave my house.'

She walked out.

Chapter Seventeen

Marian, clad in only her shift and a silk robe, ran down the stairs to her tiny library. She closed the door and fled to the large leather chair that faced the cold fireplace.

She curled up in the seat, the leather chilly against her bare feet and through the thin fabric of her robe. Tears stung her eyes, but she refused to shed them. She'd known he would ultimately not wish to marry her when he understood the depth of her views, but she had not guessed that he knew so much about the march.

She covered her face with her hands. To be fair, he did not really want to arrest her. He wanted her to call off the march because of the danger to her and to Yost.

His footsteps sounded on the stairs and soon after the front door closed.

He was gone.

At least no one in the house had known he'd been there.

Marian hugged her knees to her chest and tried not to think about how it felt to make love with him. She must think only of how he was working against her cause.

'Oh, no!' She shot out of the chair and paced the room.

She'd forgotten to ask Blanche what to do about preventing a baby.

How could she admit to Blanche that she'd bedded the captain when she must also tell her the danger he posed to her and to Mr Yost?

She glanced at the bookshelves. She'd purchased the house with most of the furniture and books in it. Perhaps the previous owners had owned a copy of *Aristotle's Masterpiece* or, if not that well-known book about all things sexual, *Culpeper's Complete Herbal*. Those books surely would explain how to prevent a pregnancy.

She found Culpeper's book and pulled it off the shelf. The light in the room was dim so she carried it over to the window and opened the leather-bound volume.

There was no table of contents. No index.

'They are listed alphabetically!' It would take her hours to pore through the pages of herbs and their uses. She closed the book again and leaned her forehead against it.

Could having a baby out of wedlock be any worse than leading a march on Parliament? At least she would not be hanged for having a child.

She pictured herself holding a tiny baby in her arms and felt like weeping again.

The baby would be *his*.

With a groan, she returned the book to the shelf and walked out into the hall.

Blanche had just come in and was removing her hat and gloves.

'Marian?' Blanche gaped at her undress.

'I—I took a nap and just returned a book to its shelf.' How easily she lied. She took a breath and forced a smile. 'I think Hannah must be out. Would you help me dress?'

A few minutes later Marian again sat at her dressing table, but it was Blanche with her instead of the captain.

Blanche drew a comb through Marian's hair. 'I am surprised that you did not remove the hairpins before napping.'

Hairpins had not seemed important at the time. 'It was silly of me.'

Blanche pulled her hair into a tighter knot. 'Well, I do not mind arranging your hair. I enjoy it and it gives me time to speak with you.'

Marian glanced at Blanche through the mirror. 'We have not had much time of late, have we?'

Blanche looked distressed. 'I have not been a very good companion.'

Marian reached up and squeezed Blanche's hand. 'I did not mean that. You are always here when I need you, and I do not begrudge the time you spend with Mr Yost.'

Blanche blushed. 'I do spend a great deal of time with him, do I not?'

Marian patted her face with a blotting paper. 'Is he dining with us tonight?'

'If you do not mind,' Blanche said uncertainly.

Dinner was time enough to tell them what the captain had said to her. 'Of course I do not mind! I enjoy his company.'

'Is Mr Landon dining with us, too?' Blanche asked, twisting a lock of hair and pinning it in place.

'No,' Marian answered in a sharp tone. She softened it. 'No, but I did see him briefly. He—he escorted me home when I called on Domina.'

'Did he?' Blanche gave her a knowing look through the mirror. 'That is three days in a row you have seen him.'

'Three days,' she mumbled. She wanted to divert the conversation away from the captain. 'What did you want to talk to me about?'

'About last night—' Blanche began.

Marian held up a stilling hand. 'You need not explain. I have seen you blossom under Mr Yost's attentions these few weeks. He brings you happiness. That is all I care about.'

Blanche's cheeks turned pink again, but she shook her head. 'I meant what transpired between you and Mr Landon.'

Marian stilled. 'Because the captain was in my room?'

Blanche nodded.

Marian pressed a hand to her abdomen—where a baby might be growing. 'It was innocent, I assure you. I heard a sound outside and he came in to investigate. It—it was the two men coming to see Yost.' That sounded plausible. She hoped.

Blanche gave her a worried glance. 'You never mentioned meeting Landon in Brussels.'

'I did not think to mention it.' Marian could feel her pulse beating fast.

Blanche's brow creased. 'I am concerned for you.'

'Why?' Marian made her voice light. 'There is no reason for concern.'

Her friend seemed not reassured. 'I am persuaded you have little experience with men. And you have told me nothing about Mr Landon—'

'Because there was nothing of consequence to tell,' Marian said defensively.

Blanche attended to another lock of hair. 'Did you know him before Brussels?'

'No.' She did not want to discuss the captain. 'Do you have a point, Blanche? Because I wish you would make it.'

Blanche put her hands on Marian's shoulders and met the eye of her image in the mirror. 'It takes time to know a man. To know if your heart is safe with him.' Her expression turned bleak. 'I—I just want to warn you that a man can deceive you. Seem one thing and be another entirely.'

Marian could feel the pulse in her body accelerate. What else was she to learn about the captain this day? 'Do you have some information about the captain, something I should know?'

Her companion looked surprised. 'No. Goodness, I know less of him than you do.' She swallowed. 'I am speaking about my husband, I suppose. He was a charming man and he quite swept me off my feet. He—' Her voice cracked. 'We were married very quickly after meeting, and it was not until later I discovered his fondness for cards and for drink.' She glanced down to pick up a hairpin. 'I merely wanted to warn you to not give away your heart too quickly.'

This warning was too late.

'I do appreciate your concern.' Marian's voice was stiff, but only because she was attempting to keep tears from flowing. 'But you do not have to worry about me.'

Blanche stepped back. 'I hope you will forgive my speaking so plainly. I know it is not my place.' Her face became the picture of distress.

Marian regretted her clipped tone. She stood and gave Blanche a quick embrace. 'I thank you for caring about me.'

'I hope Mr Landon is every bit as gentlemanly as he seems. I like him,' Blanche said.

So did Marian. In fact, she loved him in spite of what he could do to them. To her.

Allan returned to the Home Office.

It was the only thing he could think of to do.

He walked in and went to his desk. The newspapers he'd left there that morning were missing. He opened the drawers looking for them, but they were not there.

Sidmouth appeared in the doorway. 'Walked out, did you? Wondered if you'd come back.'

'A matter of importance required my attention.'

Marian.

'Matter of importance, eh?' Sidmouth pursed his lips. 'Thought the Home Office was important.'

'That is why I returned,' he replied. 'To work some more today.'

Sidmouth was behaving oddly. Allan often left the office during the day. Most times it had been to follow up on some lead.

Sidmouth slapped his thighs. 'Well. Good news, Landon. Found another gentleman to assist.'

'Another?' Who this time?

He pointed at Allan's chest. 'Need a man willing to do what needs to be done. Found just the fellow.'

Allan disliked the sound of that. Was he hiring provocateurs after all? Perhaps the rumours of Spa Fields were true.

'More men, more information. Need to know the day and location. Who else is in on it. Coming soon, I'll wager.'

Allan felt his anxiety rise. Would this new man discover Marian's part? 'Who is this person?'

'Son of a baron. Not afraid to dirty his hands a bit.'

Son of a baron? A wave of trepidation washed over Allan.

Sidmouth gestured for him to follow. 'Come, Landon. Fancy you know the fellow.'

They walked to Sidmouth's office where, lounging in a chair reading a newspaper, sat Edwin Tranville.

Edwin stood when he saw Sidmouth, his expression smug when he rested his gaze on Allan. 'Twice in one day, Landon. What did I ever do to deserve this?'

Sidmouth clapped Allan on the back. 'Trust you to fill in young Tranville here on your efforts so far.' He left before Allan could say a word.

Edwin lifted the newspapers. 'I borrowed these from your desk. Boring stuff, mostly.'

Allan glared at him. 'Cut line, Edwin. What the devil are you doing here?'

'Why, engaging in gainful employment.' He smirked. 'As you have done.'

Allan stepped closer, making the most of his taller stature. 'Sidmouth said you were not afraid to dirty your hands a bit. What did he mean by that?'

Edwin's smirk did not falter, but he backed away. 'You would have to ask him, but apparently there is another fellow I am to work with. You are on your own, it seems.'

'Why are you doing this, Edwin?' Allan demanded.

Edwin placed a chair between them. 'Because I can do a much better job than you, Landon, and I'm going to prove it.' He rubbed his scar. 'Sidmouth valued my connection to Marian. It was one of the factors in my favour.'

Allan changed his tone. 'Listen, Edwin, you must take care about Marian—'

Edwin's nostrils flared. 'I always take care about Marian. Besides, she will not know I'm spying on Yost.' His eyes narrowed. 'Unless you tell her.'

Allan doubted she would listen to him long enough for him to tell her anything.

He advanced on Edwin again. 'You will spend much of your time in taverns, I warn you. You cannot allow yourself to get so drunk that you cannot remember what you have heard.'

Edwin rolled his eyes. 'Lawd, Landon. I can hold my drink.'

There was no reasoning with him. Disgusted, Allan strode out.

A week later Marian and Blanche waited in Marian's bedchamber for Lord Ullman's carriage to arrive and take them to Domina's ball. Domina had insisted upon sending the carriage, and Edwin had volunteered to escort them.

Marian stood at the window. 'I dread this event.'

Blanche turned from checking her gown in the mirror. 'Oh, Marian, I know you do.' She lowered her voice. 'Is it because Mr Landon may be there?'

Blanche persisted in thinking Marian's heart had been broken by the captain. Marian had done her best to convince her it was not so, that she considered the captain more of a threat to the soldiers' march than a lost suitor.

Marian forced a dry laugh. 'I hope the captain does attend. He will see me acting like a lady of the *ton*, interested only in parties and gowns and gossip.'

Marian had increased her attendance at various entertainments, mixing in society as much as possible to dispel any notions that such a frivolous creature could be the mastermind behind a march upon Parliament. She had no illusion about fooling the captain about her efforts, but, if he told anyone, who would believe him?

She went on. 'It is difficult to pretend to enjoy such triviality when the day of the march is almost here.'

'I think you should forget about the march and enjoy yourself.' Blanche checked her image again. 'I confess, I am very excited. I never thought to wear such a beautiful gown in my life.'

Marian smiled at her. 'You look lovely in it. I'm glad we purchased it for you.'

The deep garnet of the gown enhanced Blanche's complexion and brought out the red tones in her brown hair. Marian made certain both her gown and Blanche's were the very latest fashion to suit the role she played. Her modiste had been delighted. Marian's gown was made of ice-blue silk with a bodice covered in lace and tiers of lace at the hem. The blue complemented her eyes.

And to be entirely truthful she hoped the captain would admire it.

'I am glad for the carriage,' Blanche went on. 'Although it seems like the rain has stopped for the moment.'

It had rained all day, matching Marian's mood and filling her with memories of the rain before Waterloo.

'Has Mr Yost seen your gown?' Marian asked, wanting to turn her mind away from those memories.

Blanche blushed. 'I will show him later.'

Yost no longer shared dinners with them and he rarely walked with Blanche. Reilly created a small opening in the wall that separated their gardens, though, so he could pass through unseen and consult with Marian about the plans. Blanche used the opening almost every night to be with him.

Marian heard a sound outside. 'Here's the carriage.' She reached for her wrap.

The ladies descended the stairs. Edwin was already waiting in the hall.

He bowed, hat in hand. 'Good evening, Marian. You are very prompt.'

Marian peered at him, looking for signs he'd been drinking. He'd seemed on exceptionally good behaviour of late. He'd called upon her a few times and had always appeared sober. Still, something was going on with him, she could tell. Once, in the middle of the night, she thought she saw him standing across the street, which made no sense at all.

'You look ravishing tonight, Marian,' he told her.

It bothered her that he said nothing about Blanche's appearance, but then he always treated Blanche as a mere servant.

'Thank you, Edwin.' Marian wrapped her shawl around her shoulders. 'I suppose we might as well leave now.'

There was a crush of carriages the closer they came to Lord Ullman's town house. They merely inched along. The captain would have suggested they walk the rest of the way, but such an idea would never occur to Edwin.

'Domina will be in raptures if the ballroom is as crowded as these streets,' Edwin drawled. 'This is her first big event.' He emphasised the word 'big' with a grand gesture of his hands. 'I suppose everyone will be scrutinising the flowers, the food, the…' He paused. 'The wine.'

'She has been talking of little else for several days,' Marian responded.

'Has she?' Edwin rubbed his scar. 'What a dead bore.'

He went on, trying to guess who would attend and who had refused the invitation. Marian barely listened. Out of the window of the carriage she had a clear view of the front of Domina's town house and could see who arrived.

She watched for the captain.

He'd not attended other social events where Marian had been present, but surely he would attend his uncle's ball. Perhaps he would not even speak to her. If he did, she knew how to play her part. She did not know which circumstance to hope for.

Their carriage reached the end of the street. They were mere steps away from Domina's house.

Marian could stand it no longer. 'Let us get out here. It will take a quarter of an hour to reach the front of the house if we do not.'

Edwin sent her a scornful look. 'Really, Marian. We are not tradesmen.'

They waited until the carriage reached the front door.

Domina and Lord Ullman stood near the entrance of the ballroom, receiving their guests. Edwin greeted them with a bored expression and limp handshakes.

Marian followed him. 'You look splendid, Domina,' Marian told her friend.

Indeed Domina had never looked better. Her gown, all white lace and silk, was trimmed with pearls. She wore a pearl-and-diamond necklace to match and a turban with a white feather.

'Thank you, Marian.' Domina's eyes sparkled. 'I am so excited I can hardly stand still. I do hope I get to dance.'

Lord Ullman patted her hand. 'No fear of that, my dear. I claim the first set.'

She squealed. 'Is he not wonderful?'

Domina turned to greet Blanche, and Edwin went in pursuit of a servant carrying a tray of champagne. Marian scanned the room and immediately spied the captain.

To her surprise he walked directly towards her. Her breath caught. There could be no more impressive a man than he, elegant and masculine in his formal attire.

Blanche came to Marian's side and spoke first. 'Why, Mr Landon. How good to see you.'

He bowed to her and to Marian. 'You are looking exceptionally beautiful tonight, Mrs Nunn.' His eyes shone with genuine appreciation.

Blanche flushed under the compliment. 'Thank you, sir.'

He turned to Marian, his expression guarded. He nodded. 'Marian.'

'Does not Marian look lovely tonight, as well?' Blanche asked.

His eyes flickered over her. 'As always.'

Marian felt her body awaken under his gaze. She fought the sensation. 'Captain.'

A fleeting sadness shone in his eyes, before he turned to Blanche again. 'Would you do me the honour of the first dance, Mrs Nunn.'

Blanche glanced at Marian.

Marian smiled. 'Goodness, do not refuse him, Blanche.'

'I do not like to leave you alone,' Blanche said.

Marian laughed and let her gaze sweep the room. 'In this crowd? I shall not be alone. Besides, we have just walked in. I may yet find a partner.'

'Then, yes.' Blanche beamed at the captain.

'I will find you when the dancing starts.' He bowed and walked away.

'Do you really not mind?' Blanche asked.

'Of course not!' Marian replied a little too brightly. 'You love to dance.'

On the contrary, when the captain had asked Blanche to dance, Marian warmed to him. Being engaged for the first dance by such a man would increase Blanche's social consequence. As a lady's companion, she might have easily not been asked at all, but she did look so lovely, Marian expected she would not want for partners this night.

She and Blanche walked through the room, exchanging pleasantries with people with whom they'd lately become acquainted. At the same time, Marian searched the room for the captain or fancied his eyes upon her when she looked away.

When it was announced that the dancing would start, his gaze merely touched hers before he took Blanche and led her on to the dance floor. As it turned out, Marian did not have a partner, so she watched them from her spot against one wall as the captain took Blanche's hand and, with the other dancers, formed two circles, one moving inside the other. The captain performed the dance without effort. His footwork was not perfect, but he danced as if he cared less for his own feet than for the enjoyment of his partner.

Marian envied Blanche.

Edwin sidled up to her. 'Oh, Lawd. Look at Ullman.'

Lord Ullman danced energetically, but was stiff and very slightly off the beat. He beamed adoringly at Domina, however.

'He appears to be enjoying himself very well,' she said to Edwin.

'He's a buffoon.' Edwin held a glass of wine in his fingers. He drank the contents in one gulp.

Marian glared at him. 'You are drinking!'

He sniffed. 'It is one glass of wine. A man might have one glass without getting drunk.'

She looked into his eyes. His returning glance was steady. 'Take care, Edwin. Do not drink too much.'

He rubbed his scar. 'I will not drink too much. It was just that one time. Have I repeated it?'

'Not in front of me,' she admitted. 'Not yet.'

He glanced around. 'Where is your companion? Isn't she hired to keep you company?'

Marian inclined her head to the dance floor. 'She is dancing.'

'I'm affronted for you. You should be on the dance floor and she should be—' He gazed at the dancers and stopped talking. 'I see her,' he finally said.

Blanche was asked by another man to dance the next set, a quadrille. Marian danced the next set, as well, and the one after that, a Scottish reel. Her dance partners were perfectly charming gentlemen, but Marian was more attuned to where the captain was at all times than to their company.

She was standing out in a line dance when she caught

Edwin snatching a glass of wine from a passing footman and drinking it straight down. Later, at the supper, his voice carried across the room. She watched him sway as he walked towards her table, another glass in hand instead of food. He carefully lowered himself into a chair next to her.

Lord Ullman and Domina had stopped by Marian's table, but Domina had dispatched Lord Ullman to fetch her one of the tiny cakes from the buffet.

'Did you ever think that I would be giving such a grand party?' she chattered on to Marian. 'Does not the ballroom look transformed? Ullie said I could spend whatever I wished so I filled the room with flowers. It is a wonder we had space to dance. Are not the musicians grand? Ullie says they have played for the Prince Regent and were once engaged to perform at the Regent's palace in Brighton. You know, his Royal Highness is having the palace entirely redone. Ullie says we shall be invited there to see it—'

'Well, won't that be grand, Domina,' Edwin said with great sarcasm and in much too loud a voice.

'There you go being a nuisance again, Edwin,' Domina countered. 'Some people never change. Tell me, who is beating you up these days?'

'You always were a shrew—' Edwin began.

Marian interrupted. 'Domina, I think your husband needs your help at the buffet. He just looked back here for you.' He had not done so at all, of course.

'He needs me?' Domina shot out of her chair. 'I must go to him at once.'

When she had gone Marian turned to Edwin. 'You are behaving very badly,' she told him in a fierce whisper.

He merely laughed and gazed around the room with a vacant eye. She twisted away completely and joined Blanche in conversing with the other people at the table. When she glanced up she found the captain watching her from across the room.

It was announced that the dancing was about to resume,

and a gentleman approached Blanche to engage her for the set. Marian followed them into the ballroom with Edwin right on her heels. With an apologetic glance, Blanche left her to take a place on the dance floor.

Edwin gazed around the room. 'You should dance with me.'

She did not even look at him. 'I think not.'

'C'mon.' He seized her arm. 'I want to.'

'You are too drunk,' she whispered.

'Have to have a couple of drinks or it is no fun. C'mon.' He pulled her.

'Release me, Edwin. You risk making a scene.' She tried to wriggle away from him.

His grip tightened and his voice turned to a growl. 'Are you refusing me, Marian? In front of all these people?'

Someone appeared behind him.

Captain Landon!

'Ah, there you are, Miss Pallant,' he said in a clear voice. 'We are engaged for this dance, I believe.'

She was almost too grateful to speak. 'Yes, Captain, I believe we are.'

Edwin was still gripping her arm when she put her hand in the captain's.

'If you will excuse us, Edwin,' he said loud enough for others to notice and to turn curious glances towards them.

Edwin released her and backed away, an angry sneer on his scarred face.

The music began, and Marian and the captain joined hands and marched into place. He bowed and she curtsied, and he took her in his arms at the precise moment the music of the German waltz required him to sweep her around the room.

She gazed up at him. 'You have rescued me again, Captain.'

His eyes were dark and warm. 'I suspect we are even.'

'Even?' Her brows rose.

'You saved my life at least twice.' He twirled her under his arm and then held her again. 'Once by tending my wounds and once from the peasant's axe.'

'You cannot do sums,' she countered. 'You picked me up when the whole French army was chasing me. You pulled me out of the burning château. And you saved me from Edwin once before...in my hall.'

'Then you owe me.' His voice deepened. 'How shall you repay?'

Her body came alive to him and ached with wanting more. 'How may I?'

The waltz was once considered scandalous because the man held the woman, albeit at arm's length. The captain breached propriety and drew her close so their bodies almost touched.

He whispered in her ear. 'Do not risk a hanging.'

Chapter Eighteen

The fire inside Marian cooled. She tried to pull away, but the captain held her firmly as he twirled her around the room. 'Abandon this plan, Marian. Make Yost call it off. Sidmouth does not yet know the time or place, but he is getting close.'

A *frisson* of fear ran up her back, but she forced herself to ignore it. 'I will not abandon our soldiers.'

'There are other ways to help them,' he insisted.

She shook her head. 'This is the way I have chosen.'

He resumed a proper distance, but she remained in a swirl of emotions. Was he truly warning her out of his concern for her, or did he simply want to stop the march? Did he care about her or about his job?

She did not know. She only knew that she felt captured by his gaze and quite helpless to look away. She yearned to be making love with him, to be held by him in bed, but he was her enemy, intent on foiling her plans.

His eyes seemed like mirrors, reflecting identical longing and regret. Time ceased and the room blurred and she could see nothing but the captain, her *Captain* again, the man who'd captured her heart.

The music stopped and he reluctantly released her.

It was too much to bear. She curtsied and stepped away from him. 'Excuse me, Captain—'

She fled into the crush of people, to the ladies' retiring room, waiting there long enough for him to have asked another woman for the next dance. When she ventured out again she threaded her way through rooms where guests talked to each other in small groups. Lord Sidmouth, in a deep discussion with another gentleman, approached from the opposite direction.

Loathe to be forced to even greet him, Marian ducked behind a huge jardinière of flowers. To her dismay, the two men paused next to the flowers, within two feet of her.

She heard Sidmouth's companion ask, 'How did you learn so much about Yost?'

Sidmouth replied, 'Sent in a spy. Knew his neighbour...' The men continued walking.

But Marian had heard enough.

Allan completed his second circuit of the ballroom and made his way back to the hallway, searching for her.

Not that he expected her to dance with him again or even speak to him. He merely wanted to keep her in sight, as if that alone would save her.

He closed his eyes as the pain of his helplessness washed through him. All he could do was try to convince her to get the march cancelled before Sidmouth discovered her involvement. With Edwin in Sidmouth's employ it was even more dangerous for her to be a part of this.

He took a deep breath and opened his eyes.

And saw Marian advancing on him like charging cavalry.

'I would speak with you alone, Captain,' she demanded.

He nodded and led her to a niche near the stairs where they could be private. 'We can speak here.'

Her eyes flashed. 'You used me.'

'I never—' he tried to protest.

'You only pretended to love me.' Her voice was low and angry. 'I overheard Sidmouth. You used me to spy on Mr Yost.'

His worst fear had come true. 'Listen to me, Marian. It is not that simple—'

'Simple? Do not say you have some complicated explanation, some convincing denial.' Her breathing accelerated. 'Like your very convincing denial of a Frenchwoman in Paris.'

'That was the truth—'

She would not allow him to continue. 'Truth? Do you expect me to believe you now? You deceived me. You were *sent* to call on me. I was merely part of a task you were assigned to perform.' She made a strangled sound in her throat. 'What did Sidmouth say, Captain? "See if she will whisper secrets into your pillow?" Or did you merely seek entry to my room to see out of the window?'

'Marian—'

She held up a hand. 'Say no more. I will no longer believe any of it. And I am not stopping the march. So arrest me if you must.'

'I do not wish to arrest you.' He emphasised each word.

Her eyes flashed. 'Oh, but you might be *forced* to.'

He seized her by the shoulders. 'Enough!' He leaned into her face. 'Remember that *you* involved yourself in this danger, Marian. Not me. I am trying to extricate you from it. I'm trying to keep you from hanging by your neck.'

Her lips quivered and apprehension flickered in her eyes. 'I cannot stop it now,' she whispered.

Their gazes caught briefly. Allan released her and Marian again fled from him.

He pressed his forehead against the wall. How was he to save her now?

His only hope was to learn what he could about the march. Perhaps Yost could be persuaded to stop it if Allan could show him that Sidmouth knew the time and place and would be ready to arrest them all. Allan now had no illusions about Sidmouth. He was convinced the man employed agent provocateurs, and suspected that Edwin had agreed to become one.

Allan was no longer in Sidmouth's confidence. He had no guarantee he could learn enough to save Marian. He did not know how much time they had before it would be too late.

He walked back to the ballroom. Marian had retreated to one of the chairs against the wall. He stood on the other side of the room, unable to resist watching her. The last dance ended and the guests filed out.

Allan followed and, in the crush of people waiting for hats and cloaks, saw a drunken Edwin approach her. Marian seemed to be speaking hotly to him.

'Carriage for Miss Pallant,' the butler announced.

Edwin seemed to glue himself to Marian's side as she and Blanche walked out. Allan pushed his way through the crowd, reaching the pavement just as a footman assisted Blanche inside the carriage. Marian continued arguing with Edwin. She ascended the carriage step, but Edwin was right behind her.

'I'm coming with you,' Edwin slurred.

She turned to him, framed in the carriage doorway. 'No, Edwin.'

'I'm coming.' Edwin demanded. He shoved her inside.

Allan surged ahead and seized Edwin by his coat collar, pulling him off the step. 'Not so fast.'

Edwin swung around with fury in his eyes.

'I have need of you, Edwin,' Allan said to him, not wanting to cause Marian any embarrassment.

Her gaze caught Allan's as the footman closed the door and the carriage moved away.

Allan took hold of Edwin's arm and walked him away from the other guests.

'See here, Landon!' Edwin cried. 'You take your hands off me!'

Allan released him. 'You are too drunk to be fit company for ladies.'

'She's my cousin!' Edwin cried, as if that meant anything at all. He made a show of straightening his coat and brushing off imaginary dirt from where Allan had gripped his sleeve. 'Trying to act the hero, eh? We'll see how important you are when this march business takes place. For once everyone will congratulate me and you will be nothing to them.'

Allan seized the front of his coat. 'What do you know, Edwin?'

Edwin shrank back. 'Wouldn't tell *you* if I knew something.'

Allan released him.

The next afternoon Marian sat behind her desk, curling and uncurling a small piece of paper. She looked up to her two most important allies, Mr Yost and Reilly. 'Where do we stand?'

'All is set,' said Reilly. 'The men know it is to be Charing Cross at dawn.' They had withheld the location until the very last minute.

'And they know there are likely to be provocateurs?' she asked.

Reilly nodded. 'Each man has sworn to be disciplined, to stop anyone who creates havoc.'

Mr Yost drummed his fingers on the arm of his chair. 'Your friend Landon called upon me this morning.'

'He spoke to me, too. Very early,' Reilly said. 'Came to the door while you and Mrs Nunn were still asleep.'

'He came to the door?' Her nerves skittered.

Yost shrugged. 'He asked me to stop the march. I didn't admit even knowing what he was talking about.'

Reilly nodded. 'Me, too, miss.'

She twisted the paper. 'He is persistent.'

Yost rubbed his forehead. 'I confess, he seemed genuinely concerned about you and desired I keep you out of this.'

'You cannot believe what he says to you.' She took a breath. 'He cares only for the Home Office.'

Yost raised his shoulders. 'He did inform us there would be agent provocateurs. That would seem counter to what the Home Office would wish.'

'He's passing the same message through his contacts,' Reilly spoke up. 'Some of the men heard him speak of his concerns as to the danger of the march.'

'He is trying to scare them,' cried Marian.

Yost pursed his lips. 'Perhaps, but it seems odd to me. Why would he want to stop it? Wouldn't he want it to take place so arrests could be made?'

Marian stood. 'It does not matter why the captain does what he does. All we need ask ourselves is if the plan will still work.'

Reilly straightened. 'The men know what is expected.'

Smoothing out the paper only to twist it again, Marian went over the plans in her head. The march was intended to be merely a show of force, a warning that the soldiers' needs should not be ignored. At the exact time of the demonstration, Yost and another man would leave the list of demands at Parliament. Reilly and Marian would be with the other protesters at Charing Cross. The early dawn traffic through the busy intersection would be momentarily halted by the crowd. No speeches would be made, but the group would be led in a cheer. Three loud *huzzahs* and then the crowd would disperse. A brief—and hopefully safe—show of force.

'How many men do you think we have?' Marian asked.

'At least five hundred,' Reilly told her. 'Maybe more.'

Five hundred men willing to risk arrest. They would move into place very quietly throughout the night. They knew to plan their way to escape.

Would it work?

She inhaled a nervous breath. 'We must hope that the Home Office is kept in the dark, but we prepare as if they know the whole plan. Does the captain know when the march is to take place?'

'I do not think so,' Reilly said. 'He is still asking for information in the taverns, but everyone knows who he is and what he wants. He almost got into fisticuffs with your cousin at the Coach and Horses Inn the other night.'

'My cousin?' Marian gaped.

Yost added, 'Your cousin is often seen in the taverns, as well, and not always in the company of gentlemen.'

So much for Edwin's promise to cut down on his drinking. At least he no longer called upon her, although that must mean he was very deep in the cups.

She looked down at the piece of paper, now hopelessly creased. 'My cousin is of no consequence. It is the Home Office and Captain Landon we must fear.'

But not for much longer, because by this time tomorrow, it would be all over.

Sidmouth sent Allan to the taverns that evening to search for Edwin. Neither Edwin nor his nefarious partner had reported in to the Home Office all day.

Unlike when Allan had searched for Edwin at Badajoz, this time there was no gunfire, no riotous shouting. No agonised screams, but something was afoot. Allan sensed it. His heart pounded with the same foreboding as it had in Badajoz. The sense of anticipation was so strong it was almost palpable.

He enquired after Edwin wherever he went. Not truly caring whether Edwin went to the devil or not, he really also sought information on the march. No one would tell him anything of that, but several men had seen a man fitting Edwin's description. Reports were that Edwin had been drinking heavily and had been in the company of a Mr Jones—Lord Sidmouth's man, no doubt.

Allan followed Edwin's trail from one dark taproom smelling of hops and sweat to another. As the night wore on, the sense that something was in the air intensified. More men eyed him with suspicion. Fewer men sat drinking. More wandered the dark streets.

Hairs rose on the back of his neck as shadowy figures passed him in the night. Memories of Badajoz filled his mind.

He felt himself grabbed from behind and swung around ready to put a fist in the man's face.

'Whoa, Allan! It is me. Gabe.'

Gabriel Deane. His friend from the Royal Scots.

'Gabe!' He clasped his friend's hand and shook it. 'I did not know you were in London.'

'I arrived not long ago.' Gabe rubbed the back of his neck. 'The battalion disbanded, Allan. I'm at a loose end at the moment.'

'Disbanded?' Allan frowned. 'I'd heard rumours that might happen. What will you do?'

Gabe shrugged. 'Pay a visit to Manchester.' Gabe had grown up in Manchester. His father and brothers were prosperous cloth merchants there. 'After that, who knows? And you? How do you go on?'

Three men slipped past them, eyeing them suspiciously.

'What the devil is going on here?' Gabe asked. 'I've been seeing men on the streets everywhere.'

Allan pulled him aside and explained about his employment with the Home Office and about the march he was trying to prevent. 'I am loathe to admit this to you,' he added, 'but I am in search of Edwin Tranville again.'

'Edwin?' Gabe cried.

'He's in the thick of it, causing trouble.' He peered at Gabe. 'Come with me, if you are at liberty. I'll explain the rest.'

Gabe laughed. 'I am quite at liberty.'

Allan went into more detail as he led Gabe to the next tavern. He explained about the Home Office, Sidmouth, about Yost and Edwin and about the provocateurs. He did not speak of Marian, telling himself he was merely protecting her by leaving her name out of it. Perhaps, though, he feared the pain of explaining to his friend what he'd almost had with Marian. And lost.

They left the third tavern without success.

'One more,' Allan said. 'If Edwin is not there, I'm going to simply follow some of these men to see where they ultimately are bound.'

'One more tavern,' Gabe agreed.

They entered a tavern near Hyde Park Corner, dark like the others with chairs filled with men who examined Allan and Gabe as they scanned the room.

No Edwin.

They were about to leave when a man raised his head from a table near the back of the room.

'More brandy,' the man cried, holding up a bottle. Enough light hit his familiar scarred face.

They'd found him.

Allan and Gabe crossed the room and Edwin lay his head back down on the table.

Allan looked down on him. 'Edwin.' He spoke as if issuing orders.

Edwin looked up and it seemed to take time for his eyes to focus. 'Lawd, it is you.' His filmy gaze turned to Gabe. 'And *you*. I s'pose you'll want to drink with me.' He waved his hand to the weary tavern maid again. 'Two bottles, wench. These fellows are paying.' Edwin laughed as if he'd said something extremely amusing.

Allan gestured for the woman to leave them. He sat and leaned close to Edwin so others could not hear. 'Something is afoot. What have you learned, Edwin? Where is Jones?'

Edwin looked around. 'Where *is* Jones?' he said too loudly. He slapped his forehead. 'That's right. He left. Went to make the report.'

'What report?' Allan demanded.

Edwin drained his glass and poured another bumper of brandy from the bottle. He gave Allan a smug look. 'Not going to tell you.'

Gabe seized Edwin by his coat and hauled him to his feet. 'Tell him what he wishes to know if you value your neck.'

Edwin's face contorted. 'Very well. Very well. I'll tell. What do I care about it?'

'Then speak up now,' Gabe ordered.

'Jones left. Told me to go to the devil.'

Allan took Edwin's face in his hand and forced Edwin to look at him. 'Where is the march to be? When is it scheduled?'

Edwin squirmed in Gabe's grip. 'This morning. Not going to tell you where. Not going to tell you when. You'll grab all the glory.' He tried to pull away, but Gabe restrained him from behind. 'Going there myself. T'watch the Horse Guards. Told Jones I'd meet him there.'

The Horse Guards? Did Sidmouth plan to release the Horse Guards on the protestors? The soldiers would not stand a chance.

Allan leaned into Edwin's face. 'Tell us where. What time this morning?'

Edwin slumped and Gabe must have loosened his grip, but all of a sudden Edwin broke free, flailing his arms. He swung out at Allan before Gabe grabbed him again.

'Leggo!' Edwin shouted. 'I'm gonna report you to Sidmouth. Have you arrested. You wait and see!' He struggled, but Gabe held him tight.

Allan moved to another table, asking the two men seated there, 'Do you know where the demonstration will be? Do you know what hour?'

'Go away,' one man growled.

He addressed the entire room. 'Tell me, any of you. Where is the demonstration to be?'

They only glowered at him.

He went back to Gabe. 'I have to find out more, but I cannot let him get to Sidmouth.'

'He'll cause no mischief.' Gabe shook Edwin like a rag doll. 'I'll make certain of that. Do what you must.'

Allan nodded his thanks and rushed out. All he could think was that he had to warn Marian that she was walking into a trap. Bryanston Street was too far to walk, and finding a hackney coach might take time.

More men filled the streets, sauntering in the direction of Westminster Cathedral. Were they headed there or to Westminster Palace? There would be few avenues of escape if the march was on Parliament.

Allan went to the stables where Valour was kept. He shouted for the stable lad to let him in and to saddle his horse.

A few minutes later he was astride Valour, skirting Hyde Park to reach Marian's town house. The first slivers of dawn were peeking through the sky.

He dismounted in front of Marian's house and pounded on her door. 'Marian! Open the door! Open the door!'

Her house was dark. He glanced at Yost's. It was dark, too, but that did not mean that they were not awake in the back, preparing for the march.

He pounded again. 'Open the door! It is urgent!'

He heard a frightened voice through the door. 'Go away, sir.'

'Hannah? Hannah, is that you? It is Captain Landon.' He used his army rank without thinking. 'I need to see Miss Pallant immediately! Let me in, Hannah.'

'I dare not!' she cried. 'She's not here, anyway.'

He heard another woman's voice. 'What is this, Hannah?'

Blanche.

'Mrs Nunn,' Allan cried. 'You must let me in. I have news of grave importance.'

There was a pause, then the door slowly opened. Blanche's face appeared in the gap. She held a candle. 'What is it, Mr Landon?'

'Let me in, please,' he said to her.

She stepped aside and he entered the hall. Hannah held a hand to her mouth, looking frightened.

'I'm not going to hurt anyone,' he assured her. He turned to Blanche. 'Where is Marian?'

The women looked from one to the other.

'Has she already left for the march?'

Their eyes grew wider.

Allan took a step closer to Blanche. 'You must tell me where she is going. I have to stop her. She's walking into a trap.'

'A trap?' Blanche cried.

'The Home Office knows where the march will be and when, but I do not. You must tell me before it is too late.'

Hannah spoke to Blanche. 'You cannot tell him. Miss Pallant said we were not to believe him.'

He faced Blanche, placing his hands on her arms. 'You must believe me. I want only to protect her. And the men, if I can. And Mr Yost. Good God, Mrs Nunn, they are calling out the Horse Guards.'

She blinked.

'Mrs Nunn, listen to me—'

'Don't listen,' Hannah cried.

Allan went on. 'She is walking into a trap. You must help me stop her.'

Blanche searched his face. She blurted out. 'Dawn. At Charing Cross. She should be there already.'

He spared her only a quick grateful look, running out the door to mount Valour and race down Bond Street to Piccadilly.

The sky had lightened. Dawn would come within minutes. On Haymarket Street wagons and carriages stood at a full stop. Valour made her way through them.

When he finally reached the intersection known to all as Charing Cross, it was filled with soldiers, hundreds of them. They kept their voices low, collectively producing a low hum.

He searched for Marian, slowing Valour to a walk. The men barely parted for him.

'I say we give them a good fight,' he heard one man say, his voice louder than the others.

'We gave our word, man,' another responded in a Scottish brogue. 'Stubble it or we'll mark you for a provocateur.'

Allan continued to pick his way through the crowd. How hard could it be to find a woman among all these men?

He glanced down Whitehall towards Westminster Palace. Years of war had made his eyesight keen.

He saw movement.

The Horse Guards were forming their ranks, preparing for the charge.

Chapter Nineteen

Marian stood at the base of the statue of Charles I inside the wrought-iron fence, dressed once again as a boy. Surrounded once again by soldiers. Her nerves bunched in her throat, making it hard to swallow. Soon she'd know if they'd be successful or hanged for traitors.

Reilly climbed on to the statue. 'Is it time now, miss?' He would lead the cheer.

Three huzzahs and they would be done.

The sky was light, light enough for Marian to catch sight of the man on the horse, the man searching the crowd.

The captain.

She turned away from him. 'Yes, Reilly, now, I think.' *Before he arrests us.*

She should have known the captain would come. He'd warned her he would.

Reilly climbed a little higher and cupped his hands so his voice would carry. 'Soldiers!' he shouted.

The crowd went silent.

'Prepare to cheer!'

'No!' The captain swivelled around on Valour and pointed towards Whitehall. 'Horse Guards! They are coming!'

Marian scrambled up the statue to see rows of uniformed soldiers on horseback starting their charge. She remembered from Waterloo. They started slow and gradually built speed. They would burst into the intersection like a fire-breathing dragon.

'Cheer!' she cried at the top of her lungs. 'Cheer!'

'Huzzah!' Reilly lifted a fist in the air.

'Huzzah!' Five hundred fists rose. 'Huzzah! Huzzah!'

'Run!' boomed Allan. 'Run now!'

The men ran. From her vantage point on the statue they were like water splattering in all directions.

The Horse Guards built their speed.

Marian climbed down from the statue, and Reilly lifted her on to the iron fence surrounding it. 'Do not wait for me, Reilly. Get out of here.'

Reilly easily climbed to the other side. When his feet hit the pavement, he reached for her.

'No,' she cried. 'Go.'

He glanced behind him.

'Get out of here, Reilly!' It was the captain.

The captain's strong arm plucked her off the fence and on to Valour's back. Reilly ran, disappearing into the remnants of the crowd. She prayed he would escape.

'Hang on,' the captain told her.

She seized Valour's mane in her fingers and pressed her knees tightly to keep herself from falling. Rather than turn away from the Horse Guards, the Captain headed straight for them, but veering off and heading into St James's Park instead. She expected to hear horses' hooves behind them, but soon the only sounds were the chirping of early morning birds. The water of the lake peacefully sparkled as the sun finally rose.

'I didn't see Yost.' The Captain sounded worried.

'He wasn't there.' With luck, Yost had delivered the list of demands to Parliament safely. She could only hope for the others as well. 'Do you think they got away?'

'I think they very well might have.' He sounded as if he was glad of it.

She turned to look at him. 'You warned them. You warned the soldiers to run.'

He did not answer, merely put an arm around her as he had done when they fled the peasants' farm.

The park seemed quite deserted as if nothing had ever disturbed its tranquillity, not even a nearby demonstration that almost ended with a cavalry charge. 'Captain, I want to stop. Might we stop a while?'

He swivelled around, checking the area. 'Let us find a place where we won't be seen.'

He left the trail and found shelter under a weeping willow tree next to the lake. They dismounted and Valour ambled over to dip her nose into the water to drink.

Marian sat upon the ground at the trunk of the tree.

'I am reminded of our resting place after running from the peasants' farm,' the captain remarked as he joined her.

She remembered every moment of their being together, but now was not a time for memories. 'Why did you warn us about the Horse Guards?'

He looked surprised by her question. 'So the soldiers might get away. If not, there would be injuries and arrests. I never wanted that.'

She shook her head. 'You did not want the march to take place at all.'

'There is no fear of arrest if no one breaks the law.' He spoke as if this should be self-evident.

'But then the plight of the soldiers could be further ignored.' She lifted her palms, realising she was starting their old debate. 'Did you not risk arrest by being there?'

He glanced away, then met her gaze. 'I had to save you.'

Valour ambled over and nudged her. She reached up and

patted the horse's neck until Valour spied a spot of grass nearby to nibble.

Marian turned back to the captain. 'I never wanted anyone to be arrested. Or hurt. That is why I planned it the way I did, to only show that the soldiers could be a force to be reckoned with if their needs were not met—'

He interrupted her. 'You *planned* it?'

She nodded and went on. 'There was to be no rabble-rousing. No speeches. Just a demonstration of force and the delivery of a list of demands.'

He touched her arm. 'You were the leader?'

'It was my idea. All my idea,' she admitted. 'I involved others only because I knew no soldier would follow a woman.'

'You enlisted Yost?'

She would not answer him.

He shook his head. 'I am not spying now, if that is what you fear. In fact, today I shall resign from the Home Office.'

'Why?' she asked, astonished.

He leaned back against the tree. 'I kept hearing my father's voice telling me to do what was right. I finally decided to listen to him.' He glanced away for a moment. 'Sidmouth's tactics were not right.'

'But you knew he was doing nefarious things like hiring provocateurs and still you worked for him,' she accused.

His eyes narrowed. 'I needed to protect you. I could only do that by remaining with the Home Office and learning what I could from Sidmouth and his men.' He took a breath. 'I did not believe the rumours of Sidmouth's provocateurs, that is, until he hired Edwin.'

Her jaw dropped. 'He hired Edwin?'

The captain nodded. 'Edwin boasted of being hired as a provocateur.' His expression turned doleful. 'But I do not suppose you will believe any of this now.'

A day before she would believe nothing he said, but everything seemed different under this tree, next to the water, no one else around. 'Did Sidmouth truly ask you to use me to spy on Yost?'

He stared at her. 'Yes. And I agreed.' He gave her an anguished look. 'But once I'd been with you, I knew I would tell him nothing I learned at your house.'

She waved that away. 'Did he ask Edwin to use me to spy on Yost as well?'

He nodded. 'I fear so.'

She dropped her head into her hands for a moment. 'Why on earth did Edwin wish to work for Sidmouth?'

The captain rubbed his brow. 'I have no idea.'

Marian felt as if her insides were shredding into bits. Her own cousin had been working against her. Not the captain.

He added, 'Edwin never knew you were involved. I am certain of that.'

Would Edwin have cared? she wondered. At least the captain's work with the Home Office had been grounded in his beliefs about government and law. Edwin had no such strong convictions. She doubted Edwin would have experienced any conflict over using her to get what he wanted. She believed the captain genuinely had. She, on the other hand, had been as single-minded as Edwin.

Marian's thoughts and emotions were a jumble. 'I risked too much, did I not?'

He searched her face. 'What do you mean?'

'I was outraged by the government's neglect of the soldiers, so I planned something grand to show they had better pay attention. I see it all differently now. I thought I was so clever, that I had thought of everything. My march would not be violent like Spa Fields. My march would succeed, unlike the Blanketeers.' She paused. 'I did not think of the cost, that men might be arrested and hung because of my vanity.'

He took her into his arms and held her close. 'It was not vanity, was it? I would never doubt your loyalty to the soldiers.'

She nestled against him. 'Do you think some men were arrested?'

'I think they all scattered in the nick of time.' His voice soothed her. 'I see things differently as well. My work had as much to do with ambition as the lofty principle I espoused.' He lifted her face with his finger. 'Perhaps I am as vain as you are.'

She smiled and settled against him once more. 'Well, I have learned my lesson. I will think of others from now on, not myself.'

'You make it sound as if you are like Domina.'

They both laughed.

She felt him take a deep breath. 'We need to get you home before anyone sees you dressed as a boy.' He helped her rise and they walked over to Valour. 'I will tell you that I am still ambitious, Marian. I still want to become an M.P., but not at any cost. It is now more important for me to do what is right. As my father said.'

She hugged him close.

He broke away, but she felt a camaraderie with him that surpassed even what they'd had in Belgium.

'Come.' He smiled. 'I will take you home, then busy myself composing my letter of resignation.'

When he moved to help her mount Valour, she stopped him. 'Wait a while before resigning from the Home Office.'

'Why?' he sounded surprised.

'If you resign today, Sidmouth might blame this failure of the Horse Guards on you. Wait a while and find some other excuse to resign.' She thought some more. 'In fact, if anyone reports seeing you at the march, you must explain that you were the one who broke it up. That is the truth, and you might as well take credit for it.'

He gaped at her. 'By God, you are scheming to rescue me again.'

Her brows knitted. 'I was thinking of your desire to become

an M.P. This must not ruin it. I could not bear it.' Then she smiled. 'And I do owe you a rescue or two.'

She threw her arms around him again, holding on tight and pressing her cheek against his chest. 'I am so sorry, Captain. So sorry for doubting you. So sorry for the things I said to you.'

He lifted her chin. 'Then perhaps you must make it up to me.'

'How?' she cried. How could she possibly repay him for what he'd done for her?

'Marry me,' he murmured.

Her eyes widened and she took a breath. 'I will not marry you to make it up to you.'

He turned away with an expression of pain.

She clutched him to her, rising on tiptoe. 'I will marry you because I love you, and nothing will stop me this time.'

An urgent sound escaped his lips before he crushed them against hers in a kiss that made her forget about spies and marches and everything but him.

'Take me home, Captain,' she whispered. 'And never be parted from me again.'

Epilogue

1820—London

Marian took a seat on the bench in the back of St Stephen's Chapel. Mr Yost sat beside her in the place designated for members of the press who report on the proceedings of the House of Commons. She stared down at her knee breeches, stockings and boy's shoes. Yes, she would pass as a boy once again. No one would remark upon Yost bringing an errand boy with him.

She glanced around the room and thought of how much had changed in the three years since she had organised the soldiers' march.

She'd never had any reassurance that her march made any impact at all. No news of it ever reached the newspapers; Sidmouth had seen to that. Still, she had to believe someone had read the petition; someone must have realised the significance of ignoring the soldiers' plight, of what soldiers could do if they chose.

In three years not enough had changed, but Marian had not lost heart. Her very reason for sneaking in to the Commons showed she continued to have hope. She kept to her promise to abandon grand schemes, instead now using her money to invest in ways to help individual soldiers find work, or to fund relief.

Other things had changed as well.

She glanced over at Yost, making notes on a sheet of paper. He had begun reporting on Parliament's activities for a new daily newspaper, one with neutral political views. He refrained from writing seditious material, now that he had a wife and twin sons who depended upon him. Marian smiled when she thought about how blissfully happy Blanche was to be Mrs John Yost.

Blanche still worried about her excessively. Her brow had creased in worry when Marian told her she intended to dress as a boy and accompany Yost to this place.

It was forbidden for women to attend these sessions in the Commons, but Marian had been determined not to miss this day. It was said that Caroline Lamb once disguised herself as a page to witness her husband's speech at the opening of Parliament. If Lady Caroline Lamb could do so, so could Marian.

This was the day Marian's *Captain*—her husband—now Mr Allan Landon, M.P., would make his maiden speech in the august body.

Her gaze took in the room with its wainscoted walls. It seemed dark and exclusive, a place where important things happened. The lavishly gilded Speaker's chair and majestic columns only reinforced this impression. In the spectator seats she spied Jack Vernon, now a successful portraitist, and Gabriel Deane. Gabe winked at her and grinned.

A door opened and suddenly the benches began to fill with countless important-looking gentlemen, and Marian shivered in anticipation.

Finally her captain entered and took his seat. Her chest swelled with pride. He'd denied being nervous, but she'd known he must be, just as she knew he would deliver an impressive speech and set the tone for what she was certain would be a great career in Parliament.

As he promised in his campaign, he would advocate for an improved pension programme, employment and housing for England's soldiers. Ironically, it was his passion for helping the soldiers that helped him get elected in a Whig stronghold; his brief stint at the Home Office was not held against him.

Yost took notes during other speeches and business, but at last the time had come.

The captain stood and walked to the front of the chapel.

'Mr Speaker,' he began.

Marian could not help but rise from her seat so she could see better.

'Members of Parliament...' His gaze swept the crowded chapel, but suddenly halted.

His eyes caught hers.

She would undoubtedly be in for a severe scold from him for this latest escapade. It made not a whit of difference to her. Nothing would have stopped her from being present to see and hear him speak. Nothing could make her regret it.

But she held her breath.

He smiled, just a fleeting smile, but one she had no doubt had been meant for her alone.

'Members of Parliament,' he repeated. 'I stand before you a wounded veteran, but one more fortunate than many, one whose life was saved—' he looked directly at Marian '—and I will speak to you today so I may help other men who fought tyranny for you and now suffer...'

He had no illusions that one speech would create change, but it was a start. Marian's heart burst with pride for him.

Who would have ever known that the lark of a foolish girl would lead to this day, this place, this *life*?

When his speech ended and several members cheered, her applause was the loudest of all.

* * * * *

Author Note

The soldiers' march depicted in the book is a mere figment of my imagination, although the plight of the soldiers after Waterloo was real enough. The Blanketeers and the Spa Field Riots did occur and Lord Sidmouth, the Home Secretary, was accused of hiring provocateurs to cause the trouble at Spa Fields. Henry Hunt was a genuine liberal orator, but Mr. Yost did not really exist.

Today we take for granted the freedom to criticize the government and demonstrate for causes, but with the Seditious Meetings Act of 1817, it was illegal for groups of more than fifty people to gather together. It also became illegal to write, print or distribute seditious material. Lord Sidmouth had been a strong advocate of these measures, but they proved to be a blight on Lord Liverpool's government and ultimately ushered in a more liberal Tory government in 1822.

Next in my Three Soldiers series is Gabriel Deane's story. From the moment he, Allan and Jack rescue the Frenchwoman from Edwin Tranville at Badajoz, Gabe is captivated by her. When he meets her again in Brussels they begin a scorching affair, but when Gabe asks her to marry him, she refuses.

Then they meet a third time in London....

Look for Gabriel's story. Coming soon.

MILLS & BOON®

Want to get more from Mills & Boon?

Here's what's available to you if you join the exclusive **Mills & Boon eBook Club** today:

✦ *Convenience – choose your books each month*
✦ *Exclusive – receive your books a month before anywhere else*
✦ *Flexibility – change your subscription at any time*
✦ *Variety – gain access to eBook-only series*
✦ *Value – subscriptions from just £1.99 a month*

So visit **www.millsandboon.co.uk/esubs** today to be a part of this exclusive eBook Club!

The World of Mills & Boon

There's a Mills & Boon® series that's perfect for you. There are ten different series to choose from and new titles every month, so whether you're looking for glamorous seduction, Regency rakes, homespun heroes or sizzling erotica, we'll give you plenty of inspiration for your next read.

By Request

Relive the romance with the best of the best
12 stories every month

Cherish™

Experience the ultimate rush of falling in love.
12 new stories every month

INTRIGUE...

A seductive combination of danger and desire...
7 new stories every month

Desire™

Passionate and dramatic love stories
6 new stories every month

nocturne™

An exhilarating underworld of dark desires
3 new stories every month

For exclusive member offers go to
millsandboon.co.uk/subscribe

Which series will you try next?

Awaken the romance of the past...
6 new stories every month

The ultimate in romantic medical drama
6 new stories every month

MODERN™

Power, passion and irresistible temptation
8 new stories every month

MODERN
tempted™

True love and temptation!
4 new stories every month

MILLS & BOON®

Why shop at millsandboon.co.uk?

Each year, thousands of romance readers find their perfect read at millsandboon.co.uk. That's because we're passionate about bringing you the very best romantic fiction. Here are some of the advantages of shopping at www.millsandboon.co.uk:

* **Get new books first**—you'll be able to buy your favourite books one month before they hit the shops

* **Get exclusive discounts**—you'll also be able to buy our specially created monthly collections, with up to 50% off the RRP

* **Find your favourite authors**—latest news, interviews and new releases for all your favourite authors and series on our website, plus ideas for what to try next

* **Join in**—once you've bought your favourite books, don't forget to register with us to rate, review and join in the discussions

Visit **www.millsandboon.co.uk**
for all this and more today!